Joyce Cary was born in London
He studied art in Paris and Edi
After serving in the Balkan W
Political Service and served in
In 1920 he returned to England
it was not until 1932 that his first book was published.

Cary's first four novels, *Aissa Saved* (1932), *An American Visitor* (1933), *The African Witch* (1936), and *Mister Johnson* (1939), were inspired by his time in Africa. He went on to write political studies such as *Power in Men* (1939), poetry including *Marching Soldier* (1945), and short stories such as *Spring Song and Other Stories* (1960). However, Cary's major work consists of two trilogies: *Herself Surprised* (1941), *To Be a Pilgrim* (1942), and *The Horse's Mouth* (1944); and *Prisoner of Grace* (1952), *Except the Lord* (1953), and *Not Honour More* (1955). He died in 1957.

'Whenever I am idle I choose a Cary novel in the way I might seek a friend's company, and it is not long before I am encouraged, inspired to write.'

Paul Theroux

'A marvellous writer — fresh, funny, popping with life.'

Doris Lessing

Also by Joyce Cary and available in Cardinal:

A Fearful Joy

Charley Is My Darling

Charley Is My Darling

BY

JOYCE CARY

CARDINAL

A CARDINAL BOOK

First published in Great Britain by Michael Joseph 1940
This edition published in Cardinal by Sphere Books Ltd 1990

Printed and bound in Great Britain by
The Guernsey Press Co Ltd, Guernsey, Channel Islands

ISBN 0 7474 0688 X

Sphere Books Ltd
A Division of
Macdonald & Co (Publishers) Ltd
Orbit House
1 New Fetter Lane
London EC4A 1AR

A member of Maxwell Macmillan Pergamon Publishing Corporation

Charley Is My Darling

I An undersized boy, in a neat brown suit, stood in the farmyard. It was harvest-time. The September morning sun, bright as wheat straw, made even a broken traction-engine, lying against the wall, beautiful and exhilarating. The hens spread their wings to bathe in the falling light. The boy, shrunk together with his hands stuck deep in his pockets, looked so wretched that he seemed ridiculous, like one overdoing a part.

A sturdy country girl, of about fourteen, in a sacking apron, stood two yards off looking at him. In one hand she grasped a bottle, in the other a pair of trousers and a shirt; over her head was thrown a green jersey, and on top of the green jersey a man's old felt hat was balanced crookedly. The jersey and the hat formed a kind of hood over her broad face, which was turned towards the boy with an intent curiosity and anxiety, like that of a nurse in charge of a foreign patient, at once very ill and mysterious. This responsible expression overcame the oddity of her appearance, so that the jersey, the hat, the bottle and the trousers, instead of being absurd, enhanced the gravity to tragic proportions. She was as dignified as Lear in rags, because of the rags.

Suddenly a young woman came out of the farmhouse door, and exclaimed in a soft sing-song voice: "Why, Charley, whatever is the matter?"

The boy jumped, drew himself up, and in a moment his whole appearance changed. He seemed even to grow broader and taller. The dejection of mouth, eye and cheek was replaced by a gay and friendly smile.

"Good morning, Miss Phyllis," he said.

"But, Charley, here's Miss Allchin 'phoning that we're to get your head shaved and throw away your nice suit."

The girl was very pretty, with dark brown eyes and a singularly pale, soft skin. Her voice, too, was soft, and though she used emphatic words she did not emphasise them. She sang them all in the same tranquil chant.

Charley was visibly shaken by this news. A kind of flutter or tremor passed over his face, and he said: "Is that Miss Lina?"

"Yes, Miss Lina Allchin—and you know she thinks a whole lot of you, Charley. The way you helped us last night. Why, I don't know whatever we should have done without you."

Charley still looks anxious and dejected. The girl with the bottle frowns at him and then glances anxiously at Phyllis, as if appealing on his behalf to the chief medical authority.

"I'm to get someone to do it or send you to Longwater," Phyllis sings. "They have the cottage hospital to Longwater —could you go on the pony, Charley? She says not to put you in the car. Isn't it turble? It's a sha-ame, Charley. I couldn't be-lieve it. I'm so sorry."

"It's all right, miss. It isn't your fault."

"And there's the pony gone up the field with bindertwine— you wouldn't mind if we did it here, Charley?"

"No, miss." But his voice is uncertain.

"It's only the other boys," Phyllis says. "You don't know them, do you?"

Charley, obviously surprised that the girl should penetrate his own anxieties, gives her a quick glance and colours slightly. He is full of that gratitude with which a child, and especially a boy of his sensitive age, fifteen, responds to a sympathy, which reveals his difficulty to himself. But he says nothing.

"But Bessie here couldn't take you to Longwater, could she, and I've got the men's dinner. If only everything wouldn't happen at harvest-time—oh dear, this war, if it could only have kept off over harvest."

Phyllis's perplexity is only in her words. Her voice tones would have served equally well as a thoughtful song of thanksgiving. But Charley responds to the perplexity. "All right about the boys, miss—they won't do nothing."

"But, Charley, Bessie said they wur calling out just now in the village."

The girl Bessie frowns and moves her lips as if to speak, but thinks better of it and frowns again.

"That's all right, miss—they was only being funny—you do it 'ere, miss."

"You really wouldn't mind, Charley?"

"I don't mind the boys, miss," Charley was anxious to take the attitude most useful and least troublesome to Phyllis. It was just readiness to oblige that had made him so useful to the distracted billeting officer, Miss Allchin, and her lieutenant, Phyllis Hawes, on the day before, evacuation day. They had soon discovered that Charley, though he had been thrown into the party at the last minute and was among strangers, knew more about its components and luggage than any other member of it. Within five minutes of the train's arrival it was to Charley that both appealed when children disappeared, women inexplicably refused to enter motor cars, and two boys fought over the same suit-case with Cockney yells which neither could interpret. It was Charley who, after quick-fire conversations in Cockney, explained to them in excellent English that Mrs. Wastie could not sit in the back seat of a car because it would make her sick, and Mrs. Wilson would not enter the front seat for fear of collisions, but that both were too shy to explain their difficulties.

"You could wear the hat all the time, couldn't you?" Phyllis says.

"Yes, you do it, miss. I'd rather you did it, really—only for all the trouble I'm giving you."

"It's no trouble, Charley—I'll get a chair, then. No, you'd better not have a chair, had you? Mother ——" She turns to the kitchen door. "Where's that box?"

Mrs. Hawes comes to the door and brings out a small packing-case. She is a stout, short woman with grey hair, but a face so young that she seems like Phyllis's elder sister. She leans on the door and watches while Charley is sat down on the box, and

Phyllis clips and shaves his head. Bessie lays down the clothes and the bottle, and brings water and soap in a tin basin.

"Isn't he good, mother?" Phyllis says. "He doesn't mind a bit."

"Ah, but however did they let un get in such a turble state ?" Mrs. Hawes has the same chanting, compassionate tone, but three notes deeper.

"He sits so still as a post. Don't you, Charley?"

Charley smiles, and the girl Bessie, anxiously watching him, also begins to smile, with gaiety and relief, just as a woman can't help smiling when a young baby makes some first sign of intelligence.

Charley, seeing this smile, turns his head, so that the woman in the door can't see his face, thrusts his tongue into his lower lip, screws up his little blunt nose and makes a grimace ingeniously ugly.

Bessie is so startled that she almost drops the basin. Then she smiles again doubtfully, ready to appreciate the joke, if it is made plain to her. Charley sticks out his tongue, whereupon Bessie, turning red, frowns, and makes a face almost equally hideous.

"Whatever are you pulling that face for, Bessie," the operator sings, "and whatever have you done with that paraffin lotion?"

Bessie continues to thrust out her tongue as far as it will go, and the woman in the doorway says: "She can't hear ee, Phyllis."

Phyllis reaches out her hand for the basin. Bessie starts, and finding herself noticed, looks astonished and turns beet colour. She looks sulkily from Phyllis to Mrs. Hawes.

"You better be careful the wind doesn't change when you're doing that, Bessie," Phyllis says as she washes Charley's head over the basin.

"She can't ear ee," the mother chants in rich compassion, "and wouldn't be no good if she did, poor thing. She's too foolish."

14

Bessie sticks out her lower lip obstinately and says in a low voice: "I heard ee, Miss Phyllis—I heard ee quite well."

Charley, under cover of the basin, makes another face at Bessie, who promptly complains of him: "It's the boy, Miss Phyllis, making faces."

"Noa, I'm sure he never did, did you, Charley?" then, without even waiting for the favourite to reply, she sings: "Do go on, Bessie, and get that lotion," and to her mother: "She's getting worse, I do believe."

"Ah, poor thing, they often get worse at that age—they goa right off."

Bessie obviously hears this. She starts, frowns at the speaker with an angry, enquiring glance, then turns and walks slowly away, with dignified steps.

Phyllis rubs Charley's head with a towel, and sings : "You don't feel too cold, Charley?"

"No, miss."

"That's a good bo-oy. You don't mind a bit, do you deeur?"

"No, Miss Phyllis."

"It doesn't matter if silly boys do call out, does it?"

"Of course it don't—I don't mind em."

"And it's a big hat—it will come right down. Bessie," she utters a lyrical note, "don't ee forget the hat." Phyllis talks West-country to Bessie, and Charley talks standard English to her.

Bessie brings lotion and clothes, and Charley goes into the stable to change. He comes out transformed, the bald skull, the green jersey which is too tight, and a pair of wide, cut-down trousers completely alter his proportions. His head seems absurdly small, the ears project like a dog's, his cheek-bones appear much higher, and his cheeks thinner, his body is shrunk by half. He is changed from a respectable looking young citizen in a brown suit, to something between the convict of history and the kind of street Arab represented in old comic papers. Phyllis looks at him with calm reflection, and says: "They arn't too ba-ad, are they?"

"No, miss, they fit very nicely." The sensible, good-natured citizen still lives in the grotesque clothes. "Thank you very much for shaving me."

"Oh, it's no trouble, Charley—it's only so turble unlucky for you. Where did Bessie put that hat? Look in the kitchen, mother. You must have the hat, Charley."

"Yes, miss."

"And you'll come back for the lotion every day?"

"Yes, miss."

"And if the boys do call out at you, you come and tell me or Miss Lina. But they won't, I know, will you?" She turns to two boys who for the last five minutes have been lounging in the doorway of the yard. "I'm sure Walter won't laugh at you, will you, Wal-ter?"

Walter, a tall good-looking boy, with very curly brown hair, touches his cap and says: "Yes, Miss Hawes."

"You won't laugh at Charley?"

"Who, Miss Hawes?"

"Why, Charley Brown here, who found your suitcase for you last night."

"No, Miss Hawes."

Mrs. Hawes brings the hat, between thumb and finger, and gives it to Charley at arm's length, as if to a leper. Charley thanks her, puts on the hat and glances round the yard as if for a way of escape. Walter and his companion, a small boy with flaming red hair and a paper-white face, fill the doorway with their legs.

Everybody looks at Charley and sees that he is nervous and undecided. Suddenly he puts his hands in his pockets and swaggers up to the gate. The two boys, however, do not move their legs, so that he cannot swagger through it. He has to go round Walter and step over the other's legs. In this way they successfully spoil his exit.

Three minutes later Phyllis hears in the deep lane below the house the polite Walter bawling at the top of his voice: "Baldy, Baldy, Charley Baldy, HE'S LOUSY."

She goes out indignantly, though without haste, just in time to see Charley being rolled in the road, clasped tightly in the same mass with Walter and his red-haired friend, whose name is Basil Siggs.

When she calls out to them over the hedge they start up. Charley scrambles to his feet, grabs his hat from the ground, cramps it down to his ears and flies up the road. But at ten yards range he turns to let fly some language so bad that both the boys look up at Phyllis as if to say: "There now, we're justified."

But Phyllis has taken to Charley, and nothing can set her against him. She sings out: "Why, what's he done to you, poor little boy?"

"He's dirty, Miss Hawes," Walter says.

"It isn't his fault that he wasn't looked after proper—I'm ashamed of you, Wal-ter."

The boys stare at her and suddenly Walter says politely: "Do you milk the cows, miss?"

"Noa, I only milk sometimes." She gazes thoughtfully at the boys and says then: "It's a long wa-ay from London to here—I've been three times."

At that moment a shrill whistle comes apparently from the little copse farther up the road and a shattering yell: "HI, BILL!" Walter and Basil crouch down and then dart into the next gate. As they disappear they utter a shout which sends all the rooks into the air and silences every bird within half a mile.

2   On this second day of evacuation, Burlswood seems to be completely occupied by its guests. This is partly due to the smallness of the hamlet and the shape of its surrounding fields. It stands in a spoon-shaped valley where every field can be seen from any part except the bottom of the bowl. In the principal lane running from the church, at the shank of the

spoon, to the point, at Hall Farm, a tall lanky boy in tortoise-shell goggles is gravely assisting a native to deliver milk. The seven cottages on the right of this lane, strung out like a row of circus waggons stalled on the incline, are set back from the road and in to the slope behind. Each bottle of milk has to be carried through a long front garden, so that the lanky boy has been at work for half an hour.

Behind these cottages in a rough steep field scarred by an old quarry, a short boy in a grey suit is bent double gazing at something on the ground. A fair-haired boy at the top of this field next the Green Man is whistling a shrill note like an engine whistle and waving to someone below, and on the left of the road, in a huge wheat-field, where the Hall Farm cutter has been rattling since dawn, Charley's figure, easily distinguished by the hat, can still be seen as he hurries northwards. He glances now and then at the harvesters but does not stop. He seems to be full of his own purpose. But suddenly he turns round, retraces his steps, runs a little way along the hedge, and begins to ascend the steep grass field towards the main road. He is still in a desperate hurry to get somewhere; but it appears doubtful if he knows where.

In the same field a small girl in a white muslin frock, followed by a small boy with bright green knickers, is trying to pull a red engine through the grass. When the engine falls down, which happens every ten seconds, she waits, gazing round her meanwhile at the cows, and the harvesters below, until the boy sets the engine right side up again. She then gives another pull and again it falls over.

In every direction a stranger can be seen. Yet there are only eight vackies in the place, and of these Walter is hidden among the big trees in the bottom of the valley, opposite Hall Farm, and his red-haired friend is climbing an apple tree in the orchard at the bottom of Quarry Field. Of fifty or sixty natives there are only five to be seen, the milk-boy, Peter Drake, now pushing his hand-cart to the top of the hill and the door of the Green Man; two men in the wheat-field, a small boy driving the tractor,

18

and Hawes himself, a huge man in an ancient straw hat, seated on the cutter.

On the other hand, the natives can be heard. There is another cutter at work somewhere behind the church. A ringing sound from the blacksmith's shop, by the lowest of the seven cottages, where three horses and a cart are standing, shows that the blacksmith, as usual at the beginning of harvest, is busy with arrears; and carts are rattling in the deep lane beyond the wheatfield.

But the effect is not that of a workaday place invaded by frivolous tourists. For some reason, probably because the visitors are children, they seem to belong to the scene quite as much as the tractor, the horses, the ringing hammer and the carts. Their business also appears appropriate to the time and the day. It is a different business only because they are young.

3 Phyllis, going to make her report to the billeting officer, meets her in the road, coming to see Charley for herself. She is annoyed to hear that he has gone.

"You were very quick, Phyllis, you're sure you made a thorough job of it."

"Oh yes, Miss Allchin," Phyllis sings, "I took off every hair. The poor liddle chap looked quite laughable."

"And you're sure he didn't mind too much."

"He diddn care a bit, he's too sensible."

"I hope so. It's so easy to make a mistake with children, and we don't want to give him a bad start. The report from London says he's very clever."

"But he've left school surely, Miss Allchin."

"He missed his scholarship by some illness, but he's been going to night classes. I had a special note from his teacher about him. She says this might be a great chance for him, to get him out of a blind alley."

Miss Allchin is a young woman of about thirty, with pretty, very regular features, which nevertheless have a look of nervous energy and quick feeling. She is as dark as an Italian and has the Southern skin, a clear pale brown. Her hair crimps in tight black waves. She has a trick of frowning and poking forward her head when she speaks. She does it now when she exclaims: "I particularly wanted to catch Charley this morning."

Phyllis answers as if taking a response in church: "I'll send him along, Miss Allchin—soon as ever I see him." She says nothing to Miss Allchin about the recent attack on Charley because she does not want to distress her, or to worry herself by having questions to answer and perhaps criticism to meet. She understands by Lina's voice and manner that the lady has already taken a strong fancy to him and that she will therefore certainly criticise any other woman's handling of his case.

"Oh, and there's another thing," Miss Allchin, having finished with the personal interest, comes to business. "You have a boy called Siggs, haven't you?—Basil Siggs, with red hair."

"Noa, wĕ put him to Wickens."

"That's very funny, because Mr. Wickens says that some of our boys let out his bull this morning—it's taken them over an hour to catch the brute, and he says that one of them has red hair—real carrots."

"There's two others with reddy hair. It med be the one they call Ginger. But it could be Basil, though he is at Wickens. He's very sha-arp and he looks wicked, too." Phyllis smiles. Her tone would have been laughter in a less contemplative nature. "Like flies, arn't they, for getting in everywhere? But it's natural for boys, too."

4   In Wickens farm at the top of the hill the old Devon bull, cranky and nervous, utters his cracked blare. His thick sides ache with bruises; his nostrils drip blood; his brain is full of bewilderment and humiliation. Only that morning someone had opened his gate and it had taken six men an hour's battle to drive him back again. Wickens' voice

can still be heard from his kitchen, threatening police and actions for damages. The yards, full of violent shadows, are empty. Suddenly a small boy in a blue cap, with a long stick in his hand, appears as if from the ground in front of the bull's stall and gazes through the heavy bars of the gate. These bars are set horizontally in a square frame; the stall is deep and narrow so that the huge brute stands in shadow. His claret-coloured flanks are still mottled with dirt, sweat and blows.

The boy stoops and gazes with round eyes; he is as still as the bull in his concentrated interest. The bull, with round foolish eyes, stares at the boy. Another boy, fair-haired, slips along the wall of the cowhouse, deep in shadow, and joins the first. A minute later there are three.

"A bull," one whispers.

"Would e go for yer, Ginger?"

"Course he would."

"Sall right if you don't show im nothing red." This is a dark pale boy with an impatient voice.

"You know a lot, Arry."

Ginger, smiling at the others as if waiting upon their pleasure, hums to himself: "Run, Adolf, run, run, run."

"Come on, Bill." Harry turns has back on the stall. "Wot we going to *do*?—there's nothing ere."

Bill, biggest of the three, is a heavy red-faced youth with red polished cheeks and wet hair slinked down across his bulging forehead. His hands are thrust deep into his pockets where his fingers can be seen fumbling and working. He laughs silently all the time and continually swings his heavy shoulders and body as if he cannot find an easy balance. He laughs at Harry's impatience and says: "Look out, Arry—e's coming for you."

Harry jumps and again turns towards the stall and says "Nao, e aint—e's only blowing is nose. No animals go for yer if ya let em alone. Wy, they got a place in South Africa were the lions eats out of yer and."

21

"He kissed me on the ship," Ginger murmurs. "And the captain kept the score."

"It's cruel to keep em locked up," Harry says severely.

"Let im out then, Arry."

"Oh, shut up, Bill—I aint funny."

"Bet you won't let im out, Arry," Bill jeers. Obviously his only method of conversation is the jeer and he has to make it serve all purposes. On the other hand, his grin is always good-natured.

"Oh, shut up, Bill," Harry pushes him with his shoulder. Bill at once charges at Harry, trying to crush him against the wall, prods him with his elbows and treads on his toes. Meanwhile he says loudly: "WASSAY WASSAY."

Harry dodges aside and says in a weary tone: "Oh, shut up, Bill, you make me tired."

"I didn't say nothing."

"Then ow did you say about letting im out?"

Bill farts and the other two collapse into violent giggles. Bill, standing with his back to the stall and his hands in his pockets, rumbles, rolls his shoulders and grins with the triumph of a comic artist. He is delighted by the brilliance of his own invention. Ginger's calm reserve and Harry's impatience have both been conquered. They double up, shake their heads and snort through their noses in the effort of holding back their noisy laughter.

Suddenly a shadow appears in the yard, beyond the edge of the barn, a tongue of blue-grey on the wrinkled dry mud shining now primrose colour in the morning sunshine. All the boys stare at it, and Bill turns and takes a step along the wall as if to escape.

A small boy in a man's hat hurries past the lower wall of the cow-house, his shoulders humped, his head swinging forward at a dejected angle. As he turns up the yard his projecting ears catch the sun and shine like rubies.

Suddenly he catches sight of the three boys standing motion-less in the shadow of the cow-house. He starts, turns as if to

22

run off, then draws himself up, thrusts out his chin and struts towards them. His listless movement of a dejected mongrel is changed into the uneasy exaggerated swagger of the same mongrel when he finds himself watched.

The three boys stare at him with totally blank faces. This blankness, by expressing no feeling at all, when feeling must be present, has the effect of the deepest contempt and the most wary hostility. Their immobility is like that of wild animals gathered together for immediate violent action in any direction.

"Ullo," says the stranger.

Nobody answers this. The stranger turns pink. He swaggers up to the stall and peers in.

"Wot you got ere?"

No one answers. The stranger turns to them.

"Bulls aint nothing to be afraid of."

No one answers this, but Bill leers at Ginger over the stranger's hat and jerks his shoulders as if hustling somebody. Bill gesticulates with his shoulders because he does not care to take his hands out of his pockets.

"Cows is different," the stranger says. "Cows go for you with their eyes open. But bulls go at you blind. Bulls is easy. You just wait till their orns is grazing your leg and then you dodge em."

"You aint afraid of bulls," Bill says, reeling towards the stranger as if to fall upon him and crush him.

"Nah, course not,"

"Let im out then. Go on, let im out."

"Course I would if I ad the key."

This offer interests the whole party. Ginger, Harry and even Bill look at the stranger with speculative curiosity. Bill says: "Wots yer name, Sinbad?"

"Charley Brown."

"All right, Sinbad Charley, don't brown me off."

"You really going to let out the bull?" Harry says.

"Yers, if I ad the key."

"There isn't a key," Ginger says gravely. "Only bolts. There you are, top and bottom."

Charley is taken aback. He had thought he was safe in asking for a key. He turns round very slowly and looks at the bolts.

"Go on," Bill says. "Bulls is easy, aint they?"

Charley is now looking at the bull, which gives a snort. He turns round, rather pale, and says in a condescending manner: "Course they're easy, but if I let im out, wot you going to do?"

"Wot we going to do?" Bills says. "Wy, we never said we'd do nothing."

They gaze at Charley in the middle of them with his back to the stall. They understand perfectly his situation; that he, an insignificant foreigner, has been trying to impress them, and that he is now in a pitiful and difficult position. They see that he is in a state of the highest tension and this excites their own senses. Ginger stares fixedly at him, Harry is flushed, Bill grins broadly, jerks his hips and works all his fingers convulsively.

"Go on," he says. "Get on with it."

Charley spits on the ground. "I'll let im out in arf a sec— nothing in that—but wots the good if you're just going to run off. Wots the good of letting im out, see?"

The boys are interested. This is a new idea, something to think about. They close in with curious and attentive looks. Bill's fingers are still. He says: "Garn, Sinbad, wot could we do?"

"Wot you do with bulls? You fight em."

"Fight em?" Bill gives an incredulous laugh and jerks one shoulder into the air. "Fight the bull?"

"Ya," Charley says, speaking with great energy and speed. "A bullfight, see—like they do in Spain—we'll dodge im all round—get some of those sacks—and wave em in front of is nose—I'll do it—I'll show you. Only you got to be my men with spears—and prod im."

"Your men, garn," Bill says, with a shiver of excitement and delight.

24

"Prod him?" Ginger asks mildly.

"Yers, stir im up, see—get im going."

"It's cruel," Harry says.

"Cruel." Charley stares at him in contemptuous amusement. "Oos this chap?"

"Don't mind im," Bill says. "E's a cissie—e's a Christian."

"I aint," Harry shouts.

"Oo tried to get in the choir down Pratt Street?"

"Cos I wanted to play billiards."

"Billiards—cor, billiards, ear that, Ginger—it was is dear Jesus."

"I aint a Christian," Harry says firmly. "I only said, well—wots the good of it."

"You can't ave a proper bullfight without prodding bulls," Charley says. "You got to make em wild—but if you funk it, you better get off."

"I aint funking it, ere, you better shut up—I aint afraid of any bulls."

"Wot, you'll stand around?"

"Yers, I'll stand ere."

"All right," Charley says with the air of a condescending prince. "If you promise to stand round, you can stay ere."

By this adroit sentence, Charley assumes leadership. Bill, noticing it, leers and says: "Ark to Sinbad."

"You better go and get yourself a stick over there." Charley suddenly takes Bill by the arm and points across the yard at a pile of brushwood. Bill, astonished, laughs and says: "Sinbad, the boss, watto." Then he sways across the ground, picks up a stick and returns slowly. "Wot next, mister?"

"You stay there," Charley commands him.

"Yessir, pleasure, don't mention it."

"Gimme that sack, Ginger," Charley commands, and Ginger runs across to fetch an empty sack from the door of the stable.

Charley takes the sack and places Ginger in the centre of

the yard. "You stay there, see—till e rushes at ya. Then you dodge off that side and I'll dodge off this side."

"And he knocked em in the old Kent——"

Harry, standing to the right, on tiptoe, with his stick held like a spear, calls out in a voice cracked with excitement: "You really going to do it, Charley?"

Charley disdains to answer. He turns to the gate. The three boys crouch like Rugby halves on the defensive; they move in sudden darts and continually jerk their heads, arms and bodies. Their faces are solemn and surprised as if they can hardly believe in their own daring. Even Bill is grave. He looks all at once like a red-cheeked infant, innocent and expectant, rather than an awkward half-grown youth.

Charley, sack in hand, peers at the bull. The bull snorts and he jumps back a yard; the three boys suddenly increase their distance from the stall by several yards.

Charley is visibly terrified. He slowly moves one foot towards the stall and then quickly leaps to one side. Suddenly he makes a spring and draws the top bolt. He stoops at once, pulls back the lower bolt and dancing backwards, holds up the sack as high as his nose. The three boys retreat another two paces.

The bull has not moved. He stares at Charley with eyes as foolish as glass balls. Charley stops his retreat, flaps the sack twice and springs nimbly from side to side. The bull makes no sign or sound.

The boys gradually straighten their backs and close in towards the stall.

"I told you e wouldn't do nothing," Harry says.

Charley goes up to the gate, rattles it, pulls it open a foot and bangs it to; the bull snorts and stares in wonder.

Bill and Harry walk boldly up to the gate and peer through the bars. Bill says: "Wot about the bullfight, Sinbad?"

"E's not a real fighting bull," Charley says. "You can tell by is orns."

26

"I told you e wouldn't do nothing, Mr. Arry Know All, Esquire, M.P.M.T."

"Well, I did."

There is silence. All appear dashed. Their expressions resemble those of dogs, who, having chased a cat across two streets, suddenly realise that they have lost their master. Bill gazes round him with a leer which has become senseless; a mere grimace. Ginger takes a rubber band out of his pocket; puts it between his teeth and plays three notes.

Harry wanders to a stable door and hooks his chin on the lower half as if to support himself. On the hill a cutter makes a crescendo, rising to a whirring scream that sounds as if it will be unbearable in another five seconds; then suddenly fades. A small child's voice shrieks in the lane: "This way, sil-lee." There is a rush of children's feet.

5 Charley has been gazing gloomily at the bull. He is disappointed in him. He feels the growing boredom and disgust of his new friends and he sees them already moving away from him. He turns suddenly and says: "Ere, less go an get some booze."

"Wot sort?" Bills asks, in a bored voice.

"Cider."

"Cor—Sinbad thinks cider is booze." He is still bored.

"So it is booze down ere."

"Nao—cider, booze—booze is beer."

"I only got thruppence."

"Wy, I thought you meant pinch it."

"Pinch it." Charley is shaken.

"Wot, you mean to buy it?" Bill says, suddenly laughing. "Sinbad and is thruppence—bottle a sugar water."

"Ya," Charley recovers himself, "if a chap knew were the booze was—of course e could pinch it."

"Wot, you would."

"Course I would—if there was any to pinch. But there aint none, see."

"All right, then, cocky. There's three cases bottled beer went into the ouse down there," nodding at the back of Wickens' farm-house, "arf an hour ago—saw em myself—into the back kitchen."

Charley looks at the house, hidden partly by the slope of the hill and there is a long pause. Then in a doubtful nervous voice he says: "Garn."

"Swear to God," Bill says. "S'truth, aint it, Ginger? Two cases anyhow."

"They took them into the back kitchen this morning."

"Go on, Sinbad—anyone could do it."

Charley is visibly in distress. He licks his lips and tries to say something and thinks better of it.

The three boys look at him with the most concentrated attention, studying his distress. Charley finally, with a visible effort, squares his shoulders. "Show me were it is."

"Go on," Bill says. "E's kidding."

But his leer is respectful and impressed. Ginger smiles with admiration. They know that Charley is trying to impress them and dominate them by his reckless deeds, but they are quite ready, even Bill is ready, to be dominated.

Charley feels this interest and expands in it. His chest swells out in the jersey, he gives his hat a poke over one eye, and cocks up his chin. "Come o-o-rn," he drawls. "Wot you waiting for—urry up—I'm thirsty."

This stroke of genius carries the party away. Bill gives a crow of laughter, doubles up, still with hands in his pockets, and says, "Good ole Sinbad." Harry's pale cheeks flush and he says, "You really going to pinch it, Char-lee?"

"Course—didn't I say so."

"Spose they catch you—it's a copper's job."

"Ere—wot you fraid of. Come o-o-rn—shew me."

Bill jostles him to turn him round and nods with his head towards the opposite corner of the yard by a barn. "There's a path there—right down to the yard—kitchen winder's in the yard."

Charley takes the path down the hill, followed at ten yards distance by the three boys. When he passes the barn he creeps along by the garden hedge to a wall which divides the Wickens' yard from a paddock. He creeps along the wall towards the house and peers over a dustbin through the open window. Suddenly an old woman in a man's cap appears at the door with a bucket in her hand. She sees Charles who at once springs upright, walks up to her, touches his hat and says: "Good morning, m. Does Johnny Smith stop ere?"

The old woman looks at him, slowly chewing with her gums and says at last: "I dunno, you better ask the missus." Then she walks through the yard with her bucket full of potato peel, and disappears into an out-house. Charley at once darts into the kitchen. His hands appear suddenly at the window holding two bottles of beer, which he lowers by the necks to the ground between the dustbin and the wall. Then he strolls out of the door just as the old woman reappears. He touches his cap to her and says: "No, m, e aint ere."

The old woman says nothing. She labours slowly towards the kitchen with the bucket. As she recedes through the doorway, Charley picks up the two bottles and darts back along the wall. Panic takes him for a moment. He feels that yells are going to sound behind him. He leaps across rows of cabbages in the kitchen garden and dives head first through a hedge of beans. When at last he stands in the cow-yard among the gang, he is too breathless to speak. His cheeks are still crimson, his eyes sparkle. He wants to shout, or dance. He has great difficulty in striking an appropriate attitude of calm indifference.

The others dance round him. Bill even takes a hand from a pocket in order to slap him on the back. "Good ole Sinbad."

"And we'll hang our washing on the Siegfried——"

Harry, almost as flushed and breathless as Charley himself, stares at him with a kind of foolish amazement. He says: "I

say, Charley, jew ever do it before—jew always pinch things?"
A deep wrinkle shows in his narrow forehead.

Charley is trying to control his breath. He looks still more
dignified. But he doesn't know what to say to Harry. If he
speaks the truth and says that he has never before stolen anything except lumps of sugar or spoonfuls of jam, he will no
doubt strike all the boys with astonishment at his cleverness.
But if he claims to be an old hand, a real thief, he will set himself on a superior plane. He will command their respect.
Since they are strangers and know nothing about his past, he
has a free choice. He can make for himself whichever position
he chooses.

"Jew pinch everything," Harry cries, screwing up his eyes
at Charley as if at a light too brilliant for them.

"Wy, of course—anything I want."

"Aint you never been cotched?"

"Garn, e's an old Borstal lag, aint you, Charley?"

"They aint cotched me," Charley says.

"You're too smart," Ginger says, apparently without irony.

"Don't need to be smart to dodge the coppers down our
way. Those flatties couldn't catch a traction engine with a bust
biler."

The boys go into another explosion of laughter, and, trying
to repress it in case of making too much noise, giggle, snort
and squeal. But to make up for their absence of whoops and
yells which the occasion deserves, they slap themselves, and
twist their bodies into contortions. These gestures are a ritual
expressive of intense appreciation.

"Cor, Sinbad," Bill whinnies. "You're a oner at pinching,
you are."

"Adam and Eve and pinch bottle."

"Best pinch I ever saw," Bill says, and suddenly jostling
against Charley, he puts his hand under his jersey and jerks
out a bottle. He moves away five yards, dodging at every step
as if expecting someone to leap at him from behind. Then he

faces round, leering enormously at the three boys, unscrews the bottle and puts it to his lips.

The others, who have not moved a step, at once call out: "Ere, ere, Bill."

"Arf a mo, Bill—your trousers is afire."

"Don't swallow the bottle—there's tuppence on it."

"Look out, Bill, there's a wapse in it."

These reproaches are also ritual, and in fact all the boys have used them so often to someone drinking that they repeat them without energy or conviction. They sound like responses in church.

Ginger sings mildly to himself, murmuring the words: "Another little drink wouldn't do us any harm."

Suddenly Harry gives a low whistle and jumps into the shadow of the bull pen. Bill whisks the half-empty bottle behind his back; Ginger steps back into a doorway.

6   Miss Allchin is walking quickly up the yard from the lane gate, with a short thick-set man in brown tweeds, with old-fashioned knickerbockers and enormous brown boots.

The boys, caught in the angle between cowhouse and barn, cannot escape. Charley leans nonchalantly against the gate of the pen; the other three, acknowledging his leadership, move inwards towards him and stand on either side.

Miss Allchin, screwing up her eyes as she peers against the sun, says in an uncertain voice: "Good morning," and smiles.

"Good morning, miss." Two caps come off; Charley slightly raises the front brim of his hat without moving the crown. Bill cannot bring himself to move a hand all the way from his pocket to his cap in order to perform an act of mere courtesy. He feels that such an elaborate ritual could be absurd and almost rude. But he blushes with embarrassment at the social difficulty. He assumes a leer which seems lecherous but is only defensive.

Lina Allchin, speaking apologetically, says: "I was just

31

going round to tell you that we hope to start classes to-morrow." Then suddenly she recognises Charley and thrusts out her chin towards him with a smile which makes her a very pretty girl. "Why, Charley, there you are—I've been looking for you everywhere—so you got the hat."

"Yes, thank you, miss."

Charley is full of gratitude to Miss Allchin for the hat and for liking him. He knows she likes him simply by instinct, the same instinct which makes dogs know their friends. Like a dog, too, he manages to convey, with very small means of expression, a great deal of what he feels. His sudden smile, and a certain lively expression of his rather hoarse voice, are enough.

"I hope you're not feeling too uncomfortable."

"No, miss."

"And you're not angry with us?"

"No, miss."

"It isn't your fault, we all know that."

Charley gives a nervous glance at the three other boys who are listening to this conversation with deep interest and curiosity. Lina notices the glance and looks at Charley. Charley's face conveys nothing, but the woman understands his difficulty and suddenly changes the subject. "About these classes—I've got you down, Charley. You're coming, aren't you? To-morrow at nine—at the house next the cross-roads. The Cedars. There's no name on the gate, but there *is* a cedar, one cedar, on the lawn. Now, who else will come. I know you, don't I?" turning to Ginger. "You were in my car last night. You're Siggs, aren't you?"

"Fant."

"Oh, yes, of course, Fant, Richard Fant." She is a little put out as if by a serious mistake. Miss Allchin, like any other young woman just appointed to war duty, without experience or training, is nervously anxious to seem more efficient than she is; or than anybody could be. She turns to her companion and says: "Please, Mr. Lommax, you have the list."

The man silently draws out pencil and note-book, takes a paper from the back and hands it to her. He then balances the pencil over the book as if ready to make notes. He is a middle-aged man with a strangely yellow face, wrinkled like a windfall, a broad, heavy-ended pale nose, and large torpedo moustache, tobacco coloured in the middle and dirty grey at the points. His expression is extremely serious.

"William Gittins," Lina reads.

Bill grins silently and twists from the hips. His hands under the cloth of his trousers grab inwards:

"You'll come, won't you?"

"I don't mind."

Lina goes through the list one by one until she reaches Henry Bean, who also agrees to come to the class. Then she turns to Lommax and says: "Now, Mr. Lommax, for your class to-morrow morning——"

Lommax makes no answer. He has taken out a letter, and, using the notebook as a desk, is drawing on it.

"You could take the names now, couldn't you?"

Lommax says nothing, but continues to draw, glancing now and then into the bull-pen with that professional important air which belongs to all men when they are doing their work.

Lina frowns. No doubt she would like to say: "Mr. Lommax, you seem to forget that you are on duty, war duty," but instead she says politely: "How many can you take in a class, Mr. Lommax?"

Lommax draws another line and looks at the effect. Then he says in a deep bass voice: "Naw, naw—ah've missed it."

The boys are all trying to peep at the envelope, Charley from one side, Harry and Ginger from another; Bill from behind. Lina taps her foot on the ground.

"Naw, naw," Lommax murmurs. "It won't do."

Over his shoulder Bill leers at Harry and pretends to kick the artist. Harry nudges Charley to make him see Bill's jokes.

Miss Allchin, deciding to humour her volunteer, looks over

33

his arm at the drawing and says: "I see, the bull. But it's very good."

"Naw, naw, Miss Lina, it's not bullish enough. Ah haven't got um yet. Wait now—let's see what an eyelash will do."

"Have bulls got eyelashes?—I can't see any from here."

"That's naw matter, Miss Lina—if this is my bull and ah wants an eyelash on him, he's damn well got to have an eyelash." He speaks with a booming but thoughtful voice, drawling out the syllables while he scratches at the envelope with his pencil broken at the end.

Bill behind, pretends to stroke a moustache; Ginger smiles gravely at Bill. Harry makes a feint to knock the artist's hat off; but though they are anxious to express extreme ritual contempt for the stranger, for his occupation, his remarks and appearance, they are also in a fry of curiosity to see what he is doing.

It is obviously not meant for them. They are getting a peep into something that is not for children; real grown-up stuff, unadulterated and untrimmed.

"Oh, dear, you're spoiling it," Lina says.

"Ah thought so—it *is* the eyelash." The artist, though Charley's fingers are on his sleeve, pays no attention to the boys, but continues to draw, deliberately and carefully. "Yes, it is the eyelashes—parrtly—and parrtly the turrn of the nostril."

Charley jumps two feet into the air, and failing even then to get a glimpse, puts his hand on the artist's wrist. "Oh, please, sir, lemme see."

"They want to see, Mr. Lommax," Lina says.

Mr. Lommax stands, glaring first at the bull, then at the drawing. Suddenly he turns upon Lina and booms in a disgusted voice: "Ah had the idea—but it's e-luded me."

"Please, sir——"

"Won't you let them see, Mr. Lommax?"

"It's not fit to see." Mr. Lommax puts the envelope in his pocket, turns round and walks off. The boys run after him and

Charley raises a hand as if to grasp at his coat-tail. Lina quickly catches the boy's shoulder and says: "Don't do that—you mustn't worry Mr. Lommax."

At this moment Lommax turns round, makes a frame of his fingers and looks at the farm buildings. Lina says to the boys: "So you'll come to-morrow—that's three of you—nine o'clock at my house—the Cedars."

Charley nods his head sideways towards Lommax and says: "Will he be there, miss?"

"He's promised to take a class, haven't you, Mr. Lommax?"

"Naw, naw, it's naw good to me—couldn't do anything with the damn thing."

"Mr. Lommax, you did say you would teach an art class for me this week?"

Lommax glances at the boys with an air of remote nonchalance. He does not even dislike them. He says: "Teach—ah can't teach, Miss Leena——"

"But you said——"

"No one can teach arrt."

"Oh, I know, of course——"

"Ah'll show em what it's about, if you like. But it won't do any good, you know, not a bit. They'll never learn anything. No one ever learns anything."

"Oh, but, Mr. Lommax——"

The man turns round again and glances at the bull, then shakes his head:

"Naw, ah had him—ah had him—ah had the idea of him— but ah lost it." He walks off, followed respectfully by Miss Allchin.

7 The boys look at each other. Bill rolls on his hips and says: "Ah aven't got it, Leener."

"The bulbul ameer."

"Oh, Leener, look at me eyelashes."

"But wot did e mean," Harry asks Charley. All look at

Charley as if for information. Charley is acknowledged leader, even by Bill.

Charley, feeling his dignity, ponders with a responsible frown. At last he gives judgment. "Not arf bad, e wasn't."

"Did you see wot e did?"

Charley has seen nothing. But since he feels the strongest interest in Mr. Lommax; since he is determined to go to the class to-morrow, and feels that some excuse for that pusillanimous act may be necessary to his gang, he sets out to make a hero of him.

"Not arf bad," he says therefore. "E can dror, that chap."

"Can you dror?"

"Yers, of course, but not like that chap—e's a real artiss, it's is job."

"Are you really going to the class?" Ginger asks.

They all look again at Charley, who spits on the ground and says: "It aint a class, that chap aint a teacher, see, e's a real artiss."

"Oh, Leener," Bill says, jerking his hands in his pockets. "Look wot I've done."

"But wot was e talking about?" Harry demands.

Charley and Bill and Ginger, who haven't the least idea what he was talking about, look solemn.

"Lot of bullshit," Bill says, and then gives a loud bellowing laugh at his own wit.

There is a thump and a clatter; the bull appears in the midst of the boys. He snorts, lowers his head, and swings round uncertainly. The boys scatter and fly; Bill and Harry for the field behind the cowshed; Ginger and Charley for the road gate.

The bull gives a blare, and suddenly three men come rushing from the road gate. A little old man in the middle with a long yellow nose and a grey moustache is shouting something in a cracked voice. And as he sees the boys he utters a kind of scream.

Charley and Ginger, cut off, stop dead; the bottle, jerked

from Charley's jersey, falls on the stones and bursts. The three men, now opening the gate, give another shout, and the next moment the two boys are running back through the yard. They pass the bull on each side. He swings round again and puts himself to a gallop after them. Ginger with his light long legs is already over the fence. Charley, shorter and in bad training, reaches the fence gasping for wind, misses a vault; then catches his foot in the top bar and tumbles head first into the paddock. His hat rolls off. The bull, close behind, gives a hoarse grumbling roar and the farmer answers with his high cackle of rage.

The boys are already far across the paddock, Charley snatches up his hat and makes a desperate sprint after them. He dives through a hedge gap and is caught by briars. He kicks wildly and rolls down a bank into a deep narrow lane. There are two boys standing in the lane watching him with surprise. But as Charley flies up the lane after Ginger, already disappearing, they, too, take to flight.

A hundred yards up the lane where it runs into the main road from Burlswood to Tawleigh, the hedge's banks have been cut back to give Wickens' carters a view as they come into the highway. A triangle of rough grass marked with deep cart tracks forms the corner, with a signpost at its forward angle.

Ginger, Harry and Bill stand at this signpost, laughing and looking up and down the three tracks to see that no one takes them by surprise. They watch Charley as, quite breathless, he staggers out of the lane on to the grass and falls back against the bank. His hat is still grasped in his hand, his bald head, marked with one large scratch from his morning battle, shines in the sun.

Bill, Harry and Ginger gaze at this bald head with interest. Bill is visibly confused. His round good-natured face expresses the most contradictory feelings. His mouth is leering, but his eyebrows are astonished and his attitude is respectful. He is not sure that a bald head may not be the latest thing among thieves.

Charley is too exhausted and alarmed to think of himself. He is completely relaxed and has no thought of appearances.

The other two have now joined the three at the signpost. All of them gaze at Charley. One of the two newcomers is the curly-headed Walter. He is a well-known humourist among his friends, and he now grasps himself by the sides and says: "Ow, wish I hadn't eaten all that breakfast." No one is amused. Bill leers at him and says: "Ullo, Funnyface."

But Walter is already pointing at Charley and singing: "Baldy-Baldy-ballocky baldy. HE'S LOUSY."

Ginger, Harry and even Bill are astounded for a moment at this outrage. They can't believe that this strange rat is insulting the great Charles. They stare at Walter. But he continues to sing Baldy, Baldy, and turning to them, he explains: "They had to shave him—and they burnt his clothes, too."

Bill, Harry and Ginger look at Charley again just as he, hastily, with a guilty and nervous gesture, puts on his hat. In an instant they see him as he is, a frightened, breathless small boy, smaller than any of them, who, in some extraordinary way, has imposed himself on them. All, even Ginger, gaze at him with surprise as if they are seeing him for the first time.

Walter, feeling that this time he has the crowd with him, laughs and shouts: "Baldy, Baldy, he's lousy."

Charley rushes furiously at him, but he dodges across the road, singing and laughing.

Bill says, suddenly recovering himself: "'E's lousy, Sinbad's lousy. Knock is hat off, Ginger."

"I aint," Charley screams. "You shut up."

"Ooo aint wot?" Bill leers at him.

Charley grabs at a stone and throws it at Walter. In a moment the air is full of sods, stones, pieces of dung, sticks. Charley, well pelted by six hands, nevertheless charges each enemy with such ferocity that he gives way. But the other five rush in from behind to prod him in the back or rub dirt on his bald head. Charley then turns and they scatter. This kind of human bullfight with a small, angry, desperate boy for the bull is popular everywhere among children. As in real bullfights, it needs only blind courage and fury on the part of the victim and numbers and agility on the part of the players.

But Bill, who does not throw because he prefers to keep his hands in his pockets, who plays the game by jostling Charles or kicking at him from behind, is not so agile as the rest. Charley, turning, catches him as he sways clumsily to one side and punches him in the ear.

"ERE," Bill shouts, "wot ya think your doing." He is not angry but offended. He takes out one hand and gives Charley a heavy slap in the face which knocks him against the bank. Charley, weeping with fury, jumps up and rushes at him again. Bill, startled by this ferocity, cries: "Ere," takes out his other hand and gives him another careless slap on the side of the face which knocks him flat. He lies half stunned and completely winded.

A cart comes down the road with a slow rattle. The carter calls out something and at once Bill and the whole party rush down the road and turn into the first field gate.

8   Charley did not come to the classes at the Cedars. Lina put this down to fear of Wickens, who had already made complaints to Lina that her boys, as he called them, led by Brown, had let out his bull and stolen his beer. Though Lina assured the old man that Charley Brown was far too sensible to let out bulls or steal, Wickens persisted that Charley was a ringleader and threatened to apply for a summons. But he did not do so for two reasons, because he was still not quite sure of Charley's guilt, and also because he had a theory, or feeling, that war, since it was a misfortune, ought to bring some hardships. Many country people had this feeling. They complained of the vackies for leaving gates open, breaking the ripe corn, letting the pigs into the garden, but usually they added with various tones of resignation or bitterness: "But there, it's the war, iddn it?"

39

Meanwhile Lina visited Charley's billet at Mrs. Parr's every day to enquire for him. But the boy was always out. Once she saw him darting through the fields as she came down the road, but Mrs. Brown told her that he had been out since the morning. Lina regarded Mrs. Brown as an enemy. She agreed with the chief billeting officer who said: "The children are easy—it's the mothers who are a problem."

In fact, though Mrs. Brown was always ready to warn Charley against any person in authority, she was not vigilant enough to do it well. Charley owed most of his escapes to a village boy called Bert Smith, who lived in the other half of the double cottage.

Mrs. Parr had nothing to do with the Smiths, who formed the lowest rank in the hamlet. In hamlets there is generally a highest and a lowest, very definitely marked; one family much richer, more powerful and important, one poorer and more helpless than all the rest. Mrs. Smith, of Burlswood, was a widow, by courtesy, who went out to work by the day, sometimes four and five miles off. From Saturday night to Sunday night she was usually half drunk, when she would wander about the village grinning foolishly, explaining her condition and apologising for it. She had two or three excuses which she used in turn, such as a stomach-ache, or bad news, or the bad conduct of her son Bert.

The village did not despise Mrs. Smith so much for her drinking fits as her public discussion of them. It held that a person who confesses a fault, without any attempt at a cure, is twice contemptible.

Bert Smith, the son, was a boy of twelve who was not much bigger than a child of eight. But his narrow face had a look of experience which gave it often the characteristic look of harassed middle age. This look was emphasised by large steel spectacles. Bert was always grinning. From the first moment of the strangers' arrival he had followed them about, grinning in a friendly and hopeful manner.

He was dressed like his mother, entirely in cast-offs. At this time he was wearing an old pair of riding-breeches which came down to his enormous boots, a huge cap, stuffed out with paper to prevent its falling over his nose, and a man's coat. The sleeves of this coat, several inches longer than the boy's arms, and the peculiar shape of its shoulders hanging from his narrow frame, gave him an appearance which could be recognised as far as the eye could see. Anyone in those days who saw a party of the vackies going up over the rolling fields above Burlswood, on some new exploration, was very likely, five minutes later, to see Bert toiling and flapping after them, with a gait reminiscent of a turtle in some thick liquid.

Bert, no doubt, saw or felt, in this arrival of a crowd of strange boys, a chance to make a friend. He was at the age when a child spends at least half his time making friends, changing friends, or quarrelling with friends, or wondering with dismay and secret terror why he has no friends.

So Bert was always in pursuit of the London boys. But he never caught up with them because he was afraid to go close. When they lingered, he lingered; when they stopped, he stopped, gazing sideways at them through his spectacles and grinning from ten or twenty yards away.

Bill and Walter, the biggest boys of the party, paid no attention to Bert. Some of the younger ones, like Basil, who had strong moral feelings, would throw a stone at him.

Bert, since he lived next door to Charley, was always at his heels. Charley could not put his head out of the cottage door without seeing Bert's hopeful grin and absurd hanging sleeves. He would then, of course, pretend not to see him and look the other way. Charley felt a strong repulsion from Bert, from his dress, his grin, his spectacles, his persistence in offering acquaintance. There was in Charley perhaps the same instinct which makes young horses in a field avoid one who is lame or sick and which will sometimes cause two such creatures, both maimed and neglected, to avoid each other. It was as though some secret nerve warned him against contamination; as if Bert's friendlessness might be catching. But though

Charley would not notice or speak to Bert, Bert, when Charley himself became outcast, was his efficient watch-dog. He would dodge under the Parrs' window at any hour and call out: "Charley, here's Bill and Walter, coming up quarry field." He always seemed to know where Charley was, so that he would come labouring up to him in a field half a mile from Burlswood and say: "Mr. Wickens allays comes round here about now, to look after his sheep."

Charley would silently accept warning and run away, followed respectfully, at ten yards distance, by Bert.

It was Bert who warned Charley when Lina Allchin came to find him at the Parrs' and reassure him about Wickens. But Charley was not afraid of Wickens. He did not come to the classes because he was afraid of meeting Walter or Basil on the road and hearing the song: "Baldy, Baldy." This song had an effect on Charley which was at once noticed by the others. It infuriated him, but it seemed also to take away both his courage and his wits. When Walter or Basil or Bill, lying in wait near the Parr's cottage, sang it out at him he would first jump and glare and then run off, but often in the stupidest fashion. He would start in one direction, change his mind, and take another. Or he would rush straight at some impenetrable hedge. This was delightful to the boys because it gave them something to think about and to do at the same time. All felt his difficulty, that he was confused and perplexed, that he could not understand exactly the nature of his misfortune, or how justly he ought to be regarded and treated as an outcast; but they were never tired of stalking him, lying in ambushes for him to see what he would do and then wondering at the foolishness of his deeds.

One morning they went to the trouble of a plot which took almost a whole morning to execute. The Hawes were cutting wheat in a field called Frenchay, just behind their house, which was in the valley below Burlswood. Both Harry and Ginger helped in the work, Harry because he was billeted at Hall Farm, Ginger because he was allowed sometimes to drive an old

Crossley without a number, used to convey small loads across the fields.

The plan was to ambush Charley from this car. Bill, Walter and Basil therefore, soon after tea-time, began to drive from Parrs', which, as they expected, caused Charley to go towards Frenchay. When at last he did try to escape down the farm land from Frenchay to Hall Farm, Ginger jumped out of the Crossley and turned him back. He behaved then exactly like a terrified rabbit; ran first into the arms of Bill and Walter, who whipped his legs with hazel twigs, and then rushed down towards the bottom of the valley, where the stream cut him off. Finally he had again to run the gauntlet of the hunters, singing with shouts of laughter: "Baldy, Baldy," and chasing him till they were too tired to run any further.

Then they had still the greater pleasure of wondering at him.

"He was blubbing," Walter said in a tone between amazement and gratification.

"Wy did e go down ill?" Bill cried. "E knew e couldn't get out that way.

"Wy does e act so funny?" Harry asked. "E wasn't like that before was e? E wasn't like that wen e pinched the beer."

"E's barmy, that's wot it is, or wat d'ya think, Ginger?"

But these questions were merely attempts to express interest in Charley's predicament and wonder at his being so foolish. The reason why he was foolish was known to all of them because they had all behaved in the same way, for the same reasons. Every child has been perplexed by some unexpected social development, if it is only a sudden question to which he does not know the answer, or a sudden charge, of which he does not know the meaning. He feels then, at least for a moment, a kind of confusion which is like a splitting up of the brain into senseless fragments, and in that confusion he does or says things which astonish him and shame him for a long time afterwards.

No doubt Bill, Walter and the rest had no recollection of their own crises of perplexity, but the experience was as much

43

part of them as their fingers and toes. Therefore when they exclaimed at Charley and experimented on him they were really re-living, with intense curiosity, bits of their lives.

It added to their pleasure, of course, that Charley had once imposed upon them, that he was obviously full of courage and intelligence. Because this made the wonder of his cowardice and folly, that is, of the cowardice and folly which had fallen upon themselves in similar perplexity, still more extraordinary and exciting.

9 Charley himself in this strange misery of not knowing what was the extent of his crime in being lousy among a set of boys who, apparently, had never been lousy, quickly began to accept the position of outcast. He would slip out of Parrs' before breakfast, after climbing out of the window by the spout of the water-butt. He would snatch some bread and margarine out of the scullery window or go hungry till dinner. He would suddenly appear in the kitchen at dinner-time, when only his mother was in the room, and snatch a piece of meat from the stew or some cold bacon from the dish. When Mrs. Parr saw him dodging out of the room before her she would draw out her thin lips and say: "If he comes for his dinner, he'll sit down for it in my house."

"Charley never sits down for nothing," Mrs. Brown would answer, laughing. "'E's a live one, e is."

Mrs. Brown was Charley's stepmother. She was a young woman of twenty-seven, with a round rosy face and a little snub nose, shiny on the wings as if greased. There was a perpetual smile on her small thick lips which were slightly pushed out as if they were tasting something nice. Mrs. Brown had offered to help in the cottage and would sometimes peel potatoes or boil a kettle. But she often lay in bed till nine or ten in the morning and then she would wheel her baby, in its smart perambulator, to the Green Man, where she would have

44

a morning wet and a long talk with two of the other women evacuees.

No words could express the bitter contempt of Mrs. Parr for Mrs. Brown, or the good-natured indifference of Mrs. Brown to anything that Mrs. Parr might think or say or do. Yet there was no quarrelling in the cottage. Mrs. Parr had the self-control and patience of the born country wife, accustomed to a little world where a moment's loss of temper or single cross word may produce a feud lasting for years and causing endless damage; Mrs. Brown had the large good nature and tolerance of a Cockney, joined to the physical contentment of a young wife.

Her relations with Charley, perfectly reasonable to her and to him, were an extreme annoyance to Mrs. Parr. She would say: "If that was my booy I'd learn him to take his hat off in the house."

"Charlie never as took is at off for anybody," Mrs. Brown would answer, as if discussing the interesting habits of some wild animal.

Mrs. Brown was much amused by Mrs. Parr's dislike of Charley's manners. She would warn him: "Look out for her, Charley—she says you slep in your boots again."

"Wot if I did?"

"She says she won't give you no more sheets if you wipe yer boots on em."

"Don want sheets."

"So I tole er, but it aint no good telling *er* nothing, no morn if you talked to an old taxi-cab. She jus goes on the same."

Mrs. Brown considered it part of her duty to Charley to warn him against all persons who wished in any way to control him and interfere with his freedom of action. One afternoon she said to him: "Teacher was after you this morning, Charley."

"Oo?"

"Miss Allchin—poke-nose I call er."

"She aint a teacher."

"Who is she, then?"

45

Charley makes no answer to this. He is too much dejected.

"She teaches, don't she?" Mrs. Brown asks, seeking the last word. "Drawing, aint it?"

"No, they got a real artiss to teach drawing."

"Well, she teaches."

Charley is scrabbling his finger on the table-top. He drags out a spot of milk into a face. Then he slides across the room, to take from the window-sill next the back door a pencil used by Mrs. Parr for writing down her memoranda. He draws a face on the wood.

"Drawing, Charley?" Mrs. Brown asks.

"No."

"Don let er catch you with er pencil."

Charley puts down the pencil and slides into the parlour where the ink and notepaper are kept.

He draws there for ten minutes until his stepmother silently opens the door and says: "Look out, Charley, she's at the back door."

Mrs. Brown, having given this warning, like one Indian brave to another, makes her own escape and is found by Mrs. Parr sitting in the kitchen. Suddenly Charley comes in and says: "Gimme a penny, mum."

"A penny? I give you a penny this morning."

"Gimme another, mum," Charley says. He leans against her shoulder: "I wants it bad."

"Wot a way to ask," Mrs. Brown says. "Don't even give a smile," and raising her voice she shouts at Mrs. Parr, who is rather deaf: "Asks for a penny and not even 'please, mum'. Manners."

"He's not my booy," Mrs. Parr says, demolishing mother and son at one blow. Mrs. Parr looks like a witch, but by doing so she makes everyone perceive that the traditional features of a witch are those of natural power and much dignity.

Mrs. Brown understands the stroke and laughs at it. "Oh, Mrs. Parr, that was a nice smack in the eye." Then suddenly

46

she says to Charley: "In the pocket of my fawn coat—and don you take more than a penny."

"Ave you got tuppence, mum?"

"No, I avent—all right, tuppence—and that's all."

Charley goes upstairs to fetch the tuppence. He is just running out of the door when he stops, comes back to his mother and says: "Ows baby?"

Mrs. Brown, understanding that this is a form of gratitude, answers: "A lot you care—but you're welcome, Charley." And she shouts at Mrs. Parr: "E's got a way with the gurls, aint e—see im dig it out of me."

Mrs. Parr scorns to answer such a speech. Charley does not notice it, he is already flying to the shop. He can think of nothing but his purpose. For the moment he is possessed by it, carried away like a rider on a wild horse. But also he possesses it. He can't hold it, but he rides it; he knows, or think he knows, what he wants to do with it. At the village shop he buys a twopenny bottle of red ink. Five minutes later he is in the old quarry.

This is a deep semicircular cut on the steep hillside to the east of Burlswood. It belongs to Wickens Farm, but it has not been used for a long time. The floor is covered with broken stones and a thick growth of brambles, gorse and alder. The ruins of a shed and a deep square pit half full of ancient grey sawdust show where the level has served for foresters to cut and saw a few boles of elm and chestnut, windfalls in some forgotten storm.

All the vackies separately and in parties have examined the quarry. Charley, even in four days, knows every inch of it. He makes for a corner, behind the saw-pit, where a thick growth of brambles screens the rock face from any passers along the farm lane below.

Charley has already marked down a shallow hole in the rock, which might almost be called a cave. But as he pushes through the brambles he is startled by the sound of music. One single note, so soft and smooth that it seems like a natural product,

47

something that belongs to the air of the place, grows on his sense. As he listens it changes to another and runs very slowly up a broken scale. Two notes are missing.

He looks through and sees Ginger sitting in the cave with a mouth-organ at his lips. Round below the cave a few stones have been piled and some rotting planks from the shed have been propped up against the rock. Ginger has been building himself a house. But he has grown tired of the work, and is now playing to himself. He looks at Charley, four yards away, out of the top of his slate-green eyes, and continues to play the notes, contriving by careful management to give them the quality of an æolian harp. Charley stares at Ginger for half a minute. He seems to be astounded by the sight of Ginger playing to himself; Ginger, though his calm gaze acknowledges Charley's presence, seems quite undisturbed by it. Charley, in fact, is astounded, but only in sense. He does not even reflect "There's Ginger." He has no time for reflection. He turns about and forces his way through the scrub to the next open space. Here there is a tree-stump in a small thicket of nettles. Charley tramples the nettles, lays out his notepaper and ink-bottle on the stump and squats down in front of it, to draw.

At once he is absorbed, concentrated, so that he holds his breath often for half a minute, and then breathes again with a great impatient sigh.

He draws first a red bull with black eyes, then a black bull with red eyes. He then draws men, houses, a cow in a field with red clouds raining black rain. He draws blue slates on the houses, blue lines on the sky above the clouds. He then makes a blue bull with black eyes set in red circles. He gives it red horns and finally draws curled red strokes like flashes of lightning radiating from it in all directions. He stares at this picture for a long time with an astonished air. He puts his head on one side and frowns at it, then tries a view out of the side of the eyes.

"Rotten," he murmurs, but it seems to him a masterpiece. He is red with excitement and surprise.

But soon he thinks, "I'll make it look lighter round," meaning that he will throw up the flames round the bull by a dark background. He puts in a blue cloud with red edges on the left and a red cloud with blue shadows on the right. The effect seems to him terrific; the bull now looks like a bull of blue fire with transparent horns full of flame. He gazes for another five minutes, enchanted by his own bull, and then puts in a third cloud and darkens the other two.

But the paper is now soaked with ink, which begins to run. The bull begins to lose its sharp lines. Charley, swearing furiously, wipes the clouds with his sleeve and finally licks the dripping ink. The sodden paper tears under his tongue. He is in tears of rage and disgust. He looks at the paper on the ground and says: "Wy, it's rotten—just rotten"; he has lost all confidence in himself. He is sure that he, Charley Brown, could never do a good drawing. "Ere, wot you bin playing at, you bloody fool—you aint a bleeding kid." He leaves everything where it lies and goes off, slouching with disgust, his hands deep in his pockets.

From the cave in the rock face he can still hear Ginger's successive drawn-out notes, as sweet as bird pipes.

IO   The Cedars was a small, low, red-brick house near the Burlswood cross-roads. An old cedar grew in a grass plot on the left of the short drive. The other grass plot on the right had a rose-garden close to the low boundary wall on the road. A walled kitchen-garden stood to the north side of the house, a lean-to greenhouse clung to the south. The yard and buildings were approached by a gate between house-and kitchen-garden, barely wide enough for a cart or car; and also by a back drive from the church road, which turned off along the churchyard wall.

One Wednesday afternoon Lina, having set her last class to work, was going through an upper passage to find pencils for it when she happened to glance from the window and saw in the back lane an unmistakable old hat and green jersey. Charley had come and was actually approaching the house.

But when she opened the window he took fright and darted off down the lane. Lina was startled and also frightened. She had asked herself a hundred times of Charley in the last few days: "Was I right to let Phyllis shave his head like that— oughtn't I to have sent him away to the hospital at Longwater? Obviously something has gone wrong."

Seeing Charley retreat she felt therefore something like panic and flew downstairs, thinking: "Perhaps if I get my bike I could cut him off at the road."

She made for the road, but reaching it, she was relieved to see the hat once more moving slowly towards the yard and the kitchen door. She therefore returned through the house, and after stopping to take breath and collect her ideas, as for an important crisis, she went quickly into the yard by a door from the little back room, used for bicycles and garden chairs. Charley, standing irresolute in the middle of the yard, did not see this approach from the flank. When Lina spoke to him he jumped and turned to her a face full of uneasy suspicion.

"Why, Charley," Lina had decided on an easy careless tone. "I've been expecting you for days."

Charley said nothing; he was still suffering from shock.

"But it doesn't matter now you're here. You're just in time for tea. Come in."

Charley muttered something which Lina caught but did not at first understand: "Brought your—what—oh, Mister Lommax!—no, I'm afraid he's not here to-day. He only comes for week-ends."

There is another awkward pause. The boy looks at Lina under his hat brim with an enquiring doubtful eye; Lina tries to think of some remark, full of psychological cunning, which will in a flash prove to him the sincerity of her will to help him, and win his confidence. But she can't think of the magic phrase. At last she says breezily, in a tone which seems to her disgusting: "Come along—we've got a chocolate cake."

Charley retreats a step. Suddenly Lina notices that he is holding something under his left arm. It is glued stiffly to his side.

"Have you brought your books?" she asks, surprised. Then by an inspiration: "A drawing-book—do let me see."

The boy stops and shakes the hat. "No, I don't think——"

"But have you brought some drawings—you'll let *me* see, Charley."

Charley looks at her and becomes, as she puts it, reasonable. He draws out two crumpled sheets of paper from under his jersey. He looks at them with a doubtful frown.

"I must show them to Mr. Lommax, mustn't I?" Lina says, holding out her hand.

Charley silently lets her take the drawing. He turns slowly pink.

Lina is surprised. She has expected something in pencil, crude perhaps but neat. She sees a mass of red, black and blue lines, with large blotches of crimson and blue-black. She takes care, however, not to show any disappointment. She says gaily: "In colour—I like plenty of colour. This is a landscape, is it?"

"No, miss, the bull—it's meant for," Charley squints over her arm at his own drawing. His expression is full of perplexity.

Lina, gazing, sees that there is something like an eye close to the finger. When the finger is withdrawn she sees another eye, with a large dim black centre, and all at once the whirling lines round those eyes form themselves into a wrinkled face, monstrous and absurd. Lina is startled. She wants to laugh, but again she controls herself. She says gently: "I see, a bull's head."

"And the bull——" the boy reaches up to plant another finger on the paper, "there's his hoofs."

"They're rather near his head, aren't they?"

"Yess," the boy admits this with reluctance. "They're bull's hoofs—meant for."

"Yes, bulls do have short legs, don't they? I think it's awfully good, Charley. I see you like drawing." She blushes slightly as she gradually perceives other details of the work.

Charley also turns red. He loses all confidence in his drawing.

"No, it's rotten, miss. I didn't really mean to show it to you."

"Oh, but, of course, I know this is only a beginning—the colours have run a bit, haven't they? And the bull is not just perfectly clear. But it's awfully good."

Charley has been gradually recovering his aplomb. Now he draws himself up and says in an easy tone, using his best English: "It's rotten, miss. I don't know why I did it."

"But I'm awfully glad you showed it to me, Charley. Now what do you say to making another drawing for Mr. Lommax. I'll give you some clean paper—real drawing-paper and some real colours—water-colours."

"Yes, miss, I'd like that," Charley takes the drawings from Lina, glances at them and then laughs. He says, in surprise: "Rotten, aren't they, miss, they really are."

Lina, greatly relieved, smiles and says: "They'd hardly do for Mr. Lommax, would they—but we'll try again, won't we?"

"Yes, miss—thank you, miss, for being so kind." Charley tips his hat brim and walks off. As he goes into the lane, Lina sees him crumple up the drawings and throw them into the hedge. For some reason, though she is glad that he has perceived the badness of the unpleasant drawings, she feels again a little nervousness about the boy. Upon an impulse she runs after him and calls: "Charley."

He turns and comes back, politely giving a tug at his hat brim, as if to show that he would take it off if he were not prevented by some mysterious force.

"Yes, miss."

"Have you had any pocket-money lately?"

"Mother gave me thrippence Monday."

"Here you are then—I really owe it you for all you did on evacuation day." She gives him a shilling.

"Thank you, miss," laughing with pleasure. Lina, seeing in the boy's delight that he has already recovered from his disappointment over the drawing, smiles with equal delight and says: "Mind you spend it all—it's for a present."

Charley runs off, forgetting even to tug his hat; Lina, going back to the house, thinks with an impulse of warm happiness: "How good-natured they are—it's wonderful." She means that it is wonderful in Charley, who is poor and unjustly treated by the world, to be so forgiving towards her, who is well off. But she could not put it that way without treachery to the political ideas which have nothing to do with her private feelings.

II Charley, with Lina's shilling in his hand, walks soberly down the back lane. But this demeanour is a courtesy to the place. The back lane is part of Lina. Inside he is in such joyful excitement that he wants to run and yell. He knows very well what a shilling means to him. It is power, opportunity. A boy with a shilling, or even sixpence, however despised and cut off from society, can always be sure of a welcome when he invites another boy to share it.

The reason is not altogether cupboard friendship. It is paltry tribal feeling. Children expect to share pleasures, and are ready, of course, to make any necessary adjustment of social relations securing that end. So a small girl, who detests another, but meets her in possession of a new toy perambulator, will be polite to her in order to lay even two fingers on the perambulator. Grown-ups smile wisely and think her a time server. But in fact she is invoking certain understood rules of conduct. The proof is that if, having been polite, she is still prevented from a tribal share in the perambulator, she will feel a bitter grudge against the owner and say: "It's not fair—she's mean."

Charley, therefore, however sedate down the back lane, is really flying in spirit, to share friendship again, and to meet his kind on tribal ground of hospitality. As he springs out of the gate into Church Lane, his whole face is transformed, and he lets out a yell to be heard a quarter of a mile away: "Hi, Ginger!"

Ginger is dawdling along the main road with Harry. They both stop and look with surprise at Charley as he rushes towards them. But they do not think of calling Baldy because the very fact of Charley's bold approach shows that a new situation has arrived in which Baldy might be the wrong move.

"See here," Charley yells. When they see the shilling they understand at once Charley's boldness. It is the natural thing. Ginger says: "What you going to buy—biscuits or pop?"

"Anything you want," Charley cries, and seeing at the corner Bert, who has no doubt been stalking him for most of the morning, he yells again: "Come on, Bert, I got a shilling."

Bert, approaching slowly and cautiously, with a sidelong grin, says: "A shillun, that's a good un." Then he gives a loud giggle.

"Wot about Liz?" Harry says.

"Liz—oo's Liz?"

"Bessie—Harry's girl," Ginger says. "At Hall Farm. But he calls her Liz—he's been taking her all round."

"She aint my girl—I aven't got a girl—she ony appens to go my way."

"She's barmy," Ginger says.

"She aint barmy," Harry becomes suddenly excited and angry. His little white forehead, star-shaped between the peaks of his thick black hair, becomes puckered with deep wrinkles. "She's got as much sense as you ave, more."

"All right," Ginger says. "You say so. Roll out the barrel."

"She aint barmy," Harry bawls as if defying the world's opinion. "She aint even ardly deaf—not so much as they say."

"Twank, twang, twanky," Ginger imitates a banjo with surprising loudness and fidelity.

"It's a shame," Harry shouts.

"All right," Charley says. "I aint saying we won't ave yer Liz—get yer Liz."

"She aint mine—and I aint going to get er. Wy should I?"

"All right then, Arry, just wot you like. Come on, boys, come on, Bert."

As they pass the corner, Harry disappears, and two minutes later both he and Lizzie Galor are members of the party. Lizzie, as usual, is carrying a basket. She is rarely seen in the village without a basket, sometimes an enormous one containing washing or vegetables, which she is carrying from one house to another, sometimes a small one, with eggs, which she is delivering to Hall Farm customers. Like Bert, she is a solitary, but for a different reason. Bert is a social outcast; Lizzie is shut in by her deafness and a certain reserve, common in children with some defect. This reserve nearly always goes with a passionate eagerness to take part in the world. Thus bed-ridden children rapidly acquire an extraordinary knowledge of events, and facility in writing or speaking affection to the most casual acquaintance. Yet they are so diffident that other children terrify them and make them obstinately silent.

Now brought suddenly among the group of boys, Lizzie's broad brown face, covered with freckles, assumes at once a look of obstinate stupidity. Her face with its short square nose, grey green eyes, thick mouth and small pointed chin, is well formed for the expression.

But Charley, finding her lurking behind Harry, welcomes her with a yell: "Hullo, Liz—wot'll ya ave?"

Lizzie, no doubt remembering Charley's former perfidy, looks at him with a disapproving face and says nothing. Harry catches the girl's arm and shouts: "She'll ave milk chocolate, won't you, Liz? Thass wot she likes."

"She didn't say so," Ginger says. Ginger plainly dislikes girls.

"Ere, you shut up. You leave er alone, Ginj."

"She can't hear."

"Yes, I can," Lizzie says unexpectedly and turns dark red. This embarrasses all the boys, who stare at her for a moment, sidelong.

"Tell Ginj to shut up, Charley," Harry shouts furiously. Charley, thus appealed to as the host and leader, at once says: "Shut up, Ginj," and Ginger accepts the command without a word. For in this situation Charley is the man of power and acts as a man of power. In fact no one even recollects that half an hour before, he has been an outcast ready to fly from any of them at a single rude word.

Charley now leads the way to the shop and buys bulls-eyes, acid drops and two bottles of fruit juice at twopence each. Lizzie, who comes only just within the door, as if she can neither separate herself from her new friends nor venture among them, advises fruit juice as the cheapest article. "Tis the same as at Longwater," she says, "but the sweets is all more." She advises Harry to tell Charley to count his change. But neither Charley nor Harry think it the proper thing, on a feast day, to count change, and Charley, when change is offered him, says only: "There's three apence over, boys—wot can we get for three apence?"

He gets acid drops. The five children wander slowly down the lane sucking and talking. No one walks straight ahead. Charley as the host and leader is always the nucleus of the swarm, but he wanders from the shop door to the field wall opposite, back again to the next cottage below the shop, obliquely to the field gate. The others, except Lizzie, who is always behind and a little separated, drift round him, sometimes walking backwards, sometimes edging sideways.

Charley is telling stories out of some crime magazine. "I tell you wot the Diamond Gang did—they went in an empty ouse—a castle it was—a duke's castle—went in by the cellars, see, through an underground passage, cos the doors was locked—and they went and pinched carpets and furniture and pictures and gold ornaments and silver frames and statues— everything they wanted for the castle, and, of course, they pinched the finest things, wy, some of the pictures was worth thousands of pounds and a lot of the chairs was all over gold with silk cushions and they ad all sorts of wines and champynes and food—and they ad their molls there, too—that's their dolls, you know."

Lizzie, fascinated by the story, has gradually, as if against her will, been drawn towards the teller with whom she now walks so closely, striving to catch each word, that she touches his arm. She murmurs; "Was this in Lunnon?"

Ginger laughs suddenly and Harry says: "Shut up, Ginj, wy shouldn't it be in London?"

Ginger takes a rubber band from his pocket, puts an end between his teeth and twangs three notes.

"Molls are so faithful," Charley says. "They're better than wives—the molls in Ammurca as saved their chaps' lives over and over again—they'll shoot it out with the G-men every time an wen their chaps get bumped off—they go on shooting until they get all shot to pieces."

Ginger looks thoughtfully at the rubber band and says: "There was a woman soldier once—they found her out when she was wounded."

"But that was a long time ago," Lizzie says.

"But wot was the good of it?" Harry asks, walking backwards. "Wot did they want it for?"

"Wot for?"

"The ouse—the castle."

"Want with it, wy, they lived there, of course—with pictures like at Windsor Castle and marble statues and golden pillars." Charley, having reached the wall again, unbuttons and waters upon it, directing the jet with one hand and waving the other to emphasise the parts of his story, "and carpets like grass all with flowers in em, yers, and great bowls full of roses and every night they ad fountains playing with coloured lights." Charley is in highest inspiration and enjoyment. His audience is now at least fifteen, including some of the village children who stand too far to hear but not too far to catch the wondering and pleased expressions in nearer faces. Young Fred Hawes, aged twelve, riding towards the harvest field with two cans of tea and kicking a bay pony's sides with his large rubber boots, like Dick Turpin on his way to York, draws up by the hedge. The expression of hurry and anxious impatience on his round face gives way gradually to a look of baffled wonder. Norman Siggs, solemnly returning to the same field from his farmhouse tea, in a neat collar and tie above, and corduroys borrowed from Wickens, below, stops at the Green Man gate and looks across the road through his round black goggles with the expression seen only in hobbledehoys of his age, who find their own company oppressively serious, but are too proud to join in children's games. A small fair girl with very pink cheeks, carrying a bunch of ox-eyes, is standing actually between Ginger and Harry. She wears an elaborate muslin frock, starched and frilled, and looks round now and then in solemn wonder, as if surprised to find herself in such rough company. She is sucking one of Charley's acid drops.

All the children have come together in a few minutes as if the knowledge of free sweets had been carried to them by a special sense. Yet at least half of them don't want sweets. Norman is too serious-minded to eat sweets except in private; young Fred Hawes on his pony is too amazed by the vackies to ask for one. Charley buttons himself carelessly with one hand and strolls off again. "And a band playing music every day—different music, like in the Pallydedance."

The audience parts in front of him but, unwilling to drop behind, walks sideways; the small girl, whose name is Irene, sucks her acid drop, and skips backwards, looking curiously at the audience and not at Charley. It has not yet occurred to her that the story is the attraction; it seems to her that free acid drops explain the gathering. Charley, with a gesture which combines emphasis on the point about the music, and hospitality, holds out the torn bag of drops to three newcomers, including Basil Siggs who at once helps himself to two drops. "Music that fairly makes your ead go round—and all the molls was dressed up in jewels and satin and they danced with em, see—and walked round looking at the pictures and listening to the music and aving drinks of champyne."

"Didn't anybody spot em?" Harry asks.

"Na-o—they was too clever, see. They ad a good blackout. You never saw a blink o light outside. Wy, people passing along the road fair shivered wen they saw that old castle all dark and covered with snow and the moon shining on it —yers, and another thing they did—they tole everybody around that the castle was aunted——"

"With ghosts," Lizzie murmurs, looking astonished. The small girl Irene, without looking at Charley, reaches up a hand and takes another acid drop.

"Not real ones, see. But wen people eard music or anything —shrieks—their air rose on end and they ran off five miles without stopping. But, of course, the shrieks was only the molls aving a grand ball with their chaps."

"Is this true?" Harry asked.

"Honest gospel—it was all down in a paper. It appened in Ammurca."

"Oh, in Ammurca—I knew it wasn't ere."

"Ah, but ow d'you know it isn't appening ere nah."

"Ow could it?"

"Of course it appens—it's appened lots of times."

"I never see nothing in the papers."

"Nah, cos they don't put it in the papers ere—the cops is afraid, see. They're afraid everyone'd start doing it—it's too easy. Wy, other day a cop thought he'd got onto one of the big shots, and e followed is car along, and it turned right up through a big iron gate, down an avenue a mile long to a castle——"

"Another castle?"

"Oh, it aint called a castle, but it was big enough—bigger than most castles——"

Bill's voice calls out from the upper road: "It's Lousy."

Walter's voice at once burst into song. "Baldy, Baldy, Ballocky, Baldy," but neither Ginger nor Harry join in with the chorus. They fall back with the startled foolish expressions of people just waked from a day doze.

Bill comes rolling among the children, with Walter behind. Walter is laughing and singing at the same time. As usual he is in the highest spirits.

12 At the arrival of Bill, the most peace-loving and timid members of the audience, both natives and vackies, begin to disappear. There is already, after the first week, a distinction in the hamlet between the good vackies and the dangerous ones. It is not yet sharp in the middle. Norman at the upper end is highly respected on account of his reputed scholarship, his grave looks, his church-going and his earnest wish to be useful. He is also pitied for his ignorance of the world, and his bad health. Ginger is ranked as a quiet boy but a regular townsman; Walter is highly popular for his jokes and friendly smiles; Basil, in spite of his piety and his membership of a Bible class, is regarded both as dangerous and comical. Even natives tease him and laugh at his fits of temper, his violent curses. But Bill with his size, his yells, his habit of leering at girls is avoided both by the good vackies like Norman, and the respectable natives. Only Sam Eger the blacksmith, and the Vicar, stand up for Bill. The first says that he's a grand young bull to come out of a dirty hole like Lunnon; the second that he is a thoroughly good chap.

Fred Hawes, as soon as he sees Bill, starts out of his fascinated contemplation; intelligence and business rush back into his features and suddenly he gives an urgent shout and kicks the bay pony with his large boots. Fred wears his rubber boots all the year round. He likes them because they are something like top-boots, a little like pirate boots; and, at the same time, distinctly farmer's boots.

The pony, which has been dozing, springs forward with a

jerk which would have unseated anyone but Fred; and the pair disappear round the corner; Fred still kicking, shouting and clattering his cans; the pony galloping. The bay pony from the Hall is used to being galloped over tarred roads.

Norman, at the same time, moves quietly and unostentatiously out of Bill's sight. Bill is apt to yell: "Hullo, old goof skin," at Norman, to which Norman has no reply.

Two other smaller boys run as if for their lives. In thirty seconds from Bill's arrival, the party in the road consists of the original members, Bill, Walter, and the little girl Irene, who is waiting for another acid drop. She looks with calm interest at Walter when he shouts again: "HE'S LOUSY."

Charley rushes at him and gives him a punch on the side of the jaw which causes him to stagger backwards with a look of amazement. Charley, full of new social confidence, is prepared to fight anybody.

"Wot you do that for?" Walter asks, holding his chin.

"Wots the game, Lousy?" Bill asks, laughing, and then he yells at two dark figures passing along the main road, just above. "HI, I SEE YA," and makes a noise like a gigantic kiss.

"He hit me," Walter explains. "Charley Brown hit me."

"All right, you it im back."

Walter, horrified by this suggestion on the part of his master, grumbles to himself. "But what he hit me for?"

Ginger says in a thoughtful way: "We'd better do it properly, the road is on a slope."

"But they aint going to fight," Harry cries, apparently as much astonished as horrified by this development.

"Come on," Charley shouts, putting down his hat, throwing up his elbows and causing his fists to revolve round each other in the air.

"I didn't do anything," Walter complains. He looks round in pathetic surprise at the circle which now surrounds him and Charley. He can't understand why anyone should wish evil to him who wants only to please.

Charley, growing more and more professional in style as he

61

sees the enemy less enterprising, now begins to prance backwards and forward with a peculiar heel-and-toe movement. This, with the waving of his fists, is very exhausting and he begins to pant heavily.

"But I don't want to fight anybody," Walter says.

"E's a Christian," Bill says. "Come on, Cissie—fight for Jesus."

"What's he want to hit me for?" Walter asks, bitterly aggrieved by this injustice.

"You cheeked me, see," Charley says. "I'm going to knock your block off——" he rushes up to Walter, who steps hastily backwards. Charley is drawing back his arm as if to knock him from the face of the earth, when suddenly Irene walks up to him, and, looking not at him but at Walter, holds up her palm. Charley, not at all surprised or even put out, at once dives his hand into his pocket, takes out a rag of dirty paper to which two acid drops are still glued, and puts it in the child's hand. "Ere you are, they're all right. That aint dirt, it's ony fluff," and in the same sentence, continued, however, in a most ferocious tone: "Knock-yer-bloody-block off."

He then assumes exactly the same position as before, redraws back his arm, probably following the motions of some film, ducks his head, and prods the air three times with his right fist. Finally he punches Walter on the arm.

Walter's retreat is now prevented by Bill who gives him a push behind and yells:"Go on, Cissie—kill im."

Charley, crimson and perspiring, breathing heavily, gives Walter a feeble punch on the nose. Walter, hurt in body and feelings, makes a wild rush at Charley and gives him a swinging blow on the ear which knocks him clean off the road into the deep ditch. He disappears into space. The spectators, except Irene, who is looking at them and not at the fight, gaze in wonder, and Bill says: "Beelimey." Walter looks round in bewilderment, gradually dissolving into self-satisfaction and relief. Charley can be heard shouting from the deep ditch, to be helped up, but no one attends to him and thus no one hears him.

"I learnt how to box once," Walter says.

"Ere, that aint a fight," Bill says. "Come on, Walt—oo'll ya take on."

"Take on, Bill?"

'Yess, we're taking em on, arn't we—it's us against them, aint it. All right, oo'll ya ave, Ginger or Arry?"

"But I don't want to fight anybody," Walter says.

Bill now takes the next step in this old routine of fight promotion. He exclaims indignantly: "Ere, you aint going back on me, are ya? Of course, if you're going back on me, I know wot to do."

Walter now has the choice between fighting his ally or his enemy. He says in a disgusted voice: "All right, I'll fight Harry."

Harry retreats across the road, bellowing: "I aint going to fight nobody."

Walter punches Harry in the shoulder, a gentle blow that is like a formal gesture. Harry ducks and turns aside. But suddenly Lizzie puts down her basket, runs at Walter and slaps his face.

Walter, horrified and astonished, falls back. Lizzie pursues him. She is dark as a plum and is pushing out her thick lower lip in an extraordinary manner. Her pale eyes, in her darkened face, shine like a cat's in the dark. Suddenly she gives Walter another quick slap in the cheek.

Bill catches the girl by the arm and pulls her back. He is exploding with delight so that he can hardly speak. "Ere, Ginj—ere, Ginj—— Cor, good old Lizzie."

"It's no good, Bill," Ginger says. "You won't teach her to fight—she's barmy."

"He's got to leave Harry alone," Lizzie says in the soft tone of the half-deaf.

"That's it, Liz." Bill bends to her like a salesman. "You'll show im, won't you? Coo, Ginger, we'll ave a proper match. Old er a minute. Come on Walt, we'll see she fights fair."

"I'm not going to fight," Lizzie says. "It's silly——"

"You got to fight, Lizzie—now you've it im. You're in Arry's gang, arn't ya? Well, you got to fight for Arry."

"It's quite easy, Liz," Ginger explains, speaking very clearly. "We'll show you what to do."

"Like this," Bill says. He takes his large red hands from his pockets, displays a few classical attitudes and punches. He says every moment: "Not like this, but like this." He obviously enjoys knowing the right movements and showing them off. He repeats each three or four times.

Ginger looks on with a grave critical air, like a young priest at an old priest, performing some ceremonial exercise. He says to Liz: "See, keep your right hand high—and you mustn't bite—it won't be any good, Bill, she's barmy, you know."

"I see," Lizzie says. Then suddenly and unexpectedly she puts up her hands in a fighting pose and says: "Anyone could do that——"

"Of course they could." Ginger takes her by the elbows from behind and begins to instruct her in the practical art. "That's the way—keep your hands up—hold your arms away from your body—it's no good, Bill, she's too soft."

"No, I can do it—you learn me, Ginger."

Lizzie is no longer flushed and she does not seem to be in a rage. Her attitude is serious and anxious, like one learning a new duty.

Bill has caught hold of Walter and now pushes him towards Lizzie. "Go on, Walt, give er one in the slats—that's the place to it a girl—in the short ribs. You knocked Lousy out—now knock out Barmy."

Lizzie suddenly aims a blow at Walter which does not reach him. Walter, in desperation, makes a wild swing and hits her in the lips, making the blood run down her chin. Lizzie hits Walter a straight left in the eye.

Then for a moment they both pummel each other with both

64

hands. Both fall. But Lizzie is first on her feet. She stands with her tongue bent over her lip, catching the blood. She still looks grave and mature, like one carrying out an important task. Walter leaps up and rushes at her, she steps aside and he falls into the mud. He jumps up again and retreats into the twilight. His voice comes back, disgusted and hurt: "I got to go home now—it's supper time."

"You can't go ome," Bill shouts.

"He ought to give her best at least," Ginger says severely.

"Ere, you give er best," Harry yells. "She fought ya fair." Harry is furious at the idea that Lizzie should be defrauded of the victory. Snorting with rage he rushes past the others down the hill. "Ere, you Walter, you come ere."

But Walter has bolted. Harry returns fuming. He has quite forgotten his late confusion and disgrace. "E ought to give er best—she won."

"It don't matter, Harry," Lizzie says. "It's silly—where's my basket?"

Ginger runs for the basket. The boys flutter round her like courtiers. Bill pats her shoulder. "Good ole Liz—not much barmy there."

"I tole you she aint barmy—ony a bit slow."

"And look at my apern—all over blood." Lizzie says severely. But it can be seen that she is enjoying herself. A childish delight in glory and popularity is urging her to smile like a small girl, who, seeing a large bun at a party, cannot help smiling at it; a serious sense of her age and responsibility as a girl of fourteen makes her frown and look indifferent to praise.

"E's got to give ya best," Harry shouts at her. "You won, didn't ya—all right—e's got to give ya best."

"It's your supper-time, Harry. You better get home quick. Mrs. Hawes don like ee to be late for supper." But suddenly as the three boys look at her, an irresistible happiness, rising from some powerful source, comes to her mouth. The thickened lips quiver and all at once she smiles. Then abruptly she turns and hastens away to complete her errand.

"Hi—hi—wot the ell—Arree—Gin-gar." All turn to the ditch with surprise and notice for the first time that Charley is speaking to them.

Ginger and Bill give him their hands and haul him up the steep brick-faced slope of the drain. He is covered with mud and slime, but he at once charges forward to assert his new position.

"Were's Walter—— Ere, fetch im back—I adn't finished with im—not by a long way."

"Nah, e finished you."

"Ere, I tripped. If I adn't tripped I'd a given im the K.O., but you can't fight proper on a road—can't do your footwork. Ere, Ginger, ere Arry, come along. I got something to show you."

Harry is doubtful. He looks at Ginger and says at last: "Ginger and me is on our own."

"Nah, you come alone ome, Arry."

"Hi," Bill shouts. "Oo'll join the lousy gang?"

"You shurrap, Bill, or I'll knock yer turnip into yer back air."

Bill, whose hands are back in his pockets, at once jostles Charley and tries to push him across the road into the ditch. Charley dodges aside and yells: "You come along with me, Arry, and we'll—we'll go to the pictures."

Bill is pushing Charley very near the ditch when the rattling of a tractor and the scrape of heavy boots give warning of the harvesters' return. The tractor turns the corner on a wide circle, and Bill at once assumes a careless attitude and gazes at the sky. Yet even in this pose, he seems to be jeering at something, harvesters, village life, star-gazers or perhaps nothing definite. The tractor is driven by Fred who, unable to reach the controls from the seat, stands upon them, shifting from one leg to another as occasion requires. It is towing a waggon full of forks, rakes, empty tea and cider cans, and womenfolk of all ages from two to sixty.

All are talking in that burst of conversation, which, at harvest time, comes between the end of rabbiting and the beginning of supper.

Behind the waggon the whole male population of the village, including the sexton and the shopkeeper, are walking together. The shopkeeper wears his gold watch-chain, but his boots and gaiters are those of a labourer. Sam Eger is roaring out one of his puzzle stories which all end in a catch. "Supper was seventeen shillun, and tips was two shillun, that makes ninteen shillun; but he paid a pound. Where did the other shillun goa?"

Suddenly he sees Bill and shouts: "Hullo, Bill, who ee waiting vor?—all the gurls be in the vields to-day."

Bill, laughing, joins him and is lost in the tide of the villagers. Harry has already run off beside the tractor. He can never get over his surprise that Fred, who can barely read, is allowed to drive tractors on the high road, and will catch, bridle and afterwards harness a pair of cart horses which, by comparison with his minute form, are larger than elephants and much stronger than lions. Fred, on the other hand, is extremely shy of Harry, whose knowledge of film stars and life in London make him feel hopelessly provincial. When, therefore, Harry calls to him: "Fred, Fred, take me up," he pretends not to hear and shouts ferociously into the valley below, already full of brown shadows: "Get out of the way there—get out of the way."

Ginger, Charley and the small girl Irene are left standing at the cross-roads, separated from each other by a few yards. Charley looks at Ginger, the small girl looks at the paper in her hand and then thoughtfully licks it, Ginger is gazing over the chimney-pots of the "Green Man" as if admiring the bright green sky.

But he is perfectly aware of Charley's anxiety to pursue acquaintance with him. Suddenly, as if by the same impulse, he turns round and stalks away towards Burlswood House, Charley takes the opposite road to Parrs', and the little girl, still licking the paper, moves slowly, with little mincing steps, towards the Cedars.

13 Charley went to bed in deep anxiety, and meeting Ginger and Harry on the road next morning, was seized again with one of the fits of nervous terror which afflict all children with imagination. He tried to pass them on the other side of the road. But at once Harry called out: "Wot about the pictures, Charley?"

"They've got an organ at Twyport," Ginger said, approaching. "But it's thirty miles."

"Ow could we go to Twyport?" Harry demanded indignantly.

Charley, raised in one moment from unnecessary panic to unreasoning happiness, cried: "Course I meant Twyport—finest cinema in England, almost."

"Twyport would be worth while."

"Go on, Charley, ow we go to Twyport—bus?"

"Motor ."

The two boys stare at him. "Motor, were you get a motor?"

"I'll get one all right—a good un, too."

"When we go?" Ginger asks.

Harry says regretfully that he has promised Miss Phylly to help at the threshing in the Glebe field, and can't go to-day. Charley, much relieved, assures him that they won't go without him. The three boys then drift up and down the road, talking about the latest pictures and the art of Richard Ford on the cinema organ, until Fred Hawes gallops up the road and Harry says that he must go to the field. All the children have been given a holiday for harvest.

Charley and Ginger go with Harry because he alone has some definite objective. Charley, from a speculation about the profits of film stars, passes to a story about a millionaire, called

Jimmy the Chink, who made a fortune from dope, and built with it a palace of solid glass.

They wander into the field where the threshing machine, driven by a long, leaping band from Fred's tractor, is already clattering in the midst of a tall column of bright dust. The huge machine has been repainted for the season, in the brightest scarlet and blue, and looks at first sight too brilliant for the open air. It makes even the western sky seem pale.

Four carts are gathering the sheaves; a dozen men and women with long-handled prongs are feeding the carts; old Sam Eger tends the lift, and Hawes himself above, with his great dark red face, is directing the flow of sheaves and clearing straw jams.

The Glebe, on the summit of the hill, is shaped like a whale back. It has been pasture, broken up within five years, and it is still full of hollows and ridges; it shows even traces of old lands. The crop is oats sown down with a clover mixture which is now bright green in the stubble, upon which the long lines of peaked stooks, tracing each irregularity of the surface by their rise and fall, glitter so pale in the sun that they seem lighter than champagne.

This clover, already hiding the stubble, gives movement to the whole field; at the crest where the rolling green curves stand up against the sky, it is like a green ocean on the top of the globe. Hawes, with his fork, on the high shaking engine, becomes a neptune on some gaudy ancient ship, being towed, with great effort, against wind and waves, by a mechanical swan. The bright dust cloud, which hangs about him and rises twenty feet above his huge straw hat, is just such a cloud of brightness as might be expected to surround a god; and the long lines of pointed stooks, rising and falling over the waves, are precisely like such fleets of nautilus as would form his escort on a ceremonial occasion. It is true that the swan, though quivering all over so that its wheel-wings shake and jump, makes no actual progress, but the field, flowing past its breast-bommet, gives exactly that effect, of moving seas and stationary ships, which sea travellers notice from the next ship in the convoy. There is even a wake of chaff streaming behind the swan's tail, and foaming round the wheels of the thresher

Hawes himself, waving his fork with a majestic gesture, and roaring across half a mile of field to the slower waggons, has no romantic ideas. He has repainted his machine to keep it from rot, and he has used the colours of the virgin because his father used them and the paint-pots stand always on the shelf, to be renewed by the order "another of the same."

Hawes owns his threshing machine and likes to have his grain bagged for the early market before any other farmer in the valley has finished cutting. Especially in fine harvest weather, with a drying breeze, he has a frenzy for work. He would, if he could, work night and day, and he has said of machinery: "Give me plenty of it—it don't want to sto-ap for dinner and it don't want to goa home to its wife." The Glebe is his last field for the year and he wants to finish it in the day.

He receives the three boys not as visitors but as valuable workers. "Goa down there by the church lane," he shouts, "and load for Peder. Gi em their prangs, Albert."

A tall, thin labourer, toothless at thirty, gives them long-handled forks and they drift towards the field corner. Charley is elaborating the glass furniture of his glass palace. "And the swimming baths was glass, too—so you could see the people through."

Ginger and Harry have already for an odd hour or two chased rabbits, set up the sheaves in stitches, and loaded carts. They are as little interested in the work as any countryman of thirty years' service; less so, for they have no standards of skill and cannot please themselves by its use, or criticise others for its neglect.

When Peter Drake brings the waggon they load without haste, and Charley, even as he lifts a sheaf, is heard to say: "And er bath was a single diamond, ollowed out. Ere you are, ole Peter."

Peter is the only native of Burlswood whom Charley calls

by this affectionate form. Peter is the milk deliverer, a tall, loose-built boy of seventeen, with a grave and rather dreamy expression. He has probably been discussing economics with Norman Siggs on the milk round and his head is still full of bank rates and gold standards. Or he is meditating on the different technique of Dickens and Thackeray. He wears, unlike any other villager at harvest time, an untorn shirt and unpatched trousers. Obliged to rearrange every sheaf thrown by the boys, to snatch every second one as it slips from the cart, to turn butts outwards and at the same time to avoid being stabbed by a prong, he makes no protests but patiently endures the distant curses from the machine. "Peder, are you aslape or only deaad." At last he jumps down himself, throws up the remaining sheaves, makes all tight with the windlass and drives away, rolling askew over the hummocks and hollows of the field at angles which seem to defy all laws of gravity. The three boys, by a simultaneous motion, stick their forks into the ground and sink down against the nearest stook.

"But, Charley, the biggest diamond in the world isn't big enough for a bath."

"But e ad the biggest, see, bigger than any of the other ones anyone knows about. I don say it was a full-size bath either."

"Did he have an organ?"

"Course, lectric—and it was glass, too—you could see the tunes opping out of it—sort of."

"When are we going to Twyport, Charley?"

"Oh, pretty soon, and another thing that Jimmy the Chink ad——"

"In a motor, Charley?"

"Yers, didn't I say so—was a Rolls-Royce all a solid gold."

"Ow you going to get a motor, Charley?"

"Ere, Arry, oo's taking ya to Twyport, you or me? All right then—an another thing about Jimmy the Chink——"

Charley was as happy as an artist can be with an appreciative following, but he found it harder every hour to put off further discussions of the Twyport promise. He had, of course, not

71

the faintest notion how he was going to transport himself and two guests to Twyport, even in a bus, much less a car. Like others who hold power by the force of imagination he never asked himself how he would fulfil promises. He allowed his imagination to gallop away with himself and his friends; relying, for the solution of all his difficulties, as they arose, on more imagination.

14   During the last three days of the week, Bill and Walter were both engaged in the Wickens' harvest. Charley was allowed peace, and when the Hawes' harvest was finished, wandered as far as Tawleigh through the lanes and fields, sometimes with two followers, sometimes with six or even ten, raising his palaces and filling them with gunmen who combined the most desperate crimes with exquisite manners and a taste for the beautiful.

Lizzie with her basket was nearly always one of the party. Lizzie was not a reader, having never perfectly mastered the art, and though she remembered every detail of the movies she had ever seen, they amounted to very few, shown once a week in the Tawleigh Hall. For her, Charley was as good as the movies; he was the source of ideas so exciting, so engaging to her mind, that she listened to them as to revelation. Her serious concentrated expression while she followed the histories of Dimond Eye, Jimmy the Chink, the dope doctor, or Ally the Phone, was like that of a devotee in church or the smallest children at a pantomime. Lizzie, from want of reading, had the same freshness of mind and power of intense enjoyment.

But the harvest at Wickens' was over on the Monday when Hawes threshed his barley for him. Nothing was left but to cart the sacks from the field. On the same morning, Charley was sitting on the bridge, over the Burls brook, at the foot of Hall Farm garden, relating a new chapter of Ally the Phone, when Bill and Walter came down the road. Harvest holiday

was not over till Wednesday, so that Bill, usually ass.
class, was free from school as well as harvesting.

He shouted at once: "Ullo, see the lousy gang."

Charley promptly jumped off the bridge rail and strutted up
to him. "Ow about it, Bill?"

"Ow about wot?"

"My gang—wot you call it."

"That aint a gang," Bill says, wriggling his fingers in his
pockets and giving a loud laugh. "Thass a Sunday school
treat," and he shouts: "Art the crald angels sing, Lousy's going
to show us something."

"He's going to take us to Twyport in a car," Ginger says,
"for the new pictures." Harry and Bert close in affectionately
on each side. Lizzie, close behind, looks at Bill with angry
defiance; Bert, on the flank, eyes him sideways and grins upon
one side of his mouth.

"Twyport, wot," Bill laughs. "E strung you along on that
yarn. Beelimey—wots your front name, Paddy Green?"

"You let Charley be," Harry says doubtfully. "E's all right,
aren't you, Charley?"

"Course e's all right—so long as you're all wrong," Bill says,
then suddenly he exclaims: "Beelimey, ere's the oly bloke—ide
me, somebody." He dodges behind Ginger and crouches
down just as the parson turns the corner from Hall Farm lane.

The young parson nods good morning to the boys, of whom
Harry and Bert take off their caps. Bill, from his hiding-place,
gives a loud guffaw. The parson stops and says: "Good morning, Gittins, why didn't you come in yesterday—I was expecting you."

Bill, having attracted the parson's eye, probably without
any conscious intention, now stands up and grins. He is
blushing. The parson says: "You mustn't be shy, you know—
I hope you'll get farther than the doorstep next time."

Bill grins and turns still redder.

"About four, then—we have tea at half-past."

Bill says nothing but, still grinning, edges slowly behind

73

Ginger. The parson walks on up the hill, and Bill walks a few paces up the road after him, imitating his gait. He then turns back, holds up one hand and says: "Gawd bless you, my children—ave you used Pear's soap?"

Then, unable to repress some mysterious excitement, he dances about the road, making obscene gestures one after another, and ends up with a yell like a railway whistle: "Hi, Mister, yer trashers is coming down!"

The others stare at him with peculiar intensity. Only Bert laughs. All the rest, even Bert, understand that Bill is in a peculiar state of mind, that he is not wholly responsible for his actions. But though they perceive this fact by intuition, they forget it at once because it does not interest them. They are interested only in the idea that Charley may not, after all, take them to Twyport to see pictures.

Ginger and Harry are starved for pictures. They have seen no work of that art for a fortnight, and they are accustomed to the peculiar enjoyments of art. Liz has not seen a picture for two months, and Bert not for a year; both would go through fire and water to see another, especially at Twyport. They turn now in one simultaneous gesture of doubt upon Charley, and Harry says: "Wen *are* we going to Twyport, Charl?"

"Never," Bill shouts.

"Ere, were did we get to. Oh, yes, and marble statues all round with lectric lamps inside their eads——"

"Are we going to Twyport, Charley?" Ginger asks.

"Course we are."

"When?"

"Wen I say."

"Nice ole German with a nastikoff," Ginger murmurs this variation to himself and ends with his banjo imitation.

"Shut up, Ginj, don't you want a story?"

"No, e wants to go to Twyport."

"SHATAP, BILL!" Charley makes a rush at Bill, who, rather than take his hands out of his pockets, runs away, roaring with laughter. At the corner of Hall Lane he turns, makes a peculiar jerk of his whole body, and shouts "SIDBAD THE BADSID." He then retreats backwards through the gate of Hall Farm, probably to leer at Phyllis, who, completely impervious to leers, will give him a letter to post, set him to clean the separator or even dispatch him, on her bicycle, to fetch a parcel from Tawleigh.

Bill is the good-natured slave of any pretty girl, and Phyllis uses him like a slave.

15 As Charley turns back to his gang in triumph Ginger murmurs: " The art of war."

"If I'd caught im, I'd ave knocked is onion off," Charley says. "Ere, were did we get to?"

"Are we really going to Twyport, Charl?" Lizzie asks.

Charley's expression becomes angry and desperate. "Course we are." He turns and begins to walk up the village lane.

But the party follows him; asking at every step, in various tones of doubt and disappointment, when he is going to Twyport.

At the top of the hill he turns upon them and shouts: "You get off Arry and Ginger, we don't want you—we're going to Twyport, Bert, Liz and me——"

"Nah," Harry rushes at him. "Nah, nah."

Charley, who has not meant to fix any time, is obliged to take the choice between anticlimax and a bold decision. He answers at once: "Yers, nah—but we aint taking you."

"Oh, Charl, you aint not going to take us?"

"You get off."

But they follow him down the road. Charley is wondering what to do.

"You really going to Twyport?" Lizzie murmurs, astonished.

"Thass it, Liz."

"In the bus."

"No, Charley's going to get a motor." Harry prances round his hero.

75

"But they're so dear—you're never going to pa-ay two pound. The bus is only two shillun each."

"You coming, Liz?"

"However could I come to-daay—there's no one to home all daay."

"Come on, Liz, we going to see the pictures."

"Oh, dear, I wish I could come. Tis a proper cinema to Twyport."

"Come on, ole Liz."

"No, I coulddn. My worst day." Suddenly she hurries away from them back towards the village.

"There's a motor coming out of the garage now," Ginger says, looking towards the Green Man. "The Vauxhall, and they've only got two on hire. We better be quick."

Charley looks down the road towards the garage. The word garage gives him the idea of walking into the garage and asking for a car to be paid for on return. But he is not sure that hire-cars are like taxis, to be paid for in arrear; and besides, he thinks it very unlikely that the foreman will allow him even to enter the garage.

The gang surrounds him, expectant and curious. Harry asks: "Wen we going to start, Charley—we don want to be too late, do we?"

Charley knows that he must act quickly. He watches a car come up the steep village lane and stop at the Green Man. The driver goes into the inn. Charley begins to move down the road towards the Green Man. But just then a more splendid car goes slowly past in the opposite direction and stops down the main road outside the Cedars. A buxom woman in uniform gets out and marches up the drive with a jovial swing of her buttocks.

Charley says suddenly to the gang: "Follow me, boys," and runs into the Hall field opposite the Cedars garden. The gang follow and crouch behind the hedge, which is several feet higher than the tallest. Charley looks round cautiously and then darts along the hedge till he is opposite the car.

"Ginger," he says, "you come with me. All you go down there to the end of the field by the gate."

"Wot you going to do, Charley?" Harry is apprehensive.

"Never you mind, Arry, you get off. Come on, Ginj."

Ginger, as soon as he is alone with Charley, asks mildly: "You going to pinch that car, Charley?"

"Thass it."

Ginger reflects a moment and says then: "It's a new one on me," meaning that he has not yet broken the law.

"You game?" Charley says.

Ginger does not answer but he follows Charley. His air, after that momentary look of doubt, seems to say: "After all, what's it matter?" Ginger is always obedient to any suggestion. He creeps after Charley through the hedge up to the car. Charley, still keeping under cover from the house, on the near side of the car, reaches up to the door-handle and slips into the front seat. Ginger follows at once. The car is pointing to the left, so that Charley, having got in first, is in the driving-seat, but he beckons to Ginger who wriggles past him.

"Can you drive her, Ginj?" he whispers.

"I don't mind."

"All right, take er along," with the air of an admiral to the chief engineer. Ginger examines the instrument board and gear levers, then he starts the engine and drives down the road.

"Stop," Charley says. Ginger is already drawing up. "Op in, boys." Bert hops into the back seat, Harry stands in the road with a look of consternation on his face. He can't believe his eyes.

"Aint ya coming, Arry?"

"But, Charley, it's a copper's job—pinching cars."

Suddenly the peewit cry of Lizzie is heard. She is seen flying up the field. Ginger says: "There's someone coming up the road, Charley."

"Ow, wait for Liz."

"They'll cop ya," Harry says urgently. "You can't do it,

77

Charley." Lizzie, panting, rushes up to the car and scrambles into the back seat, planting herself next Bert. She says with an angry frown for some imagined critic: "I don't care."

"Good ole Liz—good-bye, Arry."

Harry from outside cries urgently: "But e's pinched it, Lizzie—e's pinched the car."

"What does he say?"

"He says that we've pinched the car," Ginger explains.

"Did he really steal it?" Lizzie asks, frowning angrily at Charley.

"Yes, he pinched it—I'm pinching it, too. Want to get out —I think you'd better."

Lizzie sits silent.

"Urry up, Liz—we can't wait."

But Lizzie cannot persuade herself to give up the expedition, with the shops and cinemas of Twyport at the end of it. She frowns angrily, turns dark red and says: "I don't care—they can kill me, too."

"Go on, Ginj."

The car jerks forward. Harry, whose eyes have been fixed anxiously on Liz, now perceives that even she is leaving him. He makes another appeal for help and sympathy. "Lizzie, it's a copper's job."

Charley answers laughing: "Good-bye, Arry." The car runs forward, Harry gives a cry of despair, sprints after it, shouting: "Stop, stop," then leaps desperately on the running-board. Bert and Lizzie seize him and pull him in. Liz, though still breathless with haste and defiance of authority, finds breath to say reproachfully: "You didn't ought to do so, Harry—you med a bin killed." She speaks as one doing a duty laid upon her. Charley cries exultantly: "Let er rip, Ginj."

A car passes them on the opposite direction and a woman passenger turns to stare. Charley pulls off his hat and puts it on Ginger's head.

"Sit up, Ginj, and old a fag in yer mouth. Anyone give us a fag."

78

No one has a cigarette. Charley rolls one out of a piece of paper from the front locker and puts it between Ginger's lips. Ginger, with the hat and the cigarette, now looks like an undersized youth rather than a small boy. Nobody sees anything strange about the other children. All are accustomed to carfulls of evacuees. The only glances attracted now, when Bert bounces wildly up and down on the cushions, or leans his whole remarkable body half-way out of the window, are not curious but amused or sympathetic. Charley tries to keep Bert in order. He calls out: "Thass it, Bert—stand on your ead and wave your feet in the air. Beave like you always drive around in cars till you sick of em." But he spoils the effect by laughing and saying: "Look at Bert—acting barmy—old im down, Arry, or e'll bust the windows—it im on is silly ead."

Bert then smiles and sits still. But he neither bears malice nor feels subdued. In five minutes he is rattling the window up and down with chuckles of delight. Harry never moves, even to hold Bert. He sits beside Liz with a look of astonishment and shocked dismay frozen on his compressed features. He cannot yet believe that he is sitting in a stolen car.

Liz, beside him, is also silent. But her face has that obstinate and defiant expression for which all her Anglo-Saxon features are so well designed. Her eyes, lips, chin, even her nose and forehead, seem to say over and over again: "They can kill me, but I'm going to see the pictures at Twyport."

Charley notices that Harry has now taken Lizzie by the arm. Such a discovery demanded a ritual joke. Charley, for the last year, has been especially contemptuous of all sentiment. He is old enough, precocious from life and town experience, to be excited by girls, but the excitement is still divided into two different parts, sexual and romantic. The first expresses itself only in obscene words, jokes and drawings on walls or lavatories; the second, which is still a total excitement of his whole body, causes him to feel the most tender kindness towards actual girls or women of any age who do him kindness or even smile at him. He at once thinks such women beautiful

79

and plans to confer extraordinary benefits upon them. He is at the same time so shy of them that he can barely find words to speak to them and prefers, on the whole, to be out of their presence. He is devoted to Phyllis Hawes and Lina Allchin, but he finds it uncomfortable to be with either of them.

For Lizzie he has only the feelings due to a loyal and brave supporter. But something in her expression, as she sits upright and solid in the middle of the back seat, makes him hesitate to chaff her even in an accepted and conventional manner.

16 They reached the suburbs of Twyport just before midday. Charley ordered Ginger to drive the car up a side street and to stop opposite a garden wall. "Nah, chaps, we don't want to go opping along like a lot of kids, we want to look like we lived ere. Arry, if Bert begins to act up, it im."

The party gets down soberly, returns to the main road and follows the traffic stream into Twyport. The town proves to be nearly a mile away. Bert begins to walk backwards and flap; Harry, immensely relieved to escape from the car without being arrested, grows impatient. In ten minutes he has forgotten the late crime.

"Wich cinema we going to, Charley?"

"It aint time for the pictures yet."

"I say, Charley, aint we going back for dinner?"

"We aint going back to dinner; we came to see the pictures, didn't we?"

Ginger blows out his right cheek and thoughtfully slaps a rhythm on it with his hand. His expression on the left is reserved and deeply thoughtful; on the right it is like nothing human.

"But wen we going to ave dinner, Charl?" Harry cries, as if the idea has just struck him.

"Wen I say."

"I eat, thou eatest, he eats, we don't eat, you can't eat, they haven't got anything to eat," Ginger says. "Twang, Twang, Twankety."

"Shurrup, Ginj—I'm the boss—aint I—well then, dinner'll be wen I say."

Ginger once more blows out his cheek and plays the drum to himself.

The party arriving at last among the shops is visibly tired and discouraged. Only Lizzie turns her eyes to the shop windows. Taken at last by surprise in front of a draper's, she is seen to linger and stare at a pink satin dance frock. But when Charley calls her to follow, she shows again a face of undiminished moral dignity. It can't be told whether she has enjoyed the frock or stopped only to disapprove of it.

"Wen we going to have dinner, Charley?"

"How much cash have you got?" Ginger asks.

Charley is silent in contemptuous indignation. He rushes ahead of the party and with his hand in his pocket rattles a penny against a bottle opener. This is all the movable property he possesses. He feels the depression and suspicion of his followers and also that the time has come for another decisive act. The feeling, since it is only a feeling, is much more urgent than a thought. It is continuous and unrelenting.

He grows uneasy and absent-minded. He allows Lizzie and Harry to walk arm-in-arm without noticing this breach of manners. He ignores Bert who is again walking backwards and running into the passers-by. His face is pale and pinched and he looks about him with sharp anxious glances.

Suddenly he steps off the pavement into a traffic block. Bicyclists are waiting among the cars and buses for the lights to change. Bicycle baskets are filled with small parcels, books from the library, bags and mackintoshes.

Charley, picking his way among cars and bicycles, looks into the baskets. Some of the women stand facing forward and ready to mount. They gaze angrily at the lights. All these, even the young ones, look haggard with indignation and anxiety. Others are standing at all angles, calling out to each other, nodding to friends on the pavement; gossiping. Among these, even the old ones look young, almost childish. Charley, passing one of these gossipers, a very fat woman in an enormous fur coat, who is shrieking at another fat woman in a car about ten yards away, takes a bag out of her basket and glides at once into the high gorge between a van and a bus.

He is trembling with something more than fear; a kind of horror. He feels as if he were someone else; and as if this other person were feeling very sick and at the same time performing unaccountable feats. The bag is already inside his jersey, supported by a hand in his pocket. He doubles round the bonnet of the van, passes between two cars and turns left among a stream of foot-passengers crossing at the lights. Two minutes later he is among the gang, which surrounds him with excited cries.

"Were you been, Charley?"

"Wot you run off for?"

"Come on and not so much of it." He leads them quickly to the first back street and looks about for an open gate. Finally in a narrow paved mews he sees an empty garage standing open. He steps inside the door, beckons to the gang and pulls out the bag.

"You didn't pinch it, Charley?" Harry says.

Charley opens the bag and pours out on the cement silver, coppers, lipstick, a silver cigarette-case, a purse, powder-box and two dirty handkerchiefs. In the purse there are three pound notes and one ten-shilling note.

The four children stand round with solemn faces; expressions of that deep apprehensive gravity seen only on children's faces on awe-full occasions, such as a first communion, a visit to a death-bed, a first dance. At last Ginger says in a mild reflective tone: "You've done it this time, Charley."

Then, after another pause, in a new voice:

"Four pounds in about two minutes."

"E'll be copped," Harry says. Then in sudden doubt he looks round the circle and says again: "They'll cop im, Ginger?" But this is a question.

"And the case is silver too," Ginger says. Ginger examines the case. It is heavy, with gilt inside.

"They really always do cop you," Harry says. "In the end they cotch ya—they cotched two chaps in our street six months after."

"I don't know any more than you do."

"That's wot they tell ya," Harry says this with diffidence as if seeking to test the argument. He feels that this new moral world, in which four pounds can be juggled out of space in a moment, is unknown to him. He gazes again at Charley, screwing up his eyes as if trying to read a peculiar alphabet.

Bert alone shows no sense of responsibility. He is grinning and blushing with delight. He flops on his knees and gathers the loot together. "Here y'are, Charley—don't lose none of it."

"That aint nothing," Charley says, stuffing his trouser pockets. He kicks the empty bag carelessly aside. But his voice quivers with nervous excitement. He feels the awe and shock of his followers like something beyond admiration, and he is full of gratitude and affection towards them.

"Wot d'you want, chaps—come on, wot d'you like?" He takes Harry and Lizzie by the arm and guides them up the mews. "Watch, knife, sheath-knife—wot you want, Liza? Dimon necklace?"

Lizzie, still flushed and defiant, stares at Charley. Harry shouts at her: "E pinched it, Liz—pinched the lot." He wants to see Liz fly with horror from the scene. But Lizzie answers: "I know."

"E'll go to prison, won't e?"

"We'll all go to prison," Lizzie says.

This shocks Harry so much that he is struck dumb. He stands with pale face and open mouth, gazing at the girl.

"And hell too," she adds.

83

"You're a bad lot, Lizzie," Ginger says.

Lizzie looks doubtfully at Ginger and pushes out her lip. "I don't know, but I done it now."

Charley, who has been laughing at Lizzie, now suddenly loses his temper and cries out: "Ere, less of it, all of you. Wot you think I did it for? To give you a treat or wot? Ere, take it," he pulls out the money and scatters it on the ground. "Go and ave your dinner and your pictures—sall right—you didn't pinch it. I'm giving it to ya, see—and you don't know were I got it. If the coppers get ya, tell em Charley is a bad naughty boy wot pinches things."

He catches up his hat and swaggers off. But at once Ginger and Harry are beside him. "I'm in this with you, Charley."

"Wots wrong, Charley?" Harry asks, perplexed and ready to be ashamed of himself.

Even Lizzie makes amends. She says: "We're all so ba-ad as each other, Charley."

Bert has already gathered up the money. With one of his sleeves he carefully polishes the dust off a coin before handing it back to Charley.

"All right, then, thass all right," Charley says, mollified. "Smy treat, boys. Wot you say to dinner, the pictures, and wot you say, Arry, a watch or a knife? Wot you say, Ginj?— Liz, ere, she's for joolery."

All look serious still, but except for Lizzie, this gravity is no longer apprehensive. Even Harry has become used to the idea that money can be snatched out of the air and spent. He says: "I don really want nothing, Charley—but you ought to get a stop-watch for yourself. I know a chap got a real stop-watch for five bob."

"Yes, Charley, you get yourself something—a ukelele or a first-class harmonica."

Charley laughs and says: "Harry, stop-watch; Ginj, uke; and a dimon necklace for Liz."

"I don't want nothing."

84

"But you've got to ave something—you're in the gang, aint ya? I got to get ya something—wot does Bert want—wot you want, Bert?"

Bert grins and shifts his legs awkwardly. His eyes look everywhere except at the rest.

"Ca-a-me on, Edwud."

"I don want nothing, Charley."

"He don't really," Liz says suddenly. "He wouldn't know what to want." Lizzie takes the village view of Bert, that he and his family are negligible persons.

"Ave you got a knife, Bert?"

Bert grins with delight. "Yes, Charley, I'd like a knife."

"Got arf a crown for yourself?"

"No-a."

"Would ya like one?"

"Yess, Charley, I would."

"Ere y'are, then," handing over the half-crown with a magnificent gesture. "Nah then, boys, I'm going into the joolery shop, see—to get Arry's watch and Lizzie's doodahs —and I don want the ole crowd of ya coming in and making a row. Joolers don't stand for it—they ony ave genlemen and ladies in, see—and they'd call a cop in arf a mo if anyone started acting around."

"Bert'd better stay ere," Harry says.

All look at Bert, and Charley says thoughtfully: "Yers, I don think you'd better go into a jooler's shop, Edwud."

"E stinks awful in a room," says Harry.

"Ere, ere, Arry," Charley says reproachfully. But Bert, standing in the middle, smiles and adjusts his spectacles. His air of pleasure reminds one of those mongrel dogs who wag their tails equally when abused or caressed.

"I'll look after Bert," Ginger says. "I don't want to come in, either."

The party returns to the main street, and Charley leads Harry into a cheap jeweller's.

17 As soon as they are in the shop both are panic-stricken. Neither is accustomed to this kind of shop, and it alarms them more than a church or a police-station because they feel that it belongs to a social plane unknown to them and full of traps. The shopman himself, a pale smart young man in a black suit, is more fearful to them than a policeman. The policeman is a known function; this man's self-assured look has a quality of cynical boredom which is always terrifying or provocative to children.

Charley is also upset by the unexpected presence of two other customers, fresh-faced country girls examining alarm-clocks.

Harry stands close to the door, ready to fly; Charley retreats to the farthest end of the glass counter from the two girls, and even then, in asking for stop-watches, fails to make himself heard.

"What is it, Tommy?" The assistant is not greatly surprised to see the two children. There are many evacuees in the neighbouring villages, and he has already had visits from them to buy cheap metal pencil-cases and match-boxes.

Charley makes a strong effort and gets out a loud exclamation: "Stop-watches, please."

"Cheapest is seven and sixpence, Tommy."

"All right, mister, less ave it."

The watch is bought and handed over to Harry, who at once winds it up and begins to start and stop the second hand.

"You got any necklaces?" Charley asks. "Dimon or ruby ones?"

"Diamond necklaces, certainly."

The assistant fetches a tray of cheap jewellery, and Charley looks it over.

Suddenly Lizzie appears at the counter beside him. She has slipped through the door while the assistant was looking at the shelves. But she does not speak. She pulls Charley's sleeve and shakes her head, meaning that he is not to buy her a necklace.

"Come on, Liz—pick your choice—wot about this one—with rubies in."

"That one is nine and six," the shopman picks it off the tray and looks at the ticket. "This is cheaper—this is six and six—diamonds and sapphires—finest quality."

"See ere, Liz."

"I don't want un."

Lizzie puts out her hand and carefully takes the necklaces. "Look, this un is cracked," she whispers, pointing to a glass ruby. "They diddn oughter ask all that money for a cracked un."

"Slight flaws do occur in the paste," the shopman says. "Of course, the cheap glass imitations are different."

"Ere, Liz, this is the one *you* want." Charley takes up the most expensive necklace.

"I don't want none, I tell ee." She pushes it away.

Meanwhile the shopman and the two other customers are all looking over Charley's head into the centre of the shop, where Bert has just made an appearance.

Harry, still testing imaginary motors and aeroplanes with his stop-watch, sees nothing else; Charley is feeling too magnificent to notice his surroundings; Lizzie is staring critically at the diamond and ruby necklace, which seems to her, since it comes from a real jewellery shop, unusually beautiful. She is fascinated by the combination of its natural glitter and its ideal distinction. But when Charley offers to put it on her neck she quickly draws back with the instinctive gesture of one who is on the verge of a blasphemous act.

Suddenly a loud laugh is heard. Bert, in the middle of the floor, has been for some time gazing round him at the walls of green plate-glass within which float, like the creatures of a tropical sea, great silver-sided salvers and trays, in cheap electro-plate, scores of gilt enamel and glass clocks in full face like a school of John Dorys gazing at the diver when he has descended among them; long curving snakes of imitation

87

sapphires, amethysts, rubies and crystals, all seeming to glow, under hidden electric lights, with phosphorescent radiance.

Now he bursts suddenly into loud, irrepressible giggles.

Charley and Harry stare in horror, Liz exclaims in her broadest accent: "Goa away, Edwud, go away."

But before they can move the assistant quickly opens a flap in the counter, takes Bert by the arm and runs him into the street. Bert makes no resistance. His face, as he is whirled towards the door, expresses neither surprise nor indignation.

The assistant, having pushed Bert several yards down the street, returns to his place, dusts his palms together, and says to the two lady customers: "They've got a cheek, some of these evacuay."

Then he says to Lizzie severely: "Did you bring him in?"

Harry, with a scared face, at once goes out of the shop. Charley says hastily and humbly: "This one, mister."

"That's ten and six." Charley pulls out a note but brings two others with it. The assistant and both the customers watch while he detaches one from the crumpled bundle and hands it over. Charley, very red, says: "Ere y'are, mister. Thass for the watch too." The assistant fingers the note and looks doubtfully at Charley.

"Where did you get this?"

"Wot's wrong with it?" Charley cries in the shrill, defiant tone of a young Londoner under suspicion.

"I was wondering where you got it."

"From my ma—d'ya think I pinched it?"

"No, of course not, Tommy. But I'm afraid you'll have to wait a minute for your change." He goes into a back shop and is heard saying: "Excuse me, sir—it's some of these boys——" then a door shuts.

Lizzie is pale as sycamore. She pulls Charley's sleeve: "Come on, we'd better get away."

"Nah, I want my change," Charley says, striking a dignified attitude.

The door opens again and the murmuring voices are heard: "Just keep them a minute."

Charley loses his nerve, takes Lizzie by the arm, snatches up the necklace, and darts out of the shop with her. They rush up the street in panic, almost knocking down Bert, who is standing on the pavement at the corner of the shop window.

Charley leads the way down the first side-street to the left, again to the left and so back again into the crowded main street. Here he stops, panting, and waits for Bert and Harry toiling after them. He asks them indignantly where they are running to, and before they can answer says: "Don't you know thass the way to be copped?—never run nowere."

"But you run, Charley."

"I ad to get away from ya, adden I—four of us running we'd been sure to be copped. Were's Ginger?"

"Looking at the pianners," Bert says.

Finally, Ginger is discovered looking into the window of a music-shop. He cannot make up his mind between a mouth-organ, a concertina, and a ukulele.

"It's either eight and six or eighteen and six," he says. "You can't see the label properly."

Votes are divided. Charley says: "Never mind, Ginger, ere's a quid."

Ginger, to everyone's surprise, shrinks from entering the shop. "You get it, Charley."

Charley is alarmed at this suggestion. He feels that all the shops are now on the look-out for him. He rallies Ginger.

"Wy, wot you fraid of—they can't eat ya."

Ginger looks again at the shop window, where there is an absurdly small grand piano. He shows no apprehension, but his cheeks are still flushed and his mouth is set. He is determined not to enter a shop with grand pianos in it. Just as he had balked at the jeweller's. Lizzie says: "Don't be afeard, Ginger—they've got to give un to ee if tis marked."

Ginger is so much disturbed between desire and fear that he does not resent these remarks. He looks round at the circle and says quite humbly: "Perhaps there's another shop with ukes—toy shops have them."

"Aw, ga-a-arn, wot you afraid of?" Charley cries. "All right, I suppose I'll ave to get it for ya." Trembling he swaggers into the shop. But the girl behind the counter does not even look at him. She gives him the ukulele, takes his pound and changes it, during a day-dream, in which her eyes pass over all objects with equal blankness and only her hands seem to have purpose and understanding.

She holds out the change from the cash register without looking to see if Charley is waiting for it. Charley runs down the shop to take it from her hand. He comes out in triumph and hands the ukulele to Ginger who at once strikes a chord and says: "My uncle had one, but he took it to France."

18 Charley, exultant with this happy and glorious situation which he has produced, is now afraid of nothing. He offers to lead the whole party, including Bert, into a restaurant, for a half-crown lunch. Harry and Ginger both oppose Bert's inclusion on the grounds that he is too dirty. They are not thinking of the danger of attracting notice, but simply of the social impropriety. Bert himself feels this, for when Charley recklessly urges him to come in, he says with his usual friendly smile: "I'm not dressed right, Charley."

Finally Bert is sent to Woolworths with a shilling to buy buns and lemonade, and the others follow Charley into the principal restaurant. Lizzie is still nervous and pink, Ginger silent, Harry anxious. When Charley looks round for a table, they huddle together and stare about them.

People smile from all sides at the group. Their mouths form the word "Vackies." These smiles abash and anger Ginger. They are just what he has expected. He scowls and turns paler, so that freckles, formerly unnoticed, appear all over his cheeks. Something bitter and savage appears suddenly in the form of his expression.

Charley, whose social nerves extend no farther than his own circle, is enjoying the smiles. Catching one, he grins back, as if to say: "What a game it is," and already he has won the heart of a stout country waitress. When a table is found for four, he shouts across the restaurant: "Come on, boys." Liz, looking fierce, Harry, visibly in terror, stumble after him. Ginger does not move. He is fixed in his place by a kind of catalepsy.

The other children are now safely at their table. The customers all round stare at Ginger, who is so white that his freckles are like a rash.

"Wots wrong with Ginger?" Harry exclaims in anxious surprise. Charley, feeling suddenly that Ginger is helpless, jumps up and goes back. "Go on, Ginj, we got a table," and steps past Ginger to be behind him. This adroit movement obliges Ginger either to block Charley's road or move. He moves forward, slowly and awkwardly, like an automaton. But he reaches the table. Then suddenly his colour returns, he looks like himself and says: "I didn't know you had a place for me."

This lie carries off the awkward moment of reunion after a crisis. Ginger has recovered his social aplomb. Harry shouts: "Wot'll we ave, Charley?"

"Anything you like."

"Coo, just look at the paper—there's four kinds o puddin."

"Roast beef for me."

"Can we ave soup too?"

"Clear soup for me—that's the test of good cooking."

"A shillun for meat and potatoes, and it ony costs em but four pence—no wonder some people gets rich."

Five minutes later Ginger is strumming his ukulele between mouthfuls, Harry shouts, looks round for attention, sticks a spoon in his mouth and tries to balance a roll on the handle. Charley, who still wears his hat, is laughing at him so violently that he chokes. Only Liz keeps her adult dignity. She asks Charley for the necklace, examines it carefully, holds it up to the light, spits on it and polishes it with her frock. Then she

91

says: "I don't want it, Charley—but it's a good un. You put un away and give un to your girl some day."

"Go on, Liz—it's for you."

"Noa, it's too fine for every day and I couldn wear it on Sunday, could I?" She continues to play with the necklace, holding it up, rearranging it on the tablecloth. Her expression of serious disapproval becomes more an apology for this pleasure than a sense of sin.

The boys, no younger in age, appear childish in comparison. Having recovered from shyness they become at once exuberant. It is as though their energy, always pressing upwards like a fountain, having been artificially frozen for a moment, now springs into the air with violence, making new and fantastic shapes.

Glances and smiles are now accepted as compliments and encouragement, even by Ginger. He does not look round like the others; but he feels an audience and strums more loudly, singing as if to himself, but really for the benefit of general society. "Aint she sweet walking down the street."

None of them knows how to express his happiness, his sense of being on top of the situation. They want to dance and sing and all their gestures and words, Harry juggling with his spoon and shouting, Ginger swinging his head to the rhythm of his song and throwing in new chords, Charley calling out: "and did ya see the chap's face wen e sees Bert come in?" are all performing a kind of dance and song. Charley's song is a saga of their adventures; his dance a play with danger. He likes to call just when the disdainful head waiter is passing their table: "Like a fag, Arry?" and pull out the stolen cigarette-case. But this no longer frightens the others, not even Harry. All are convinced that Charley is a genius who can do anything. They do not even thank him for their presents or for lunch. They take them as gifts from God, from luck.

Gratitude is replaced in the boys by dependence and confidence; by affection in Liz, who when they reach the darkness of the picture-house, at half-past two, pushes past Ginger in

order to sit between Harry and Charley. But she makes only
one remark during two repetitions of the whole programme.

"Oh, dear lord, I hates this un."

They are looking at an enormous half-naked woman with
three-inch teeth tumbling in a rood of bed.

"Cut it out," Charley mutters beside her. "Aw, cut it out
and give us the real stuff."

By the real stuff he means gunmen living dangerous lives
and their molls faithful to death; that is, anything but gigolos
pursuing love-affairs and women pursuing millionaires.

19 At eight they come into the streets. They are in a
silent reflective mood, which is far removed from
dreaminess. Their eyes gaze before them with the confused
expressions common in children after the pictures, as if they
find the real world more extraordinary than the one they have
just left.

After a few minutes Harry, passing most rapidly from this
surprised mood, asks: "Wot we do now, Charley?"

Charley makes no answer. He is in front, edging his way
through the crowds which have poured out of other cinemas
or are making their way there. Ginger plays soft chords and
murmurs to himself: "If you were the only girl in the world,"
but his voice does not agree with his reminiscent expression.
Bert is smiling, with a delighted satisfaction. He says to
Charley: "I liked the shooting, Charley."

"Come on, Bert—keep in."

"And they little pistols."

"Yers, did you. Oh gawd, I do wish people wouldn't walk
so wild."

It is growing dusk. The sky is as bright as a paper lantern
showing its own colours in every shade from the palest water-
green to ink-blue, but giving little light to the streets. They
are full of grey shadows in which grey people hurry with preoccupied faces. The children, moving at another *tempo*, at

their own level, feel rather than notice their difference, actually more fundamental than difference of race. As they dodge aside from single hurried passers, or step off the pavement to get out of the way of young men marching four abreast, arm in arm to some rendezvous, their faces change quickly from reflective animation to weary disgust. This expression might be seen on the faces of philosophers or poets, who have come out from some private gathering of their own to find themselves in the midst of a jostling race crowd. Like such, too, who, whatever their recent differences in questions of science or art, are now more conscious of common sympathies and common weakness, and strive to keep in touch with each other, the children begin to cling together. They resent separation, and struggle by various means to keep in contact, falling into single file, or taking the shape of an es in which Harry is holding Charley's jersey, Lizzie is holding Harry's coat, Bert is holding Lizzie's skirt and Ginger, though he holds nobody, is so close behind Bert that he treads on his heels.

This flexible line is broken every moment by sailors taking a diagonal line to some pub, by complacent women in barrel-shaped coats, whose eyes look out far above the children's heads, by black overcoated citizens in pairs, discussing the evening news. But it re-forms at once. Ginger steps back from the gutter; Bert dodges sideways back to Charley; Lizzie calls urgently to Harry, for whom, since he belongs to Hall Farm, she seems to feel responsibility; and Harry, with the expression of a long lost child returning home, escapes from between a tower of coat and two militiamen in battle dress to grab at the nearest member of his own tribe.

"Were are all the car parks got to?" Charley asks in a despairing voice.

Charley is growing tired and cross. He feels his responsibility and it annoys him.

"Were's that car park you see, Ginger?"

"Behind the trees."

"Were is the trees?"

94

They find the trees and the park, but very few cars in it and those watched by an attendant who shoos them away. When Charley goes round behind a tree and makes a dart from there a special policeman in a tin hat suddenly pounces: "What are you playing at there?"

"All right, I aint done nothing."

"Leave the cars alone."

"Can't a chap go to is car?"

"Now, none of that, me lad."

"Boo, take it ome to mother for the soup."

The little group on the pavement is discouraged. Ginger yawns and says: "The art of walking."

"Wot'll we do now, Charley?—we're late already," Harry is worried.

"Come on, chaps, I wouldn't ave any of those old sausage machines for an en roost."

He leads along the pavement. But no unattended car can be seen in the darkening street and no more parks are found.

"We're going the right way anyhow," Ginger says.

"But we can't walk ome," Harry cries. "It's thirty miles."

"I can walk thirty mile easy," Bert says.

"Nobody aint going to walk," Charley cries. "Wot d'you take me for? It's my party, aint it?"

A large car passes them and draws up on the opposite side of the road. The driver gets out, leaving his engine running, opens a gate in the house railings and goes to ring at the door of a house about ten yards back from the road. Charley catches Ginger by the arm and says: "Come on, Ginj—there we are. Op in."

Harry protests: "But e'll see, Charley."

"I'll wait till he goes into the house," Ginger says.

"E aint going in—can't you ear is engine running?"

"And e's got a torch," Harry says, much alarmed. "Look there."

"E's looking at us, Charley," Liz warns as the man flashes his torch at his car and the beam crosses the road.

"Oo cares—let im look—e can't ear and we won't go straight at it, see—we'll go beind, sif we was just crossing the road. Then I'll go along the pavement to the gate, see, and you go up the other side in the road and Ginger gets in—quietly Ginj—and takes the weel and you all op in and I shuts the gate, see, and ops in—and off we go."

"Go on, Charley—you couldn't—e'd catch you."

"I've never drove at night," Ginger says. "Only in the garage. You better drive, Charley."

"Nah," says Charley who has never driven a car at any time. "Don you see I got to shut the gate and stop im running out before we makes a getaway; and look ere, Ginj, you say 'All right, Charley,' see, wen you're ready to get off. Come on, chaps."

"Go on, Charley—you don't mean it—you couldn't."

"You ready, Ginj?" Charley sets out across the road. The others, after a moment's hesitation, follow, unwilling to be left behind. At the opposite kerb behind the car Charley stops Ginger by a tap in the chest and waves him towards the off side. Ginger obediently slips round behind the car and creeps towards the front offside door under cover from the house. Charley goes along the pavement and waits. He sees the car door open, hears a thump as somebody's boot strikes the running-board.

The man at the house door also hears it and flashes his torch down the garden path. Charley says aloud in a conversational voice: "You all right, Ginger?"

"All right, Charley."

"Were's Liz—she aint lost?"

"She's here."

The torch light falls on Charley and the man's voice, in a tone of mixed uncertainty and indignation, a conditional threat, exclaims: "Keep away from that car."

Charley shuts the gate, darts across the pavement and dives into the front seat of the car. Ginger lets in the clutch and accelerates. The wheels jump forward. The man is heard shouting something and rattling the gate, but before he has turned the handle the car is twenty yards away, going at fifteen or twenty miles an hour. As he rushes up the pavement, still shouting, Ginger changes gears and the car accelerates rapidly to thirty, forty, and disappears at sixty.

Bert explodes into a shout of laughter.

"Wot you laughing at?" Harry says angrily. "E saw us—I said e would."

"Ow d'ya like the car, Ginj?" Charley asks in a lordly tone.

"She's all right—you're not sitting on my uke, are you?"

"Nao, you and your uke. I'd buy you another if I did—a good un."

"They're after us," Harry cries in a voice of despair. "It's the police."

But the car, overtaking them at a high speed, passes them and proves to be a private sports car, driven by an A.T.S. girl.

" 'Sall right, Arry," Charley says. "Nobody'll catch us—you'll soon be in your little bed."

The exhilaration of the escape passes off within five minutes into renewed sleepiness and boredom. Lizzie dozes on Harry's shoulder. Harry murmurs: "We're late aready," only Bert is in his usual lively spirits. Now and then he utters his giggling laugh. He is recollecting the pictures. "Ullo, Charley, you see the chap that shot the other chap."

"Yers," in a sleepy voice.

"He stuck it in his side, didden he. Chap was proper frightened, wassen he. He didden expect that, didde, Charley?"

"Go on, Bert—go to sleep."

Bert reflects for a time and then laughs again. "Proper surprise it was, wassen it, Charley? You see his face?"

"Wassay, Bert?"

"The rich chap, I mean—what had the darter—wen he got bumped off."

"Oh, yers, go on, Bert. Go to sleep."

But five minutes later, Bert explodes into another giggle.

97

"He wur surprised, wadden he, that un never thought to get bumped off, he didden."

Ginger is driving now in the country roads at thirty-five to forty. At sign-posts he slows down to fifteen so that he or Charley may read the directions and make sure of the way. They are already on the Burlswood road, and Bert recognises familiar marks.

"There's Crocombe Church, Charley."

At long intervals a car passes. One of these cars, having passed at speed, swerves into their headlight and rapidly slows down.

"Is that the police?" Ginger asks, without apparent interest.

"Gawd, stop, Ginj—we got to op it."

But Ginger, almost touching the tail of the police car, brakes and turns, skidding into a farm track. Then he accelerates again. The track is down a steep hill. The car seems to jump into the air. Harry gives a cry of terror and at almost the same moment the bonnet strikes a gate with a loud crash, and the engine stops.

"Op it," Charley cries, "along the edge." All the four doors of the car are flung open as the children throw themselves out. Charley and Ginger run along a hedge, creep under a gate, and crouch down by a new straw stack. Here they wait for twenty minutes. The police car lights are still shewing on the road above; the beam of a torch glides over the hedge at forty yards' distance, and a man somewhere in the dark background calls out: "It's no good, Ritson—they're miles away by now."

After that there is a long silence. Then the police car, on the road above, darts away.

Charley goes back towards the wrecked car, calling softly for Liz, Bert and Harry.

20 Harry is found in the ditch, Bert and Liz in the next field. The party sets out to walk into Burlswood by the fields. Bert acts as guide, running on before and leading

them by stiles, hedge gaps, bridges and gates as if he carried in his head an illuminated ordnance map. But the other four are now very tired. They roll against each other and, catching hold of each other's arms or waists or shoulders, stumble through the rough fields like one composite animal. Their talk becomes dreamy and erratic as if their minds, half asleep, wander also in half-dreams, full of reminiscence and obscure fears, loves and ambitions. They cling together like small, sleepy children, and their thoughts also reach out instinctively for that comfort of sympathy and warmth.

"It was nice in the pictures," Lizzie murmurs.

"Steak an pudden—I like that better than roas beef."

"The big all with pillars in——"

"We med fall in a hole—is that your arm, Charley?"

"No, it's mine," Ginger says. "Hold on, Liz."

"It was warm in the pictures, waddn it?"

"It cost a million pounds, that picture. A million pounds."

"Ow late is it, Ginger?"

"It doesn't matter now."

"No, it's too late now," says Liz, in a meditative voice. "Won't I catch it when I get home." She speaks as if this event were still far distant in the future.

"Will they take a stick to ya, Liz?"

"I dunno. Father beats me with his belt."

"I ad an awful wopping from my father once," Charley says. "E nearly killed me, e did."

"Wot for, Charley?"

"Cheeked im—father can't stand cheek."

"Did you really cheek un, Charley?"

"Yers, I did."

"Bad enough to be wopped."

"Yers, I deserved it—I was an awful cheeky kid."

"Kids are awful cheeky—you got to learn em."

"But I wasn't cheeky," Harry says, "and e took a wip to me. E's awful strict, my father is."

"Poor Harry," Liz murmurs. "You got a cruel father."

99

"E aint so cruel, e's only strict. E thinks I'm going to the bad all the time, and, of course, e as to stop it, asn't e?"

"But he must be cruel to beat you so ba-ad. I do wish people weren't so cruel, too."

This remark produces a silence. It surprises the children from the mature and serious Lizzie who has before shown so little feeling. "Why are they so cruel?" she asks in the same novel tone. "It aint no fun hurting people."

"They wip Jews to death in Germany," Charley says. "Jus go on beating till they pass out."

"It's so wicked—arn't they afeared to do such turble things."

"You don't believe in hell, Lizzie, do you?"

"I don know."

"Wot, don you believe in ell, Charley?"

"Burning fire for ever and ever. Thass cruel if you like."

"But what you going to do with cruel people like they?" Lizzie gives a deep sigh. The second Lizzie, tender-hearted and confused in mind, seems to be gaining rapidly on the first, the competent and responsible. Of the two chief beings wrapped up in Lizzie, the child, grasping the world by reason and precept, seems for the moment to have given place to an emotional woman, living by heart and dream. "If there iddn no hell, Ginger, what you going to do with those people that beat poor old men to death."

"I don't know, Lizzie. Shoot em. But they might shoot you first."

"Perhaps there isn't no god neither," Charley suggests.

"Course there's a god," Harry says. "Oo made everything—someone must ave made it."

"All things bright and beautiful, All creatures great and small."

"Ah, it's too pratty, that one."

"It's a good tune."

"Abide with me. That's a turble sweet hymn, too."

"I like that one, too, Liz. Sad, aint it?"

"It's nice."

The moon is as bright as an arc lamp, with white fire at the edge. The children draw closer together and dawdle more slowly. Liz now between Harry and Charley, Harry holding Ginger, with arms interlaced, they wander at every step out of their course and out of line. The wings curve in so that Ginger and Charley are walking backwards, both talking together.

"Did you ever get wopped, Ginger?"

"Only at school."

"On your trousers, that aint nothing. It's on your bare skin it urts, don't it, Charley?"

"Will you scream wen they wop ya, Liz?"

"I dunno—I suppose I shall, too. But he don't like me to scream because of the neighbours."

"You scream, Liz, loud as ya can. Or e'll go on till e makes ya. It's wot they want, see, to make ya oller. Then they feels they're doing some good with it."

A long pause follows. The little party is clasped so tightly together that no one can guide it and it takes its course by a series of accidents, turning suddenly to the left because Charley trips against Ginger, then slowly to the right in a long curve because Harry on the right, with his shorter legs and anxious thoughts, drags back.

Bert comes rushing up to them, flapping indignantly. "Were you going, you've turned right about." He seizes Harry and, by pushing at him, brings the party to the right direction. "There," he says, delighted with himself on this his occasion of authority and responsibility. "Now goa straight and think were you going."

"Wips is the worst," Harry murmurs.

"Father used a stair rod on me once," Charley says, "a brass one—the marks lasted six weeks."

"And there's blind cord, with knots in."

They begin to discuss canes, whips, sticks, and varieties of beating. They discuss foreign tortures, and every now and then Liz says with wonder that she doesn't know what the world is coming to, that it gets crueller and crueller. But soon she, too, is talking again about whips and beatings.

"He'll take the belt to-night, I espect."

"Wips is worse—make ya scream right out."

"Thass it, Arry—you don forget a wip in a urry—or a stair rod."

Bert comes running back, and speaks in a severe tone: "Were you bin, Charley—I thought you wur all lost."

"All right, Bert, we're coming."

But again they wander, closely bound together not only in body, but in sympathy. They feel something more than affection and tenderness; a closeness deeper than any family relation; and as they talk they try to increase this feeling; they try unconsciously to work upon this rich secret nerve which aches in all of them. They describe their beatings not only in self-pity, but to create this rich sympathy, inventing and enlarging on their sufferings. They exaggerate their helplessness as children, they dramatise their weakness, without bitterness or malice, but simply for their own immediate pleasure.

"Wots the las time you was wopped, Arry?"

"I dunno. E used to wop me almost every day for something."

"Got any marks?"

"Daresay I ave."

"You got any marks, Charley?"

"You bet—permanent ones."

"You got any marks, Liz?"

"I dunno—but it feels like I have."

"On your bare bottom did e do it?"

"Yess, on my skin."

"Show us, Liz."

"Bant nothing to see. Only bruizes."

"If I show you mine, you oughter shew me yours, thass only fair."

"Come on, Liz—we'll see who's worst."

"I should think Harry was the worst."

"But I got permanent marks, like a chap oos ad the cat. Ere, I'll shew you."

21 They are in the middle of an enormous, rolling field with rising woods at one side. Two cart horses, an old swag-bellied mare and a shaggy colt are looking at them from a little distance. The moon picks out the frilled edge of the tree-line with a white fur of light, and beyond the road, in the valley, the outline of the cottage chimneys and the upper part of a village spire. The white light glitters on them like the artificial frost of a Christmas card, it covers the bare ground with snow and gives a pale blue tint to the shadow of the hedges and trees, as if the printer, having to limit his colour scheme, had made one set of tints do for the shiny sky, the shadow on the ground, and the picturesque roofs of village and spire. The artificial frost, in the same way, does duty both for stars and icicles.

Harry, taking down his breeches, stoops with head between his knees and shows his bare behind; the others, a little block of darkness, stoop and gaze closely at the skin. Nothing can be seen.

"Does it urt ere," Charley says, prodding. Harry gives a squeak.

"Thass the place, see, Lizzie—you can see it if you look from the side."

"Poor Harry, diddn you scream?"

"Yes, I screamed right out," Harry says, rising and gloomily pulling up his breeches. "E did it twice that week."

Charley then unbuttons and is examined. Nothing can be seen, but again the party expresses respectful horror and sympathy.

"Poor Charley, wy, it's all black."

"Yers," Charley says between his legs. "And see ow it curled round—e nearly ad my knackers orf."

"Yers, belts is dangerous," Harry says. "They didn't ought to use em—might do ya an injury."

"Did you scream out, Charley?" Lizzie asks.

"Course I did—or e'd a done it arder."

"So did I—I couldn't help hollering."

"No, gurls can't help it," Charley encourages her.

"They oughtn't to beat girls," Ginger says.

"Wy not?" Harry says fiercely. "Wy shouldn't girls cop it if they deserves it? Wy not?"

"Lizzie aint a cissie—see ow she beat Walter. She don mind a wopping, do ya, Liz?"

"I didn't say she did—I said I did. But it don't matter."

"I did mind, too," Liz says, "I diddn expect it. Father never hit me before all my life, ony mother with a slipper."

"Wot e do it for, Lizzie?"

"Cos I went with you vackies. He says I'll go to hell if I go with you vackies."

"Cor, wots e think we'd do to you?"

"You aint going to leave the gang, Lizzie?"

"I coulddn, could I? I'm in the gang now, aint I?"

"Course you are."

"Come on, Liz—show us your marks."

Lizzie hesitates a moment, frowns, then suddenly picks up her frock. The boys gaze attentively with a professional interest; Charley exclaims: "Wy, she's got a great bruise; look ere, Arry."

In fact Lizzie's marks can be seen.

"Coo," Harry says. "E did lay into yer."

"Ow do you sit down?" Charley asks.

Lizzie's voice, muffled in her frock, answers from near the ground: "It's all right if you sit crooked."

"Coo, glad I aint you, Liz."

Lizzie lets her frock down and, with a gesture full of grateful affection, takes Harry and Charley by the arms. "I did cop it proper, diddn I?"

"Coo, like ell you did."

Then with a generous impulse: "But not so bad as you, Charley, or poor Harry."

"Oh, well, we're boys, we can take it."

"Do boys feel different?—perhaps you don't feel so different."

The party is already wandering forward again.

"Must be funny to be a girl."

"I think boys is funnier—they're proper queer, boys is."

"Wy, Liz, ow d'ya mean?" in a serious tone. The ritual of cross talk, answer and answer back is abandoned. No one feels it appropriate to the time and the occasion. Voices are grave and mature, and every statement is received with thoughtful interest.

"They're proper funny, boys is," Liz says.

"I know what she means," Ginger says. "She's right, too."

"They are funny, too," Charley says. "Yers, the way they're made. Cor, it's queer, too."

Bert appears before them in the moonlight, his spectacles flash at them and then he flaps a sleeve towards a distant hedge. He calls indignantly: "That way over there."

The group, without looking at him, inclines slightly in the direction pointed out, and Ginger says: "My mother's been married three times, and she'd soon have another husband if this one died."

"Is she pretty, Ginger?"

"No, but men always like her a lot. She could have as many men as she wanted."

"How does she get em, Ginger?" Liz asks.

"She's very attractive to men. She gets all sorts of presents and she's quite old." There is a pause, and then Ginger murmurs: "The art of love."

"Wot is the art of love, Ginj?"

"I don't know—it's just something they say. Hoke, I should think."

"You can get un at Twyport fair," Liz says, "for sixpence—in a book—but it's silly—all rhymes."

"It isn't silly if you want a lot of husbands. Everybody has to learn how to do things," Ginger says.

"Wot you going to be, Ginger?"

"Engineer."

"Motor engineer?"

"Lectric—they'll soon be driving everything by lectricity."

"I'm sure you'll get a good job, Ginger."

"It's just luck."

"You wouldn't rather go in a band?"

"I wouldn't be good enough—you have to be awfully good for a good band. It's a gift."

Bert's voice comes to them faintly. "Mind the ditch."

"You get born with a gift. You get born with money and everything," Ginger says. "Money and everything."

"You wasn't born deaf, Lizzie, was you?"

"No, it come along of the fever."

"It wasn't someone it you on the ear?"

"No, it was the fever."

"Bad luck, Lizzie. But you aint really barmy, are you?"

"She don't act barmy—way she fought Walter."

"It's the way it happens, iddn it?"

There is another pause. Then Charley says: "It's a pity, aint it?"

"Wot is, Charley?"

"Gangs can't go on for ever, our gang."

"Ere, but it is going on, aint it?"

"Course it's going on," Liz says, waking from some dream. "It's got to go on now, haddn it? It couldn not go on."

"It's a nice night," Ginger says, apparently without irony.

"It's nice in the fields at night. The moon makes em look so pratty. It's bin a nice day too."

All seek confirmation of this in order to express their happiness.

"I liked it, Liz. Do you like it, Arry?"

"Yes, I liked it. Wot about ole Ginger?"

"I liked it all right."

But this is not enthusiastic enough, and Charley insists: "Did you really like it, Ginger, honest?"

"Honest, I did."

"Garn, Ginger aint never appy," Harry says.

"Abide with me, fast falls the eventide——"

106

"Don't ee, Gingarr. Tis too pratty."

"It's cos we're a real gang, see," Charley says.

"Faithful and true," Ginger murmurs as if repeating a song.

"Yers, sos we'll never squeal on each other. Cross my heart. May I die."

"Cross my heart, too," Liz says.

22 Tightly clasped together, with eyes cast down, they wander first to the right, then to the left. Liz gives deep sigh. "Father bant cruel neither—he don't like belting me."

"Nor my father aint cruel—ony strict."

"My father takes me to the pictures and gives me a beer after," Charley says.

"Noa, they arn't cruel. It's because they want us to be careful. Mother told me that if I went with you vackies I'd end in the streets. And look at me now."

"Your father'll take your skin off to-night, Liz."

"Yess, he will, too. But I don't mind. I bin so turble happy to-da-ay. I'll never forget it."

"Ere, it aint over yet."

"Noa, it's early, ant it? Look at the moon. Tis only back of steeple down church lane."

"We won't go home till morning."

"Shall us sit in the straw stack to Frenchay. Tis still dry."

"Wot'll we do there?"

"Just sit—we could talk, too."

"I'd like that, woulddn you, Ginger?"

"It's all right by me."

"What about you, Harry?"

"I ain't going ome."

Bert comes running back and says: "Ere we are, Charley." He points across the field and they see the top of Burlswood spire over the beech wood, which looks like a low cloud of grey smoke. The children stop, visibly disconcerted.

"Are you sure, Bert?" Charley asks.

"There ain't a spire on our church," Harry says.

"Yess," Bert nods. "That's it—that's Burlswood." He looks at the group, still clasped together, with a cheerful grin. Bert has no sentiment.

"We aint going ome, are we?" Charley says.

No one answers. Ginger says softly: "I will be dreaming of my own bluebell."

"I don't want to go home," Liz says, in a frightened voice. Her resignation to fate has vanished at sight of the home spire.

"But we aint going ome," Charley says.

Bert hovers before them. He flaps one sleeve like a hen that thinks it will fly but suddenly remembers that it can't. Then he says: "Just struck eleven, Charley. I'm afeared mother'll be coming after me."

"Ere, you aint going ome, Bert."

"Yess, I go that way. You can't lose yourselves now, can you? This field is big Whiteboys and over there is little Whiteboys piece."

"Thatss all right, Bert. You go ome."

Bert recedes backwards, apparently uncertain of the proper ritual for the occasion. Bert never says good-bye, good morning, or good night, probably looking upon these forms as too high toned and pretentious for his rank. But he feels the lack of a substitute.

"Good night, Bert—you're a proper good scout for finding the way."

Bert trips and nearly falls backwards; recovers himself, his spectacles flash dimly and it can be seen that he is grinning; then he turns round and lumbers away, flapping in a slow and dignified manner.

There is a pause. They wander slowly through Whiteboys, the big field on the top of the hill, between Burlswood House and wood.

"I don see why we should go home," Liz says defiantly, as

if answering some mysterious authority which is commanding them all to go home.

"We aint going ome," Charley says.

Another minute passes. Then Ginger says: "Getting cold, isn't it?"

"No, Gingurr, get in closer then."

"Wonder wot they ad for supper at Hall Farm?" Harry says.

"Oh, it's lovely here ant it—look at the spire going right through the moon."

"I can't go ome anyow—till all you is at ome," Charley says.

"Gingurr is nearest," Lizzie says. "It would be Gingurr first."

"I just go down here, don't I?"

Then there is silence. There seems to be nothing to talk about. Their ideas are divergent and even their group seems to loosen, Harry drags away in one direction, Ginger turns in the opposite.

"All right, Ginj," Charley says resentfully, "if you want to go to your ot bottle."

"I don't want to go, but the party's finished."

"No, Gingurr, don't say so."

"We'll spoil it, Lizzie, if we try to keep it up."

Lizzie throws off his arm. "Oh, goa then——"

"We'll come with you, Ginger," Charley says.

Lizzie takes his arm again and says: "But we won't go home, Gingurr—you'll be sorry you went away from the party." She warns him with anger in her voice.

They wander to the edge of the Burlswood House garden.

"There you are, Ginger."

"Good night, Charley."

"Good night, ole Ginj."

"Good night, Liz."

Lizzie does not answer. They watch Ginger stroll into the shadow of the tall house, towards the back door. They hear it open and shut, and they still stand looking towards the house.

Liz sighs suddenly: "Poor Gingurr. I wish I said good night to him."

"I dunno," Charley turns away.

"E's all right," Harry says. "E can go in wen e likes and no one says a word to im."

"Funny ow e got stuck in the caffee—e was shy."

"Ginger—e aint shy."

"I like Gingurr—I do wish I'd said good night to him," Liz sighs again. "Poor Gingurr."

As usual with this expression of pity she seems to be expressing an emotion much wider and much more deeply felt than a passing sympathy with the object mentioned. Children use the same tone, when, on the loss of a doll or a boat, they say: "Poor doll, poor boat." They do not pity the doll or the boat so much as wonder, sometimes with curiosity, sometimes fear, at the circumstances within which dolls and boats can be so helplessly smashed.

Both Charley and Harry, without consideration, feel what she means, and Charley says again: "It ain't too bad for Ginger. Is father as a garridge. E'll always ave a job."

"I wish I'd said good night to him. Do you think he noticed?"

"Course not."

"It's all right for Ginger and me. It's you oo'll cop it, Liz."

"I don mind—it's bin so lovely—don't go in yet, Harry."

"I don want to go," Harry says in a voice of agonised perplexity, "but it *is* late, aint it?"

"Jess down the lane," Liz coaxes him.

"Aw right, Liz—I don want to go really."

They turn into the lane and Lizzie presses their arms to draw them closer together. "O-o-o——bant this nice."

But Harry answers: "I don want to go, Lizzie—it's ony that——"

Lizzie suddenly drops his arm and flies into a temper. "Oh, go on, go on to Phylly."

"I'm sorry, Liz, but Mr. Awes——"

"Oh, go on, do—now you've spoilt it all," in a trembling voice.

Harry retreats backwards, through the gate into the Hall yard. He complains: "I didn't want to go ome—I didn't go first either."

"Sall right, Arry," Charley says. "Liz didn't mean nothing —good night, Arry."

"Good night, Charley. Goo ni, Liz."

"Good night, Harry. I diddn mean nothing."

"Goo ni again, Liz." The again is an assurance of forgiveness.

"Good night again, Harry." The again is an assurance of undying affection.

They watch the back door open, letting out a glare of yellow light and then they hear Phyllis Hawes' mild voice singing: "Wherever you bin, Harry—without your dinner or supper or nothing—poor boy, you must be starved," and then a call: "Mother, here's Harry come back—he'd better have the pie, hadden he?"

Charley and Liz sigh together as if from one impulse, and Charley says: "E's all right, wish I was at All Farm."

They stare at the house for a moment and then Liz says: "Poor Harry."

"You did give im a start, didn't ya?"

"I got an awful temper, Charley—something turble. It's a cross." She takes Charley's arm and says: "We needn't go home yet, Charley."

"Ain't no good anging about, Liz—the party's bust."

"But there's me and you still."

"Yers, but there isn't no party—it's bust."

There is a pause and then Liz says mournfully: "Yes, it's over, ant it? It's bin so sweet a day I wouldn't believe."

"Come on, Liz."

"I'll see you home first, Charley."

"I'm all right—I'll op in by the window."

They are climbing the hill road. Lizzie's step gets slower

and slower. Finally both children come to a halt. Lizzie says in a new flat voice: "They'll be waiting for me."

"Get in at the back."

"There bant no back." She means that the Galors' cottage, built into the flank of the quarry field, has no back door and almost no back wall.

"It's the way they jump out at you," Lizzie says.

Charley perfectly understands this. "I know—my father goes shouting at me sometimes—to bust yer ear-drums."

"They don't need to shout. I know when I didn't ought to have done something."

"Can't you get in at the window, Liz?"

"'Tis easy to get in—but they mun know I bin out all day, and they allays roar at me, both on em at once. I don't know what to do when they roar at me—it makes me so stoopid as a hen."

"Come on, Liz—less try the window."

"It won't be no good," Lizzie sighs. But she allows Charley to lead her up the back of the lane into the steep quarry field on the right. She cannot face the door with both her parents in ambush behind it.

Charley climbs rapidly in the moonlight, which does not lie directly on the slope. It strikes upon the apple trees of the Hall Farm orchard, at two or three feet from the ground; so that they seem neatly painted dark blue, to that height, instead of limewashed.

In ten minutes the children stand above the Galors' garden patch, sunk like the cottage into the hill-side, so that its inner sides are banked to a height of seven or eight feet. It is a neglected garden, full of overgrown raspberry-canes and dead gooseberry stems, which stretch up through the pool of dark-blue shadow the white, straggling tips of their branches, like an underwater vegetation, bleached above the surface.

Shadows of these stems and the heads and shoulders of the children are silhouetted on the cottage wall, less than six feet high, rising blank of windows straight out of the broken soil.

The roof, sloping high, has, on the left side, a very tall brick chimney, with a tin chimney-top, cowled to make a draught, and next the chimney a flattened low-browed dormer.

The roof is singularly long as well as bare. It covers, actually, as well as the cottage, an ancient cyder press-house, disused for half a century, which is part of some buildings and sheds once belonging to a small farm. The farm has been absorbed by the Hall. The buildings, where they come down to the road in front, are partly ruinous, and partly used to store machinery. But the cyder-house, though it has long ago lost its press, still keeps a sound roof; and a three-room cottage for the Galors has been contrived at its southern end; by boarding-up the apple loft, putting a window-frame into its apple door, and on the lower story cutting off space enough for a kitchen and bedroom, now occupied by the Galor parents.

This bedroom on the rising side of the hill is three steps above the kitchen, on its own staircase. The apple loft above has kept its old ladder, boarded between the steps; now, by courtesy, the staircase.

The loft is the girls' bedroom. Though, on the outside, its window is six feet above ground, the space from dormer to ground used to be open, and the wall beneath its sill is a rough construction of elm boards nailed to the framework of the old apple door.

As the children climb down into the sunk garden and approach the window, a low rumbling can be heard rising from the cottage, or rather from the ground. On a little reflection this noise might be recognised as a man's bass voice, distorted by partitions of dry wood and old rotting stone.

"Father," Lizzie whispers, suddenly coming to a stop. "He's bin sitting up for me."

This voice has the same effect on Lizzie as a blow on the head. She becomes dazed and clumsy. She stumbles among the garden rubbish and when Charley whispers to her: "Look out,

Liz—old up," she gazes at him with foolish eyes and open mouth.

Charley makes her lean against the wall. Then he drags a broken hurdle up to the wall below the window and props it edgeways against the sill. He pulls open a few toe-holds and hand-grasps in the rotting fabric, climbs up to the window and knocks on the glass.

The window, an old wooden casement, is opened inwards, and a young girl's face, round and serious, with level dark brows, appears in the moonlight. Susan Galor is ten.

"Is that you, Bess?" she says in a low but very distinct voice.

"No, it's me, Charley Brown—I brought Liz ome."

The girl frowns at Charley and says: "You ought to have more sense. Mother and father have been looking all over."

"Yes, poor old Liz is a bit worried—couldn't you ide er for now, Sukey?"

"However could I hide her?"

"You know you could, Sukey. You're clever enough for anything."

But Charley's flattery has no obvious effect on young Susan. She says impatiently: "What the good of it, anyhow? Oh dear, how stupid. You've got no sense, you boys. Bessie," she calls in a soft, tired voice: "Come up, quickly."

Charley climbs down and helps Lizzie to mount the hurdle. She is trembling as if with a chill, so that Charley has to place her feet in the holds. At last she slips or tumbles through the window and disappears through the curtain.

"You all right, Lizzie?" Charley asks after a moment.

"Oh dear, haven't you gone away yet, you boy?" Susan's voice says behind the curtain.

"You all right, Liz?" Charley can hardly believe that the party is over. He feels as if he had suddenly been deprived of all that makes existence bearable. Loneliness falls upon him as if he had never known it before.

Lizzie makes no answer. She doesn't hear. But Charley cannot bear to go.

"You all right, Liz?"

Susan's voice says in resigned disgust: "Your boy is talking to you, Bessie."

There is a short silence. Then Susan says again: "You better say good night and get rid of him."

The curtain is drawn back and Susan appears in the moonlight, drawing Liz after her. Liz is in patched combinations. She looks so changed by fright that Charley can hardly recognise her.

"Sall right, Liz," he murmurs. "They can't kill you, see."

Lizzie looks at him blankly. Her teeth are chattering. Sukey says impatiently: "Oh dear, say good night, Liz, so he'll go away."

Good night, Charley."

Lizzie looks at him and her expression changes slightly. She has recollected him. She gives a deep sigh and murmurs: "Poor Charley."

"Ere, I'm all right—ere—ere's your necklace." He takes the necklace out of his trouser pocket and pushes it into her hands.

"Do go now, boy, for gracious' sake."

Charley descends slowly, grumbling aloud, and goes through the garden. Then he remembers the hurdle and returns to take it away. He listens under the dormer for several minutes but nothing can be heard from the cottage except the same bass voice rumbling in the same monologue, somewhere below stairs.

At last he turns away and charges up the field like one making the shortest possible work of an unpleasant duty. Reaching the Parrs' cottage, he quickly ascends to his mother's bedroom by the usual route, the water-butt and its down-pipe."

Mrs. Brown is asleep. But she wakes enough to hear Charley's entrance by the window and to say in a voice thick with sleep and sleepy amusement: "That you, Charley?"

"Yes, ma."

"Better not let Mrs. Parr ear you."

"No, Ma."

He takes off his boots and gets into bed. As he wears no underclothes he usually sleeps in his jersey and breeches. Mrs. Brown gives a sound between a fat wheeze and a snore; a sleepy laugh: "Teacher was after you again, Charley."

"Wot teacher?"

"Miss Allchin."

"She aint a teacher."

"Wanted to know were you'd been. You better look out for er."

"All right, ma," Charley murmurs. His eyelids are falling together. He is suddenly tired.

"Were you bin, Charley?" This question is so unexpected that Charley, for the moment, is almost awakened. He wonders where he has been in order to know what answer to give, whether truthful or not. But he can't remember. The day belongs already to the distant past. He mutters: "Jus round." Then he falls suddenly asleep. Mrs. Brown is also asleep.

23 Charley lay in bed late next morning, planning new exploits. But all of them ended in long parties, in which Harry, Ginger, Bert, Lizzie and himself motored to splendid hotels, ordered immense meals, and at night went to the pictures together in the grandest cinemas. His ideas combined the magnificence of royal palaces, as seen in the pictures, with the continuous society of as many friends as possible. He wanted the magnificence, partly as a dignified setting for friendship, for he always dressed his whole gang in new suits by the best tailors, Lizzie in a silk frock and diamonds, but also he liked it for its own sake. He had just planned a floating castle on an island made of empty oil-drums, when he heard a low, shrill whistle outside the window, Ginger's whistle.

He jumped out of bed and saw Ginger below. Ginger tried to shout to him in a whisper, making very strange faces, and failing to convey a meaning, pointed at his head. Charley, touchy on this point, shouted: "Wot d'ya mean—wots wrong with my ead?"

Ginger called faintly: "Your hat."

"My at?"

"Did it have your name in it?"

"Course it ad."

Ginger at once hurried away across the fields, towards Burlswood House.

Charley, feeling a shock of terror, ran to look for his hat in its usual place on the floor under the bed. But he knew already that he had left it behind him on the night before, either in the car at the time of the crash, or nearby. He could remember when he crouched in the straw noting its absence, and making a resolution to look for it.

Five minutes later, breakfastless, with an old cap belonging to Mrs. Brown on his head, and a long face ridiculously dismayed, he was flying to the Cedars. On the way he passed Harry, who, catching sight of him, jumped and rushed away from him as if from a plague victim.

Charley's flight to the Cedars was instinctive, as a small child, on the first rumble of thunder, flies to the nearest skirt. He was extremely startled when, in the path from the gate, Basil, dawdling towards the door with Walter, turned and said: "You'll be copped, Charley, and serve you right."

"Ere, wot you talking about?"

"Were's your at," Basil asks with a grin which is both malicious and righteous. Basil shows his feeling that Charley deserves every misfortune, by a look of contempt; his pleasure in the justice of the punishment, by the malice in his voice.

"Pinching cars," he says. "Wot'll they think of us. I've a good mind to put the cops on you myself. Bill knows, too."

Charley, shocked out of his aplomb, says feebly: "E knows wrong, then."

"It's no good, Charley, Harry told us," Walter says coolly. He has not forgiven Charley for his beating. "And where's your hat?"

"In the ands of the police," Basil says.

The two go in. Charley is left so depressed that it is a long time before he can bring himself to approach the door.

Classes have already begun. A murmur of children's voices comes from the drawing-room on the right, and from some window on the left a loud contralto, saying with confident emphasis: "The rivers, of course, are *very* important." A maid, old and spectacled, with the blank expression of a servant whose work has been interrupted by some unnecessary duty, lets Charley into the hall and calls through a door: "A boy for you, Miss Lina."

Lina comes out with a book open in her hand and seeing Charley, cries: "Why, Charley, you've come at last, have you?"

"Yes, miss."

"I'm so glad—this is nice. Where would you like to start? I know you're a clever boy. You won't mind if you find things a bit slow to-day—until we can place you?"

"No, miss."

"How is your head now?" Lina takes off Charley's cap and looks at Charley's head. "You'll soon have plenty of hair again—but what an awful old cap. Did you lose the hat I gave you?"

"Yes, miss."

"Never mind, I must get you a new cap."

Charley, still terrified, anxious and humble, feels the girl's warmth of kindness and blushes. He grins to himself. His "Yes, miss" is intended to convey affectionate gratitude. The grin is an apology to himself for sentimental feeling.

But at this moment a middle-aged lady comes slowly downstairs into the hall. She is small and dark eyed, like Lina, with a flat obstinate face and sharp chin. She is dressed in very old stained tweeds and wears a ruinous felt hat, reminiscent both of Queen Victoria and the Wild West. As she passes Charley she gives him a look of ferocious disgust and says: "Is that the boy who stole Laura's car?"

Lina turns red and looks angrily at her mother. "Nonsense,

mother, no one knows who took the car. It probably wasn't a boy at all."

Mrs. Allchin, to Charley's surprise, looks snubbed and says in a defensive tone: "I was only wondering." She then swerves aside and disappears obliquely into the garden.

Lina says quickly to Charley: "I don't believe it was a boy, do you? But the police put everything on to you poor boys."

"Yes, miss."

"Very well, Charley. Now would you like to meet Miss Small who is taking the English classes?"

"Yes, miss."

Charley is introduced to a class of seven curious children, of whom one, Irene, puts out her tongue at him so calmly and, as it were, correctly, that no one but Charley even notices the expression of contempt. Miss Small, the teacher, is a red-cheeked young woman. Her fresh cheeks look as hard as cheese. She receives Charley with a series of little enthusiastic cries which, nevertheless, sound formal, as if she meant nothing very much by them. "Yes, of course—Charley Brown—I had him on my first list. Where would you like to sit? Back to window is best for light, isn't it? Pencil, paper—we were just doing a little jography."

Charley proves to know almost as much about British nominal geography as Miss Small. She gives Lina an enthusiastic report, and Charley receives a large cream bun with his milk at eleven o'clock.

After the lessons Charley, instead of dashing away like the rest, lingers in the hall until Lina, flattered and touched by his reluctance to go from her, is obliged to hint that his mother will be expecting him. Charley, thus driven from his bolt hole, creeps home by the fields. But Basil is waiting for him again that afternoon in ambush by the cross-roads, and when he calls out, Bill and Walter come from the dry ditch where they are smoking their cigarettes to shout with him: "Oo pinched the motor car—were's your at, Charley?"

Basil, ten years old, is drunk with spiteful joy. He is already an artist in his chosen medium. It is he who varies the formula and aims it not at Charley but at the windows of the Green Man and then at any passer.

"Oo pinched the lady's car," Basil screams next day at the Cedar's gate as Charley darts into the hall.

"What *do* they mean?" Lina asks, turning round and looking at Charley.

Charley, even redder, says: "It's just joking, miss."

Lina laughs and says: "Oh, well, we don't mind jokes, do we?"

But for two days Charley suffers agony and despair by this ingenious torture. "I aint telling on ya," Basil screams. "But oo pinched the blue car?"

Charley never sees Ginger, and Harry, who is luckily going to classes at the vicarage, flies from him. But he hears through the milk boy, Drake, that Liz has been beaten for going with the boys. He does not approach her cottage.

But when Basil tries to bring the campaign home to him, shrieking his slogan over the front wall, Mrs. Parr goes out by the garden into the field and takes the enemy in the rear. Mrs. Parr detests all foreigners, but especially those who are not domiciled under her roof. She gives Basil a slap on the ear which sends him howling, and silences Walter, although he is twenty yards away.

After this, while Basil screams insults at Mrs. Parr, Charley goes peacefully to school by the fields. In two days he has devised a routine, or new system of life, in which Harry, Ginger and even Liz belong to a past existence, in which Bill, Walter and Basil are no more troublesome than the rain. He cannot always escape them, but when he is caught he has refuges at hand.

It is true that Mrs. Parr makes him wash his hands and sit down to a meal, undress for bed, and even change the jersey which he has worn day and night for eighteen days and grown to love. But Charley is obliging. He is incapable of long sulks simply because he is too occupied. He is now quite restored in spirits. Basil, Bill and Walter may shout their loudest in the hearing of Lina, Mrs. Parr and all the villagers: "Oo stole the lady's car?" but he does not even turn his head. Since no catastrophe has arrived in three days he expects none.

24 At the Cedars both Lina and Miss Small notice a falling off in Charley's work. He is still, as Lina describes him, a charmer. His hair is growing, his cheeks are rounding; he is losing his appearance of a shrivelled bald old man. He is almost good-looking, though, as Lina says: "It really doesn't matter about his features, it's his expression that gets you. You can't help seeing that he's a perfect dear."

"I hope he won't trade on it," Miss Small says.

"Oh, I'm on guard," Lina says, touchée. She knows that Miss Small thinks her a favouritiser. She thinks the same of Miss Small. "I'm not going to spoil young Charley. That reminds me, how is Philip getting on?"

Philip is Miss Small's favourite. Miss Small murmurs in a lively amused tone which is the armour of attacked ladies. "He is a young rascal, isn't he?—he knows he's clever."

"Mustn't let him be a prig, must we?"

"A prig." Poor Miss Small is hurt. She turns pink. "Poor little dear, he's only eight, after all."

"It's a dangerous age, they say."

"Oh, would you say so? I always thought fourteen was the really dangerous age for boys—look at Charley Brown, for instance, I couldn't get him to do a thing to-day, and scratching himself all the time—with his hands in his pockets. Really a little horrible."

Both Lina and Miss Small turn suddenly red and Lina says sharply: "How can the poor child help growing up?" They both stand breathless as if about to discharge some weighty remark, suddenly think better of it and fly apart without a word, as if charged simultaneously by the same electrical disturbance.

The truth is that Charley, relieved of terror, finds it difficult to keep his mind fixed on the industrial revolution or even the chief rivers of England.

"What is the river on which Bristol stands, Charley?"

Charley is gazing dreamily out of the window across the garden where Mrs. Allchin is laying a brick path between rose beds.

"Charles, you're asleep. What did I ask you?"

"Yes, miss."

Young Philip, with a face as white as milk, hair like cotton boll, eyes like periwinkles, suddenly gabbles: "Oh, Mith Thmall, itth another Avon, ithnt it?"

"Yes, another Avon, Philip. Very good, Philip, you always attend."

Charley's face remains turned towards Miss Small, and even keeps an expression of interest, but his eyes are twisting towards Mrs. Allchin's brick walk. He knows all the rivers and towns in England. He has learnt and forgotten them at least twenty times.

"It meanth a river, dothnt it, Mith Thmall?"

"Does it, Philip? That's very interesting, and now can you tell me——"

Philip is trying to give information. "My father saith ith becauth the firth people didn know any other river tho they called their river THE river."

Charley, gazing at Philip with the greatest interest, bursts out: "Same way as we do in London."

"Yeth and thame way we got all the Thmiths becauth eath village thought *their* Thmith wath the *only* Thmith."

"And Brown, like me—but ow did London get its name?"

"Now, boys, this is very interesting, but we must get on with our work, mustn't we, and we can ask questions afterwards. Irene, can you tell me which is the chief river that runs out into the Bristol Channel—no, Jimmie, don't you say. I want Irene to answer."

Irene, with her bright cheeks like a Dutch doll, with hair tied back so tightly in a blue ribbon that her eyes seem to be squeezed from her head, looks blanker than wood. It is a dynamic and positive blankness, a Siegfried line erected to defeat all invasions of external suggestion.

"Now, Irene, I've just told you."

Charley is already looking out of the window where Mrs. Allchin has reached a crisis. She has put the same brick down three times and taken it up again. She now stands with it grasped in her hand, pondering. Charley aches for her. He feels as if a strong rubber band was stretched between him and Mrs. Allchin, dragging him to solve her problem.

"Charles, that is the third time I've asked you." Charley jumps and says politely, apologetically: "Yes, miss."

Miss Small is not to be charmed out of her just annoyance. But after the lesson, when she tells Lina that Charley is growing impossibly lazy, Lina says only with a puzzled frown: "I know, Doris, it's a nuisance. The truth is that the poor child hasn't had a chance to form any good habits."

Miss Small looks cold and answers: "It's not so much his bad habits as his total indifference to anything I say."

Lina, equally indifferent, as Miss Small bitterly observes, once more assumes that perplexed brow which is the defence of every headmistress in the same position, and gives the necessary answer: "So worrying—one of the most difficult of our problems. I suppose we can only be patient. Thank goodness you can deal with him—you are wonderfully good with the problems."

Charley, meanwhile, who ought to be eating his bun, has slipped into the garden. He forgets even buns in his anxiety to see what Mrs. Allchin did with the brick. He approaches the lady from behind. She is stooped double in the act of laying a brick. But by some mysterious influence, some sixth sense, or merely an acute ear and nose, she suddenly detects his presence. She starts up, brick in hand, and turns upon him, crimson with exertion and anger. "Go away, boy, go away at once," with a vigorous wave of the brick.

Charley retreats backwards, too startled to be hurt.

"Boys are not allowed in the garden." Mrs. Allchin makes another angry wave.

"But, Mother—really." Lina has darted to the rescue. "After all, it *is* war-time."

Mrs. Allchin, daunted, mutters angrily: "It was distinctly understood."

"Really, you know, we ought to dig up the garden," Lina says.

Mrs. Allchin looks as if she is going to cry. She wrinkles up her eyes and mutters in an uncertain voice: "No one to dig anything."

"There are plenty simply longing to dig—there's the two conchies at Wickens who have nothing to do—and the A.R.P. people who don't know how to fill in their time either."

Mrs. Allchin is now in retreat. She hurries towards the most distant part of the garden. But the angry Lina, still taking vengeance for Charley, calls after her: "And you know they said this was the best place for a village shelter."

Mrs. Allchin stoops suddenly into a tool shed. The effect is that of a beaten dog slinking into its kennel. Lina, flushed and muttering to herself, in a manner very like her mother's, turns to Miss Small, who has just come from the door and says: "What are you doing about your garden, Doris?"

"We're putting most of it in potatoes."

"Ex-*actly*."

"Of course, Father doesn't like it, but as we told him——"

"Exactly."

"Though I suppose your mother did order these stones before?"

But on this subject, Lina, usually so doubtful of her own judgment, is sure of herself. Everything and everybody, the news in the papers and the opinions expressed in them, all convince her that she can't be wrong. "I don't see that it matters, Doris, when she got them. This is not the time to play about with gardening when men are being killed every day."

Miss Small agrees enthusiastically with her friend. They are friends again in sympathy and disapproval of unpatriotic and frivolous pursuits.

Charley has slipped away into the house, where he is furtively, with bun-sticky fingers, pulling a picture-book out of a shelf. He can't resist pictures in any form. This book is labelled on the back *Great Pictures of the World*.

But hearing a maid coming, he quickly puts it back in its place. He is sure, by the binding, that it is not for him.

25 Charley now flies to the Cedars, every morning and all afternoon, only to see what Mrs. Allchin is doing with the bricks. One afternoon, during a whole English lesson, he is absorbed in the laying out of a new rock garden, with pegs and string, at the end of the lawn, near the wall. Mrs. Allchin, painfully stooping, does the work, but Charley, in imagination, piles the stones, lying ready by the shed, and digs the pool.

Next morning, the boredom of arithmetic is entirely removed by the discovery that pegs and string have been taken away. When, about lunch-time, he is almost distracted by curiosity, two A.R.P. men from Tawleigh and the conscientious objectors from Wickens Farm, arrive with picks and spades and dig an enormous trench across lawn and rose-beds. Mrs. Allchin has disappeared. Charley sits in a fever of wonder and excitement which is highly pleasant. Miss Small is obliged to send him out of the room for gross inattentiveness. He retires to his final refuge, the W.C., plays with himself for a little, draws anatomical and flower pictures with his fingers on the damp tiles of the lavatory wall, and then perceiving a likeness between the forms of their sexual members, elaborates these patterns till they run together into a tropical forest of human orchids and flowering flesh.

He is as silent and absorbed as a monk in contemplation of the visions produced by his own devotion; yet, like a monk, he is secretly bored, and he knows it. His contemplative peace floats like a golden cloud on a hill-top; within it is grey mist and the hill is a dreary solitude.

Outside in the yard he hears Lina explaining to Miss Small why it is no longer possible to avoid the digging of the shelter.

"I'm sure Mother thinks that I did it deliberately—but I had to ask them if they still wanted a shelter here. Suppose we had a raid and there was no shelter—Mother simply has no imagination."

"I quite understand, dear, no one could possibly blame you."

"And this is far the best place. *I* didn't choose it. *They* chose it long ago. It was only because Mother was so obstinate that it wasn't done before. I really had to make her realise that there was a war on."

The two young ladies stroll into the house, talking about the necessity of making people understand that there is a war on, especially at this time, when the armies are not fighting. Mrs. Allchin appears from the kitchen yard and approaches the diggers from that side. Charley is suddenly noticed gliding from the garden door which leads from the back passage. Mrs. Allchin flutters round the trench and then suggests mildly that it be extended in the other direction. The diggers pause, the A.R.P. men argue, the conscientious objectors look calmly submissive to fate, and finally all agree that for their part they don't mind which way the trench runs. The A.R.P. men then go away with Lina Allchin, to fetch timber for revetting, and sandbags. During the afternoon Mrs. Allchin continues the work herself. About four o'clock, Charley, freed from lessons, appears with a spade, taken from the tool shed, and also begins to dig. Mrs. Allchin gives him an indignant glance, mutters to herself and turns her back on him. She can't bring herself

126

to speak to a boy of the garden-destroying age. The trench is now a very odd shape. Landslides have taken place at one end which has become a shallow hole seven or eight feet wide and four deep. At the other end Mrs. Allchin has dug a huge hole into the clay about a foot beneath the parapet. When this, too, threatens to fall in, she props it up with stones. Charley rushes to her help and places a flat stone upon the side walls as a roof.

"It's like a cave, m, isn't it?" he says.

Mrs. Allchin makes no reply. That night it rains. The next day the A.R.P. men, coming with bags and timber, find the whole system in ruins, with two feet of water in it. They declare indignantly that some unauthorised person has destroyed their dug-out. Mrs. Allchin, much agitated, disappears. Lina, in distress, apologises for her mother and hints that she is well-meaning but not well up in military engineering. The A.R.P. men answer that they are sorry, but they cannot be responsible for a dug-out on the site. The soil has been too much disturbed. Burls must do without a shelter. They go away with a self-righteous air.

Lina gets on her bicycle and rides into Tawleigh to make explanation to the group warden. Mrs. Allchin suddenly appears and begins to throw large stones into the muddy trench. Charley joins her and assists with energy. Together they build walls against the sloping sides of the trench; complete with cave. When Lina comes back, she finds them both up to the eyes in mud.

"What on earth are you doing, Mother?"

"We couldn't leave it like that, darling," Mrs. Allchin protests nervously. "Such a mess—it's really scandalous—those men——"

"But what are all the stones for?"

"Well, as they were here, I just thought——"

"Oh, Mother, I did think you'd given up that ridiculous scheme—really and truly I should have thought you realised that this was hardly the time for rock gardens. And even if there wasn't a war, we could never carry out such a plan—it was much too expensive."

"But, darling, it hasn't cost anything. Wickens gave me the stones."

Lina is answering with warm indignation that rock gardens are not going to win the war, when she is called away to a farm-labourer's wife, whose vackie, a schoolgirl from Plymouth, has demanded a hot-water bottle in her bed, and refuses to eat margarine.

Mrs. Allchin at once returns to work with a desperate energy. Charley, who understands perfectly well the nature of the crisis, also throws himself upon the work. "It's all right, m," he tells her. "We'll get it finished and then they can't take it down."

Mrs. Allchin says nothing, but takes out one of Charley's stones, and puts it back again at a different angle. She says to the air: "I don't know how plants can grow if they've got no earth round their roots."

"I see, m," Charley says. "You put em in sloping back like."

Mrs. Allchin has already turned her back upon him. But Charley is too happy to be repressed.. He gazes into the cave and says: "Cor, it's a real cave—look at the water dripping from the top—it ought to ave a pipe to make it drip all the time."

Mrs. Allchin glances at the cave and then reflectively at the shed. Charley, feeling her thoughts, exclaims: "It's only ten foot to the pipe in the shed, and it would run out of the front, too—like a real waterfall."

On the next afternoon, while Lina is going her rounds of the cottages, Sam Eger suddenly appears at the Cedars with a length of rusty iron pipe and lays it in a shallow trench from the cave to the tool shed, where he screws it by a T-piece to the garden supply pipe. The trench, by frantic labour, in which Eger assists, is filled in only a minute or so before Lina rides up to the gate.

The blacksmith, like everyone in the village, has followed for years the conflict between Mrs. Allchin's ambitions as a gardener and her daughter's commonsense. He winks at Charley and says: "Just in time." He goes to put away his spade and gathers his tools. Lina greets him pleasantly and asks what he is doing.

"Come to look after a pipe, miss, garden pipe."

"I didn't know anything about it." The suspicious daughter.

"No, miss, just looked in as I was passing. Won't cost you nothing."

"That's very kind of you, Sam." Lina is won over instantly by Sam's good nature.

"Not at all, miss. Pleasure to do anything." Sam, who has received five shillings from Mrs. Allchin, goes home in great satisfaction. The whole affair, being slightly crooked, is much to his taste.

As soon as Lina enters the house, Charley goes to turn on the tap; the cave drips and the waterfall pours into the rocky gully below.

Mrs. Allchin sits down on one of the boulders in the new river and stares at the cave for a long time. She does not smile. Her worn face, in which the arched wrinkles of the forehead reproduce in deep folds the faint tracings of self-doubt on Lina's, shows only a kind of apprehensive surprise. It seems to say at the same time: "Has it really come true?" and, "There must be something wrong somewhere."

Charley, sitting modestly behind, but equally oblivious of the rising flood round his ankles, is trying various viewpoints of the cave; sideways, from both sides; through the eyelashes; and by a sudden glance. The sudden glance is especially pleasing.

"It's like real, aint it, m?" he says.

Mrs. Allchin says to the cave: "What's your name, boy?"

"Charles, m, Charley Brown."

Mrs. Allchin says nothing to this. Then she suddenly springs

129

up and begins to arrange the stones lying about them in the long narrow pool.

"They want to look natural," she mutters, "but they never do."

"Yes, m, like the Grand Canyon, aint it, m, in Ammurca?" Mrs. Allchin takes up the stone he has just laid and says indignantly: "I said natural." She then turns it twice round and puts it back again in the same place. Charley says with a great appearance of pleasure: "That's better, m, aint it? Perhaps if we just threw em down, from the top."

Mrs. Allchin does not seem to hear this suggestion. She fears all communication with boys. But a few minutes later, while she and he are together struggling with their largest prize boulder, she mutters: "Some people tell you to throw them down in the natural way, but that *always* looks unnatural. Of course, if people want to save themselves trouble."

Half an hour later when the cold rain is falling in sheets and the pair are as wet as they can be, with blue noses, scarlet fingers and yellow cheeks, Mrs. Allchin stands embracing a very dirty stone in her arms and mutters: "It's the drainage that's the real trouble." She looks helplessly at the pond in which she is standing and at the waterfall now augmented by rain. "It's so deep down."

"Yes'm, but if it wasn't so deep you could see the 'ouse from it. Twouldn't be a real canyon."

After a pause Mrs. Allchin remarks, laying down her stone: "I meant it to be even deeper, but those wretched A.R.P. men didn't know their own job. They *said* nine feet."

"Ain't so deep as the road," Charley says, "and there's a good ditch down the ill."

Mrs. Allchin ignores him and continues her work. She says sadly: "It's always the drainage."

"You only want fifteen foot of a drain-pipe, m, wy, I'd do it meself."

After ten minutes Mrs. Allchin says: "People try all sorts of drainage—but it never works in a garden like this."

Fortunately, Lina is extremely busy finding new billets for the evacuees quartered at two neighbouring large houses, soon to be closed for the winter. For a week of afternoons, Mrs. Allchin and Charley work, almost undisturbed, at their rock garden. The drain is contrived from bricks covered with old tiles, and proves a complete success. The waterfall, by the most careful and elaborate expedients of both artists, working in complete disunity of mind and perfect harmony of taste, is caused to leap from stone to stone as if it had followed its own track for thousands of years. Charley places for it to tumble into a waterworn hollow stone, which Mrs. Allchin removes at least twice a day, and then, compelled by that same masterful taste, puts back in exactly the same position. Charley praises each repetition of his original scheme, as an artistic revelation.

Lina still carefully supervises Charley's lessons, but in the evenings and on his free afternoons she finds time only to apologise to him for the hard, uninteresting work imposed upon him by her mother. To her mother she threatens every day a doctor's order that she give up the whole project.

"You'll catch another of your colds, mother—and you know what that means, flu and pneumonia. You really mustn't go on getting your feet wet, it's madness."

"Perhaps if I borrowed a pair of these gumboots."

These are the A.R.P. gumboots stored at the Cedars. Lina is a senior warden and keeps the Burlswood stores. She is visibly shocked at the suggestion that her stores, provided by Government, might be used for garden work. She says coldly: "Those are A.R.P., mother, and you know I'm responsible for them."

Afterwards she tells the story to Miss Small and says: "As if I were going to encourage her—I oughtn't really to have allowed it at all. It's becoming a scandal to the whole village."

Mrs. Allchin and Charley are now planting the sides of their canyon. Charley has actually learned the names of many of the plants and is one day discovered by Miss Small in the small plot of ground between the rubbish heap and the coal yard where Mrs. Allchin propagates her alpines. He is gazing at two small green leaves, not much larger than clover leaves, growing apparently out of bare earth under the bowl of a wineglass with a broken stem.

"What are you doing, Charley?"

"Just looking at the *Daphne Neorum*, miss."

"At the what?"

"It comes from Greece, miss. It's just got a new leaf."

Miss Small, repeating this story to Lina, says: "Aren't they quaint—you never know what'll they say next."

Lina, smiling fondly, murmurs: "I always said Charley would be perfectly easy to manage if we went the right way about it."

One Monday, going back eagerly to school with a large mossy stone, looted from Burls House drive, wrapped in brown paper, under his arm, Charley hears that Mrs. Allchin is in bed with flu. He is disappointed to think that she will not be able to enjoy the stone at once, but he takes it to the cave and arranges it where the water will drip upon it.

He then sits happily through the entire day, in spite of angry reproaches from Miss Small and gentle appeals from Lina, thinking about the stone, picturing its bright green under the drip of water and fancying Mrs. Allchin's delight when she sees it.

"Cor, she will be surprised," and he invents a story in which he steals many more stones and completes the whole rock garden, cave and canyon. Mrs. Allchin, staggering from her sick bed, sees this work with amazement, is carried away by her feelings, expresses her gratitude and appreciation. "An the ole lady gives a sort of gasp—er eyes is all shining—it's a fair knock-out, see—and she says to me: 'Charley, thass the best rock garden I ever saw'—and she says: 'Thank you, Charley.' Ere, ere, come off it. She couldn't say that, not my old lady wouldn't—she's a real snorter——"

"Charley Brown, do you hear what I say, or must I ask Philip to pinch you?"

"Yes, miss."

"What is the capital of Yugoslavia?"

"Sofya, miss."

"I've just told you. Philip, what is the capital of Yugoslavia?"

Philip triumphs again. Charley bears him no malice, for Mrs. Allchin is already receiving the King's first prize for rock gardens at Buckingham Palace.

But Mrs. Allchin remains in bed. The doctor comes, Lina looks anxious and the housemaid tells Irene, her favourite, that the old woman has got pneumonia and will probably pass out.

"But what did she expect—getting er feet wet day in, day out, in that nasty mud-ole."

Charley goes to look at his stone. It is greener than ever. The cave is still more like a real cave, more damp, more gloomy, more richly smelling of decay; but Charley cannot enjoy it for more than two minutes. He feels so sad that he could cry. When in the evening he asks if Mrs. Allchin is going to get well soon, his voice is so low and his face so unhappy that Lina, too, nearly cries. She wants to kiss him, but fearing that this would show favouritism, she contents herself by touching his hair with her hand and saying: "I'm afraid not, Charley, not very soon—but it's very nice of you to ask."

She tells Miss Small the story and says: "Isn't it extraordinary —you know mother hates boys. I don't think she even thanked the poor little boy for slaving for her in the mud the whole week. And now he's really heart-broken because she's ill——"

"Ah, but she's *your* mother."

"Oh, but I don't think——"

"Of course, he's devoted to you, and so he ought to be," this with a little tartness.

Lina notices the prick, but she is too moved to resent it. She can't help smiling. She can't hide a pang of pure happiness. She murmurs: "But how good they are—how loyal—it's the queerest thing."

26   The rock garden is being covered in with planks and sandbags. The A.R.P. men have agreed that the solid construction of the walls and the efficient working of

the drain make it suitable for a temporary shelter. Charley is wandering along the hedges of the Glebe, now ploughed up. He is so bored and depressed that he feels ill. He wonders if he is going to be sick. His feet, turning aside of themselves, lead him gradually to the main road, down the quarry field, through the copse in the valley, over the Burl's stream, to the back windows of Hall Farm. He stands there in the yard and hears Mrs. Hawes calling: "Phyl-lis, Phyllis—your i-ern is hot!"

Charley presses his nose to the window but the curtains are drawn. Suddenly he glides down the stone passage into the kitchen. The high room is full of heat, light and rich smells. Enormous pots are bubbling on the stove. The long table by the wall is covered with plates, bottles, saucepans, dishes, partly eaten cheeses, ruined joints, basins of milk ready to be scalded. The Hawes family is always a meal behind with its washing-up.

Phyllis is sitting on a form in the light of a single candle, knitting a mitten. Charley, looking at her, feels suddenly an irresistible desire to touch her. He thinks she is beautiful, and he feels that she can cure him of whatever is wrong with him. He goes up to her and says: "Ullo, Miss Phyllis."

Phyllis starts and says: "Why, it's Charley—however did you come here, Charley?"

"I came in."

"Your hair's growing proper, isn't it, Charley?"

Charley is afraid now even to touch this dreamy girl who looks at him with placid eyes, so beautiful that he cannot help staring at them. He feels such longing that he can hardly speak; but he is so shy that he wishes that he had never come.

They gaze at each other and suddenly the girl sings in her caressing voice: "What's the matter, Charley—has that Walter been worrying you again?"

"No, miss."

"What's the matter, dee-urr—you've never bin crying, have you?"

"No, miss."

"Would you like some chocolate?—it's milk chocolate."

Charley wants to throw himself down and bury his head in her lap; but suddenly a bass voice says from the dark corner behind the table: "Your iron'll be setting the house on fire, Phyll."

"Then why don't you go and take it off, Ar-thurr," cries the girl, in a voice so different that Charley is visibly surprised. It is the nagging voice of a shrew. It is also the traditional voice of a properly engaged girl in Burls and Tawleigh, and some people hold that the most tyrannical engaged girls are precisely those who, a week after marriage, will be slaves to their husbands.

"Arrthurr," Phyllis cries shrilly. "Arn't you going, then—whatever's wrong with you—are you dead or only stupid?" This is a family phrase.

An enormous blond young man slowly unrolls six feet of himself from the corner behind the table and goes submissively into the back kitchen. Phyllis throws after him: "And if the table's burnt, you can get me another, Arrthurr, lazy great lumper."

Arthur reappears: "Noa, it's not burnt, Phyll."

"And that's not your fault, Arrthurr."

Arthur sits down beside her, takes the knitting out of her hands and continues the work. His huge fingers move as deftly as hers. Phyllis stares at him indignantly and says: "I'm to i-ern your trousers, am I—so's you can dance with all sorts down to Tawleigh."

"You're coming, too, an't you?"

"I'm not coming to be trodden on with your gre-at feet."

Phyllis gets up and goes into the back kitchen. A moment later her shrew voice cries: "Arrthurr—if you don't come quick and show me where to crease em, I'll do em crooked, and make you a guy for all the Tawleigh girls. And you on't like that."

Arthur disappears into the back kitchen. The forgotten Charley goes out of the back door, and now he is really tearful with depression and boredom.

Charley is wandering past Wickens. Even Basil's sharp voice would be a consolation for him. But though he prowls through the yards for an hour, he never hears it.

27 On the next night he sets out to look for Harry, but turns aside through the orchard. He descends into the Galors' garden, climbs the hurdle and says through the window curtain: "Ullo, Liz." His voice is cheerful because he expects to make a sensation. But Liz, being two yards away and unexpectant, does not hear him. It is Susan who answers in a loud indignant voice: "Who's that? Is that you, Charles Brown?"

"No, it's Lord Gort, V.C."

"What *do* you want now?"

"A Rolls-Royce and a million pounds with dimons in."

"Oh, dear, Bessie—here's one of those boys wants to see you again. But do be quick."

"Who is it?"

"Charley—the baldy one."

In ten seconds Liz is at the window. She draws back the curtain. But she doesn't know what to say or do, and neither does Charley.

There is a long pause. In the bright moonlight, the two faces are illuminated in strong light and shade. The children stare fixedly at each other with an air of surprise, embarrassment and disappointment; the common look of childish friends meeting after a long time. They have expected they don't know what of pleasure, of revolution in their case; and now they haven't found even words.

Susan's voice says from behind: "Hurry up, do. There's father now."

Heavy boots can be heard thumping and scraping in the road down below in the valley.

"I better go," Charley says.

"No, he won't come yet, Charley."

There is another pause. Charley ponders and looks past Lizzie into the attic room. It is a narrow attic, just long enough for the bed, which fills up a whole side of it from front wall to back. The bed is fine old mahogany, of the French pattern, about four feet six wide, from some local sale. A guttering candle is stuck by its grease to the top bar. The only other furniture in the room is a chair without a back and a packing-case standing on its side. The floor is bare elm boards, immensely wide, with uneven joints.

Susan is sitting up in bed with a lesson-book, revising her home-work by the candle-light. Her hair is falling across her eyes, and now and then she looks up at Charley with a frown. Then she scratches her chest vigorously through the front of her woollen vest. She is obviously annoyed both with Charley and chest for interrupting her work, and is anxious to punish the chest with her nails.

Lizzie has jumped out of bed in her woollen combinations. Her hair, being just too short for a pigtail, is tied on the top of her head with a piece of tape. This gives her the appearance, in the dim light, of wearing a kind of Chinese hat. She, too, is obviously at a loss for something to say. Charley, after long reflection, says at last: "You all right, Liz?"

"I'm all right—how are you?"

"All right."

"They didn't catch you yet?"

"No, they aven't copped me yet. Did you cop it, Liz?"

"Yes, father gave me a hiding."

"But you didn't mind it, did you?"

"Noa, I'm all right now. Is Bill going to tell on us?"

"I dno. I don't care wot Bill does."

"He keeps on shouting after me."

"Don't you mind im, see. You don't mind im, do yer?"

"No, I don't care for Bill—if he wouldn't keep on pinching me."

"Pinching's nothing to a tough un like you, is it?"

"No, it isn't nothing. Bill's silly."

"Ere don't you let im worry you, see. You tell im you're in my gang, you ony got to say the word and all the gang will get after im, see."

"I did, but he only laughed. He says you dursn't do nothing."

There is another pause.

"He's been after Ginger too," Liz says, "down that old hole of his."

"Wot was Ginger doing in the ole?"

"Nothing. He never does nothing. I asked him to stop Bill pinching me, and he said he wasn't big enough."

"I aint afraid a Bill," Charley says, but in a flat voice.

There is another long silence. Charley and Liz stare at each other.

Susan suddenly breaks off her tables to say: "Oh, dear, I knew you'd make her cry—I really do wish you boys 'd leave Bessie alone."

"She ain't crying. Wy should she?"

"Noa, I ant."

"And I aint coming after er—she's in my gang, that's all."

"She cried enough last week."

"I never did."

"Oh, well—" Susan scratches still more vigorously, and returns to her book.

At the window Charley and Lizzie are dumb. Charlie says at last: "I better go now."

Liz is silent.

"About time, aint it?" Charley wants support from her. He feels obscurely troubled about Lizzie, and at the same time he feels that his visit has been a failure.

Galor's heavy step turns in at the door; there is a sound of boot-scraping, then suddenly the whole cottage shakes to his tread in the kitchen.

Liz says: "Quick, Charl, he med come up!"

She vanishes behind the curtain. Charley, no less startled, falls down the hurdle, which clatters loudly on the wall.

But Galor turns into his own bedroom below. It is Mrs.

138

Galor's voice which screams up the stairs: "Put out that candle, Susan—how offen I got to tell you? You want the hair-brush, missy, that's what you do."

The candle goes out. Charley, forgetting the hurdle, is already falling over the wire; with a loud curse he rushes blindly forward, stumbling uphill, towards home.

But as he approaches home his legs falter aside. He recoils from home, from bed, from accepting the day's end. He feels like a man whose life has been a failure, longing for escape and yet reluctant to die.

He wanders for another hour in the great Whiteboys field, tired, hungry, but tormented still by this feeling which he can't interpret, of blind energy and frustration. Something within him is resolved upon not going to bed until it has achieved some task. But there is nothing for it to do, Charley stops and looks about him in the large field. The moonlight falls upon the grass like a frost. The waves of its old lands seem like an ocean swell frozen in some new glacial epoch. The sky is like a gun-barrel, dark-blue steel at the zenith, pale grey at the down curves. The moon is a ball of ice hanging by a miracle in the emptiness, freezing the very sunrays to white ice-light as they glance off its sides.

Charley looks about him and gives a sigh. "Poor ole cave."

His tone is full of tender sympathy for the lost rock garden. He is feeling for a friend, put upon and neglected, but still a friend.

28 Charley's disinclination to go home extends to a dislike of going anywhere. He is late out of bed every morning and late at school. He wanders home to midday dinner by the Hall yard, half a mile out of his course, or Burls House wood, which is the opposite direction. The last journey of the evening is always especially prolonged, because of the nearness of bed and the end of another futile day.

On a dark evening, without either object or any conscious impulse, he wanders about Burls House grounds for an hour, then climbs on the garage roof, ascends a fire escape, and succeeds, by help of a spout, which affords a hand hold, in leaning out as far as Ginger's window on the third story. But he is not much disappointed when Ginger proves to be not yet come to bed. He is not looking for Ginger. He does not know who or what he wants.

On the next night after this sudden feat of house climbing he wanders into the quarry. He explores all his old haunts like a ruined statesman visiting the scenes of his distinction. He spends ten minutes hunting in the cracks of the stump for any trace of the red ink spilt upon it when he drew his picture. He breaks through the thicket of briars and hawthorn to visit Ginger's hole.

For a long time he can't find it. Brushwood has been piled on its roof and against its open sides. He detects it at last in the twilight, only by footmarks in the ground.

He peers then under the brushwood, and going down on his knees, puts his head into the darkness. He remains for some reason quite still and holds his breath. Then he says, "Ullo, Ginger!"

At once Harry's voice shrieks: "It's Charley—we thought you was Bill."

Ginger, saying nothing, strikes a match and lights a candle stuck on the rock at the back of the recess. Charley sees Harry crouching on the ground, Ginger sitting on the rock shelf.

The ground is covered with straw, trampled and muddy; the roof has been propped up on a broken window frame; the new covering of brushwood provides a side wall and fills the gaps in the roof.

"Cor," Charley says. "It's a real cave."

"It drips a bit," Ginger says.

"We thought you was Bill," Harry says, gazing at him still with hare's eyes, astonished and terrified.

"Cor, it's a real gang cave like Diamond Eye ad in Ammurca."

The others say nothing. Harry is still suffering from shock;

Ginger has a reserved and thoughtful expression. He gets down from the rock shelf as if vacating the captain's seat. As naturally, Charley sits down in it. "Coo," he says, looking round. "We ony want a lamp and carpets and a chair—and it'll be a real gang cave."

"I believe Bill is on to us ere," Harry says. "E saw Ginj coming out."

"Course e isn't," Charley cries, unwilling to admit any disadvantage in so fine a cave.

"Ow d'you know, Charley?"

"Cos if e was on to it e'd be after us ere, and e aint been after us."

"E knows. E's just waiting," Harry says.

"Bill don't wait for nothing—why should e?" Charley answers. "Garn, we're safe ere as if we was in Bucknam Palace—and comfortable too. All we want is the furniture, a carpet and a chair—yers, and pictures. Dimond Eye ad real old masters in is cave—worth millions o dollars."

Harry stares at him with an expression at once woeful and alarmed. His lips are still miserable but his eyes and forehead are amazed. "Pictures," he mutters and looks round wondering at the brushwood, the oozing rotten boards, the straw underfoot, smelling already like the rubbish of a brewery.

"Wy not?" Charley cries. "It's a cave, aint it? Wy, we could live ere."

Charley cuts school the next day in order to rebuild and patch the shed roof with old planks torn from the sawmill. He manages even to excavate the cave a few inches deeper by breaking down the looser stones, flattens the floor, and steals an old square of carpet from the Cedars garden shed to cover it.

That evening he persuades Lizzie to slip out by the cyder house and brings her to admire. "Good as a ouse. Come in— you can stand right up." He stands under the roof, with his head bent to one shoulder and his knees crooked, to show Lizzie the convenience of the space.

"There isn't a lot of room," Lizzie says.

But Charley is outraged. "Wot d'yer want then? Come on in and see. Stand ere." He pulls Lizzie into the shelter. Lizzie, who is an inch taller than Charlie, is obliged to kneel. Seeing now what is her proper part, she agrees: "Yess, you can stand, can't you, amost."

But Charley is already depressed. Like other artists, he praises his own work only to still his own doubts and the least criticism destroys his confidence. He looks round with a disgusted air. "Nah," he says, "it aint much, not yet it aint. But you wait. You see wen you get a chair and a lamp and some pictures. We aint poshed it up yet, Liz. Ginj says they got undreds of things in Burls Ouse—lamps and spears and carpets; they got three lumber rooms full a stuff."

"You couldn take em from Burls House."

"Wy not, Liz—borrow em, of course. Don't you want to make the place nice? See ere, Liz—spose we was to come and live ere."

Liz stares at him through her rat tails. "How could we?—they'd find us first thing."

"Wot, down ere? Bet you they never would. Nobody never comes ere. And if they did we'd just say: 'Thanks, but we aint coming ome no more. This is our ome. We live ere, see.'"

"Noa, we never could. But we med have a fire, too."

"Course we'll ave a fire—you couldn't ave a real cave without a fire, could you? To sit around of an evening."

"And cook supper. We could make tea, coulddn we?"

"Yers, if you like."

29 Ginger brought a lamp from the Burls House lumber room, a bronze lamp on chains, with red-yellow glass panels, intended to be hung in some corridor. Its bowl was lost or broken, and when Charley hung it from the roof it reached so close to the ground that no one could even creep beneath it. But for an evening, with the candle stuck inside it,

it gave so much pleasure that Harry forgot his terrors and Ginger himself expressed some appreciation.

"It's nice," he said, "at least the yellow is," and after long thought: "Yes, I like it. It's not bad here. It's a fairly good cave."

" It's a real cave," Charley says.

"Bill knows we come down the quarry," Ginger says doubtfully.

"Wy don't e come after us, then?"

"He's planning something. Or Basil is. Basil is always planning."

"E'd better not come round our gang cave, that's all," Charley says. Suddenly he takes out the silver cigarette-case from the bag stolen in Twyport. He hands it round with the gesture of a big-shot. "Ave a fag, chaps—they're cork tips."

Then he pushes the case into a crack in the rock. Harry and even Ginger are surprised.

"You aint going to leave it there, Charley?"

"Course I am. Aint this our cave? Well then, and wots the good if you don't ide your loot in it?"

Ginger's cave now becomes the daily rendezvous of the gang and all depression at once is lost, or rather it is merged into a new experience which transcends it. For they share their fears, and talking to each other of danger, make it a strand in their fondness.

They visit the cave not only all together at fixed hours but singly, drawn by the attraction which belongs to any place where people have been happy. Ginger turns aside in the morning to dig the ditch a little deeper; Charley to admire the lamp and polish the cigarette-case; Lizzie to leave a bundle of dry twigs in a sheltered corner; Harry simply to sit and wonder at the whole construction.

The autumn has been dry, but now there are days of rain. The hollow is flooded, and Ginger, when he digs the ditch deeper, finds that the walls slip. Twice after a night's rain the whole hut falls in; but once Ginger, once Charley and Ginger, quickly rebuild it. Neither does Ginger tell Charley that he has once before found it collapsed, nor Charley tell the rest that he has helped to rebuild it. They treat the hut exactly as devoted admirers treat some hero, hiding his faults from each other, from the world, and even from himself.

The evenings are drawing in and this pleases them all. They go early to the hut, light a fire of twigs, boil tea in an old meat tin, and say over and over again each night: "Coo, see how dark it is—aint it nice in ere with our fire."

What this means is—the darkness has shut out all Burlswood from us, the bare quarry, the rusty scrub, the broken wire along the lane, and not only Burlswood, but our whole lives in the outside world. It hides, too, the meanness of this hut. Here we are alone in the world and it is a world full of affection and beauty. See this beautiful lamp, this carpet, this convenient fireplace, this sofa where two can sit side by side; these things are ours.

In the same way when Lizzie says, having been pestered by Bill: "Why does that Bill go on so? How can anyone be so silly," and repeats the new idea three or four times in the evening, she is not expressing anger against Bill but wonder at a certain kind of conduct which, for some reason, strikes her as discordant. She does not blame Bill for his obscene tricks, she only wonders why such things should be. But she can't express the wonder except in a tone of voice and repetition. Probably each time she says a thing the words seem to her charged with an increasing significance, to come nearer to her feeling.

But all their talk is full of repetitions, attempts to catch in a few worn words feelings as strong and deep as they are fresh. Thus they are like four dumb poets to whom the smallest experience has the effect of a revelation but who are compelled to express these powerful original feelings in mere sighs or cries. Moreover, they have not the faintest idea that there is anything remarkable in the force of their wonder, their affection, their hope, their criticism of the world, and so they try to express them, not for the sake of each other but only for themselves. Their talk is half ejaculation.

"It's lovely to-night."

"That was Phyllis Awes in the lane and Arthur Veale. Just before the rain stopped."

"They going to be married next week."

"But it was raining."

"Wy does she go at im, she don't go on at anyone else."

"E's gone on er, see."

"She's pratty, Phyllis. She was born pratty, too, and she's never had nothing wrong. Never had a toothache even."

"I wish she wouldn't go on at Arthur, it makes him look so silly."

"Wy does she, Lizzie?"

"I don know, Harry, and she screams turble at Twyport fair. Every day she goes on they whirlies and screams so—till all the people is looking at her. I've heard Mrs. Hawes tell her a hundred times."

At least half the sudden remarks express like this a feeling that dignity should belong to the life of the people to whom dignity is so important and a wonder at the strange lack of it even in the most fortunate existence.

30 Charley's disappearance every evening amused Mrs. Brown. One wet night when she caught him getting his tea from the scullery shelf she laughed and said: "Wot a boy. Going on the tiles in this weather."

Charley did not answer. He was offended by the word tiles and his mother's grin.

"Oo's your lady friend?"

"Aint got none." Charley is sulky because he feels suddenly guilty. He realises that Liz, as well as the cave, is an attraction. For the first time he combines in one, two kinds of feelings about women: he likes Liz and he also likes to be close to her.

But according to his own rule he ought to despise this weakness in himself and he does not do so. He is thrown into confusion of mind, and he resents any jibe which increases his discomfort as an unfair blow.

Mrs. Brown smiles at his embarrassed sulky face and says : "Go on, think I don't know—the funny one down the ill with the big mouth. Wots er name, Bessie, aint it?"

Charley is silent. He perceives that he must not show his anger if he wishes to keep his dignity.

"All right, mister man," Mrs. Brown says. "No offence meant and none taken. Even if she is a bit funny. Any gurl is better than none, aint she? You're getting a big boy now, aint you?" Mrs. Brown at this remark goes into fits of laughter. Charley scowls and says: "Gurls is a lot a good, I don think."

This is the only defence Charley knows, the traditional pretence that girls are nothing to real he-boys. But it is not what he feels, and it makes the situation still more disgusting to him. He therefore grows sulkier and ruder. He humps his shoulders, pokes out his neck and assumes an ugly position.

Mrs. Brown suddenly loses her temper. "Ere, wots wrong with ya? Can't ya answer a civil question? Got a pain or something?"

"Well, wot you say I got a gurl for?"

"Good for you if you ad—she might teach you some manners."

Charley, gloomy and embarrassed, puts on his cap and goes out. He can't bear the presence of Mrs. Brown another moment. She calls after him: "Ere, I needn't be nice to ya for nothing you know—I aint going to throw away my trouble— not bloody likely. Life's too short."

Charley darts away in flight. He is now so eager to reach the quarry, to escape from the grown-up world, that he can't wait to take his raincoat from the hook behind the door.

Beside the gate of the Green Man paddock, his usual route to quarry field beyond, he sees Harry and Ginger crouching under the hedge. He shouts to them with delight: "Ullo, Ginj!—ullo, Arree!"

They rise, and he remembers the ceremonial duty of a leader,

146

the dignities necessary to their society. "Ere, wots the pass-word?"

But Harry is too troubled to care about ritual. He says in a shaking voice: "Bill's there now."

"Were?"

"Down in the quarry—with Liz. He catched er coming along."

"Garn."

"Honest, you come and see."

"It's Bill," Ginger says, "I saw him quite close."

"E's bin after Liz for a ole week," Harry says.

"I know—but e ony pinches er—Bill's always pinching gurls—e can't elp it. Liz don mind Bill—she's used to im."

"It aint Liz—it's the ole."

"I aint afraid of Bill," Charley says. "If e comes round the cave I'll eave stones at im."

They are standing in the lane below the quarry mouth. A tall uncut hedge leans over them from the high bank. Suddenly the spreading beam of a torch falls on the wet lower stems of the hedge, throwing their shadows on the three boys. They drop down and almost at once the gate rattles as somebody begins to climb it.

Bill's voice calls: "I see ya, Lizzie. Can't you wait a minute?"

"No, I got to get home."

"You weren't going ome just now. Wait a minute, Lizzie."

"You leggo of me, Bill."

"Wy, Lizzie, I aint going to urt you. It's only a bit o fun. Ere you are, look ere—know wot that is?"

"Of course," with warm contempt.

"Wot, you bad girl. I say, Liz, like to ave a bit o fun? Ere, I'll show you."

Lizzie gives a sudden exclamation and the next moment Bill cries out: "Ow! you're urting—leggo." Lizzie tumbles over the gate and flies down the lane past the boys. Bill, swearing loudly, flashes his torch up and down the lane, but finally goes off on the inside of the hedge, towards the road.

The three boys get up and stand for a moment in silence, peering at each other in the fluttering light of the moon. Harry says at last: "I tole ya." And then breathlessly: "Wot Bill do to er?"

"They have you up for that," Ginger says. "Bill's a fool."

"Wot e do?" Harry asks again.

"Lizzie tole im off proper, didn't she?" Charley says.

"I ates that Bill," Harry says. "E's a dirty beast."

"Bill's all right," Ginger says, "It's Basil who's the bastard."

"E aint all right, e's a dirty beast."

"Twang, twang, twanky."

"Come on," Charley says. "Wot are we waiting for?"

He leads the way to the cave. When all three have crept into it, and Ginger is trying to strike a match on a wet box, Lizzie's voice is heard from outside: "Hullo, Charley! Hullo, Harry! Hullo, Ginger!"

"Ullo, Liz!"

"I was hoping you'd come."

"Yers, of course we come. You all right, Liz?"

"I'm all right."

Charley, not knowing why, makes no reference to Bill. Harry bursts out: "I say, Liz, wot did Bill do?"

"Shut up, Arry," Charley says. "E didn't do nothing, did e, Liz?"

"But she ollered—I eard er. You ollered right out, didn't you, Liz?"

"Shatap, Arry, she never did. Come on Ginj. Were's the matches?"

"Wot's the good if Bill's been ere? We better ook it."

"Was Bill ere, Liz?"

"Yess, he followed me."

"E wasn't inside, was e?"

"I dno—I ony just come."

"That's done it," Harry says. "Aint no good us coming ere no more."

"Course we'll come ere," Charley says angrily.

"Wot, and let Bill cop us? E'll bring the ole lot."

"I aint afraid of Bill," Charley says, but in an uncertain voice.

"He's gone, anyhow," Ginger says.

Suddenly the torch flashes again across the bushes. Charley, Harry and Liz, as if by one impulse, crouch down in the hollow floor. Bill calls: "You there, Lizzie?"

The four children crouch in the dark, scarcely breathing. The torch flashes once through some crack in the side wall; Bill's boots clatter on the stones.

Then for a long time they hear nothing.

The hut smells of foul, rotten straw, like the fermenting rubbish of a brewery. The rain pours through the roof and forms pools of mud underfoot. One corner of the roof has slipped from its support of sods and rests on the ground. But no one can bear even the thought that it is their last evening there; that they have no longer a private place.

"It's bin nice here," Liz says in her reflective voice.

"It's not such a bad cave," Ginger says modestly.

"Fines cave I ever saw."

"With the lamp and everything—turble nice."

"Not so nice as Burls Ouse."

"I'd rather be here," Ginger says. "Besides, they're going to turn me out of Burls House."

"Go on."

"Going to shut it for the winter. They've got about four other houses."

"This is good enough for me. Wot you say, Arry?"

"I'll live ere if anyone else will. Wot about you, Liz?"

"We couldn't really, could we?"

"How could we get food? We've got no money."

"We could pinch it," Charley says without conviction. He is so depressed that he wants to shout or cry.

"Oh, it's cold," Harry says, pressing in more closely among the others.

All, as if the words suggest the idea, squeeze inwards. They wriggle and clasp each other more closely.

"Last night of the piece," Ginger says.

"Tell us a story for the last night, Charl."

"About Diamond Eye's cave and the fountings."

"You were going to tell us how he worked the fountains."

"No, tell us about the palace made of glass."

Charley is silent. He is not in the mood for stories. Suddenly he exclaims: "Wy should we go ome? I aint."

"Were you go, Charl? Aint nowere."

"Aint nowere. There's the ole world. You ony got to op a lorry."

"You really going, Charley?"

"I aint going ome, I know that."

"Nor me neither," Liz says. "If Charley don't, I don't. I hates this place. I'm tired of it."

"Wot, you going to run off, Liz?"

"Yes, if Charley runs off, I'll run off."

"Is it cos of Bill?" Harry asks.

"Noa, of course not," with deep scorn, "Bill's only a booy."

"He's a nuisance if he knows about my cave."

"No, we can't stop ere."

"You come along a me, Ginger, and we'll get another cave. There's undreds of em. The obos uses em every night."

"Go on the tramp," Ginger says.

"Yers, we'll just go off. You coming, Ginj?"

"Yes, I'll come," Ginger says to everyone's surprise. "But I must go and get my uke first."

"You really going, Charley?"

"How much money have we got?" Ginger says. Ginger is already preparing, in the most matter-of-fact way, for the road, and again all are secretly surprised.

"I aint got none," Charley says. "But wots the odds? We'll easy get some money."

"Can't do nothing without money."

"I could pinch it."

"Don't you go stealing no more bags, Charl. They'm sure to catch you next time."

"But you needn't do nothing. I'll pinch for all of ya."

"They'll cotch you, Charl—and then what should we do?"

There is another long silence. Another stone falls with a splash and the water begins to trickle into the hollow beneath their bodies. Harry says suddenly: "Oo—it's cold—the water's coming in."

"It'll get warm, Arry."

"Move Arry up a bit."

"Lie on me, Harry."

"I'm all right, Liz. You're wetter than I am."

"I got two pounds," Ginger says. "Two pounds three and fourpence."

"Go on, Ginj, were you get it?"

"Saved it."

"Wot for?"

"You never know when you'll want money. But we could use it now, couldn't we?"

"Two pounds—we could take the bus to Plymouth or Southampton."

"Is it cheap to live at Plymouth?"

"No, it's were the ships go from—we'll go on a ship, see."

"Where to, Charl?"

"Anywhere. Africa, Ammurca. Ammurca's the best. We could get jobs in Ammurca."

"Talk sense. It costs twelve pounds third class."

"Cor, we wouldn't pay—we'd just go on board and ide. Thass wot you do—stowaway."

"They'd catch us."

"They couldn't throw you in the sea."

"But they'd send you back again, if you wur children."

"Or all over the place," Ginger says. "Even if we'd got some money, they'd see that we were children and send us back."

"They allays sends children back," Lizzie says.

There is another silence. Water can be heard dripping steadily upon some pool within the hut. Suddenly another sod of earth gives way and the window-frame slips sideways. The roof tilts and swings upon two corners, letting in two pale green triangles of watery moonlight. Charley says suddenly: "Well, we aint going ome anyow."

"I ant," Lizzie says. "Never no more."

"Wot about you, Ginger? You all right?"

"I'm coming along with you—I can get the money any time."

At this speech everyone for some reason becomes hopeful again. Ginger, though he never leads any enterprise and follows every suggestion, seems to have the power of inspiring enterprise in others; of giving to their wilder aspirations the appearance of possibility.

"Yes, we will go, won't we?"

"I'm ready when you are. Where shall we go, Charley, London?"

"Yers, good ole London. I know the very place. We could get a room for ten bob a week and no one'd say a word to us, and Lizzie can cook."

"Has it got water laid on?" Liz asks.

"There's a tap on the landing."

"Has it got a stove?"

"Gas. You ire a stove, see."

"Furnished?" Ginger asks.

"Sort of—arf a bed and arf a chair. But we'd ire—see, you can ire anything and pay after."

"Let's go, Charley—let's go now."

"We can't go till the bus goes."

"But that iddn till morning. We can't stay here all night."

"Wy not—aint it all right? Ere, aint ya comfortable? I'm all right. Ere, aint ya warm enough?"

The roof swings in the wind, slips and falls across Harry's back, sending a flood of water on the four children. Harry cries out: "We'd better get out of this."

Impatient voices reproach him.

"Wots wrong, Arry?"

"Only a little drop."

"I don't feel nothing."

"There you are, Arry. If you want to go away. We're satisfied."

"I think it's all right," Ginger says. "I built it with stones all round so that it couldn't fall in. I couldn't stop all the holes, but it's quite strong."

"It's a lovely house, Gingurr."

"Ere, we're not going ome again, are we?"

"Noa, but we mustn't be catched here. They med be coming now—we ought to be going."

"Sall right, Liz, we'll go first thing—soons the busses start."

"I'd rather go now."

"You can't walk."

"I can then. I could walk to anywhere."

"You couldn't—they'd see you on the road."

"Tramps walk all over England."

"Not children," Ginger says. "If you tried to be a tramp, they'd take you up at the first town."

"And the pleece'ud send you ome."

"I wish we wern't children," Lizzie says.

"That's the trouble. You don't get a chance till you're grown up."

There is another silence. Harry's teeth suddenly chatter loudly and he says : "Are you warm now, Liz?"

"I'm warm."

"It's not the roof," Ginger says. "It's the rain—it's coming at the wrong angle. It blows under."

"That's all right, Ginj. We aint worrying."

"I won't go back," Lizzie says. "That's certain sure."

A gust of wind swings the roof and suddenly the walls of mud and stone fall inwards with the roof on top of them. Gallons of water which have filled the ditch and undermined the walls pour into the cavity. Harry gives a scream of terror. "I'm drownded."

All the children are struggling desperately in a pond of soft mud. Charley, finding his way out by some instinct, is the

153

first to crawl from beneath the fallen roof into the green twilight of falling rain. He catches the nearest roof plank and tears it away. Ginger, smooth as an otter with wet mud, creeps out. He and Charley together rescue Liz and last of all, Harry, who is almost suffocated, so that all beat him on the back for several minutes, while he retches and coughs.

At last when he has pulled himself away from them they all stand looking at the ruins.

"It's really only slipped down," Ginger says. "We could put it up again in a minute."

This gives them their cue. Charley says: "Thass all right. There wasn't nothing wrong with the ouse."

"It's a lovely house, Gingurr, but this turble rain would work in anywhere."

They stand for another moment, as if waiting for another cue to give them direction. Then Harry says: "Charley, if you don don, I'll go ome now—I'm so cold."

"You'd all better go home quick as you can," Lizzie says, "or you'll get numony. This wind is a regular numony one."

"Wot about you, Liz?"

"I'll have to go home, too, won't I? Wouldn't be no good to stay here by myself and get cotched in the morning."

"All right, Liz, but don't you let em wop you."

"I can't help what they do."

"Shall we come ome with you?"

"You can't help what they do neither—none of us can't."

3 1   Mr. Lommax, returning to Burlswood for his usual week-end, was reminded by Lina Allchin that he had promised to give a drawing lesson to her pupils.

"Ah did not promise to give a drawing lesson, Miss Leena, for that would be impossible. No one can teach drawing—or anything else. But if you would like me to see what they can do for themselves, ah would be very glad to give them the materials. Send them up to-morrow afternoon at four o'clock."

Lina therefore appointed twelve children, including Charley, to go to Burls House on the next afternoon. Charley was much excited. He had never before had a lesson from a real artist.

The lesson was fixed for half-past two. The party of children arrived punctually, but no Mr. Lommax could be found and no one at the house had heard of his undertaking a lesson. Messengers were sent to find the artist. Mr. Wandle hurried to the village shop to buy its whole stock of pencils, colours and paper; the children stood together tightly grouped in a corner of the hall, staring about them.

Burls House is a tall Victorian villa with no distinction except large windows and rooms, which serve Wandle to show his collection of fine furniture of all periods, old china and modern pictures. The effect of this mixture offends pedantic tastes, but is both splendid and lively. The children could not understand the interest of an exhibition chosen by no standard but that of a single plastic taste, but they could appreciate the magnificence. They looked about them with expressions of awe, which in simple and frank minds answers every relevation of power, whether in religion or beauty. Charley, who had never before seen or imagined such splendour, who had never been into a picture gallery in his life, was so visibly taken aback, that Mrs. Wandle, deputed to keep the children out of mischief till Lommax was found, said to him kindly: "Do you like pictures?"

Charley is not seeing the pictures. He is simply feeling his whole surroundings as shapes of bright colour and receding forms. He does not even notice Mrs. Wandle as a separate object and he has no idea of her. Above all he does not know whether he is liking these new feelings. He has not had them long enough. He gazes at a tree like a green bomb explosion in a sky on fire with little thin flames and he feels a shock as if something has actually exploded, silently but violently, somewhere inside him. He is shocked and amused, but he does not know whether to laugh or look solemn.

"You like my tree?" Mrs. Wandle says. Charley grins uncertainly and says: "Yes, 'm."

Mrs. Wandle seeks a more responsive child. Charley returns happily to his obscurity, where he remains, gazing now at a picture, now through a door into another great room crowded with wonders, now along the high curtains to the ceiling, until a messenger comes back from Lommax.

Lommax has been discovered in a field painting the portrait of a disc-harrow. He sends back orders that the children are to draw what they like and that he will then come and tell them what he thinks of the work.

The result is, of course, that the children, sat down round a parlour table, do not know what to draw, and ask Lina Allchin what she would like. She suggests various subjects, a ship at sea, a naval battle, a lighthouse, a farm with cows, a train. Charley, like the rest, assumes that these subjects are given him because they will please Mr. Lommax. Lina, as a grown-up, will know what the grown-up Lommax would prefer. He takes not the least interest in any of them, but he decides loyally to do the neatest possible lighthouse in the bluest possible sea, as blue as chalk pencil can make it.

But in fact, he takes no interest, at that moment, in drawing. He is still full of confused excitement, wonder and shyness. Burls House has caused an effervescence in his imagination so lively that he cannot give form or name to one impression before it is succeeded by another, equally disturbing and elusive.

Meanwhile he draws the lighthouse, with a beam of yellow chalk falling upon a small Woolworth cutter lost in a sea of blue shavings.

When Mr. Lommax, red and blue from the wind, and explosive with energy, marches in from the fields, he gives Charley's work one glance and picks out young Laurie's as the best. Laurence is a small, pale, black-haired child, aged seven, with a large mole on one cheek. He has been sitting in happy isolation, doing his work with a smile of self-satisfaction. Laurence is extremely shy and much put upon. He seems bewildered by Lommax's compliment. His smile disappears instantly. He turns painfully red and stares at the artist with a perplexed frown as if suspecting him of some kind of joke at his expense.

"This is the only drawing that has any interest for me," Lommax booms. "I take it that this young man has hitherto escaped all so-called instruction in arrt—he is extremely fortunate and I do not propose to ruin his talent now. I will, however, be very pleased to make an offer for the worrk to add to my collection. Mr. Laurence, will you accept a shilling, cash down——" He holds out a shilling to Laurence, who is too startled to take it until half a dozen childish voices shriek at him, furious with impatience of his stupidity. He then hastily puts out his cupped fingers, still black with pencil and chalk. Tears show in his lashes and at once excite derision. Irene points her neat tapered forefinger at him and says with righteous scorn: "He's crying—oh, what a cry-baby."

The children crowd round to stare at Laurence's drawing. Their faces show curiosity, disgust, suspicion and disbelief. Artists rarely appreciate another's success. Charley is disgusted because he thinks Laurence's drawing of a very crooked train among a forest of cabbages, entirely bad, and his own quite good. His boat is extremely neat, and the curves of the lighthouse, difficult to match, are almost as good as if he had drawn them with a compass.

"Please, sir," a little girl asks in a grieved and bewildered tone, "why is Laurie's drawing good?"

"It is good because it is interesting to me," Mr. Lommax booms. "It excites my emotions and attracts my intellectual curriosity."

The anxious Lina says mildly from behind: "Mr. Lommax means that he likes Laurie's train and the way he has got his effect."

"Aye," Mr. Lommax says, "put it like that if ye like." His

tone suggests both that Lina has no idea of what he means and that it does not matter in the least.

"But it's all crooked," a boy objects.

Here Mr. Wandle comes in and is shown the drawing. He gives it his closest attention, the more impressive because of his air of lively surprise. Mr. Wandle is a very tall man with a deep stoop. He has a pale face, a long sharp chin and a very large white broad hooked nose, of which the tip is depressed almost to his upper lip. It is the nose of a sheep. He wears very large black-rimmed goggles, and his black eyebrows are arched high on his wrinkled forehead as if in perpetual surprise. But the surprise is not wholly painful; it is also eager. Mr. Wandle is like a man who is always being astonished both by good and evil, but is still sensitive to shock.

"But this is really amazingly good!" he says in great surprise. "It really has direct observation." His voice is a high quack, resembling that of Donald Duck.

"Naw, naw, I wouldn't say that—I would say, inspiration. Children do not observe—they feel."

"Ah, you think this is a romantic and poetical train—a symbolical representation?"

"Naw, ah think," says Mr. Lommax, whose rule is never to accept a suggestion, "ah think it is the arrtist's idea of a train —and that his idea was a good one."

The children, bored with this discussion, are now wandering about the room. Two are boxing; Irene is trying to pinch Laurence through his thick knickers, while he, at last convinced of his triumph, is sitting on his chair with a smile of happiness mingled equally with enormous surprise and a certain diffidence, which seems to pervade not only his flushed cheeks and bright eyes, still wet with tears, but his whole frame. Even the hollowness of his back and the inclination of his thin neck are joyful and questioning.

Irene, defeated by the knickers, plunges her hand into the waistband. Her small mouth is pursed into a button of determined cruelty. Only Charley and Ginger, the two oldest present, are still listening to the men. They turn their backs indeed, and pretend indifference, but they gather every word. Ginger gazes at the wall with a thoughtful mild expression; Charley, with his head bent forward, frowns and scratches himself fiercely inside the thigh. He has forgotten his manners and everything else in curiosity; he frowns in the effort of catching out of this grown-up expert talk something which he will be able to use: a clue to artistic glory, triumph and fame. He knows that it means something, and he feels every moment that he understands it, but when he tries to grasp at his understanding, it escapes him. He peeps sideways at the child's drawing on the table and frowns angrily at it. Ginger's eyes with an even more stealthy expression turn now and then the same way.

"Yes-yes-yes," Wandle says. "The *naïveté* which makes a train skip like a young lamb is an excellent equivalent for the genius which overcomes conventional boundaries of fact."

"Naw, naw, Jimmy, equivalent nothing—it's the simplicity of mind which takes the shorrtest cut to expressionism. You can see it there——" nodding at the picture on the wall—"in my 'Brittany Harrvest.' "

"One of the best things you ever did, Johnny."

"Ah wouldn't say that—but it is certainly characteristic of my firrst period."

The two boys are looking at the picture, Ginger sidelong, Charley full-face, with open curiosity. For the first time he is looking at a picture by Mr. Lommax, certified by Miss Allchin and Mr. Wandle to be a real artist, a famous artist. He stares at it as a prospector stares at the formation from which, he is told, millions have been dug.

"When, if you'll excuse me, Johnny," Mr. Wandle says, "your inspiration was fresh and exceedingly original."

"There is naw such thing as inspiration, Jimmy," Mr. Lommax never minds contradicting himself, "and orriginality is merely a fashion among the young leddies in the arrt schools —naw, naw, naw, but look at the corrn—it's sunk a wee bit, but it's rrich still—it's the corrn that increreeased a hundred-fold —d'ye see that—it's trremendous, that corrn—you can hear it grrowing—you can smell it, warrm and fusty, like a fox—you can even see it trrembling as the scythes come nearr—you can see the heaviness of it, like a gravid wumman when her hour has come—naw, naw, that's metaphysical—ah'm talking non-sense—it's not a wumman, it's corrn—the corrniest corrn ah ever pented—and how did ah do it, Jimmy?—come here, and look——" drawing Wandle to the canvas and making him stoop. "Now look up this way—d'ye see now—those strokes of red—vermilion, nothing else but pure vermilion—drrawn through the chromes and the ochres——"

Charley, under Wandle's elbow, is almost rubbing his nose on the picture "drrawn thrrough—with a wet brush on the wet pent—now that's the sorrt of thing ah couldn't do now— ah wouldn't do now—it's a trrick—it's an expeedient—it's a shameful deed. But man, how it succeeded—how it came off —man, it was a strroke of genius and how did ah do it? God knows." Lommax shakes his head in a regretful sadness. "How did ah devise such a technical shorrt cut—such a perfect means of expression—for my idea—when to tell ye the truth, Jimmy, ah was nothing but a conceited young fool wasting very impermanent colours upon a forrtunately impermanent misconception of everything in the worrld including the arrt, so-called, of penting, and the privileges of the artist. When I had neither the modesty to learn by my own mistakes or the instruction of others. And yet, I brrought off that corrn— the finest corrn in penting. I do not forget that Van Gogh has trried his hand at corrn eether."

Charley's eyebrows are almost in his hair as he gazes not at the picture but at the speaker. Lommax, quite unconsciously, gives the boy a tap on the shoulder and says: "Ah don't believe in genius, Jimmy, but if the worrd has a meaning, it means the intuition which perceived that that expedient of the brush would give precisely that quality of rrichness which it needed; and see here——" Suddenly he lifts the picture off the wall, turns it upside down and props it on a chair. "The composition and colour composition—look at this bit of blue—like a dumb-bell."

He waves his thick red dirty finger, the colour of old brick, at a patch of blue and then at a cloud—"Ye see, there's relation —a pattern."

At this word, Charley, staring at the picture, for one moment sees the corn, the sky, the clouds, the trees, the mowers disappear, they are not present even upside down; in their place are strange new shapes and colours which seem suddenly more intense, and more exciting, so that their vividness makes him want to exclaim. Then Lommax comes between him and the canvas, stooping down to rub his finger on it and say: "Cracking already—pented in a hurry by an ignorant young fool."

Charley, trying to butt his head between the men, touches Wandle's hip, who is also prevented from seeing the picture.

He looks down at the boy, smiles and quacks in the same phrase as his wife: "You like pictures?"

"Yes, sir. What is it, sir?"

"It's a cornfield, upside down at present."

"Yes, I know, sir, but what——" Charley, unable to explain that he wants to understand Mr. Lommax, wags his head towards him.

"You'd like it explained, is that it? Johnny, here is a pupil for you."

Lommax stands up and looks at his finger. "It's powdering too—in fifty years it will be in rruins—and the National Gallery."

"Here's a pupil for you, Johnny. He'd like to know how you do it."

Lommax does not even glance at Charley. He is not interested in children, but only in his painting. He says: "Ah never take pupils, Jimmy; Ah haven't sunk to that level. Ah'm a fraud but not an abortioner."

"But——" Wandle is annoyed. "I thought you wanted a grant for art education, Johnny, in the French style."

"There is no such thing as education, Jimmy. It is a racket. Money for penters, yes, but for God's sake, don't educate them—don't educate anybody. Ah had the best education in the worrld myself—and what do I know—nothing."

"You know how to paint."

"Naw, Jimmy, ah don't like to contradict you, but if there's one thing ah'll never be able to do, it's pent."

He has stood aside from the picture and Charley glances at it again. But it is only a row of men, upside down, cutting an upside-down field. Charley is full of derision. He feels a violent urge to laugh. Ginger suddenly moves his lips at him as if to utter his twanky-twank; Charley, startled, jumps, and then, when the twank does not come, explodes through his nose. Wandle and Lommax both turn in surprise. The boys dart away and as Charley rushes after Ginger up the corridor, he says: "Ah doant bulleeve in genius, Jimmy, but if the worrd as a meaning, it means bullock shit." He wants to abuse the grown-ups in the rudest possible words, to make fun of them and all their ideas. What else can he do with them since he can't get hold of their meaning?

32　They had run upstairs into Ginger's room, on the third storey. From this, after Charley was tired of acting Lommax in various undignified attitudes, they ascended to explore the attics, part of the roof, two of the maid's rooms, including their chests of drawers, the tank room and a lumber room. Ginger showed his domain to the visitor.

Charley was delighted with the lumber room, and examined every cranny of it; tried on an old helmet, draped himself in a velvet curtain and threatened to chop Ginger's head off with a cavalry sabre. In passing, he drew pictures in the dust on all window-panes, table-leaves, bookcases, and, finding an old exercise book, delighted Ginger with caricatures of a naked Lommax and a naked Wandle arguing about a picture.

Lina Allchin was now hunting him through the house. A maid came to call his name and Ginger's in the upper corridor.

"You'd better go, hadn't you?" Ginger said. Ginger was now deep in an old magazine, just discovered in a corner. He spoke without raising his eyes from the text.

Charley, with his elbows spread out on a box, and his nose almost touching the exercise book, did not answer. He probably did not hear. He was improving on the Lommax-Wandle picture in a new version.

Charley was not seen again at the Cedars till the next day, and when Lina asked him where he had been on the day before, he answered innocently: "I went ome, miss."

"But Miss Small expected you back—at the English class."

"Yes, miss."

"You forgot about it, did you?"

"Yes, miss."

"All right, Charley—I know drawing rather goes to your head. But don't forget again, will you?"

"Yes, miss," Charley says, so full of the wish to be agreeable that he can't bear to use the negative even when it is appropriate.

33   The second housemaid at Burls House, packing for Ginger who was to be sent to a new billet at Wickens', found Charley's caricatures of Lommax and Wandle and took them to her mistress. She complained, too, that the boys had been in the lumber room and drawn more pictures there, of the same kind, in the dust.

Mrs. Wandle was surprised and very much interested. She liked Ginger, but she had found him extremely reserved. He had spent most of his time at Burls either out in the fields or sitting in his bedroom practising softly on a mouth-organ, an accordion, a jew's harp or a ukelele.

She took the drawings to her husband who, since Lommax was in the next room, was careful not to give any definite opinion on them. "Yes, very interesting," he says. "Still waters run deep, Johnny, look at these efforts by our young friend." Lommax looks at the drawings and says with emphasis: "That's remmarkable worrk."

"Don't you think so?" Wandle quacks, encouraging him. Wandle likes people to be enthusiastic.

"Very remarkable."

"What is it exactly?" Mrs. Wandle asks.

"Adam and Eve."

"Or two Adams."

"It's certainly Adam in the spectacles."

"A curious conception of the male figure—almost neolithic or negro."

"Naw, Wandle, it's neether neolithic or negro. It's original. It has the force of an original experience——"

"Extraordinary piece of work for a child."

"It's just what ye'd expect of a child. Almost any child can knock off a masterpiece."

"By accident," Mrs. Wandle suggested.

"Naw, it's simply because children starrt with the rright idea. They starrt off rright away to make something—to express some kind of an idea——"

"Yes, yes, indeed—the creative instinct," Mr. Wandle quacks. "You can see that in everything they do."

"Naw, naw, Wandle—keep instinct out of it. They just want to express their feelings. That's why they don't copy— in fact, a healthy child takes no real interest in nature—he's only interested in his own ideas about it."

"But really, Johnny, in order to express something, you require a means, a symbol which must be made, created. Even words are symbols."

"Naw, James, you're not going to put your symbols over again with me at this late date."

An animated argument followed during the next hour and the drawings were forgotten.

Mrs. Wandle, with more personal interests, when she went

to see Ginger to make sure that he was ready for departure, took the drawings back to him and asked him when he had done them. Ginger was even more reserved than usual. He hated the change of quarters because he had enjoyed the comfort and peace of the big house. He said: "I didn't do them, Mrs. Wandle."

"Oh, who did them then?"

Ginger was silent, but after a little reflection, answered: "A friend of mine."

"Your friend draws very well."

Ginger looked at the drawings and asked: "Are they good?"

"Mr. Lommax thinks them very good and he ought to know, oughtn't he?"

"It was Charley Brown did them."

"The little boy who had his head shaved?"

"Yes, Charley Brown."

"Oh, did he do the drawings in the lumber room, too?"

"Are they good, too?"

"I've not seen them." Mrs. Wandle is amused by Ginger's caution, and smiles. Ginger looks at her with a blank cold expression which no duke, offended by bad manners, could have bettered. It was not offensive or provocative, merely untouched, far from her.

But this, too, amuses and pleases her. She enjoys character. She invites Ginger to visit the lumber room, where she looks with some surprise on the drawings. They are more anatomical than she had expected. Ginger, beside her, though still perfectly dignified, turns red. At this moment the second housemaid, fretting all the time, comes in and says: "And they've taken away things, madam."

"What things, Jinnie?"

"The lamp, for one—the old lamp from the back passage."

"Who took it?"

"The boys, ma'am—you can see—it's gone."

Mrs. Wandle is again surprised and curious. She wonders

what Ginger can want with an old hall lamp. She turns to him: "Do you know who took the lamp?"

"Yes, Mrs. Wandle."

"Was it Charley Brown?"

"No, it was me." Ginger becomes scarlet, but is otherwise perfectly collected.

"Never mind." Mrs. Wandle smiles. "You should have asked me, that's all."

"But it's no good to him surely," the housemaid cries. Housemaids are always attached to those objects, however much they have detested them in use, which they have once cleaned.

"Yes, where on earth did you put it—it's quite a big thing?"

"I'll bring it back," Ginger says.

"Not if you really want it," Mrs. Wandle cries. "It's no good to us here. Do keep it if you can make use of it."

"No, I won't want it any more," Ginger says. "I'll go and get it."

He goes off at once. Almost as soon as he is gone, Lina Allchin arrives with her car to take him to his new billet. She prefers herself to take billettees to their new hosts in order to be present at the first interview. When she hears that Ginger has gone to fetch a lamp taken from the Burls lumber-room, she is painfully surprised. She apologises for the boy.

"But he behaved beautifully," Mrs. Wandle cries.

"He's an odd boy—an only child—and I believe his mother drinks—I know he's had an unhappy home life. But I'd no idea he'd take things—what on earth can he have wanted a lamp for?"

"He's got it in the old quarry," the housemaid exclaims. "The boys have got a hut there."

Jinnie, who is repeating merely what the rest of the village has known for a fortnight, that is, from about twenty-four hours after Ginger has first chosen his secret hiding-place, explains that the boys go there every night.

"What for?" Mrs. Wandle asks.

"Smoking and all that," Jinnie answers, with prim disgust.

Lina is startled. She says to Mrs. Wandle: "I think I'd better go down—I'd no idea."

Ginger, met in the field, carrying the lamp towards Burls, is therefore compelled to return to the shed, where not only the carpet is found and recognised, but the cigarette case, pushed into its crack in the rock.

Ginger refuses all account of the case, saying only that he didn't put it there. At Mrs. Wandle's suggestion it is sent round to all the billets. No one can recognise it, and Mr. Wickens hands it to a special policeman from Longwater on his evening beat along the electric cable. At Longwater station it is at once recognised, and a plain-clothes man comes to interview Ginger and Charley. Lina Allchin sends for the boys. She is apparently unsurprised. She jokes with the policeman and says: "I suppose you're having a terrible time with all our vackies?"

In fact she is overwhelmed. She feels that somehow she is responsible at least for Charley's crimes; and that a more efficient person, even Doris Small, would have prevented them and saved the boy from a criminal career.

But like all diffident beings who, at thirty, have not yet accomplished anything in the world, she is doubtful even of her doubts. She cannot be sure whether she is not condemning herself too easily; or whether perhaps she is not making too much of the whole affair.

But doubts and self-doubts all increase her sense of responsibility towards Charley.

When the boys are brought in, Ginger pink, Charley very pale and almost blue about the nose, she suddenly runs at them and says: "Now don't be frightened and it will be all right— it will be all right as long as you don't do anything silly."

This, as she herself realises, is aimed at Charley. The moment she sees Charley she feels such a painful anxiety and pity that she can hardly control her breathing. She is surprised by the warmth of her feelings for Charley and excuses it to herself.

167

"He's so helpless—and he really is good natured. But I'm sure that if they have been doing anything wrong, it's the other was the leader. That Fant is a thoroughly bad type. But I must be fair, I mustn't show my preference."

When she tells the boys to sit down, she takes the opportunity to give Charley a pat on the head, and repeats urgently: "Now, *you* mustn't be afraid, Charley—it's perfectly all right."

The policeman begins by questioning Ginger, who answers with skill and care.

"Did you drive a car at a farm here?"

"Yes."

"Did you drive the car that was taken from here to Twyport?"

Ginger reflects and seeing no way of denying this, says: "Yes, but I didn't take it away."

"Who took it?"

"I don't know."

"What, you don't know who took the car?"

"No, I just drove it."

"Did you take the lady's bag?"

"No."

"Do you know who did?"

"No."

Charley, meanwhile, at whom Lina glances anxiously, shows the most cheerful indifference. His colour has come back. He looks from the policeman to Ginger and smiles at all Ginger's obstinate "Noes."

Lina is relieved. She feels confident that Charley is innocent and also that he will not be frightened or fail to do himself justice. In fact Charley is not reflecting at all. He has, at the first summons, been so frightened that he cannot think. Now, finding nothing terrible in this questioning, by a fair-haired young man in plain clothes, in a warm room, he is no longer frightened, but still he does not try to make up any story, or to imagine what is going to happen to him. The whole situation is novel to him, he has no experience, no knowledge of the proper ritual or rules, and so, like other children faced by some problem of life or art, he is obliged to be original. He has to improvise.

He is still smiling at Ginger when the policeman turns to him and asks: "Did he take the lady's bag?"

"No, sir, course e didn't."

"Do you know who took it?"

Charley looks at the policeman and says nothing. He raises his eyebrows slightly as if enquiring: "What is he after?"

"One of you took it, didn't he?"

"Why, there was five of us," Charley cries.

"Five. I see—what are the names?"

Charley looks startled; and then smiles broadly as if at the detective's cleverness. He says at last: "I don't know."

"We'll soon find out," the detective says. "We have a list of your crowd. Was it Henry Bean?"

"No."

"Was it Edward Smith?"

"No, it was me."

"Ah, now we're getting on. You took the lady's bag?"

"Yers, sir, and the car and the other car and everything."

"Charley," Lina exclaims, "are you thinking what you're saying?"

"Excuse me, miss, I think it's better left to me."

"Yes, but the boy doesn't realise what he's saying."

"I think he's telling the truth, aren't you, sonny?"

"Yers, of course—I wouldn't say it if I adn't done it, would I?"

"You took the cars and the bag?" The detective is pleased with himself.

"Yers, and I let out the bull, too."

"A bull, what bull?"

"Mister Wickens' bull—I let it out, see." Charley is also pleased with himself.

"Charley!" Lina exclaims.

"Yes, miss?"

"Excuse me, miss, I think you'd better leave this to me."

"Yes, but the boy doesn't realise his position—he's not thinking at all. Charley, you don't mean that you *planned* all this?"

Charley looks confused. He has a moment of doubt. He has made his improvisation, he has hit upon free confession as the most striking and interesting expedient. But he is not sure what details will please his friend Lina. The question of truth does not arise because he has not the faintest idea whether he planned the expedition or not. It was much too long ago. Finally, after looking anxiously and enquiringly at Lina, he says: "I don't know, miss."

The result is to destroy the excellent effect of his former candour and to fill him with the depression of perplexity and the sense of failure. His fine, clear-cut idea is muddled and spoilt.

"But, Charley," Lina says in her anxious, urgent voice, "you must know whether you meant it or not."

The detective intervenes. Miss Allchin must really leave the examination to him. He says to Charley: "Were you the leader then?"

Charley is now distressed and anxious. He hesitates for a long time before he answers: "Spose I was." Then suddenly he improvises again. "I promised them a treat, see—and then we adn't no money in Twyport so I ad to pinch the bag." He has not noticed this point or thought of it before, but he feels interested in it and enlarges it. "That was wy I took the bag, see—I ad to take it, cos I'd promised em a treat, and wen we got to Twyport we adn't no money and nothing to eat either. That was wy I took the bag—I ad to get the money."

"You understand that I'll have to arrest you, and the charges will be taking a car from Burlswood without permission of the owner, larceny of petrol and oil, larceny of a bag." The detective recites a list of charges and at the end arrests the two boys.

Charley is now in great distress. He appeals to Lina: "But

I told im everything, miss, they won't send me away, will they?"

Lina, now knowing the meaning of the technical phrase, sent away, is greatly touched. She answers: "We want to keep you, Charley, and we will if we can."

34 Charley and Ginger were taken to Longwater, charged and released at once on bail. Meanwhile, Lina Allchin appealed for help in all quarters. Her energy pleased everyone, who considered that it was wonderful how she had changed since the war. Even in the village it was noticed. "How Miss Lina's come out of herself with they vackies. Got something to do. Quite enjoys herself."

In fact Lina did not think of herself at all. She was only horrified by the idea that Charley Brown might be sent to an institution for young criminals, and that she herself might be partly responsible for his ruin.

"I feel it's my fault," she told Wandle and Lommax. "I ought to have known what he was up to."

Wandle reassured her, but she insisted that she had failed. "I don't feel I know anything about children—I'm really the last person for a job like this. And you can do such frightful harm by not knowing."

"You couldn't know that this young rascal was a car-thief."

"I might have got to know him better—but children are so elusive, and I don't like to impose myself on Charley—he's so delightfully independent."

"He seems to have a genius all his own."

"Is stealing really so bad in children?"

"I should think that depends on the child and his motives."

"Charley is a dear, I really mean it."

She asked for their advice and they advised her to swear that Charley had all the virtues. They, too, would swear, if she liked.

"Mr. Lommax will support a fellow artist, won't you, Johnny?"

"Ah, is that the lad that drew Adam and Eve in the garrden of innocence?"

"But not in innocence."

At once they begin to discuss the artistic question.

"If you'll excuse me, Jimmy, ah should say it was the completest innocence."

"I see what you mean, the primitive frankness."

Miss Allchin now asks: "Did Charley draw something for you?"

"He did, Miss Leena, a most remarrkable worrk, which ah would be very glad to purrchase for my collection."

Lina turns red with pleasure and excitement: "But is he really good, Mr. Lommax?"

"His drawings are good. Ah cannot vouch for his robberies."

"Do you think he is really artistic?"

"Everybody is artistic, Miss Leena——"

"But, Mr. Lommax, don't you see, this is very important to the poor boy in his terrible trouble. He comes before the Court to-morrow. His whole life depends on what happens in the next few hours. If I could tell the magistrates that he has promise as an artist, they might agree to put him on probation."

"You can certainly say that, Miss Leena."

"Oh, thank you, Mr. Lommax."

"Because all children have prromise as arrtists, as I said before, everybody is arrtistic."

"But Miss Allchin would like to know, Johnny, if you could advise a special education for her protégé."

"What, bring him up to live by arrt? Naw, I could not advise anyone to condemn any child to be an arrtist. It is a hundrred to one that he will be a bad one. A thousand to one."

Lina looks angrily at Lommax. She thinks him frivolous. She would hate the man, as she hates all frivolity, if he were not, in her belief, eminent, and if he had not such a fine voice and assured, grave manners. Wandle, on her behalf, says: "But, Johnny, if we do not take the risk of allowing children to become artists, there will be no artists."

"Aye, and ye might add that if there were not hundrreds of bad arrtists, there would be no good ones. Look at Frrance, where the Government deliberrately manufactures bad arrtists by the thousand, and therrefore leads the worrld in penting."

"Then hadn't we better say that young Charley Brown might be risked?"

"Ah would not take the rrisk for a child of my own. Ah would rather put him in the submarrines."

"You don't give me much help, Mr. Lommax."

"Ah will do anything to help you, Miss Leena, so long as you know what you're doing."

"Can I say that you think him promising as an artist?"

"Ah will come and swear it, if you like—perjury has no terrors for an arrtist—he is damned alrready."

"It only means a few extra drawing lessons for the boy," Wandle says.

"Which will, in any case, rruin any ability he may possess."

35 Further evidence gathered by the police from some of Charley's victims caused the arrest of both Harry and Lizzie. But Charley claimed from the beginning to be the ringleader of the party, and even Lina was obliged to admit that Ginger had not prepared the expedition or snatched bags. Harry, barely twelve years old, was discharged; Lizzie was placed under supervision, with her parents, and Ginger was ordered six months probation in his billet.

Charley's fate, because he seemed to have enterprise and imagination, was doubtful till the last moment.

Lina who, in her anxiety, had begun to seem absurd, brought Wandle into court, and sent for Charley's father, offering to pay his fare. But what, in the end, had more weight with the magistrates than Mr. Wandle's and Lina's own certificates of character, was a visit from Charley's late teacher in London. She arrived fifteen minutes before the case and stayed less than five minutes afterwards. She was a thin woman in pince-nez, the very type teacher of the comic papers; in a badly-fitting tweed skirt and a green jumper. She was obviously worn out by the effort to keep in touch with old pupils and also to teach an evacuated school in the Home Counties; she spoke abruptly and impatiently to Lina and did not show great enthusiasm about Charley. "Charles," she said, "had been a disappointment to her and the school. Measles was not only to blame for his missing a scholarship. He had always been too fond of street life. But he had ability, and he had not before committed any crime. So she had come to get him off if she could." Lina detested this dry tone as much as the woman, and feared the effect of her evidence. But suddenly Wandle, who had just come out from giving his own tribute, asked her: "What time did you start this morning, Miss Pedder?"

"Half-past five. Why?"

"And what time will you get back?"

"I haven't an idea," with a glance which snubbed this impertinence.

Wandle, raising his brows, smiled and bowed himself towards the lady. "You seem to have a high opinion of our young criminal."

"He's one of my boys, that's all."

"A nice boy, we think."

"I can see he's been getting round you—he gets round everybody."

"He didn't get round you, Miss Pedder?"

"Of course he did, they all do—I'm a perfect fool about boys."

"Wouldn't you like to stay and see him after the case? I would be delighted to put you up for the night."

"I should love it, but I've no time." For one moment the woman's nervous exhausted face, the face of a devotee, relaxes, and she says: "I never have any time to see my boys—not really to see them. And, of course, it takes a long time for children to thaw out with me. I suppose it's the pince-nez or something. For boys you want to have either charm or time —but I don't suppose the Board would see it."

"You'll do your best for Charley, won't you?" Lina asked.

"I'll stick to facts—if I let the magistrates think I have a personal interest in Charley, they'll write me down as a silly spinster with a pash for boys." Then, just as she was called in, she relaxed again and said coolly: "Of course I have a pash, but what on earth would be the good of me in this job if I hadn't?"

Miss Pedder certainly gave very dry evidence; she seemed to grudge the admission that Charley had not been actively criminal in London. "But he was much too fond of the streets and street gangs."

She agreed that he was clever, but asserted that this made his conduct worse. "He really has no excuse."

She then hurried away to catch her train, refusing even tea. "I've no time."

Her parting from Lina and Wandle was that of one who could not waste time on improving an acquaintance for which there was no time. Lina, to whom such a woman was as strange in all her thoughts and ways as a different species of mammal, was still more embittered against her. She was surprised to hear afterwards that her evidence had had great weight with the chairman. "The only thing that counted against it was the lady's obvious partiality for the boy."

When Charley's father, on the other hand, said that Charley was a young devil who had to be kept in order, he carried no conviction to the magistrates, but when he promised to beat the boy well, he made them feel that he was a serious and responsible citizen who had some conception of the grave dangers of juvenile crime.

They also felt that Charley would not be let off too lightly. They agreed, therefore, to put him on probation, provided that he lived in quarters approved by the probation officer and attended regularly the local classes provided for evacuated children.

Lina Allchin at once suggested that Charley should be billeted at the Cedars, where he would be under her care. She explained that she had meant to take him in the first place, and had been prevented from doing so only by her mother's objection to boys of the destructive age. "But now my mother has had to go away for her health, and so there's no reason why I should not have him."

The probation officer, a young man, of the new school, immensely serious and greatly overworked, agreed heartily with this plan.

Lina had also a private plan, to intercede for Charley with Mr. Brown. She approached him the same day. She asked him if he were sure that beating was good for children.

Mr. Brown was a short, square-shouldered man of forty with a hooked nose and a face like weather-worn teak. He had blue eyes even brighter than his son's. It seemed also that he had as much intelligence and character. To Lina's surprise he knew all about the controversy between beaters and non-beaters.

"But if you're not sure it will do any good, Mr. Brown?"

"Can't be sure about anything, miss, these times. Thass the trouble, see. The kids don know were they are and nor do us parents. I seen kids go all wrong after a licking and I seen some that was a lot better for it."

"It depends on the boy's character, doesn't it?"

"Depends on such a lot o things, aint no good worrying about em," Mr. Brown said, not pertly, but with the manner of one speaking from experience and reflection. "But one thing is, I know it won't do Charley no arm because e's a good-tempered kid. E'll get over it all right, never you fear, and it got im orf with the beaks. It's a sure call with the beaks, parental correction."

Lina was obliged to leave the responsibility to Mr. Brown

who at once, out of a delicacy which again she had not expected, took the boy from the Cedars, to Mrs. Parr's; beat him there thoroughly and delivered him again at the Cedars the same night.

36 Lina, nervous in her new responsibilities towards Charley, asked advice of all the experts she could find; the probation officer and one of the magistrates. All said in various forms: "Win his confidence."

"How do you do that?"

"You must show confidence in him."

This policy accorded very well with Lina's own inclination towards Charley. A few days after his arrival at the Cedars, when she felt that he was growing used to her, to his new suit of clothes and a new routine, she took occasion one day to tell him that she was not going to regard him as a prisoner. Characteristically, she had not prepared a speech or arranged a set interview. She spoke on an impulse, in the upper corridor, chiefly because she was nervous of speaking at all, and wanted to get it over.

"I don't want you to feel that I'm watching you, Charley. That would be stupid, wouldn't it, because you're quite clever enough to deceive me. Of course, there are certain rules about not meeting Fant or Harry or Bessie Galor, or going where you might meet them—but they're not my fault. The Court made them."

Here she stuck for a moment, embarrassed by Charley's embarrassment. Charley, red in the face, was playing with the handle of the bathroom door.

"Yes, miss."

"And we must trust each other, mustn't we?" Lina made another plunge. "I'll trust you to keep the rules and you can trust me——" she hesitates, wondering in what Charley can trust her, and says at last—"not to spy on you and to bother

177

you as little as I can. To trust you, in fact. For I know you are trustworthy."

"Yes, miss, thank you very much." Charley was greatly moved. What he understood from the girl's speech was that she liked him and meant to be his friend. His thanks were so plainly sincere, that both were moved to further embarrassment. They stood for a moment, then separated unexpectedly, without another word.

This shyness between Lina and the boy, natural to both at their ages, was no drawback to their mutual liking. Charley was growing sensitive in certain matters. When Lina, obliged by a sense of duty, enquiring about ear-washing, nail-cutting, and what she called regularity after breakfast, showed nervousness and coloured, he also blushed. This expression of a common modesty of feeling, not before noticed by Charley in himself, created a peculiar tie of sympathy; something much deeper than any verbal agreement.

On the other hand, his new sensitiveness made him loathe the housemaid Plant, a long-faced, bony old woman in spectacles who detested him, and would tear open his bed in the morning with a furious gesture. She accused him of wetting it, but Charley said indignantly: "It aint wet—I mean, it aint that kind a wet."

Two spots of purple appeared in the old woman's cheeks, and she muttered that she had not bargained for boys and their nastiness. But Charley disliked Plant so much that even her step in the corridor made him feel a warmth of repulsion. It was there before he recognised it.

He did not set himself to plague the old woman, but he was a nuisance to her. Instinctively he did everything that annoyed her and hindered her work. But he set himself deliberately to please Lina Allchin. He found one obstacle in Lina's shyness, which prevented her from giving explicit directions. But native quickness usually made him able to understand her. For instance, when Lina passed him coming out of the lavatory and said, "The water is quite warm now in the bathroom," he gathered that he ought to wash his hands after going to the lavatory. He picked up table manners in a couple of days, but not the art of waiting on a visitor, until a young Allchin boy came back for the mid-term exeat. Lina apparently could not bring herself to make Charley wait upon her when she was the only lady present.

The young boy, Brander, was an enigma to Charley. He was a pale child of twelve, very thin, with large grey eyes. He never smiled, and he spent half of each day taking prodigious walks by himself, and the other half reading. To Charley he was extremely polite, unless Charley touched his books, when he would curse him and shout: "You dirty beast, I'll kick you."

Charley and he, on the second day, came to blows when Brander, who was half a head taller, receiving a punch, at once took up a hockey-stick and aimed a blow at Charley's head which, though it luckily missed, was meant to kill. Its murderous fury shocked Charley so much that he avoided Brander from that moment. But he studied the boy's manners. They were not good manners. Brander opened a door for a lady with a careless jerk and handed her the bread and butter with a gesture which said: "You are a bore and I wish you to the devil," but he knew the ritual.

What Charley could not understand in Brander was his indifference to friendship. For Charley the world had always been divided into three parts, his relations, his friends and his enemies. For Brander it was divided, apparently, into people and things which interested him and those that did not. When Charley, puzzled by his remoteness, asked him: "I suppose you got a lot a friends at your school?" he reflected for a moment before answering: "Not friends—but some of the chaps are all right."

"Avent you got no friends?" Charley asked, thinking already that he would be a friend to Brander. But the other, who wanted to go on reading an encyclopædia article, answered shortly: "No, except one chap, but I don't like *him* much. He jabbers. Besides, he's an ass."

To Charley, Brander's existence seemed so dull, so lonely so friendless that sometimes he pitied him and more often he despised him. To Brander, Charley was a savage who did not even know how to amuse himself. He complained ten times a day to his Aunt Lina: "He's always butting in just when I'm doing something. Can't you give him something to do for himself?"

"You might at least take him for a walk sometimes."

"Oh, lord, but he talks the whole time, and I've only got till Monday."

"I only wish he'd talk more."

"Oh, he doesn't talk to *you*, but he talks to *me* all the time."

"What about?"

"Oh, lord, it isn't *about* anything. It's just talk."

Lina lectured her nephew about his social duty as a host, but Brander, at twelve, was indifferent to class distinction. He knew Charley simply as an individual, another boy, who threatened to spoil the two chief pleasures of his holiday from school, solitary walks across country and reading, and he therefore detested him. Charley, on his side, though wary of Brander, was always attracted by him. He was curious about him, as about a foreigner. He was interested by his queer habits, his learning, his strange relation to his aunt, whom he treated with formal politeness and open contempt. When Lina made any remark at table about the weather, the war, about anything at all, Brander would wrinkle his nose as if someone had hurt him and cry out in an angry, sorrowful tone: "But, Aunty, you've got it all *wrong*. Strategy is what happens before a battle, and tactics is what happens in a battle."

"It doesn't matter so long as Charley knows what I mean."

"But it *does* matter. If you don't get the words right you can't think right." His high treble voice, as it rose towards the word think, seemed full of tears, and once he said not to Charley but to the air in Charley's presence: "Women are really *perfectly* useless."

37 Charley himself, though cut off from all his old acquaintances, was too busy to feel lonely. He was working hard at all his classes, especially at his drawing. Every afternoon he was shut up in the room still called the study, where the late Major Allchin had written his pamphlets on archæology, to work upon a large still life of a wax pear in a glass bowl, a black bottle and a crumpled napkin.

This drawing gave both Lina and Charley a great deal of pleasure. Lina was astonished by the accuracy and the skill with which Charley had learnt already to shade or to take out a high light; Charley was astonished to see how easily he could give the effect, merely by pencil and rubber, of solidity and texture.

It was true that now and then while he worked and while his face had the intent concentrated expression of one who dutifully lends his whole mind to his task, his hand would begin to draw little comical figures on the margin of the paper. One drawing, of strange arabesques, dancing girls, naked Wandles in horn-rims, murders, rapes, and film stars with eyelashes like bicycle spokes, which he had inadvertently drawn on the top of the table in ink, he had to keep hidden by various subterfuges. He could not imagine or even remember how he had come to draw such a picture in the Cedars. Yet every now and then he awaked as if from a dream to find a smile on his lips and a pen or pencil in his hand, adding new details to this picture which had become so shocking that he himself could not bear to think of it on the Cedars table.

He knew, of course, that this drawing must be discovered and the idea filled him with terror, but only for a few seconds. Then he abolished it from his mind and continued in perfect happiness and serenity, acquiring the ritual of manners, learning quadratic equations and picking out the high lights on the black bottle.

At night he would lie in bed, after Lina had come in upon some excuse to say a last good night, and imagine the glorious future when he would exhibit at the Royal Academy and drive about in a blue Rolls-Royce with silver wings. "And one morning Miss Leener will be looking out of the winder, just after breakfast, wen she says: 'Just look at that beautiful car—I wonder does it belong to the King or wot. I wish I ad a car like that,' and then she says: 'Wy, it's turning in at the gate—it muss be a mistake—oo can it be?' An then the shover—e as a blue coat juss like the car—e gets out and rings the bell, and Miss Leener says to im: 'You've come to the wrong ouse—hhouse,' and e says: 'Miss Leener Allchin I pressume,' and she says: 'That's me.' Ere, ere, she wouldn't say that, she says: 'I am Miss Allchin,' and the shover says: 'That's right,' e says, 'wen you want the car, miss,' and she says: 'Wot car?' and e says: 'This ere car, miss, wich is yours,' and she says: 'Wot do you mean?' and e says: 'Mr. Charley Brown as sent me,' and she says: 'Do you mean the famous Mr. Charley Brown, Royal Academy, the great artiss?' and e says: 'Yes, miss, Mr. Charles Brown.' Ere, Sir Charles Brown, Bert,' yess, that's it: 'Sir Charles Brown, Royal Academy, as ordered me—commanded me's better—commanded me to present you with this ere car for Christmas an to be your shover, and e's paid me, too,' and she'll say: 'Oh, gawd!' Ere, go on, she wouldn't say that—she'd say—ere, ere, she wouldn't want a shover nor a big car, she ates swank. All right then, I'll send er—aint nothing you *can* send er—she don't want a dimon necklace nor nothing—aint nothing she wants."

Charley's stories for some time had all run aground in this manner, upon some shoal of fact. They no longer encouraged him. Often they left him with a sense of depression, as if unexpected obstacles had risen in front of him. But his fits of depression did not last long because if they came upon him during the day he forgot them at once in curiosity, and if they touched him at night he fell asleep.

38 Lina had been anxious lest Charley's old associates, especially Ginger, whom privately she blamed for his crimes, should tempt him away from the Cedars. She was

relieved to find that he never sought their company. It seemed that her plan of removing him to the Cedars had been successful in isolating him from bad companions. In fact Charley was so much interested in his own surroundings, for the first fortnight, that he had no time to think about gang affairs. He heard, of course, all the latest news. Basil and Walter both came to classes at the Cedars, and though they never brought their feuds within its doors, further than to whisper into Charley's ear as they passed, "Lousy," or to scribble some threat in his exercise book, they kept him posted in the latest phase.

Class-rooms, as distinct from halls and playgrounds, are neutral in gang warfare, and deadly enemies who in a school hall will slyly stick compasses into each other or, in the playground, batter each other with satchels or stumps, will exchange gossip across a desk lid. They act so in the spirit of lawyers at the courts or brokers in the exchange, who divide their lives into the professional and the personal.

Thus Walter, in the intervals between one lesson and another, before the fire in the study, would tell Charley that Ginger had sworn at Harry, and that Bill had a new friend, a Tawleigh boy called Mort, bigger than himself and much more violent. A few days later Charley heard in the same way that Ginger, who was now billeted at Wickens, was friends with Basil, and that Harry was going about with Bert. Basil told him, in the lavatory, with spiteful contempt, that Bill and Mort spent all their time in Tawleigh chasing girls in the lanes and whispering various obscenities in their ears.

"Ope they get copped," Basil said, "I ates that Mort—e's a bloody swine. E's worse than Bill. Ope one of them girls' chaps catches im and gives im a kick in the belly. That's wot e wants; e's a sod, e is."

Charley, thoughtfully making patterns on the slate, answers: "Wots the next class?"

"Jography. I ates jography—they just does it to keep us shut up. It's a dirty trick, that's all."

"Miss Small aint a real teacher."

"Miss Small—Miss Bloody Cheeks—I owe er one, Miss Small, I'll give er something, you just see."

But Charley is not interested enough even to ask what revenge Basil is planning against Miss Small for trying to teach him the capitals of Europe. He is in another world, enclosed by the invisible walls of imagination and purpose which shut off one special group or class from another.

To Walter and Basil, of course, the daily news of alliances and forays is the chief interest of their lives. They are more excited by the rumours that Bill has had his face smacked by a girl in Tawleigh than by the air raid on Heligoland. Even the war news from Finland is forgotten when Walter brings the story that Mort has chased Ginger and smashed his uke. All day while Walter and Basil sit in class one can see upon their interested faces, the question: "What will Ginger do now?"

Charley is trying to please Miss Small by knowing his seas, and Miss Lina by getting his kings and dates right.

One day Walter, full of excitement, beckons Charley to a window and, hiding behind the curtain, points out to him the dangerous Mort sitting on a baker's cart in the yard. Charley sees a tall fair boy with a long pink nose, a stooping back and one shoulder much higher than the other. He is smartly dressed in a brown tweed coat and grey flannel trousers, and his long hair is shiny with oil. He is smoking a cigarette and scratching his nose with an air of mild astonishment as if some odd thought has just struck him.

"He's a terror," Walter says. "He took a knife to Bill once. Stick you for tuppence."

Charley is more interested to notice that the Tawleigh baker's cart has called at the Cedars because this means a party. The Allchins order only sweet cakes from Tawleigh.

39 A few days later, on a cold afternoon, Charley is sitting in the study in front of an octagonal pot in a soup plate, a difficult study in perspective. As he stoops over

the table, from which the cloth has been turned back, his drawing-board is resting on the top of his head. His tongue is hanging out as far as it will go, he is lost in concentration while he draws some new improvements to the scene on the table top, which has now, after a fortnight's work, covered two square feet of wood with every variety of naked savage, Wandle, dancing girl, man-tree, wild bull, rape and murder, the whole forming what seems at a first glance, like a complicated forest of flowers, a tropical garden.

Charley, who has just discovered a bottle of red ink in the study desk, is astonished by the new effects which can be obtained by dipping his pencil in the ink and drawing thick red lines round parts of the design. His experiments excite him so much that he holds his breath. He is just drawing a shower of red rain falling from a black tree, with leaves shaped like hands, upon two little black figures, possessing only one leg apiece, when he hears Lina's step in the corridor.

Instantly he jerks back his head, the drawing-board falls, covering the table top, and he begins to shade the soup plate. He is red with shock. He had thought that Lina was out.

She comes in, dressed for Twyport, and looks over his shoulder. "Very nice, Charley—very good indeed. You could almost lift it off the board. You are getting on."

"Yes, miss."

"Really, it's almost good enough to frame. Will you finish it this afternoon, do you think?"

"Oh, yes, miss, easy."

"I really will see about a frame—it's just a wee little bit smudgy in the bottom left-hand corner, isn't it? I suppose you can't help rubbing it, can you? But we'll soon clean that up, won't we? Really it's awfully good, it's a wonderful drawing."

"Yes, miss." Charley, satisfied with himself, looks at his drawing first from one side, then from the other, bending his neck. He thinks it a very good drawing.

"Very well, Charley, you're a good boy—here's just a little present—you've deserved it." She gives him a shilling.

"Oh, thank you, miss. Oh, you are kind."

"Not a bit, Charley—it's a great pleasure to teach you. Now good-bye for the present."

Charley jumps up to say good-bye. His manners are improving every day. "Good-bye, miss, I hope you has a nice party."

"Thank you, Charley, but I'd much rather be here all the same."

Charley, by a second inspiration, opens the door and Lina, moved by affectionate happiness, smiles down at him, says: "Thank you, Charley—I wish everyone had such nice manners."

Charley, blushing, murmurs: "Oh, no, miss—that's nothing, miss."

He walks about the room smiling to himself with pleasure until he hears the car start; then he lifts up his board again. But the red ink has smudged and run, it covers the back of the drawing-board.

"Ow, damn it all," Charley says, disgusted: "Ow, blast." He drops the board again and goes to the window. On the crest of the hill, where Whiteboys raises its turtle back to the sky, Albert is ploughing with the Wickens tractor. Charley watches Albert out of sight, over the crest, and then gazes at a small late flock of starlings, wheeling over the vicarage elms, until five children come running down from the vicarage by the church road. One of them is Harry and behind him Ginger can be seen dawdling with his usual idle gait. Suddenly he runs forward past the other children. Charley hastily throws open the window and leans far out to see where Ginger has run to. But the corner of the lane is out of sight. Charley jumps hastily out of the window, coming down on all fours among the little drooping wallflowers just planted for next spring, and darts down the Cedars back drive.

Ginger has disappeared. But he remembers now that Harry was also in the procession. He turns to run towards the cross roads, when suddenly he catches sight of Harry walking down-hill through the Hall meadow. He rushes after him, shouting at the top of his voice: "Ar-ree."

Harry turns in surprise, and Charley shouts: "Ullo, Arree."

Harry looks at Charley with disgust, wrinkling his small forehead. He still blames Charley for leading him into crime.

Charley feels to his amazement that Harry is not pleased to see him. He says again: "Ullo, Arry, ow is it?"

"All right."

"Don't seem all right," Charley says. But suddenly catching sight of Walter at the lower end of Frenchay field, he shouts HI WALT I WAS LOOKING FOR YA.

Walter, in the open field, knows that this is a challenge. He answers: "Hullo, Lousy, has mother Lina let you out?"

Charley dashes across the muddy field, bawling: "All right, just you wait a minute, thass all, just you wait."

Harry, suddenly starting after his old leader, calls out: "Come back, Charl—they're all there."

"You just wait, Walter," Charley shouts, now within ten yards. He skirmishes towards Walter who retreats a few paces down the lane towards a large elm bole. He faces Charley at last. He does not put up his fists.

Like other boys, Charley finds it difficult to hit Walter in cold blood, without some equivalent to the boxer's handshake; some ritual marking clearly the passage from peace to war. But Walter still refuses to put his fists up. He only looks alarmed and amused and repeats: "Hullo, Lousy—they let you out again, did they?"

"Look out, Charley, it's Bill," Harry yells. "Behind the tree."

Bill and Mort at once rush out from behind the tree. Bill, laughing, gives Charley a heavy thump on the side of the head, which knocks him down.

Charley, however, bouncing up again like an acrobat, darts between the two big boys and is twenty yards down the lane before they can turn.

"Whoops," Bill bellows. "After im, Walt, after im, Mort."

Walter, Bill and Mort follow the hunt down the lane, each giving tongue in his own language.

"Tear is trahsers off," Bill cries, roaring with laughter.

"Lousy," Walter yells.

"Kick is tripes out," Mort bellows. He has never seen Charley before in his life, but he is raging against him. He makes great leaps after him, so that in spite of his thick clumsy legs, he travels fast. Charley is now in the high-banked lane and can't escape. He is just about to be caught when Phyllis Hawes' young man, Arthur Veale, in his best blue suit, turns into the lane from the main road.

At once Mort, Bill and Walter and even Charley himself stop running, and, holding their breath in order not to pant, assume the dawdling gait of tourists. Mort even stops to look into the hedge as if at some flower or nest.

It is the local rule, or rather, simply the instinct, among all the gangs, to stop their fights, chases and even their conversations, at the first appearance of a grown-up. This is the more strange that none of them have followed the same custom in Town. Charley, Bill or Walter, in their own streets, have carried on their campaigns among the very legs of the general public. But in the country they behave like visitors in a foreign land who are not sure of the laws.

Charley receives a sideways nod from Arthur to which he replies with a smile and nod. He strolls carelessly into the main road, turns to the left and at once darts across the bridge and takes cover in the coppice. When Mort and Bill dash into the road, he is already half-way home.

He arrives there with his tie under one ear, a cut on his cheek-bone, one side of his new suit muddied from top to bottom, and he has lost his new cap. He explains that he took a short cut to Hall Farm, lost his way and fell down a bank into a ditch. Lina is sympathetic and plasters the cheek-bone. Charley laughs and says: "Sall right, miss, thank you, miss."

All the evening he keeps smiling to himself, and when Lina, delighting in his pluck and good humour, catches his eye, she, too, smiles as if to say: "We understand each other, don't we?"

40 The next morning, Charley spends much time looking out of the window. He sees nothing but the usual scene, Wickens' red cows in green Little Whiteboys, the baker's cart with a shaggy pony, the tall vicar striding along in black knickerbockers and grey stockings. Peter Drake pushes his go-cart full of milk-bottles as far as the cross-roads, and turns back. Once Ginger's pale red head goes smoothly and slowly past the hedge-top towards the vicarage for the morning class. But Charley knows that Bill must have gone to the same class and that between classes, and going to and from classes, all among the lanes and fields, Ginger, Bill, Basil, Walter, Harry and Lizzie are deep in a life of anxieties, triumphs, plans and secrets.

He wonders if Harry has escaped from Bill. Lina says to him at breakfast: "Isn't it terrible about these air raids on Helsinki, Charley?"

"Yes, miss."

"I don't see how they can go on fighting against Russia."

Charley does not even try to remember where Helsinki is. He is too anxious for news of his own world. He waits impatiently for the arrival of Walter and Basil to tell him the news.

Walter says that Bill has chased Harry, but Basil is furious with Harry for coming to see Ginger. "E aint got nothing to do with Ginger—I ates Arry. Wy can't e mind is own business. If I catch im anging round Ginger I'll put Mort on to im."

"Mort—you wouldn't."

"I would, too—both on em is swine."

Charley cannot sleep that night with excitement. He is like a man of the great world who, after a long exile, has gone back to society. Nothing has happened. He has only met a few people and heard a little gossip. But the kind of people and the quality of the gossip goes at once to his head. He feels that only this kind of people is alive and only this kind of talk has any meaning. He is full of excitement, about he knows not what; expectation of he knows not what; sympathies without

189

an object and amusement without a direction. Charley has nothing to look forward to among the old gangs, nobody wants him there, and new dangers are lying in wait for him; but he feels so impatient to return to them that when he hears seven strike, he can't believe that it is not breakfast time.

At every spare moment during the day, he is slipping down the garden to the lane, or peering over the wall into the road. He dodges about the hedges all evening until he sees Ginger and Basil come out together and walk down the lane, arm-in-arm.

This astonishes him, and for Charley astonishment is a pleasure. He marvels for at least five minutes at this extraordinary friendship.

He is back at the Cedars in order to finish his drawing. But in the evening, after tea, he disappears and is not seen again until ten o'clock. His excuse is that he went to see his mother and lost his way coming home.

"But, Charley, it's an absolutely straight road all the way."

"Yes, miss—but I come along the field."

"You ought to know the field path by now."

"Yes, miss."

Charley is so obviously absent-minded that Lina is annoyed and says sharply: "You haven't been going with those boys again, Charley?"

"No, miss."

In fact Charley has spent three hours in the quarry with Ginger and Basil, who, it appears, are close friends. Harry and Walter are also friends, and they are carrying on a feud against Ginger and Basil, who do not want to fight anybody. Their only enemy is Mort.

Every now and then Basil, who is lying against the rock tightly clasping Ginger's right arm, breaks out in rage against Mort: "I'll kill im, e's a beast."

Ginger is breathing into a mouth-organ which he holds in his left hand, playing faint broken notes. "E it Ginger," Basil says. "The bloody sod—in the stummick. I'll kill im." But when Ginger tries to shift his right hand to the mouth-organ, he complains: "Wot you opping about for, Ginger? Just wen we was comfable."

He has planned a life's friendship with Ginger. "Ginger and me's going in the same job—we're friends, see. You aint nothing to do with Ginger, now—e aint going around with you, Charley Brown."

Ginger continues to breathe a ghost of the song "Run, rabbit, run."

"You better leave Ginger alone," Basil tells Charley. "E don't *want* you coming round. You tell im, Ginger."

Ginger says nothing, and Basil complains: "Go on, Ginger —tell im wot you said you would."

Ginger continues to play. Suddenly Basil leaps up, snatches the mouth-organ out of his hand and screams:

" SHUT UP, YOU SWINE ! " Then he flies at Charley with such spiteful fury that Charley hastily steps backwards. " YOU GET OFF, LOUSY. GETOFF, GETOFF, LOUSY, LOUSY. IATEYA. GINGER ATES YA."

"Ere, ere," Charley says astonished. He looks at Ginger. But Ginger, having picked up the mouth-organ, is calmly playing again. As Charley retreats backwards, Basil once more sits down and takes Ginger's arm, snuggling up against him like a cat against a cushion. He looks at Charley with an expression so tranquil, so catlike in its self-satisfaction, that Charley is silenced and defeated by surprise. He turns round and slowly makes his way home, saying to himself at every step: "Thass funny. Fancy. It's queer too. E's a start, Basil is. And so's Ginger. E's a cure."

41   Charley was surprised by the friendship of Basil and Ginger, but he was not surprised to find himself excluded from all friendship. He wondered at people, but not at events, because in his experience, anything might happen, at any time, to anybody. He felt lonely, however. Once

or twice, in the twilight, he even approached the Galors' cottage, from the back, with a strong impulse towards Lizzie.

But when a light showed in her window, he turned away among the bushes on the hill. He still looked over his shoulder towards the light, but he retreated from it as from a temptation.

Charley was ashamed of the impulse which carried him again and again to the Galors' cottage patch; but Lizzie began to obsess him. He made up stories about her and drew her picture on the table top, among the flowering naked Wandles, the excited bulls and the film stars.

One evening, when Charley was wandering through the bushes behind the Galors', with his hands in his pockets, disconsolate, excited, and full of confused sensation, Basil leapt up from the quarry mouth with a scream. "Ere e is, Bill, we got ya, Lousy." Bill and Walter came rushing from ambush just above the quarry and Charley, terrified out of his wits, flew down the hill. Whereupon Mort sprang out of cover by the blacksmith's shed.

Charley doubled back to the Galors'. He knew his way among the rusty wires and gooseberry bushes which confused Bill and tripped Walter. The two girls put their heads out of the window and Susan cried angrily: "Go away—oh, dear, it's those awful boys."

"Mind the gate, Charley," Lizzie shrieked. By some extraordinary quickness which belonged to all her senses except her ears, she had recognized Charley and perceived the situation.

"Mind the gate—it's got the lock on," and a last desperate yell: "Go in the kitchen."

Charley darted through the Galors' back door, through the kitchen, luckily empty, and out of the front door through the old farm-yard into the village street.

Bill was already climbing over the gate and Walter was coming down the hill. He was obliged to run down-hill towards the bridge. But just as he reached the bridge, Mort sprang out from the trees, took him by the neck and threw him into the pool.

Bill and Walter, running up, were startled by this act. Bill, almost ceasing to laugh, so that his mouth kept only the shape of laughter, said: "I say, Mort, can e swim?"

"Let un drown then," Mort says. Charley, coming up to the surface, makes a grab at the edge of the bridge and holds on to the planks. He says in a tone of mild anxiety: "Give us a and, mate."

"Go on, drown," Mort shouts. He jumps on Charley's fingers. Charley, with an agonised yell, lets go and drops back into the water. This time, by good luck, he lands on his feet and discovers that he can stand with his head above water. Mort leans down and tries to push his head under, Charley retreats. Mort pelts him and drives him slowly to the far end of the pool where the Burls stream runs out through an iron grille. Here the pool has been walled in. Charley cannot climb up or escape down stream. He stands up to his neck in the freezing water while Mort throws rubbish at him and shouts furiously: "Go on, you baastard, drown. I'll freeze you."

Bill not laughing, but still with the formal face of laughter, remonstrates: "I say, Mort—is clothes'll be all spoilt."

Walter, too, is not whole-hearted in the sport. He calls at Charley: "Is it wet down there, Lousy?" but he does not throw stones and his voice is perplexed. Only young Basil is delighted. Mort hunts and shouts and threatens with a kind of sullen obstinate rage, as if he had a bitter grudge not only against Charley, but against everything. He curses the stones for sticking in the road, just as savagely as he swears at Charley, but Basil shrieks and dances with pleasure.

"Ow you like that, Lousy—ow you feel now, Lousy?" he screams. "Ere's a present for you," throwing a piece of dung. "I say, Mort, lemme go and poke im with a stick. Poke im in the middle see, were it's deeper."

Basil actually does creep through the fence and poke at

Charley from the top of the wall with a stick, so that he is gradually driven back into deeper water.

Bert, Harry, and Ginger have now joined the spectators. Bert dodges from one view to another, grinning with curiosity and excitement. Harry stares with round horrified eyes and keeps shouting: "Let im out—E's ad enough. E'll catch is death." Ginger asks with mild surprise: "What's wrong with Mort?"

Some of the village children are looking on, in a group some distance apart. Fred Hawes calls out: "They've got someone in the water," as if referring to a foreign game; another boy remarks in a broad accent: "He did summat to Morton."

Girls' voices are heard in the shadow of the trees, laughing and asking questions. The villagers cannot decide whether the affair is a joke or something that ought to be stopped.

"It's they boys agen."

"Some of em's in the water."

"There's bin a fight."

Charley is so cold, miserable and bewildered that he does not utter a sound. He stands in the water, with his arms tightly folded to hold in the warmth and tries to dodge the rubbish thrown at him by Basil and Mort. Suddenly he sees a dark object in the water close to him and hears Lizzie's voice: "Zat you, Charl?"

Charley can't say anything. When he tries to speak, his teeth chatter violently.

"Gimme your hand."

In the twilight he can just distinguish Lizzie's round face and the soaked dress clinging over her shoulders. The water is up to her breast. A spurt of gravel strikes the water and Basil screams from the bridge "Duck im—drown im."

Charley ducks and says to Lizzie: "Look out, Lizzie—they're throwing things."

"Gimme your hand, quick, Charl." Lizzie pulls at his arm. Charley lets her take his hand and at once she leads him towards the bridge. "We got to go under. You follow me."

She ducks her head under the bridge and turns to encourage Charley. "See—there's lots a room."

Charley ducks under the bridge. He hears Basil's scream of rage. "'E's gone under—somebody showed im—oo's that in the water?"

"Get the other side and poke im," Mort advises.

But Lizzie, who knows the pool, leads Charley along under the bridge, and emerges on the down-stream side. Here the bank slopes gently up to the road. While Mort and Basil, armed with their poles, are still looking over the railing, up stream, Lizzie pulls Charley up the bank.

"Look out, Mort!" Walter cries. "Other side!" Although he gives warning his voice is still full of doubt. He acts like a man whose nerves respond to a stimulus, while his mind is still in suspense about the value of the whole experiment. Mort and Basil turn in fury, but Charley and Lizzie are already slipping through the trees. Before Mort can give chase, Bill suddenly makes up his mind, and says: "E's ad enough, Mort, let im alone."

"Who are you?" Mort turns on Bill. "You looking for a smack in the snout?"

Bill, laughing, with his hands in his pockets, lunges heavily into Mort and treads on his toes. Mort screams out a curse which brings a murmur of protest from the village. A man's bass voice, Galor's, from the wall of the Hall garden, just above the bridge, says gravely: "You keep that language to yourself, boy, you hear? Keep it to yourself. And get off from here. I know ee, so get off, quick. Get along to Tawleigh, where you belong."

Mort screams another curse, but he is already on the other side of the bridge. Bill, Walter, Ginger, Harry, at the sound of Galor's voice, have disappeared like shades into the surrounding shadows.

Lizzie and Charley, breathless, are climbing out of the copse into quarry lane. Charley is so cold that he cannot fit his toes into the cracks between the stones. He tumbles back, and

Lizzie pulls at him. She is frightened, urgent, and like many frightened children, full of resource and power. She clambers back over the wall to push Charley upwards. She encourages him like a small child. "You're all right, Charley, ant you?"

"I'm all right, Liz."

"You bant too cold?"

"Mort's a cure, aint e?" Charley murmurs in a voice of tired wonder.

"I hate that Mort—I told you he wur wicked. Oh, dear, however shall I get this booy dry. Is your feet dead?"

"You all wet yourself, aint you?"

"What you want is a hot bath front a fire. Mum give Su one last week. But I can't take you home, can I? I can't go home."

"E got me in the deep end, see." Charley is still preoccupied with his adventure.

"Pity you bant to Mrs. Parr now. She allays keeps a good fire."

"We could get in er kitchen—she can't ear—she's deafer nor you are."

"However could we go in another person's house like that, Charl?"

"Off the barrel. Done it undreds o times."

"We coulddn. Oh dear lord, how this booy do shiver. He'll get numony next."

"Jes as you like, Liz. But it'd be warm at old Parr's."

"Oh dear me, come on, then—I bant going to let no one say I let ee die of numony."

"Where we going?"

"Mrs. Parr's, but I wish it was anyone else. What did you go and get in the water for? Boys is wonderful for getting into trouble. Whatever shall I do with him if Mrs. Parr hasn't gone to bed?"

Mrs. Parr had not gone to bed. When the two children, dripping and shivering, reached the cottage and peered from

196

the top of the water-butt through the top of the back window, by a chink well known to Charley, they saw that the old lady was still in her bath.

This was one of those zinc baths, shaped like a baby's coffin, which are still used in the country in preference to the chilly flat bath or the clumsier hip-bath.

Mrs. Parr, dressed in nothing but her spectacles, was sitting in this bath, which was placed exactly opposite the fire-basket of the stove. A large kettle stood stewing on the hob. Every now and then Mrs. Parr reached out her arm, and, lifting her legs into the air with surprising agility, tilted the kettle till it poured a stream of boiling water into the bath beneath her. The operation, full of danger and the nicest skill, was carried out with the nonchalance of many years' practice. Each time it was performed Mrs. Parr, having let the kettle fall back with a loud clop, quickly seized the bath by the sides and lifted herself several inches into the air. At the same time her old witch's face assumed an extraordinary expression, her eyes were screwed up till they disappeared while her mouth stretched almost from ear to ear in a grin of agony.

She then gradually lowered herself into the hot water, and with every inch of descent, an inch came off the grin. At last she reached the bottom. The grin vanished with a speed which showed that for the last few seconds, at least, it had been merely ceremonious, a tribute to the bath, and the old lady's face fell instantaneously into its usual austere shape. She then poured the hot water over herself with a tin cup.

Charley, too cold to know what his feet were doing, slipped off the butt with a clatter. Lizzie jumped down after him, and both cowered under the window-sill.

Mrs. Parr screamed "Shoo" and then again "Shoo"; after that there was a long silence. Charley climbed once more on the butt. The old woman had just put on a nightgown of blue flannelette and was in the act of pulling a man's stocking over her grey head. The bath had disappeared and the fire door of the stove was closed.

Mrs. Parr picked up her candlestick and the skirts of her nightgown and went briskly out of the kitchen.

Charley at once began to clamber up the spout.

Caution was not needed on the narrow spouting, far detached from the wall. He wriggled quickly through his mother's bedroom window.

"Oos that?" Mrs. Brown asked, and added at once: "You won't get nothing ere!"

"It's me, mum, Charley," in a subdued voice.

"Wy, you did give me a start—thought you was burglars. Wot you doing ere, Charley?"

"I fell in the water—I want to dry in front of the fire."

"You look out for Mrs. Parr, Charley—she may be deaf but she's sharp."

"All right, ma." Charley speaks quietly and sadly. He is still oppressed by Mort's fury against him. He is just letting himself out of the door when Mrs. Brown gives a shrill laugh and asks: "Ow's the old bottom, Charley?"

Charley, who knows the proper answer to this, says: "Sall right cept for sitting on." In fact his bruises and weals are almost cured.

Mrs. Brown roars with laughter. At last she manages to say: "Tanned ya proper, your daddy did, diddnt e?"

"Yers, e did, I don't want no more from that shop."

This again is the correct answer. It excites the imagination, gives a picture of violent feeling and treats the whole episode in a facetious spirit.

There is a short silence. Charley is waiting to know if his mother has heard Lizzie's voice. Mrs. Brown says sleepily: "There's a fire in the kitchen."

"Yes, ma, I was just going down."

"Poor ole Charley—like beating carpets." She is already half asleep.

42 Charley shuts the door carefully and feels his way down the narrow stairs to the back door. In a moment Lizzie, with a scared face and the deliberate steps of a cat in a strange house, moves into the kitchen. She is shocked even to see her skirts dripping on the oil-cloth. She has a country girl's respect for another's home. Seeing Charley, who has lit the lamp, putting back the chimney with his wet fingers, she quickly takes it from him, whispering: "You'll break it, you silly. Don't you see it's all wet?"

She dries the chimney carefully and replaces it with an anxious frown. But the next moment, seeing Charley's purple nose and blue cheeks, she rushes at him. "I believe you got the fever, I know you'll get numony. It's just what would happen."

Charley opens the fire door and holds his hands in front of the fire, but Lizzie pulls him back. "Don't go too close—it ant safe when you're froze."

"Wy not, Liz?" Charley in his subdued condition is ready to take advice.

"Your flesh will all come off—ony thing is a hot bath. Where she put the bath, Charl?"

"You aint going to make me ave a bath."

"You must have a bath or you'll get numony. Quick, get off your clothes while I heat up the kettle."

Liz is now poking the fire, filling the kettle as if she owned the house. She drags out the bath from beneath the sink, places it in front of the stove and pulls down Mrs. Parr's towel from the rack. Then she hastens to strip the protesting Charley, whose cold fingers are still fumbling at buttons. "You're just as wet as I am," Charley protests.

"Never mind me, hurry up and get your things off."

"You're shivering, too, Liz."

"I'll dry after."

"You better ave a bath, too."

"Hurry up, Charl."

"Ere, spose you get numony."

Lizzie, with a troubled frown, is still unbuttoning Charley. She says: "How can I have one when you're having one, too?"

"I won't look, Lizzie, honest."

Lizzie says in a severe maternal tone: "Never you mind about me; wait a minute till I put the water in and then I'll turn my back."

She pours out the water and sits down on a stool with her back to the fire. Charley pulls off his breeches and gets into the bath with several loud oos and ohs.

"Is that nice, Charl?"

"Not arf—I'm boiling. Wy don't ya op in, Liz?"

"How could I, Charley? Talk sense." Lizzie's voice is more impatient than shocked. Her modesty is the robust simple country modesty of rules rather than feelings. She has a code of manners but nothing shocks her.

Charley, having finished his bath, wraps himself in an old horse blanket which Mrs. Parr has spread over the meal box. He squats in front of the fire while Liz lets down the ceiling rack and hangs out his clothes. Liz then undresses behind his back and hangs up her clothes beside his, by stretching her arms over his head. She gets into the bath.

"Is it ot, Liz?"

"Proper hot."

"Want some more water?"

"I'll look after that, Charl."

"Ere's the towel," holding it over his head. "Is it ot enough?"

"Proper hot. I love a hot towel."

"Wot will we do wile the clothes get dry?"

"Quat in front of the fire."

"You sit with me, Liz. There's lots of room in the blanket."

"All right, shut your eyes."

Charley shuts his eyes. A violent commotion takes place beside him and Lizzie is under the same blanket.

Charley clasps her firmly to him and says: "You warm now, Liz?"

"It's nice, ant it?" She gazes at the fire with a surprised expression as if she can hardly believe her own enjoyment.

Charley is moved, and for some reason, he wants to crush Liz still closer to him. He tightens his arm with all his might. Lizzie is obviously being hurt but she does not complain. She lets herself be crushed in silence. Suddenly she asks: "Whatever did they do it for, Basil and all?"

"I dunno—they was chasing me, see."

"And Basil poking—it was a cruel thing to do."

"Go on, Liz, Basil's only a kid."

"I never knew what was happening—I jus ran down the hill. A good thing too. I never knew you was in the water till Ginger said."

"Ginger didn't do nothing."

"What they do it for, Charl, a cruel thing like that? Wur Mort drunk?"

"No, he ran straight enough."

"Do you hate this place, Charl?"

"I dunno." There is a long pause. They lie warmly breathing against each other. Then Charley asks: "Will they wop ya for spoiling your clothes?"

"Noa, but they will when they find out I've bin with you. I ant bin out of the house for a week." Lizzie, under supervision, is not supposed to leave home except in charge of some responsible person.

"Ere, they won't find out, will they, Liz?"

"They would any minute if Mum goas to look for me. I mun go home, Charley, and quick, too." But she does not move.

"Don't you let em wop ya, Liz. You tell the police. It's against the law to wop gurls wen they stop being kids."

"But the police is agen me, too, since Twyport."

"It's a shame to keep ya in for that—you aint a kid."

"I wur ba-ad, too. I knew what I was doing."

"Ere, Liz, lets cut off—it's easy."

"When could we?"

"Wy, nah. Soons our clothes is dry."

"Where we go? Lunnon?"

"No, Ammurca. I want a good job, see."

"Aint Lunnon far enough," with a faint note of irony.

"All right, laugh, but I'll be in Ammurca this day nex week."

"But how we get to Ammurca?"

"Thass easy—stowaway. You don't pay nothing, see—you just go on a ship and ask for a friend. Say you got a nuncle in the crew, then ya just get in a W.C. and ide till the ship starts off. Then you go around with the crowd and ave your meals and all, and when anyone asks you for a ticket you say ya gives it up. Lots a chaps done like that."

"But not gurls."

"Yers, and gurls, lots of em."

"But don't they catch you after?"

"Nao, and if they do they can't do nothing. Course, they make you work a bit. But I wouldn't mind that. Climbing the masts is easy—they ave ladders all up, and then you ave to wash the floors, too, decks. I've seen em down at the Pool."

"I could do that."

"You'd ave to elp in the kitchen—galleys they call it."

"I wouldn't mind that—they has grand kitchens on them big ships."

"All right, Liz—soons our clothes is dry we'll get off."

"To Ammurca."

"Ere, Liz, I mean it." He presses her tight in his arms. "You and me, see."

"You and me going to Ammurca."

She says this in a peculiar voice which seems at once to laugh at Charley and to invite him. He feels her hard body grow tense in his arms. She makes a brusque movement as if to release herself, and then he finds they are closer than before. She says in the same half-jesting tone: "To-night, Charl."

"All right, then you needn't come, see. Trouble is, Liz, you aint nothing but a gurl, see; you don't believe nothing till you sees it, and then you says, it aint nothing neither."

"Well, I am a gurl, too," in a sharp voice.

"Ere, ere, temper."

"And you're a boy. I hates boys—dirty cruel villains that spoil all." She tries to spring away from Charley who protests in surprise.

"Ere, ere, wots all this abaht. I ony said you was a gurl."

"So I am—I wouldn't be a boy if I could. Gurls is worth a million boys. The cruel tricksy varmin." She struggles angrily.

"I never did nothing to you, Liz," Charley says in astonishment, and then in sad tones: "Praps we'd better go now."

Liz at once lies still. Her breathing has stopped. She seems to be in rigid suspense. Charley says: "We're warm now—we better go."

"Where shall we go?" she asks.

"Ome."

"But you said we could go somewhere else." Her mood forbids her even to say America.

These changes of feeling are beyond Charley. But he feels the new tension in Liz both of muscle and resolution. He is excited by that nervous warmth and readiness, by the spring of her muscles, which mean only that Lizzie, too, is growing up.

"You'll come, Liz?"

"How could us go so far?"

"Easy as opping a lorry. First Twyport, then Southampton —wont be no more than going over the ferry at Longwater."

"And never com℈ home no more?"

"Yes, of course we will. Wen we're rich."

"Rich—how could us be rich?"

"Everyone's rich in Ammurca. Wy, father says chaps wot cleans the streets get a pound a day—a pound a day—three undred and sixty pound a year."

"How could they—to jess ornary chaps—three hundred pounds a year. That's a ta-ale, Charl."

"They got the money, see—they got gole mines, and oil

wells—they got all the money in the world. They got such a lot a money they as to bury a lot of it."

"Bury it, that's a ta-ale, Charl."

"They can't use it, see, aint nothing they avent got. Aint nothing in the shops they avent bought already. Thass wy all jobs is a pound a day in Ammurca. Ya couldn't get anyone to do nothing for less."

"A pound a day—would ee get a pound a day too?"

"Course I would. I'd ave to. They all does."

Lizzie reflects, tense and full of obstinate caution. But obviously the details have moved her. "Truly, Charl," she breathes.

"Course you got to work."

"I could work too."

"You'd ave the ouse work."

"House!"

"We'd ad to ave a house, wouldn't we?"

"To ourselves?"

"Course it'd be a little un to start with."

"But, Charl, children couldn't have a house."

"Course I'd dress old, see, and you'd ave to put your air up."

"I could too. Yess. I could"—with another tremor of delight as belief forces itself upon her incredulity—"I don it already—rolled behind with two skewers—and I could put a handkercher down my front—I don that, too, on Longwater fair day."

"Course yar could—thass easy."

"But a house——"

"Yers, and they as real ouses in Ammurca. Everyone as a bathroom and a garridge."

"A bathroom—like at the Hawes."

"Better—with silver taps—silvery, of course—that don't want no cleaning. Big ones with ot and cold on."

"They coulddn, Charl, not all of them."

Charley begins to swear to the bathrooms, but Lizzie brushes aside this fantastic suggestion. She returns to common sense.

"If we go in a house together, people will talk, we'd have to get married."

"Course we will, silly."

"D'you want to marry me, Charl?"

"I said so, didn't I? Twyport day."

"But not playing. It iddn a game now, is it?"

"Oo said it was a game—didnt we go to Twyport? All right then, ave it a game and stay at ome."

"I'm sorry, Charl—tis easy, ant it. I hopped a lorry once with Su, half-way to Twyport."

"Thass it, Liz—you got a spunk for anything, aven't you?"

"And you'll go to parson."

"Wot—go to parson?"

"For to get married—you won't mind, Charl. In Ammurca, I mean—I wouldn't know how to talk to parson about getting married."

"Go on, Liz, you ony got to say. It's is job, see. You pay im."

"But he med think I wur too young—he med get talking at me and when they people talks quick I can't hear un proper."

"All right, Liz. I don mind. I don mind nothing."

"No, you don't mind. But you been raised in Lunnon."

"That aint nothing—aint nothing in getting married—it's the ouse, see—our ouse we want to make it nice."

"We couldn't have oilcloth on the kitchen floor, could we?"

"I'm going to ave oil pictures in the parlour."

Lizzie doesn't bother to follow these poetical fancies. She is concerned with the wonders that are incredible only to her ambition. She murmurs: "Bathroom."

"Bathroom! I'll ave a swimming-bath—ere, don't think I'm being funny. Swimming-baths is easy. You dig a ole in the garden, see—and put cement round and paint it blue with fishes swimming and then you put a greenus over and flowers in the greenus—palm trees—little uns, of course—you eat the water so you can swim all day and, of course, you'll ave the gramaphone playing like Ginje's uke."

"With silvery taps," Liz murmurs.

"And I'll ave a rock garden, see, and yers, I'll ave the rock garden on top of the greenus, see, on iron bars. It's easy—course you'd ave a little un to start with. Big iron bars'd cost too much—and wen you'd go in the greenus, you'd go in a kind of cave, see, and you'd open a little iron door like in a dungeon, and suddenly all the lights comes on—yallow like the sun and the palms wave—course, we'd ave a fan in the roof."

"You don't mean it really, Charl."

"All right, don believe me, and go back and be wopped."

"I won't, I won't, I do believe you, Charl—I do truly."

"Thass it, Liz—I knew you got spunk."

"I bant afraid, Charl—if you'll learn me. I'm a good learner if you tells me exactly. All us Galors is good learners, but Mum speaks too quick and loud. Su tells me better than anyone, but she's not time, poor deurr."

"You'll come with me, Liz—you'll come to Ammurca."

"I will too—this very night."

Charley seizes her in rising excitement and gratitude. "And you believe me—you believe it's easy, Liz. Wy in Ammurca, people wouldn't think nothing of it. With all the gold and silver and the dimonds and the shops full a things—they give em away because there aint no room to keep em no more. And we'll ave the swimming-bath too, and the greenus, and Liz, spose we ad some statues in the garden—I don mean big uns like in the park—but jess little uns, cheap uns, to begin with—two or three—course, they'll ave to be wite uns, to show, and we'll put em up agin the edge—in little oles cut out. Ere, Liz, you aint listening."

"You learn me, Charl." She holds him tightly and murmurs apologetically, as if to herself: "It wur the bathroom I couldn't get over. I coulddn see how they got the money for all they bathrooms."

"Bathrooms is nothing in Ammurca. D'you believe in the greenus—afterwards, of course—after we've saved a bit?"

"I believe it all, truly I do and we'll go this very night."
Lizzie, having reached belief, believes with energy. She clasps
Charley firmly as if to catch hold of belief. "Why shouldn't
we, Charl, of course we'll go, and we'll have the little house—
it's easy in Ammurca, iddn it?"

"There you are, Liz." Charley exults in her belief which
makes all his works of imagination seem real to him. He
crushes Liz in his arms, crushing his own muscles in the same
act, as if trying to express in pain a pleasure too keen and
triumphant for words.

"You and me, Liz."

"I do, I do be-lieve, Charl—I don't know how I do, but I
do truly, and we'll go this very night. Oh, Charl, must ee do
so?"

Lizzie has been dimly aware for some time of a purpose in
Charley's movements. But, confident of her strength and
unafraid of boys, she has given it no attention. She has had
more interesting things to think about. Now, looking angrily
at Charley, she sees on his face a mixed expression of mischief
and resolution. At the same moment he looks like a boy trying
some impudent trick and a man set upon his object.

But the moment she speaks and thrusts him away, he releases
his pressure. He says in a strange voice: "Believe me, nothing."
It is the tone of a child snubbed in a moment of happy and
careless invention.

At the same moment, Liz, looking up, sees his eager laughing
face, half mischievous and half triumphant, flash into a kind
of sulky embarrassment. Instantly she gives way to him. She
is his in mind even before she draws him to her arms and meets
him with her body. She will do anything to save the happiness
which belonged to them both a moment before.

"But I do be-lieve," she cries.

Charley does not move for a moment. She realises how
deeply she has wounded some sensitive nerve. She presses him
gently to her. "I do be-lieve ee, Charl—the liddle house and
the bathroom, too, with silvery taps and all."

"And the greenus," his voice hovers between suspicion and rising hope. But, like a snubbed child, he puts the test high. He wants the strongest reassurance.

"And the greenhouse, Charl—even the statues."

She is no longer, as she was three minutes before, dependent and humble; at the mercy of his imagination. She is humouring, consoling a sensitive child. She sighs. "The garridge, too."

She gives a slight shiver of pain and at once recovers herself. "Tis all right, Charl—and the garridge and the moty car."

"That aint nothing in Ammurca," Charley murmurs as if in a dream.

"Noa, of course not." Liz wipes his damp forehead with her hand. "Poor Charl."

Charley lies limp and trembling in her arms. She is startled by this collapse. She bends back her head to look at him and says: "And the swimming-bath. I believe ee, deeurr. Cross my heart."

"With the palm trees—little uns," Charley murmurs. He is almost asleep. Suddenly he opens his eyes, and seeing her anxious face bent over him, he smiles and says: "You all right ole Liz."

"Yes, it's all right." She presses him again in her arms. She is suddenly frightened. Her elation has sunk away. "You won't leave me, Charl."

Charley is already asleep on her arm. He smiles and frowns at the same time, like a small baby after a meal. The girl looks at him with a perplexed forehead. The wonder-worker, the hero, who has filled her with faith and happiness so strong that they still vibrate in her nerves, has suddenly turned into a dependent child.

Her arm is aching beneath him, but when she tries to move it he stirs and half opens his eyes. Involuntarily, by the instinct of the natural love that lives and grows in her for all dependent things, she bends her arm to shield his eyes from the light with her hand and is careful not again to move her aching arm.

Charley's eyes close and he breathes evenly and smoothly. But Lizzie's expression as she looks at him is still full of responsible anxiety. She touches his forehead again with her hand and frowns a little. She does not really think that he is feverish, the gesture expresses only the concern which takes her, an anxiety which binds her to Charley and Charley to her. Then for a long time she gazes at the fire. Her arm beneath Charley has become so painful that she is sure she cannot bear it another moment. But she goes on bearing it. Gradually her forehead smoothes, her lips close upon the lines of endurance. She is not thinking of anything. Pictures pass across her recollection: the black water of the pool; Charley a small dark patch in the water; her father and mother waiting for her at home; and then, again, a little house in America, painted white, an oil stove with four burners painted blue.

But the house is so small that it is like a doll's house from a long way off; the stove is like a toy in a shop window. Lizzie doesn't believe in them any more.

Her father and mother, on the other hand, are as large as life and searching all Burlswood for her.

Charley stirs and sighs, throws out an arm. Responsibly she gathers him again into the blanket. A definite thought occurs to her and she frowns. "They can't really do nothing to me— not to matter."

43 Mrs. Parr, coming down at her regular hour of six to clean the house and light the fire, found the two children asleep on her hearth-rug and wrapped in her horse-blanket.

When she waked them up they stared at her in amazement. The boy then scrambled out of the blanket, grabbed his clothes from the line and rushed out of the door; the girl, crimson, pulled the blanket still more tightly around her.

Mrs. Parr was not surprised. It was her foible, as an old

woman, to be surprised at nothing. She said only: "A nice lot of trouble you're laying up for yourself, Betsy Galor."

"I fell in the water."

"I bant asking no questions, you bant my gurl, thank God, and this bant my trouble. Get in your clothes do, and be off home afore worse happens to ee—if worse can happen."

Lizzie still stares at her.

"Hurry up, chile." Mrs. Parr pulls down the clothes from the rack and throws them at her.

"Please, I bant got nothing on." Liz does not want to dress in front of the old woman.

But Mrs. Parr, though she is not vengeful, has fixed categories of idea. She has placed Lizzie among the lost, the bad, and therefore she considers that she has no right to modesty. Modesty in such as Liz is conceit. She says only: "I can see how you are and I see how that boy Charles was, too. I bant saying nothing. Bant none of my business, thank God. But you better hurry, young missy, if you don't want Mrs. Brown in the kitchen telling all the rest of em at the 'Green Man.' "

Lizzie is forced to creep out of the blanket. Mrs. Parr stares at her with a contempt which the child feels over every inch of her skin. Scarlet, trembling, with tears in her eyes, she creeps about the floor, gathering her clothes and putting them on in the clumsiest fashion.

"My lord," Mrs. Parr says, "that a human being can be so pitiful—it's a moral."

Lizzie, fully dressed at last, creeps out of the back door and runs home. She is once more a bewildered child, overwhelmed by immediate fears and completely forgetful of everything else.

She approaches through the quarry field, by the back way already discovered and contrived by Charley. As she climbs to the window Susan pulls back the curtain and opens the sash. Susan, with dark shadows under her eyes, is indignant. "Wherever you bin, Bessie? I bin waiting for you all night."

"I fell in the water. Did father come home?" Galor now

and then, when some animal was ill, spent the night at Hall Farm.

"Of course he did, but I told mum you were in bed with a headache, and when she came in I said you were in the garden." The garden, for the Galors, means the jakes, housed in a garden shed.

Lizzie, almost crying with relief, climbs through the window and gets into bed. "You wur clever to think a that."

"It wasn't clever—twas a lie. I'm always telling lies for you, Bessie. Whatever didn't you come for?"

"I fell in the water."

"I suppose you went off with that Charley?"

"Nobody didn't see me."

"Course they did. I saw you and Phyllis Hawes saw you and a lot of those boys did. They were all standing there when you went in the trees with Charley."

"How could I come home? I was all wet."

Susan has got back into bed. She says in a nervous and impatient voice: "I don't know which is worse—sisters or chilblains."

"Oh, Su, are they very bad?"

"Teacher said she couldn't read my sums and she gave me a nought again. I'll be bottom this week. And then you don't come home and it keeps me awake all night. However shall I do my Shakespeare revision?"

"You could a gone to sleep, Su."

"How could I sleep when you weren't here? I couldn't think what you were doing."

Susan's affection for Liz was as unconscious as the motions of her arms and legs. She did not know whether to be more annoyed with Lizzie or her headache or the chilblains. "Whatever have you been doing, Bess?"

"I wur afeared to come home. I wur sopping."

But Susan's question is a form of protest. She is not really interested in the answer. She says mournfully: "And on a Tuesday, too, when I got arithmetic."

"I'm ever so sorry, Su." Lizzie suddenly puts an arm round Susan, who is so much surprised by the caress that she is silenced for a moment. She says at last, suspiciously: "Did you want to borrow my cold cream again?"

"No, I don't want nothing."

Susan shakes off the arm and turns her back. She says gloomily: "I spose I'd better try to get some sleep."

Lizzie lies close to Susan. She wants to touch her, not for warmth but because she needs the contact. She wants to soothe, to caress Susan, to make her happy, and at the same time to satisfy a longing within herself which can only find happiness in that exchange of feeling. She thinks of Charley with fatalist resignation, as something that has happened to her; part good, part bad, but already in the past. She does not rely upon Charley for anything, even affection. He is, after all, a boy. She is glad at last when her mother thumps on the bottom stair and shouts upwards: "Su-san, it's seven gone."

This is the signal for Lizzie to begin her day's work. Since the supervision order she has done the whole work of the house. This has arisen naturally from the Galors' view of their duties under that order; to keep Lizzie, at all costs, from contact with the London boys, and to reform her by strictness.

At the same time Lizzie is well accustomed to housework. She has done much from her earliest years. It has come before all other tasks, even when she was at school. Galor's hours are those of a cowman, from five in the morning till any hour at night. Mrs. Galor helps at the shop. But the Galors are saving people, who are very ready to earn an odd shilling.

But Lizzie finds no hardship in work. She has always enjoyed cooking, sweeping and cleaning. Like other children, she likes any task which has immediate results in use or beauty.

But though Mrs. Galor now does little work in her own house, and even, when she is not helping in the shop, would rather chat in somebody else's kitchen than sweep her own, she keeps up from habit and convention the manner of an overworked housewife. She therefore refuses to let Lizzie into the kitchen until she has at least poked yesterday's ashes, and when she is there treats her as a nuisance.

Lizzie, at the second thump and call: "Now then, Bessie," springs out of bed, pulls on her boots, runs downstairs and begins to fill kettles and cut bread. Mrs. Galor, bustling about with a broom, shouts at her: "Now hurry up with that tea." She has never discovered that Lizzie can hear one person's speech, at a normal loudness, from several yards. "Your father'll be here directly." Galor comes in to breakfast after the morning milking and the Tawleigh delivery.

Liz, to her own surprise, says with sudden tenderness: "Poor mum, it is a job, ant it?"

"You're a job," Mrs. Galor bawls. "Look at that frock all tore out again; it's bin wetted, too." She takes Lizzie by the arm and pulls her across the floor to examine the hole. "More trouble than six Susans. Can't even put you in good service. Better if you'd been blind, it would. But it'll have to be service somewhere, soon as this miserable war's over. You'm big enough. They'd take ee now for vegetables at the sylum— they on't be too particular bout a charcter. Here, gimme them pins, and don't ee catch it in nothing till I get a minute to sew it."

Lizzie is used to these speeches. She knows she is a family anxiety. But now, for the first time in years, she is hurt. Her mouth trembles and she says: "I bant so bad at hearing, mum."

Mrs. Galor, naturally kind beneath the rough layers of worry, looks at her in surprise and says: "Now don't ee take on now— grizzling and grussling. What's wrong with ee this morning? I'm behind as it is." She darts away to the oil stove to alter Lizzie's setting of the wicks. "Where's that kettle? Oh, my laws, not that one—the little one. It's for your father's tea."

Lizzie brings the other kettle and Mrs. Galor, putting it on, says again: "Whatever is wrong with ee this morning? But I haven't the time."

She would like to say something tender and consoling to Lizzie, but she has lost the art for lack of practice. She can't find the form of words. Even "dear" sticks in her throat. But suddenly she says: "Like a piece of seedy cake?"

"Oh, please, mum," in an astonished voice. Mrs. Galor darts away to the cupboard.

"Hurry up, then, if Susan comes she'll want a piece and we can't afford seedy cakes for breakfast every da-ay."

Lizzie sits down to eat her cake. She can enjoy the cake and still remain in terror of the retribution hanging over her.

Susan is her only means of communication with the world. She suggests to her that it would be a good thing to speak to Charley Brown.

"I think you better keep away from that boy, Bessie. You don't want the police in again."

"I will, too—but he med know if anyone's telled on me."

"How would he know?"

It is beyond Lizzie's diplomacy to make Susan useful. But Susan, like other small girls, apparently has unexpected powers of understanding. She comes back at tea-time with the news that no one is talking about Lizzie; that the boys are interested only in a new feud with Morton.

"Is Charley's friends going to fight Morton?"

"No, Charley has no friends. It's that horrid little boy with carroty hair—Basil they call him."

"I hope he kills un—I hates that Morton."

44 Charley had been elected chief of the anti-Morton faction, by Basil, simply because he seemed to have reason to hate Morton. Basil's own quarrel with the boy was a new one; Morton had pushed him into a ditch.

Basil had a new deadly enemy and a new close friend every week. No one was surprised by his sudden rage against Morton. But neither Ginger nor Charley, whom he claimed for allies, was anxious for a fight. Ginger never fought anybody. His steady refusal to take part in battle, except as a critic and adviser, might have given him a reputation for cowardice. But for some reason it did not do so. Ginger was highly respected and continued to be respected even when he flatly refused to attack Mort.

Charley, however, not only agreed to fight, but suggested half a dozen plans for destroying the enemy, by ambush, flank attack, lassoo, boomerangs or clubs.

Basil at once became his enthusiastic friend. Yet Charley disliked Basil and felt no desire for revenge against Mort. His instinct, when he was abused, was to forget about it and fill his thoughts with more amusing stuff. He was terrified of Morton. His mind was not running on gangs and gang-fights, but upon Lizzie. He felt safe with Lizzie. He knew by now that Mrs. Parr was not going to tell upon them and his mother had loyally explained to Lina his whole night's absence from the Cedars by declaring that he had been too wet and cold when he came into Parr's, to be allowed to go home. He did not fear trouble and he did not want to see Lizzie, but she was always in his feelings. He did not think of her often and he carefully excluded from his recollections all the events in Parr's cottage; but at short intervals during the day, she jumped into his mind as if from ambush. Then he was filled with nervous uneasiness and restlessness. He wanted at the same time to know what Lizzie was thinking of him, and never to see her again. He was glad that Lizzie was kept closely to the cottage because she would have no chance of coming after him, and asking him about his promises, but, two nights after Mrs. Parr's discovery, he slipped out from the Cedars in order to go down by the quarry and hang about in the bushes behind the Galors' patch, on the chance of seeing the girl. He felt curious to see her face as if he had never seen it before.

He saw nothing, however, but the candle being lighted in the attic window, and he dared not go nearer the cottage.

Meanwhile his active mind and the whole day had been filled with schemes for defeating Mort. At lessons in the morning, Basil held war councils in every interval, and even passed a note during history. "Sunday is the best day for M," to which Charley answered, "I'll take his K off him any time."

He did not want to fight Mort. He felt a miserable certainty that Mort would beat him with contemptuous ease and that he would have no mercy on a beaten enemy. Mort was capable of anything. Cruelty, and boys like Mort in whom he felt a ruthless quality, always terrified Charley. His imagination gave him penetration, by intuitive feeling, into the dangers to be feared from those who take a delight in cruelty; their persistence, their desire always for greater cruelties, their complete lack of scruple, their enjoyment in giving pain.

He was wretched with fear. But when Basil, choosing the best and most reasonable of Charley's own plans, made arrangements for the battle on the next Sunday afternoon, in Church Lane, he said: "Ere, we aint going to wait till Sunday, are we—wy not now?"

"Cos you can't get out afternoons by yourself cept on Sunday, and cos Morton won't be ere till Sunday."

Morton was accustomed, on most Sunday afternoons, to hang about in Church Lane in order to accost Milly Roy, or some of her friends, on their way to service.

Charley, of course, knew very well that he was not supposed to go into the village, except with an escort, on a weekday.

Basil, having arranged for the fight, told everyone about it. For the next week, the villagers, going about their business, noticed that the yells of the noisier vackies, to which they were already accustomed, were a little more frequent. But they could not detect any difference in their form. They did not know that hi, Bill, wait for me Sunday, which had been an invitation, was now a threat, or that the answer, I'll be seeing ya, was a defiance.

In London, both these speeches, uttered in the same tone, would have brought instant inquiries to know if there was going to be a fight and where it might be found.

Among the vackies, even those, the great majority of the

thirty billeted between Tawleigh and Burls, who had taken no part in the active gangs, there was much excitement. All of them, even the prim little girls like Irene, who had never spoken to Charley, knew that gang warfare had broken out among the factions in Burls.

The Cedars, as a whole, supported Basil and Charley; the vicarage was for Bill and, therefore, Walter. But a good part of the Cedars party deserted to Bill when Walter gave them to understand that he and Mort had promised, for his part, to smash Charley so that his own mother wouldn't know him.

45 On the famous Sunday, Charley, in the morning, had no supporters except Basil and Bert. Basil came to him, after midday dinner, armed with two stakes, into one of which he had driven a four-inch nail. He proposed that Charley should hammer this nail into Mort's body.

Charley chose the plain stake, partly from chivalry, but also from conservatism. He had used a club before, but not one armed with a nail.

"The plain one'll do—you don't want to murder the chap."

"Thass wot e deserves."

"Ere, got to fight fair."

"Not with Mort. E wasn't fair to me, was e, or Ginger." Basil's idea, or feeling about law, is that the man who wilfully breaks the law has no legal rights. "You take the nail—I chose a rusty one on purpose, so it'll poison im."

Charley protests. "E only pushed you in the ditch." He has forgotten his own misery in the same distress.

"But I done nothing to im," screamed Basil. His pale cheeks seem green with spite. "I done nothing. E just did it for wickedness. E thought e'd get away with it—cos I was too little for im. But e aint going to —e's going to pay for it, Mr. Bloody Frog-face. Were's Arry and Ginger? Wy aint they come? The dirty blasted funks—I knew they wouldn't. You can't trust em—nobody but you, Charley." He recollects suddenly how much he depends on Charley to secure justice, and turns to him with flattery. "But you can do it, Charley—you can do it by yourself. You aint afraid of Mort. You could fight ten Morts—ony thing is—it im first see, ketch im from behind and slosh im under the ear. Knock im silly first go off —then you poke is silly eyes out with one finger."

"Yers, but wot about Bill?"

"I'll take Bill on—Bill ain't no good—I'll *nail* im," flourishing the stake. "You'll ear from Bill—I ates im, too—but not like Mort. Bill's a dirty swine, but e aint a wicked swine."

At six o'clock, time for the evening service, a fine clear evening, when Basil and Charley were already in ambush behind a broken wall in Church Lane, Mort and Walter came through between two groups of girls going to church. Mort was jumping about in a most extraordinary way, pulling his long pink face into absurd shapes and shouting what he would do to Charley Brown and Basil Siggs.

"I'll murder the bastards," he shouted in a terrible voice; then suddenly turned round and walked backwards, leering at the girls behind and performing a kind of jig. It seemed as if his threats were a kind of joke; he appeared to be laughing at them himself. Then he drew himself up, strutted importantly and shouted again in a terrible voice: "I'll take the knackers offen them."

The girls are pretending not to hear, but walk close together, peep over their shoulders and laugh and wriggle among themselves, so that the two parties, in their winter Sunday clothes, look like two groups of velvety moths, brown and blue, shaking their wings and fluttering about some object in their midst.

Mort is suddenly annoyed by the giggles, his nose turns redder, and he scowls at the girls, hitches his thick shoulders, lounges from side to side of the road and bellows: "I'll take their tripes out of em and tie em round their bleeding necks."

Walter, walking behind, is laughing and dancing sideways

from enjoyment of Mort's ferocity, the girls' fluttering excitement, and the fine evening. His good-natured face is full of frank careless pleasure.

Suddenly Charley and Basil start up from behind the wall and rush upon the pair; Walter gives a loud laugh, shouts Bill, and flies down the lane to take cover at the back of the lych-gate.

Mort, dodging Basil's first blow, catches his stake, twists it out of his hand, gives him a kick in the groin which sends him rolling on the ground with a scream of pain, and turns on Charley.

Charley shuts his eyes, aims the stake like a lance and charges home. He receives a stunning blow on the head and hears a yell. He opens his eyes and sees Mort leaning against the wall with his hands clasped over his stomach. He is gasping like a fish. The girls have run ten yards away and are watching from that distance. One of them, Milly Roy, carrying her prayer book, calls out: "Give un another, Charley—the ugly to-ad." Charley, grasping the situation, swings his stake and hits the foundering Mort over the head. Mort gives a hoarse scream, turns away and, covering his head with his hands, rushes down the lane. Charley follows closely, slashing at him. The girls scatter. Walter behind the lych-gate, is bellowing: "Bill, Bill, urry up—Bill." His voice is urgent with terror.

Just as Mort scrambles over the stile behind the lych-gate and joins Walter in the sanctuary of the churchyard, the organist, a cobbler, called Sale, comes out of the parish hall at the corner of Church Lane with half a dozen choir boys in their black gowns and surplices. Charley steps into cover on the outside of the lych-gate, divided only by the stile from Walter and Mort on the inside. But he watches his moment, with the stake held ready for another prod, as soon as the choir has passed.

Suddenly Walter's shouts of "Bi-i-i-ll" quiver away in the midst, and he says in a small astounded voice: "Bill." One of the choir boys turns a grinning face towards the stile, and

Charley, Mort and Walter all at once see the red shining cheeks and flattened black hair of Bill.

Neither does he seem in the least ashamed of himself. On the contrary, he has obviously been looking forward to some such moment of triumph, for he exclaims joyfully: "I'm seeing ya—wot ho!" Walter, Mort and Charley, forgetting their war, are now all on their feet, staring. Bill, rolling along with his usual round-shouldered heavy gait, roars with laughter in their faces and says: "Won't mother be pleased."

Even after he has passed them he can't help turning round again and walking backwards several paces in order to enjoy their amazement. He touches his little black tie, pushes forward his chin from his Eton collar, smooths down his surplice, and then raising the first and second fingers of his right hand towards them, jerks it into the air with the final gesture of triumphant scorn.

"The bleeding skunk," Mort says. "I knoo he had some dirty game on."

"I knew he'd been going to church," Walter said, "but he said he had to, living with the sexton."

Suddenly a yell is heard. "Smash im, Charley. Go on, stick im in the liver." Basil, as pale as chalk, is limping towards them. In his right hand he carries a large stone taken from the wall.

Mort and Charley, as if by a simultaneous recollection, turn towards each other. Charley aims his stake, but Mort, hitching his thick shoulders, says in an impatient tone: "Ow, chuck it, we ant kids. What you playing at, anyhow, knocking me about —damm near poke me guts out and then lay me head open. Look here." Mort suddenly stoops and presents his long narrow skull at Charley's face, then tenderly parts the long pale hair with his knotty fingers. "Look at that."

In fact there is a long jagged cut across the scalp, bleeding slowly into the hair. Charley looks at it with awe. Basil, lowering the stone, advances and peers suspiciously at it. He pouts out his crimson lips and says: "It's bleeding all along."

Mort stands up again and says in a mournful, disgusted voice: "It's a ospital job. You can't go knocking people about like that; and what for? What you think you playing at?"

"Go on, oo chucked me in the water?"

"I dunno. Who chucked you in the water?"

"You did—week before las."

"Week before last—heogh." Mort snorts and spits. "You mean that little game we had—around the pool. Why, we wur all laughing, and then, fortnight after, you come along with a club and bust me block open. A police job. I knoo Bass was a toad, but I diddn spect it of you."

"You look out, Mort," Basil squeals. But Mort stands in the gloomy, sullen dignity of one actually bleeding. His blood cries to heaven and obtains protection. "So that's why you come at me in the road here—in me Sunday clothes, too. Bash me when I aint specting it. Look at me, all over blood—and all for nothing."

Charley is indignant. He says to Mort: "You it me, too."

"Course I did. When I saw you coming at me with that club. It's lawful. If I'd bloody well killed you it would a bin lawful—coming at me like that. I haven't time to go to court, but I ought to do it, too. It ought to be stopped."

"Wot ought to be stopped?"

"Chaps like you going round and bashing fellows over the head—it's grievous bodily harm."

"Ere, you come along to my mother and she'll wash yer ead."

"No, I ant going to have nothing to do with you, Charley Brown. I'm fed up. You act too dirty for me. A bloody good thing if none of you vackies had ever come here—a lot o murderous toads, that's what you are."

Mort puts his hand to his head, withdraws it covered with blood, looks at it for a moment with a grand, mournful anger, and then walks slowly away towards the Tawleigh road.

Even Basil is left subdued. He says: "A good thing if you ad cracked is cokernut," but his voice is not convinced. He says uneasily: "Wot did e mean about a police job?"

"I dunno." Charley, finding the stake in his hand, suddenly throws it over the churchyard wall. He then rubs his hands together in the manner of Lady Macbeth.

"E better not," Basil says mysteriously. "I could tell the cop something about Mister Morton—an his friend Bill. I know wot their game was—I seed em at it in the quarry."

Charley walks thoughtfully along the road towards the Cedars. He feels no triumph even when Walter suddenly looks out from the cross-roads corner and cries: "Good ole Charley. You licked him in style. My eye, didn't he cop it."

Walter's admiring voice, even more than his words, expresses his desire to be on good terms with Charley, but Charley takes no pleasure in it. He answers: "I ad to do it, adnt I? E it me first."

"Wot did e mean," Basil says gloomily, "a police job?" And then after a pause: "Course, you bashed im proper, Charley—e was a orrible sight. But a police job—yah. Wot the police want to come putting their noses in."

Suddenly, without a word, he turns down the road and makes for home. Walter, alarmed by Charley's strange manner, turns off to the left towards Wickens lane. Charley arrives at the Cedars in good time for supper and it is not till bed-time that Lina discovers to her shocked distress that his scalp has a three-inch cut under his thickening hair, which is stuck together with blood.

"Who did that to you?" she asks in angry surprise.

"Wasn't nobody, miss. I run into a post."

"You're too headlong, Charley. You'll kill yourself some day."

Charley is silent. He is still wondering if he has not been too severe with Mort.

46 On the Monday morning Charley found himself the hero of Burlswood, or at least of that part of it which knew of the Morton feud. In the morning he was con-

gratulated by several members of the class; in the afternoon, while walking sedately through the village with Lina, he was stared at by such superior beings as Norman. Fred Hawes, walking past him as he stood outside the shop, turned round in order to walk past him again on the other side, and finally called out in a shy, hoarse voice: "Hullo, Charley!" He then ran off, tripping in his large boots, towards the Hall. But his speech, from so shy and proud a boy, was a high compliment. In the evening Charley heard, from his bedroom window, for the first time in six weeks, Ginger's shrill whistle. He could not resist it and he did not want to do so. He ran downstairs into the yard, already in twilight, and slipped into the back drive. Ginger was behind the gate-post. He said only: "Some of the chaps are there."

"Were?"

"Corner of the road."

"I say, we can't go there—we'll be seen."

"It's pretty dark," and he added: "they're all there."

"Oo are all?"

"The whole lot. Coming?"

"I'll come."

Charley understood at once the meaning of Ginger's invitation to the cross-roads. It was as though a humble marching colonel were asked to take command of the guards at Windsor. The cross-roads had been Bill's headquarters.

In five minutes he was at the cross-roads, standing only a little back from public view, in the screen of the gate into Hall field. In front of him, like courtiers in the ceremonial circle, stood Ginger, Harry and Bert. While he was still appreciating the meaning of his position, that he was the undisputed master of the Burlswood gangs, Mort and Walter came over from the Green Man and joined the party.

"Hullo, Charley! What a game about old Bill, wasn't it?" Walter's method of ingratiating himself is to be lively and to have always a topic of conversation flattering to his new master.

Mort says nothing and looks extremely sulky. His shoulder

is more humped; his nose seems to hang lower as he swings down his long neck. Mort has an enormous star of sticking-plaster on his head and wears no cap. Charley, who is also plastered, wears, by order, a cap.

All are startled by Mort's appearance among them, like a pike among sticklebacks. They edge away from him and stare at him with various expressions of blank precaution and open curiosity. Charley says at last: "Ullo, Mort!—ow's yer ead?" Mort answers with tragic dignity: "Never you mind my head, Charley Brown. What you going to do?"

"To do?"

"He wants to come along with you," Walter explains.

"Ya, I will, too. It's my right. I bant so set on pinching, neither. But you bant going to leave me out. If I choose to come."

The small boys ostentatiously turn their heads and look at each other; this is a rite, expressing a high degree of surprise and perplexity. Mort says in a sullen tone: "So I'm asking you, Charley Brown, what you going to do next?"

"We haven't seen any pictures lately," Ginger murmurs.

All look at Charley, who is too much surprised to speak. He is not accustomed to suggestions from outside, and it makes him uneasy to find that he is regarded as a natural provider of treats.

"I'll get a car," Ginger says. "But not like last time—better from Longwater. They don't know us there."

"Course I'll take ya to the pictures," Charley says.

"Pictures," Mort says with disgust. "What's the good of that—I can go to pictures any day."

All stare at him in his turn. Mort, apart from his reputation for ferocity, has a peculiar influence and attraction, arising perhaps from his voice and manner. His voice is a rich bari-tone; his manner seems to say: "No nonsense, please, this is a serious world and I'm a serious person."

"Were can you see the pictures?" Harry shouts suddenly as if astonished by this statement. "I aint seen none for six weeks."

"The real stuff is in Burls House," Mort says.

There is another pause. Charley feels a peculiar anxiety, not deep, but persistent. He seems to be waiting for some inevitable crisis.

"You'd never get in," Ginger says, "with old Roy in the kitchen. He has ears like a microphone, too. You can't get near the place."

Roy is the Burls House caretaker and gardener, occupying, during the Wandles' absence, the kitchen on the ground floor and an attic bedroom. His home is in Church Lane.

"Couldn't get into Burls House," Mort grumbles, "and Roy goes to the Green Man every night and home after."

"You get in then—there's iron shutters on all the windows."

"I diddn say I'd get in—I said climbing chaps could get in— but Charley Brown doesn't fancy that job. He's afeared of the officer."

"I aint afeared. I could climb in easy." Charley, having said this, feels his anxiety grow stronger so that he gives a sudden deep exhalation. All eyes now turn towards Charley.

"Wot, Charl, you aint going to bust into Burls Ouse!" Harry cries in a tone of horror and amazement.

"Cavee," Ginger says suddenly, and nods towards the road. Mort and Walter turn round; Charley looks up and sees a little group of natives, including Albert, Sam Eger and the old sexton, watching them from the middle of the road. They have just come out of the Green Man. Sam Eger, seeing Mort turn, calls out: "Don't ee be telling, Mort, they'm too young."

Charley is already over the gate, Ginger round the corner. Mort humps his shoulder and lounges down the road with the disgusted air of a big dog insulted by an unexpected noise.

47 Charley reached the Cedars in time for tea. His absence had not been noticed. He carried tea cups and the cake-basket to Miss Small and two lady visitors in the most graceful manner and afterwards, when Lina drew him

225

into the conversation, said with all sincerity how much he enjoyed the country and what a change it was from London. He felt all the time the same anxiety, but now it was becoming an habitual settled thing like a chilblain. He was used to it, and he felt also that it would come to a normal end in due course.

In fact, that same evening, while he was dozing over a book in front of the fire, he heard Ginger's whistle. He paid no attention to it. He was too comfortable, and he could not think of an excuse to go into the back drive on a cold, wet evening.

But he was not at all surprised to hear from Walter, after the first lesson in the morning, that he had undertaken to rob Burls House. Walter was at once excited and shocked. He treated Charley still with respectful smiles, but they were nervous, embarrassed smiles. He avoided being left alone with him.

At five o'clock, in the middle of tea, Ginger's whistle was heard. Charley joined him at half-past five, actually in the Cedars wood shed, and in another two minutes it was arranged for him to break into Burls. Charley himself made the arrangements, and it seemed to him, without particular reflection, that there was no other course open to him. This was the point to which events had been bringing him for the last three days, or even three months. But he did not undertake to steal anything from Burls except money, and possibly drink. When Ginger reported that Mrs. Wandle had jewels worth many thousands of pounds he said only: "Yah, but ow you going to change em into cash? Sides, wot you take me for, a bloody thief?"

He felt strongly, like the lawyers, that stealing property from houses was quite different from bag snatching. He only differed from the lawyers in his feeling that money was not in the same class as other property. Possibly even a lawyer, finding half a crown in the street, would put it in his pocket and tell his friends about it as a lucky strike, whereas he would not dream of misappropriating so much as a gold safety-pin found on the same pavement.

226

48 At seven he stood in the Whiteboys field under the big hedge. Ginger, Harry and Bert breathed close to him in the darkness. The boys stood round him, firing questions. Even Ginger had asked three or four times: "How are you going to do it, Charley?"

Harry was almost crying with excitement. He kept on saying: "Don't do it, Charley, you'll get copped."

"Oo'll cop me if Roy aint there?"

"Roy went along half an hour ago—saw him myself."

"Yes but, Charl, e always tells Mr. Arrison to ave a look round."

Mr. Harrison was the village policeman from Tawleigh substation, who now and then rode slowly through Burlswood on his bicycle looking on each side of the road in turn. This did not convince anyone, even himself, that all crimes would be detected. Obviously if a crime happened to take place at the one time in the half week, or week, during which he was passing through Burlswood it was still possible that it would occur when he was looking at the wrong side of the road. Mr. Harrison knew this as well as anybody. But he still turned his head from side to side as a mark of authority and an assurance to the public that their interests were receiving attention.

"Mr. Arrison," Charley cried. "E couldn't catch a kipper with a toasting-fork."

"But they can see you from the road, Charl."

"Nobody wouldn't look and if they did they wouldn't believe emselves."

Charley was full of bravado arising from the sensation which always throbbed in his veins and muscles at such a moment, something between triumph and terror. Now, of course, that he was confronted by the occasion, when he had to answer at once the question how he was going to do it, he saw that there was only one way, the way he had partly followed before, from the garage roof up the fire-escape to the third storey, where it turned back towards Ginger's old room. At that corner, as he had noticed during the afternoon, the rain-water spout went up to the top storey.

Burls House had a roof walk round the top of its walls inside a low coping. The spout entered this coping. Charley thought, or hoped, that it might be possible to reach the top of the coping from the top of the spout and somehow to pull himself over it.

The idea of the feat made his legs shake and brought out the sweat on his forehead. Heights frightened him. He had climbed innumerable spouts into second-storey windows, ten feet from the ground, but he did not care to look downwards, even from that altitude.

He saw himself clinging to the Burls spout four storeys from the ground and the picture made him feel sick. He was meanwhile leading the way to the garage. He said with calm triumph: "Ow am I going to do it? Wy, up the spout."

"Charley, you couldn't."

"You'll be killed."

"That aint nothing," Charley answers. "That's easy—the real job is coming down with the beer. Were you said they kept the beer, Ginger?"

"Pantry cupboard next the sink. You don't want to bother with beer, Charley, do you? Besides, it's probably locked up."

"Course you don't want no beer, Ginger. All right, Arry and me'll drink it. I brought my tools."

Mort's voice out of the darkness says suddenly: "If you wants to pla-ay the fule."

All are startled, and Morton says, in the same solemn and warning note: "You didn't think I wur here, did ee?"

"What d'ya mean, Mort—oo's playing the fool?"

Mort says nothing. But his silence accuses Charley of frivolity and light-mindedness. Charley, feeling this charge, asserts himself: "You shut up, Mort—oo's doing the job?" He flashes a small pocket torch, a present from Lina, at the boy.

"All right, Charley Brown, I bant knocking anyone over the head with iern crows."

228

"I didn't it ya with a crow."

Morton makes no answer. His silence seems to make Charley's objection trivial and factious.

"Ere, come on," Charley says sharply. His nerves are jumping. "Show the way, Ginj."

Ginger leads a way through a gap in the hedge and the house-garden to the kitchen yard. They stand here under the garage. From its flat roof the fire-escape goes to the third storey.

It has been raining, and the sky is still full of clouds, but they are now broken into small jagged pieces, like ice-floes, bright-edged against the dark metallic blue of the cold sky. These grey fragments, with their glittering edges, are being carried south-westwards towards the Atlantic, at a speed which seems great because of the immense mass and weight of the objects in movement. The moon cannot be seen. It is still low. Little light falls on the house or into the yard. No lights, of course, are showing from the house. But the house itself can be seen sharply outlined against the rushing clouds and the dark-blue starlight. It looks immensely tall. Charley, after one glance upwards, does not raise his eyes again from their own plane. He says suddenly, in a sharp tone of command: "Gimme a leg, Ginj."

Ginger takes him by the legs and hoists him up the side of a water-butt. He puts his feet upon the rim and at once swarms up the pipe to the flat roof of the garage. Then he disappears into the shadow of the house. The fire-escape rings faintly. A moment later Harry says in a tone of horror: "There e is— see im, on the spout."

In fact, Charley can be seen clearly, against a cloud, as a small flat projection on the edge of the bare wall. This projection is moving slowly upwards. It reaches the coping and sticks. Minute after minute it remains there, as if the boy has been frozen to the wall.

Harry gives a moan and says in a panic-stricken voice: "E can't get down—e'll fall."

"We can't do anything," Ginger says.

"E's stuck at that there elbow were the wall comes out," Bert says with interest. "I thought e'd find it awkward."

Charley, in fact, has stuck under the coping. He cannot bring himself to let go of the spout and reach up across the bare wall to the top. Neither can he go down, and every moment he grows weaker. His arms are trembling, his fingers are losing their power to grip. He begins to pray: "Oh, God, oh, Jesus, save me, don't let me fall—don't let me be killed —I don't want to be killed. Oh, Jesus, you save me, I never do anything bad again—I never climb no more spouts."

He is astonished at his folly in offering to climb spouts. One hand slips off the spout. Charley is beginning to tilt backwards when he makes a spring with his legs and grabs the top of the wall. A minute later he is lying across the coping on his stomach, see-sawing to and fro, kicking wildly in the effort to throw himself forward. At last, by some extraordinary contortion, he gains a few inches and tips gradually, head downwards, till he tumbles over upon the leads.

He lies there for a long time, completely exhausted, worn out in nerve and muscle; shaking like an old man exhausted by eighty years of effort.

Then he thinks: "I've done it, I've done it," and the idea flies through his nerves like electricity. He jumps up and glides along the roof wall, trying each window. An attic window is open six inches at the top. He pushes it down, raises the lower sash, and creeps through.

He turns about the small spotlight of the torch and sees that he is in a bedroom, the caretaker's. The bed is made and a small alarm clock ticks on a box beside it.

Charley opens the door and passes quickly along the passage to the stairs. On the floor below he enters three bedrooms in succession. The light falls on dressing-tables in sycamore and ivory; and mirrors which, at the touch of a switch, light up within and show him his own face so brightly illuminated, without a single shadow, that he cannot recognise it. Having discovered this new kind of looking-glass, he examines all the looking-glasses and turns on all switches in order to see the lighting of the rooms from cornices and standard bowls.

He remembers only at the last moment to open drawers; he is not disappointed to find nothing in them. He is now impatient to explore further, to explore some of those rooms which still, from the time of the drawing lesson, remain in his memory as glimpses of a real magnificence, not equalled by the made-up films.

He does not turn on the lights in the rooms below, for fear that the tall windows, facing the road, may let out some gleam. But the torch illuminating and isolating with its small circle some brilliant object, a gilt Italian table, a painted chest, some bright painting, surprises him each time as if by a new and particular revelation. It seems to say: "Look at this—here's something you didn't expect."

The torch has discovered a strange woman in stone, with painted eyes; when Ginger's whistle is heard. Charley jumps and runs to the window. But he does not open it, and there is no chink from which to look out. The heavy, old-fashioned shutters, wood within, sheet metal without, are barred half-way up with flat strips of black iron, padlocked to a staple in the shutter-case.

He listens for a moment, then looks at his watch, also a present from Lina. It is a quarter to eight. He has wasted at least half an hour playing with his torch. He becomes at once business-like, looks in the bureau drawers, opens cupboards. Nothing is to be found except a stamp-book half-full, left in a blotter; some little ivory figures, no bigger than walnuts, in a drawer; a paper-knife, made like a miniature sword, which seems to be silver; and a gold, or imitation gold, pin, with a fox's head.

He puts the stamps, one of the figures, and the pin in his pocket and makes for the service door of the dining-room. He means to escape from the basement.

But a light is coming from beneath the door. Charley puts

his ear to the key-hole and listens for two minutes. He turns the handle slowly, then opens the door with equal slowness, to avoid a creak. At last he can see through the opening. The light is a single naked bulb at the top of the cellar stairs. A door beyond on the right is ajar and the room within is lighted. Charley presumes it to be the kitchen. The pantry door on his left is wide open. He can see glass-fronted cupboards within and a sink at the far end.

Charley hesitates and looks again at the light from the room beyond. But a whim has seized him and he can't resist it. He feels even the beginning of a laugh; a movement in the bottom of his throat. He opens the door a foot, passes sideways through into the passage, and so into the pantry.

He carefully shuts the pantry door and tries the cupboard next the sink. It is locked.

He opens the glass-fronted cupboard above, which has four shelves. On the upper three, spread with brown paper, stand rows of wine-glasses and tumblers, on the lowest a pile of trays.

Charley lifts the trays and takes a gimlet, with a cork screwed over its point, from his pocket, carefully removes the cork and bores a hole in the shelf. When he has bored four holes close together, he begins to chop between them with a knife. He has brought a fine saw, the upper six inches of the carpenter's key-hole saw, broken off and wrapped in a bundle of thick brown paper. But he dare not use it so near the kitchen.

It takes him ten minutes of careful, rapid work to cut round three sides of a square six inches across. Then he puts his coat over the hand which holds the knife, and with a quick push breaks the flap upwards. He flashes the torch through the hole and sees rows of bottles, some standing, others lying below in a rack. He puts down his arm and draws up four bottles of beer. He places the flap of wood down among the remaining bottles and sweeps all chips into the hole.

He replaces the trays, and is just about to pick up the bottles when, as an afterthought, he climbs on the sink, takes all the glasses from the top shelf, removes the brown paper, which is secured by drawing-pins, puts the glasses back, and pins the paper on the bottom shelf under the trays.

Then he puts two bottles in his coat pockets, takes one under his arm and, carrying the other in his left hand, slips down the cellar steps.

The cellar, as he has noticed that afternoon, opens upon a small sunk yard, formerly the basement yard. An empty, deserted kitchen stands on one side of it, empty larders on the second side, the cellar on the third. The fourth is occupied by a diagonal flight of stone steps leading to the modern kitchen yard. Charley passes through the cellar to its outer door. This proves to be locked, and the window, covered with black cobwebs, is barred. Charley therefore ascends the mountain of coal, pushes up the iron trap of the shoot, and climbs out into the yard. He eases down the trap upon his toe to avoid a clatter. Nevertheless, it drops the last half-inch with a sharp clang. A roaring bass voice is instantly heard from the kitchen window: "Hi! Who's there?"

Charley does not run. He slips along by the wall, turns the corner of the garage, and passes into the back avenue. The boys have disappeared.

49 The moon has risen and the whole countryside, the trees on the neighbouring hill-crests, the fields sloping into the valley, with their various textures of plough grass and root; the Hall Farm orchards and its sharp roofs, set at all angles like cut logs in a river jam, are as bright as a lantern slide in black and white. Charley does not notice this beauty, but it affects him. He feels glad that the boys have disappeared. He is pleased to find himself alone. He blows out his cheeks, in the accepted gesture of relief, and says to himself: "Thass over—and well over." He strolls along, not looking about him but feeling the stillness of the illuminated trees; and the rush of the clouds overhead, carried on the tail

of some north-eastern storm. He laughs suddenly and says to himself: "Cor, those eyes give me a start—that's a new one, that is." He is remembering the painted eyes on the stone woman.

Suddenly Harry springs out of the hedge and catches him by the sleeve. "Charl, wot you bin doing?"

"Ullo, were's the chaps?"

"They run off wen Roy ollered. You all right?"

"Nah, I got two broken legs and two broken arms. Like some beer?"

"E didn't see you, Charl?"

"Yers, e copped me proper—I'll be in jug tomorrer."

"E didn't, Charl."

Suddenly the boys dash round them in a swarm. "Charley."

"You got away, Charley?"

"E did, e did—coo e's got a bottle in is pocket."

"We thought you'd stuck, Charley."

"You were so long, and wen old Roy began ollering, we ared off."

Charley swaggers among them in glory. "Ave a drink, chaps —ave a drop—it's on the ouse—Burls Ouse—ere y'are, Ginj— ere y'are, Arry—come on, Bert—all welcome."

"Is that all you got?" Mort asks.

"Cept one and thrippence in stamps. Aint nothing in Burls —they put everything away."

"Did you try the safe?" Ginger asks.

"Didn't see one."

"It's in the pantry—with a wooden door in front."

"Aint nothing in it," Charley says. For some reason he does not want to rob the Burls safe.

"They sent the silver to the bank, I expect."

"Did ee look?" Mort asks.

Charley turns angrily on Mort. "Ere, oo's running this show?"

"You are, Charley Brown, but you bant much good at it."

"All right. If you don't like it, op it and run your own."

"I bant saying nothing, Charley Brown. I never cracks chaps over the head, from behind."

This produces an uneasy silence. Charley is embarrassed. But Mort, having spoken with great dignity, suddenly bends his long legs till he is actually shorter than Charley, rounds his little greenish eyes, thrusts forward his face and grins. Nobody else smiles at this joke. No one can tell what it means; whether Mort is deriding them for having fallen to his plea for sympathy; or making a fool of himself to amuse them, or a fool only of them, and perplexing them, out of a kind of humour. They feel that there is something of all these elements in the fixed idiotic grimace and straddling pose. But none of them knows how to deal with this expression of them.

Charley, after staring at the boy for half a minute, turns away. "Wot about a fag?" He pulls out a packet of cigarettes.

Ginger has already pulled out his own packet of cork tips. "Here you are, Charley—you deserve a good one."

Morton, who has slowly drawn himself up again, and allowed his face to change into its normal expression of a tranquil sad dignity, says: "Ant no one going to give me one?"

He takes the cigarette without thanks. "Don't you make game of me, Charley Brown. I bant so fulish as I look."

"I wasn't making game of ya, Mort."

"Yes, you wur—you think I'm a fule. So I may be a fule, but you're a bigger one. Lunnon is the biggest town, and Lunnon fules are the biggest fules."

"It's nothing to do with the size of London," Ginger says.

"Noa, you'm quite right, Mr. Fant," making even Ginger look foolish.

Charley, half an hour late for supper, excuses himself on the grounds that he has been with his mother. He knows, of course, that his mother will support his statement. Lina doubts this story, but she takes care not to show it.

Charley, for half a minute, feels a slight uneasiness, almost amounting to shame. He wonders why he is always being obliged to tell lies to Lina Allchin. It seems to him that he cannot help himself. Things are always happening to him, and involving him, which cannot be told to her. Fortunately, he thinks, she is not curious or suspicious.

50 Charley in fact, on the next day, was full of consideration for Lina and even for Miss Small; he was the picture of attention in class, but he could never answer a question or get a sum right. His drawing of the octagonal pot entered its third week and looked very much more unfinished than at the end of the first. It was also much dirtier, and somebody had dropped a blot of red ink on the soup plate.

Lina was perplexed. She knew that the boy's politeness was not hypocrisy. She could tell very easily the difference between the cold forms of Brander, who, as she knew, cared nothing for her, and the affectionate good nature which prompted Charley's clumsy service.

"It's the age," Miss Small suggested.

"It's an awkward age—of course—one forgets how old he is."

"I don't trust Master Charley very far."

"That's where I think you're wrong, Doris—you've got to trust them."

"Not blindly. I'm pretty sure it was young Charles I saw last Sunday slinking down behind the lych-gate—you know that's where all the local riff-raff lurk on Sundays, especially after dark."

Lina turned suddenly very red and said: "I know it wasn't Charley because he was here—doing his drawing. You've never been fair to the boy, Doris. I think it's a shame."

"My dear Lina."

"It's a shame—it's a damn shame."

"Well, if you take that tone."

"I don't care what you say—but that's the way to ruin a child's character—especially a boy like Charley who's really

236

affectionate and good-hearted. You've never given him a chance."

Miss Small then left the house, not in a rage, but with a cold and calm resolution never to forgive Lina, which she had found, by experience, much more satisfactory than temper, both for her own pleasure and her enemy's discomfiture. In fact, the hot-tempered and careless Lina was obliged, after only twenty-four hours, to accept every kind of humiliation, to apologise in a dozen forms, to write, to phone, to call, to send flowers and finally to cry; or at least to look as if she was about to cry.

Lina was angry with Miss Small because she was uneasy about Charley. She felt rather than knew that he was breaking the rules of his probation. But she was determined not to spy on him and she could not think of any other policy but the one she had followed, of complete confidence.

She did not, of course, ask herself exactly what she meant by this. She did not say: "Am I trying a new scheme for making a child into a little puppet; a kind of confidence trick which is designed to govern him even when nobody can see what he is doing; or do I want only to establish a personal relationship in which he will come to me for advice and help?"

The question did not even occur to her. She could only follow the advice, which agreed so well with her inclination, and trust the boy; that is, as she interpreted it, refuse to see his delinquencies.

When one evening, after Charley had gone to bed, she saw his figure, apparently fully-dressed, come up the back staircase and slip into his room, she decided that for some reason he had chosen to go to the servant's lavatory downstairs. He was wearing his overcoat for a dressing-gown.

Charley knew, of course, that Lina gave him extraordinary licence, that she avoided intrusion, and swallowed any excuse that he liked to make.

In return, he felt a deep and unquestioning confidence in her friendship.

51 Charley, when he slipped in at midnight from the side door, had not come from an expedition, but from wandering. He had not seen any of his gang since his climb into Burls House. He did not wander now to look for Ginger or Harry, but from restlessness, like a young colt through whose native field a hunt has passed. One night he went to the quarry, simply to gaze at the site of Ginger's cave; another, he climbed the Burls fire-escape and stood for a long time gazing over the landscape. The night was cloudy, nothing could be seen but the edge of the horizon, outlined against a streak of old copper and shadowy masses of cloud above, brown as peat. The trees below were blue-black, as if drawn in ink; the fields like smudges of the same ink. Yet Charley stared for a long time before going back to climb the kitchen roof into his bedroom window. He preferred looking even into this dim cave of a world to going home. On several nights he visited the Galors. One evening Lizzie found in her bed, wrapped in a page torn from an arithmetic book, a silver paper-knife, shaped like a sword, engraved with the crest of an eagle and the initial W.

Two days later the *Twyport Gazette* recorded the first robbery of what came to be known as the Tanborough gang. This was only because the first house robbed was Tanborough; and showed details common to half a dozen succeeding robberies, spread unevenly over the next two months. In all, entry was made by an upper window; only unoccupied rooms were searched, very carelessly, and left in great disorder, and some of the articles taken were of no value whatever. At Tanborough House, for instance, a brass water jug disappeared; at Crocombe, in the next week, a china windmill with movable china sails.

The thieves seemed to be amateurs in their methods of search; but they left no finger-prints and on each occasion were far away before the theft was discovered. Footmarks in a garden bed at Tanborough showed that one of the gang was a boy or very small man; another was a man's size and probably tall.

Inquiries were made at Burlswood. The probation officer called both on Charley and Ginger and gave them a little speech of warning. But the boys' reports were excellent; and the police inquiries pointed more to Longwater where a doctor's car had been missed for two hours one night. True, it had been found less than half a mile away, but the doctor believed that at least half a gallon of petrol had been used. The police formed the opinion that the gang consisted of young men, possibly of good class, who were clever enough at planning and carrying out a robbery; but not enough interested in the profits to take much risk. They made their next inquiries in the villa district beyond Longwater.

In fact Charley had taken no care to plan another expedition. The first was arranged in a few minutes one foggy evening, when he happened to meet Ginger in the road and Ginger happened to remark that Wickens had 'flu. Ginger, though he slept on the ground floor and should have found it easier than any other member of the gang to get out when he chose, had been nearly caught on several occasions on account of Farmer Wickens' nervous light-sleeping temperament.

The peculiar rhythm or order in the succession of robberies afterwards, which puzzled the police, was actually due, quite as much to the weather, or to gang quarrels, as to Ginger's difficulties in escaping from Wickens. Charley was prevented only on one occasion, by the pure accident of late visitors strolling in the garden, from climbing out of his locked and ordered villa, where no one dreamt that boys could creep down a roof at forty-five degrees.

Night-wandering children of any courage and determination, as all probation officers knew, seldom find the least difficulty in getting out of their homes, even when they are supposed to be under special supervision. Getting in is often a greater problem. It is easier to know what the inhabitants of any house are doing, when one is inside, than when one is outside. Charley took far greater precautions in entering the Cedars than in leaving it.

Harry, at Hall Farm, a huge rambling manor-house where half a dozen doors were open often to midnight, while Hawes entertained, often lost his nerve at a critical moment and failed to keep his engagements. But Harry was rather a danger to the gang than an asset. Ginger was indispensable. On half a dozen occasions expeditions had to be given up because Mr. Wickens was wakeful and Ginger dared not even open a bottom sash or move about his room.

But on this first evening, he escaped as easily as Charley, for whom houses of any kind were rather challenges to gymnastics than containers.

The pair met in Hall Farm orchard, after ten o'clock, below the old cyder house. They walked to Longwater, took the car, drove seven miles to Tanborough, of which Charley had heard from one of Lina's visitors, as a fine house, and robbed it, all within an hour. They found very little of value. Even a pearl necklace, taken by Ginger, proved to be a sixpenny counterfeit. Neither took any great pleasure in the evening, and Charley, when he went to bed just before midnight, resolved never to go robbing again. He had enjoyed the drive and the climb; but he had detested the walk home from Longwater. He also disliked very much, after climbing into the Cedars, tired bodily and nervously, the necessity of cleaning his shoes on the bottom of a carpet, and examining his clothes for stains.

But Mort had asked about the necklace the same evening. He would not believe that the necklace shown him was the one taken, and he insisted that he must be told of the next expedition and given his proper share of the loot.

Thus within five days after Tanborough Charley was climbing into the Cedars again, with bruised knees and elbows; boots caked with red clay; tired, bored; and full of a sour wonder at his own folly.

It was on the morrow of this expedition that Susan walked into the Cedars garden, after morning lessons, and coolly ordered Basil to fetch Charley to her. Basil who knew, like everyone else, that Charley and Susan's sister Lizzie had been close friends, was delighted to take the message. Charley came out of the house, in his neat grey suit and knitted blue and white tie, and said with a preoccupied air: "Ullo, Susan."

Charley appeared too sleepy to look at Susan. He stood gazing at the heap of sand-bags, now beginning to rot and burst, which had once been Mrs. Allchin's rock garden. In the middle of Susan's first sentence he suddenly yawned. Susan had said that Bessie did not want his presents and never wished to see him again. She then handed Charley the silver paper-knife. Charley put it in his pocket and said: "Did she say that erself or did you put er up to it?"

"If you go on stealing things, she never wants to see you again. She's quite right too."

"Wen did I ever steal anything?" Charley said, smiling at the little girl.

"It's not a joke, Charley. I think you're a great fool and so does Bessie."

"She didn't say I wasn't to see er again?"

"Don't you come around, Charley—or I'll tell on you. You're not to worry poor Bessie—tis pestering her to death."

Half a dozen children watched their conference and saw Susan march out of the gate, jerking her two short pigtails as if shaking dust from them, and Charley turn away from her with the same sleepy expression which his face had worn all that morning.

"Wot she give ya?" Basil shouted, rushing up to him.

"Wot she give me?" Charley gave him a look dazed with stupidity, as if his brain were really anæmic with sleep, and passed slowly into the house.

For ten days there were no more robberies in the district, then in quick succession, on the same night, three suburban villas on the outskirts of Twyport were broken into by a gang which entered by the roof, and took jewels and silver. The loss was small because it happened that there was little of value

to take. But the police suspected that the Tanborough gang
had been at work, not only by the method of entry, swarming
up a stack pipe and opening a dormer; but by the fact that in
each case small trifles were carried off as well as money. From
one house a coloured print, frame and all, disappeared; from
another, a clockwork speed-boat.

The car used for these burglaries had been stolen from
Longwater and its number was recollected by a garage hand
who had repaired the wing. When, seeing the car in a lane
near Twyport, he went up, out of curiosity, to look at the
wing, four persons, of whom two appeared to be boys, got
out of the opposite doors and ran away through the fields.
The man then suspected that the car had been stolen and
reported it to the police. Nothing was found in the car, not
even finger-prints; but a woman who saw the thieves rush out
of it, flashed a torch and reported that one had reddish hair,
and that another, the big one, had a long face, and one shoulder
higher than the other.

52 This flash of a torch nearly caused the break up of
Charley's gang. Ginger and Mort had felt the light
on their faces and Mort was sure that he had been recognised.
Mort was already disgusted by the poor returns of half a dozen
robberies, each involving discomfort and danger. He was
extraordinarily lazy and would complain if he had to walk three
miles to a rendezvous or a mile from the car. Even while he
rummaged for loot, he was often too careless to open bottom
drawers. He would throw out a drawer on the carpet, and stir
the heap with his foot. Yet he complained when he found
nothing of value and would say: "I be a fule to come along
with ee, Charley—you'll get copped and what for? Nothing."

"Then wot d'you come for, Mort? You needn't come if
ya don't want to."

Mort would then either look sulky and answer that he wasn't
going to be left out, or bend his legs, goggle his eyes, grin like

a professional face-maker, and say: "I'm a fule, ant I, Charley Brown, but what be you?"

It was doubtful if Morton cared how much or how little he received; so long as he got his share, or more than his share; but Ginger was surprised and disturbed by the smallness of the gang profits.

Ginger, it seemed, had hoped to make a fortune out of house breaking. He dreamt of jewel boxes, ten thousand pounds in a portable form.

Meanwhile several boys in the village, both natives and foreigners, knew that Charley's gang had been breaking into houses.

Bill accosted him one morning, as "Ali Baba" and several times called after him in the village "Ba-Ba, Blacksheep." In Bill's mind, almost any idea which referred to any other also meant that other. Sinbad, since he was cast up on a desert island in a turban, was any solitary and dejected person in any strange hat. Because Baba was connected by name not only with black sheep generally, but with forty thieves, he was a general term for thieves and blackguards. When Bill called Charley Baba Blacksheep, he was expressing his sense of Charley's criminality, in the strongest terms.

Basil also, moved by conscience at least once a day, threatened to tell Mrs. Wickens that Charley went robbing, Walter liked to hint at special knowledge in order to say: "But, of course, I shan't say anything."

Charley was more afraid of Walter than of Basil. The latter, though he was spiteful and righteous, was also a Londoner of his own tribe, from the next street. Bill, even though, as a declared Christian, he still made strange gestures, uttered loud yells and pursued the Tawleigh girls, had changed greatly in other ways. He no longer amused himself with small boys or girls. He was looking for a job and when he rode into Tawleigh on the vicar's bicycle, it was usually to meet some actual girl; Rose or Lily or Gladys. His intentions, though still dishonourable, were expressed in an acceptable and reasonable form. Decent and honest girls, knowing his kind, after many years' close study and discussion, had judged him to be good and sound material upon which a married career, for themselves or any other, might later be established.

Charley knew that Bill's shouts were in the class of familiar greetings. Neither Walter nor Bill could frighten him from a course of life, which, though it often bored and disappointed him, was at least a definite course.

53 But one evening when the gang was conferring at the Whiteboys corner, Peter Drake, coming from the kitchen garden with a spade over his shoulder, said: "Keep your eyes open, Charley—Mr. Harrison's been here twice to-day."

In less than a minute Morton was scurrying across the field paths to Tawleigh. He did not dare even to take the road. Ginger and Charley waited only long enough to agree that they had better not risk being seen together for the next few days.

Charley was not sorry to break off with Mort and even with Ginger. He had found no great pleasure in the last expeditions; hurried, muddled, profitless and dangerous. He had been oppressed from the very first enterprise, the Burls House climb, by the sense of futility. He enjoyed planning and forcing an entry into a house, but he had no taste for rummaging or looting. After each robbery he seemed to be exactly where he was before; and though he never allowed himself to think "This can't go on for ever—sooner or later I'll be caught," he felt it continuously. It was a drag on all his enjoyment even of some extraordinary feat of climbing, as at Twyport.

But Peter Drake's warning, while it gave him an excuse to break with his followers and dependants, had peculiar influence upon him, because of its source.

Peter Drake had a special position in Burlswood. He was not amusing, he had no accomplishments; he was not striking to look at. His pale brown face had no good features except a passable chin, small but well shaped, and dark brown eyes.

His job was humble enough; anything that anyone would give him to do. He was extremely poor. The Drakes, mother and son, were probably poorer than the Smiths. Mrs. Drake was bedridden with arthritis, and made only a few shillings a week by sewing and mending.

But everyone in Burlswood spoke of the boy with respect. Phyllis Hawes had a special tone for Drake; her words were the same, but the music was different; even Sam Eger, the blacksmith, a cynic who liked to roar at everybody and to humiliate rich farmers by recalling in public their bad bargains and their neglected machinery, paid a certain respect to Drake. He grinned at him through his enormous white moustache, but the blubber lips which hid behind that aggressive front were a doubting shape.

No one knew exactly why Peter, at seventeen, enjoyed so much respect and even influence in Burlswood. He was well read, he had read everything he could borrow in the village, but he did not quote his reading. He did his work carefully, but he was slow from mere lack of muscle. His ambition was to enter a grocer's shop in Twyport, where a place was waiting for him as soon as some means could be found of taking his mother to the town. The Drakes seemed to feel, without any discussion, that it was impossible for her to go into the workhouse infirmary. They also refused relief. Yet the late Mr. Drake had never risen above cowman at the Hawes', and he had married a labourer's daughter. Peter had not inherited his position.

It was true that every native of a very small hamlet like Burlswood had a much more definite place in society, both for good and evil, than any Londoner. Everyone's character was known so thoroughly that the smallest oddities were noted; and changes, as children grew up or middle-aged men grew down, were recorded almost from day to day. This gave to the village life a colour and texture never found in a town; a rich personal quality. It was not sad; it had probably much more gaiety in it than any suburb. But like family news, which has the same primal interest to all feelings, it was full of important events; love affairs, marriages, births, rumours of fatal illness, sudden strokes of luck or disaster, and those slowly developing tragedies which could nevertheless be followed step by step from the beginning, in a debt or quarrel, to the end in bankruptcy or the break-up of a household.

In this rich drama, lived and discussed every day, everyone in the village, Bert Smith quite as much as Sam Eger or Phyllis Hawes, had a well-understood part. Drake was not peculiar in exciting curiosity, but in the respect given to him, which seemed to be offered to some purely personal quality. It was not what the boy did which made villagers, who had been near him all his life, like Mrs. Hawes or Galor, say with pleasure apropos of a figure on the skyline, or a rumbling noise in the lane, "There's Peter."

Charley, like everyone else, was fond of Peter; of talking to him or merely being with him. He had often helped him to push his milk cart up the hill or discussed current affairs with him in some kitchen garden, where Drake was at work.

He thought him slow and countrified; yet now he was so anxious to know what Drake knew about him, and thought about him, that he could barely wait till next morning to see him again.

54 An hour before breakfast he jumped out of bed and, without troubling to wash, went down the lane to Hall Farm. Drake arrived almost at the same moment, trundling his cart, but Charley, now that he was close to him, was suddenly afraid to make a direct approach.

It was a cold morning with a fine drizzle of rain floating overhead in drifts which seemed rather to cling to all surfaces than to fall on them. Walls, earth, horses, carts, trees and people all were as wet as if they were under deep water; which was not, however, perfectly clear but slightly clouded like snow water. Even the light resembled that peculiar illumination seen in zoo tanks and goldfish ponds; it was bright without any heat and it seemed to belong rather to the atmosphere itself and the objects within it than to any luminous source. It was as if the white-washed walls, Peter Drake's yellow oilskins, Charley's pink cheeks, crimson nose and blue eyes, were all giving out a subdued radiance into the greenish ocean which surrounded them.

In the little dairy, Phyllis and old Mrs. Smith were bottling the milk as it ran out of the cooler. Phyllis seemed to have been made for the duty by a nature with a high sense of the beautiful and also a sly humour. One would have said that the girl was made of milk; the cream of nymphs. On the other hand, Mrs. Smith seemed to have been put together by a careless dustman, out of two sacks full of rubbish tied round the middle with a piece of rope. Even the rope was dirty. Another sack, also dirty, folded into a hood, formed the headpiece of this other, less subtle piece of humour. The two arms which stuck out of the smaller bale of sacking were like the knotty and twisted stems of old ivy, grey and dusty with age, torn up by the roots, which now waved in the air their broken stumps, thick, black and crumpled together as if by blows of a mattock. These were Mrs. Smith's hands, which had done, as yet, only thirty years of work and would be expected to do twenty more.

Mrs. Smith was allowed to bottle the sterilised milk in the spotless dairy only because she had always done so and none of the Hawes family had had the heart to turn her away, or even to suggest that she wash herself. For she was a touchy woman. Her self-respect had to live on such small rations that it was extremely delicate. As Mrs. Smith brought the bottles to the door, Peter filled his hand-cart; and Galor, the old gig, which, since the war, had been used for the Tawleigh delivery. The churns for Longwater had been picked up already by the milk company.

247

When Peter filled his cart, Charley made himself noticed. He peeped into the dairy and said good morning to Phyllis, causing her to say without the least surprise: "Oh, Charley, what a surprise—whatever has brought you here so early?"

"I was just passing, Miss Phyllis."

"You've been a bad boy, Charley, haven't you? I'm ashamed of you. What terrible things you been up to," Phyllis said, skilfully filling three bottles and handing them to Mrs. Smith, who capped them with the jerk of a lever, punctuating each of Phyllis' sentences with a loud clop.

"I'm sorry, Miss Phyllis" (clop).

"Look at the booy, his nose is quite frozen (clop), run in, deearr, do to the fire (clop), and get Mother to give ee some hot tea."

"Thank you, miss, but I got to get back to breafass now."

Phyllis, having finished the last bottle, turned, wiping her hands in her apron, and gave Charley her attention. "I can see you're up to some mischy again. But don't ee go stealing any more, or you'll be breaking Miss Lina's poor heart." Her tone suggested that she was more thoughtful of Miss Lina's heart than of Charley's morals.

"No, Miss Phyllis." Charley was looking sidelong at Drake who had now loaded his hand-cart. He paid no attention to Charley.

Suddenly he stumped out and began to push the heavy load up the hill. Charley ran and joined him. "It's heavy, aint it?"

"Tis better than a yoke."

They pushed it from cottage to cottage, with immense labour, as far as the Galors'. Drake, in spite of the rain, was running with sweat and panting heavily. Charley was always surprised at the enormous labour required day after day to bring the milk up the hill. He felt still more shy of Drake. To speak of his private affairs to this panting boy was like troubling an invalid.

But suddenly Drake said to him: "This is a change for you from Lunnon."

This was a favourite subject between them, and Drake usually opened with this remark. Charley was much relieved.

"I likes it."

"Do ee? I'd rather be to Lunnon."

"It's nice in the country," Charley says, out of politeness—to Drake he always affects this preference.

"Have you ever seen the docks in Lunnon?"

The docks is a new subject. The last had been Westminster Abbey and Poet's Corner.

"No, but I seen the Pool."

"That's where the butter boats come, ant it, and the bacon boats. I've seen pictures of it. That med be a fine sight."

At every halt Drake talks of the docks, especially as a port and storehouse. He describes the docks to Charley, and the methods of distribution from the dock warehouses. Charley admits that he has never seen any of these wonders. Drake says: "Ah, but you woulddn—they're too near you. I daresay now you see more here to Burlswood than I ever do."

"People are too busy to go and look."

After a little pause as if for reflection on this idea, Charley ventures to say: "Miss Phyllis seems to think I'm always up to something."

Drake turns and glances at Charley, a slow mild glance which says clearly: "So you are and I don't think much of it," then he remarks: "Tis none of my business what ee do for yourself."

"You don't think I'm up to something, Peter?"

"If you'll excuse me, I hope you'll not take Bessie Galor with you again. She'm a good soul, too good to spoil herself."

"But who says I'm going anywhere?" Charley cries.

"I don't know, but don't ee let Bessie come with ee. She'm at a restless time, like a lot, I reckon. Leave her alone and she'll settle."

Charley decides to change the subject. "Will you settle down, Pete?"

"Me? I'm settled, on the grocery to Twyport. I bant only stopping here."

"I shouldn't think you'd like to be shut up in a shop all day."

"'Tis a clean dry trade—I'm lucky to get a place in a good firm. I could be married by the time I'm twenty-five."

"Do you want to get married?"

"Well now, Charley, I'll tell ee something—but don't ee tell no one—I'm fixed to marry Su Galor when we'm saved enough. Between ourselves. But you med tell it, too. I believe tis well known enough."

"I wouldn't get married. If I'd saved anything I'd go round the world."

"Noa, Lunnons far enough. We'm going to Lunnon for the honeymoon. Afore us settles down. Won't be able to afford any more travelling, I reckon, when the family begins to come."

Charley, astonished at this dull scheme of life, cries: "And that's all you want to do all your life."

"Noa, tis not what I want, but I reckons tis what's good for me—and for most others, too." Again he looks at Charley with a slow glance, suggesting rather than accusing. "That Morton is another restless one—he'll end in jail for certain. Tis a pity, too, for he was clever to school. But he don't have consideration for himself."

"I shouldn't think Mort would settle down anywhere."

"He would, too, if Milly Roy would take him. I reckon Morton has the nature of a settler—a soft, easy soul. You find Burlswood too dull for ee?"

"Me, no I likes it."

"Ah, you woulddn live in Burlswood nother sixty year. You'll go back to Lunnon where you belong. What will ee do Charley? Reckon I'd goa on a ship; I'd like to see Chiny. They say they be the most civil people in the world and the wisest. With an old kind of wisdom. But that med be talk, too."

Charley was amused by this suggestion. Yet for some reason, perhaps only because it was from Drake, it interested him. For nearly a week he sought the boy out, got up early to help him with his barrow and followed him into the fields to spread muck. Lina, highly approving of the friendship, took care also that Drake should spend some afternoons in the Cedars garden.

All this time they discussed travelling, the odd sights to be seen in the world, and the odd customs of faraway peoples. Peter, in his slow, calm way, revealed bit by bit a large knowledge of races and their history, of their strange religions and peculiar laws. Charley spent hours inventing voyages of discovery for himself, and even examined the Cedars Atlas, and read the ancient encyclopædia, not to check Peter's facts, which he accepted as gospel, but to feed his own imagination.

After a fortnight, when Morton suddenly reappeared one day, demanding to know why he had been neglected so long, Charley told him flatly that the gang was broken up. Charley, at that moment, was a trader in the Pacific Islands, smoking long cigars on a snow-white deck, in his own swift schooner, which danced over blue seas with a hold full of copra and shell.

What made this new ambition so delightful was its possibility. Charley had even found out from a yachting magazine in the dentist's parlour at Longwater that his schooner could be bought for seven hundred pounds. Peter Drake warned him that he would also need working capital, but they were agreed that, with a native crew of five, at a pound a week a head, a thousand pounds would be enough to begin with.

"Say two thousand to make sure," Charley would say.

"Ah, better to make sure—you mustn't run out of working capital. That's bin the ruin of many fine businesses, at the very start."

"Three thousand then, for safety."

In these words Charley gave the project not only ease of accomplishment, but certainty of success. Miss Small, during a fortnight, was as pleased as she could ever be with Charley for his new attentiveness at geography and arithmetic.

55 At the end of December there was a strong frost which put the Hall Farm dairy out of action by stopping the main feed pipe. The milk, except one churn left for local distribution, with an old-style dipper, was all sent to Tawleigh. At the same time Galor was needed at the farm, for the extra labour of winter-feeding the stock. Churns were short. Drake therefore took the gig to Tawleigh, spent the morning on the milk round there, and in the afternoon went on to Longwater with the surplus; gathered the churns, already collected that morning by the milk company, and brought them back at night.

He returned long after dark, so worn out that he went straight to bed.

Charley, at the Cedars, deprived of Peter's collaboration, continued his South Sea plans only for a few days. They died then of their own reasonableness. For Charley, having now discovered the advantages of this new test, in giving pleasure and soundness to an imagined scheme, began to apply it more strictly. He asked himself where he could find three thousand, or even seven hundred, pounds, and he could not invent a plausible answer.

Thus once more he became gradually bored at lessons and unable to take pleasure in anything but his secret drawings.

Lina had discovered, and caused silently to be removed, with sandpaper, the Garden of Eden on the study table. Charley, after the shock of finding the masterpiece gone, had drawn nothing for three weeks. Now, once more, he scrawled his fancies, but only at odd moments, on odd sheets of paper, which he carefully destroyed in case Lina might see them. He was ashamed of his arabesques.

He formed a habit, puzzling to himself as well as Lina, of sitting in his bedroom. It was freezing there. There was no comfortable chair; no books; nothing but the glittering brass bed, a white-painted chair and dressing-table; chintz curtains lined with black sateen. But Charley spent hours sitting by the window gazing on the snow-fields and playing with the blind-cord. He was, though he did not know it, escaping from a boredom which had now gradually infected even material objects in the house; so that the hall-stand, with its coats, the shiny varnished doors, the pretty drawing-room, with its flounced and frilled covers, all gave him the same feeling of emptiness and dissatisfaction as if he had been a hungry Eskimo in a vegetarian restaurant.

But since he still considered himself a lucky boy to be among such luxuries, he did not know why he retreated from warm rooms and bright fires, to his own company in the bedroom.

One afternoon, when he was sitting there, playing with the blind-cord, in a state of boredom approaching imbecility, he heard Ginger's whistle from the yard. In less than half a minute he was on the stairs. Ginger was leaning against the wall beside the back door. He had heard of a house where, according to the reports, there were chests full of jewellery.

"I don't know if you want to do anything about it, Charley, but it seems like a wonderful chance. It's on two main roads, too, so that we needn't worry about the snow. Go by one, get away by the other."

"I'm with ya, ole boy."

56 The same night he and Ginger broke into a villa at Crocombe. They took seven pounds in money, a ring set with small diamonds, a collection of old-fashioned brooches, and a pair of brass fire-tongs, which Charley pushed, at one o'clock that same night, through the Galor girl's window.

He performed this feat, to Ginger's mild disgust, upon a sudden whim, like that which had caused him, in Burls House, to risk everything for two bottles of beer. It was like one of those sudden, absurd exaggerations with which, by a similar whim, he had sometimes embellished and often spoilt his best stories. It was like the glass organs with tunes hopping out of them, or the diamond bath.

It was also a contact with Liz. It would make Liz angry; it would enrage Susan; but Charley, in the new mood which had carried him away from the moment when he had said to Ginger, "I'm with you," found enjoyment in this kind of practical joke. He had never been so reckless in climbing, so daring and careless in walking about an invaded house, so impatient with Ginger's fits of caution, or so careless of his feelings. When Mort and Harry joined them, too days later, he received them both with roars of laughter.

"Ere they are, the Siamese twins."

"Wot you mean, Charl—wot you mean?"

"Ole Mort stops when you begin—that's poetry, too."

Morton detested chaff. He looked furiously at Charley and said: "Don't ee laugh at me—I don't like it—what I came for was ma money. Seventy pound you took to Crocombe—that's twenty-three pound six shillun and eightpence. Call un seven."

"Wot you mean, Charl—oo begins wot?"

"You don't know nothing that ever appened and Mort knows everything that never appened."

"You give me my money."

"I'll give ya a kick in the left eye for fourpence ha'penny —five years' credit and sixpence off for cash."

Mort opened his mouth to speak and Charley burst out laughing in his face. This laugh, and something new and reckless in Charley's air, silenced Mort. He shut his mouth again and looked only sulky.

The Crocombe robbery, which was not at first attributed to the Tanborough gang, was followed by three more in the same week. Then after a week's pause there were two on successive days. In the third week of January four different houses were entered in three days.

The police and the local papers had now recognised the gang, both by a comparison of footmarks and its idiosyncrasies. But they were still convinced that one at least of its members, probably the chief, came from Longwater.

This was not only the largest centre of population, with a

few authentic criminals, but the robberies were on all sides of it. An average of the distances from Longwater to each house broken into worked out roughly at ten miles in every direction. Longwater was a focal point. The last and strongest argument was that no house in Longwater itself or within three miles of it was ever touched.

It was Charley's idea to leave Longwater houses untouched and to treat it as a centre. Charley now spent his whole time planning robberies and keeping his followers in order. He was so changed in spirit that even Harry noticed it and complained: "Wot you laughing at, Charley—you always laughing at us?"

"I ain't laughing at ya."

"Wot you laughing at then?"

"I just laughing."

"He's laughing because he's going to get us all copped," Mort said.

"Ere, wot you want me to do, cry?"

"You won't find it so funny when we're copped."

"Cheer up, cully, you'll soon be dead."

"You're off your nut."

57 Charley was perfectly sane. He knew very well that he was not behaving sensibly, that he was taking absurd risks for very little return. He knew that Ginger's and Harry's criticisms were well founded, and that he was bound to end in the hands of the police, probably very soon. But he paid no attention to criticism or common sense. He felt "that's all right if I was a different sort of chap." He smiled at good advice as an old rheumatic man smiles at an acrobat. It was as though a wall of glass stood between him and everything rational. He could look at reason, appreciate it, but he was obstinately prevented from making any use of it. It was through this wall of glass that he could examine at will his relations with Lizzie, and Lizzie's own position, while he contrived at the same time to play the stupid game of putting

stolen goods through her window, even large objects, difficult to hide, like a fire-screen. He knew that Lizzie must be dreading each dark night, and the report of any new robbery; he would say to himself: "It's a shame on poor ole Liz, putting er in a stew," but every time he entered a strange house he would at some moment find himself laughing and saying: "Wot about that for Liz?" Then again, to the fury of Ginger and Mort, he would drag home some heavy object of household furniture, in order to give himself the mysterious satisfaction of playing another practical joke on the girl of whom he was most fond.

But the will was not like a partition. It was a tunnel of glass set on an incline, down which he was flying. He knew where it ended, in a police-station, but this amused him more than anything else. He made jokes about it in the same tone and manner as his stepmother was accustomed to make jokes about thrashings.

Charley's red-rimmed eyes and pale cheeks, during the mornings, worried Lina. She diagnosed his illness as low 'flu. She took his temperature and gave him a special breakfast food, full of vitamins. In return he laboured at the drawing and even struggled to please Doris Small. He felt more guilty towards Lina Allchin than anybody else in the world. She was perhaps the only person towards whom he felt any guilt. He did not feel guilt to Lizzie. It was as though some private knowledge told him that she and he were in league.

He could not, with all his efforts, keep awake at arithmetic or make any progress with the copying of pots, but the sincerity of his will to do so was so obvious to Lina's intuition, quick in any affectionate relation, that she very easily forgave him the absence of practical results.

58 After a fiasco at Crocombe, where the whole gang was chased across the fields by a dog, Charley proposed a return to the Twyport district. They were at a

new rendezvous, in the wood behind the churchyard. It was also a new time, just after two, before afternoon lessons. Mort, Ginger and Harry were already there; Bert, though he had never been allowed to join an expedition, or was told of its plans, was roving about them at a few yards' distance.

"You ain't going out again, Charley?" Harry said. "Wy, we was out Satday." Harry was terrified as usual. It was astonishing, though no one was astonished, that Harry should join in the mildest crime.

"I ant going to Twyport," Mort says. "That's flat. Why, it's in all the papers that bitch seed me and Ginger—but I suppose you wants to get me copped."

"Oo said we was going to Twyport?" Charley says, rapidly changing his ground. "Nah, with the cops watching all the roads for pinched cars. Nah, we going to do a job that doesn't need a car, see."

"You got some sense at last," Mort says. "I bin saying Burls House for three weeks.

"But I tell you there aint nothing in Burls."

"We might try it, Charley. We ought to go for a real scoop —this chicken feed's no good. We're bound to get copped, anyhow. Let's get copped for something worth while."

"Ark at Ginj," Charley says, laughing. "E's blue about is wistle. Go on, Ginj, I'll get you a real good un nex time. Wot about a bugle—a silver bugle?"

"Don't you let him make a fool of you, Ginger," Mort says, "with his silver bugles."

Charley makes a sudden dart at the boy, who, taken by surprise, winces backwards and then turns and runs away among the trees.

"Buzz," Charley shouts, laughing at Mort's strange disjointed antics. He then strolls back to the gang, with a reflective grin.

"That chap's as good as a play—e's a fool, too. I got something good. Down at Longwater. Full a money and jewels. Two old ladies, stone deaf and half dotty. They couldn't ear

257

us if we let off guns. Two old servants sleeping in the basement, and deafer nor the old ladies."

"Sounds too good to be true," Ginger has grown suspicious
of Charley's projects. All of them are full of jewels and guarded
only by imbeciles or cripples.

"Ask Bert, then—is mother as washed there for years."

"And I thought you didn't want to go near Longwater?"

"Oh, wots the odds, so long as we're appy?"

There is a pause. Ginger understands the suggestion under-
lying the last remark and says at last: "Short life and a merry
one."

"Yers, and bes chance we'll ever get of making our pile, or
somebody's pile. They got dimonds on their nighties."

"Draw it mild, Charl."

"Sort of—course, they're a bit eccentric. Bert's ma seen em
coming down to supper with their eads sticking out of dimond
drain pipes."

"And rings in their noses," Ginger says. But his expression
has changed. His face is at once smoother and sharper. He
begins to hum, a sign of returning confidence. "Sounds better
than the last—what's the time for it?"

"Arf past seven wen they as supper or after ten wen they go
to bed. Supper-time's best for me. Miss Lina's out to dinner,
and I'll say I'm going to mother."

"All right by me." He hums. "Every cloud is silver."

"We won't take a car this time, and we won't go together.
We'll meet at the bridge this end, seven o'clock."

Bert, appearing from somewhere, says breathlessly: "Shall
I come, Charley? I knows a back way in the garden—over the
wall."

But all three at once reject Bert. Ginger says: "He'll do
something silly."

"I got a botany class at three with the parson," Ginger says.
"I must run. Seven at the bridge."

"Thass it, Ginj. I can give ya some gloves. Miss Lina just

give me a pair a new ones, knitted em erself. You can ave my old ones."

"Thanks, Charl, but I got some new ones, too."

"Slong, ole Ginj." The ole is an apology.

59 At seven, without having given another thought to the scheme, Charley is by the bridge, on tiptoe with joyful tension. It is a dark night and he says: "Bit a luck the moon's gone in. I'm a lucky one, I am."

Mort lurches out of the dark and stands silently between Ginger and the trembling Harry, who jumps and utters a little cry of fear.

"Ullo, Mort!" Charley says. "Didn't know ya was coming."

"Course I wur coming. And look here, Charley Brown, why diddn you tell me the time? I had to go and ask Ginger."

"Thass all right, Mort, but don't go banging round, see, and don't go smashing any winders like las time."

"I never smashed nothing. It was Ginj."

"That's a lie," Ginger says coolly. "Say it again, you swine, and I'll stick my knife in your belly."

There is a short silence. Mort gives a heavy breath but does not answer. Ginger has never made a threat before or offered violence. But all feel that he is ready, at that very moment, to murder anybody without the slightest hesitation and that is, somehow, exactly what they have always known of Ginger.

"Come on," Charley says suddenly, feeling that action is required. "We gotta get off the road."

He leads them through a field to the back of the house and leaves them there behind the garden wall while he explores the garden. As usual, he has never seen house or garden before. But he finds on the right of the house a stack-pipe which, as far as he can see in the twilight, passes close to a second-storey window, open at the top. There is a door into the garden from a room below as well as the back door opening into a kitchen yard.

Charley returns to the party and says: "All set, boys? Got on your gloves?" All are wearing woolly gloves except Ginger, who has somewhere obtained a pair of lady's brown kid gloves. Charley puts on his new gloves, presented by Lina, with great satisfaction. He enjoys wearing such handsome gloves and he feels again his gratitude to Miss Lina.

Mort, who has taken a watch as his share of loot from Tanborough, gives the time, and Charley quickly climbs the pipe and leans out to the window. But it has a catch which prevents it being pushed down from above or up from below. Charley leans further across till both hands are on the sash, then suddenly springs upon the narrow sill. He can now put his arm through the narrow opening and reach the safety screw. The sash slides down. Charley climbs slowly and carefully over it.

He finds himself in a small sewing-room or linen-room. The door is half open. He pulls a pair of socks over his shoes and passes silently into a corridor. He reaches the stairs, and now he can hear high-pitched voices below. But he is no longer startled by voices. He is used to moving about occupied houses. The tension of anxiety is no longer fearful but joyful it gives him quickness instead of perplexity.

The hall below shows two doors on the left; the back one must lead to the room with a garden door. He slides down the balusters in a flash and opens the hindmost door. A voice says from within: "Is that you, Ella?"

Charley shuts the door again and darts across the hall through a door which, standing ajar, shows a dark room within. He shuts the door behind him and flashes his torch. He turns the key, goes to the window, opens it and chirrups like a small bird. After a moment Ginger appears below and he stoops down and whispers: "Aint no good for Mort and Arry. Tell em to wait down ere."

Ginger runs away with the message and returns. Charley looks through cupboards, Ginger examines a large bureau. They hand the loot: a small cash-box, stamps, five shillings in postal orders, a silver paper-knife, a silver ink-pot, a silver photograph frame, two fountain-pens, out of the window to Mort. Then Charley cautiously opens the door and they dart upstairs. They pass through the bedrooms independently, ransacking dressing-table drawers. Suddenly Mort appears behind Charley. "Wots the game, Charley Brown?" he asks.

"Aint no game, but we gotta be quick."

"What am I to do?"

"Do; wy, wait around for the stuff."

"Where you expect us to wait? You done all the work already, and got all the stuff, I'll be bound."

Charley and Ginger, eagerly seeking, pay no attention to him. He goes off to the next room, not yet reached, and they hear him dragging out the drawers and turning them upside down. Suddenly there is a crash. He has knocked over a jug.

A voice downstairs calls out: "Who's that—who's there?" Then a man's voice says: "Don't go up, aunt, I've telephoned the police." He probably wants this to be heard for he repeats a moment later in a loud voice: "Don't be frightened, Ella, I've telephoned for the police."

A woman's voice, uneven with fright, says: "I knew I saw somebody going upstairs."

Charley and Ginger look out of the windows, but there is a sheer drop to the ground and no pipes on the side of the house.

Morton comes rushing into the room and says: "Ere, you ear that? We're copped. Oh, my gawd, and you tole me it was safe."

"We got to run for it," Charley says. "Put something over your faces and run down the all."

"The door's locked," Ginger says.

"We got to open it, then. Ere, I'll look after the door."

Charley and Ginger snatch up garments from the nearest drawer and hold them over the lower part of their faces. They rush downstairs followed by Mort's thundering steps. Screams are heard, and the man's voice says: "Don't be frightened, it's all right, they can't get in here."

Charley finds the door secured only by a Yale. He turns the handle and all three rush down the gravel drive towards the gate. A woman's shrill voice from behind screams: "Stop them, thieves—thieves, stop them. "

Charley, rushing through the dark, grasping a brass bedroom jug under one arm and holding his left-hand pocket, bulging with small trinkets, with the same hand, bursts out laughing. He can hardly run for laughter. He hears Mort somehow close by in the dark garden cursing and this also makes him laugh.

A car flashes across the bridge from Longwater and stops at the gate. Ginger takes Charley by the arm and wheels him to the left. He murmurs: "The cops."

Charley is still laughing and arrives at the garden wall so breathless that Ginger has to push him over it. He falls on the short grass in the field and says: "Ole Mort, wot a cure!"

"Come on, Charley," Ginger drags him towards the open field. Charley collects himself, gets up without great hurry and says: "No, not that way, keep to the wall. Ere, Mort—come on, you great elephant—follow Ginj. Were's Arry? Arry— Arry got the jitters agen; Arry—aint no good waiting. Buzz along, Ginj—ere, follow me." He darts along the wall, rounds the corner at the back of the garden and only then turns through the fields. As they scramble through the first hedge they see a car's headlights flashing across the fields and along the side wall of the house. Ginger says: "Good thing we came this way."

"Aint any other way," Charley says, to whom their course has been obvious from the beginning, as a map ready drawn in his mind's eye.

"Now get along to the left."

"The left—but that goes to the water."

"Yes, that's it—we got to get over the bridge, see. They'll never look that way—way they came."

He leads the way along the muddy shore among tangled roots and overhanging scrub to the bridge. "Now—one at a time"—crawling—"and if anything passes get up and look like you aint barmy."

Ginger crawls away, keeping below the level of the parapet. He is invisible in its shadow.

"Go on, Mort."

"I aint going. What's the good of going Longwater side? How we going to get back?"

"All right, op it and get copped."

Charley stoops double and passes on to the bridge. A car comes down the road. He stands up and leans over the parapet, holding the can upon the outer side of the bridge in his hands. As the car lights fall on him he spits into the water. The car passes and he runs across the intervening distance, joins Ginger, and they take once more to the fields, following the shore of the Longwater for two miles until they find a boat and ferry themselves across. An hour later, extremely tired, they reach Burlswood. Charley is exultant. He says every few minutes: "Cor, that was a good un."

He bursts out laughing. "Poor ole Mort, ear im coming down the stairs."

Then again he marvels at the events of the evening. "Crikey, wot a night—that was a winner."

Ginger, calm and tired, makes no comment.

"An I got me brass jug. Poor ole Liz, she'll ave a fit wen she puts her feet on it, and Susan'll ave two fits."

When they arrive in the rendezvous, at the site of the old cave, they find Harry there, in the last stages of terror and misery.

He has escaped over the garden wall and been hunted through the fields behind the villa for two miles.

"That gives us away," Charley says. "Wy did you run towards Burls?"

"I wanted to get ome. Oh, Charley, you don't think they'll cop us?"

"Nah, sall right, Arry. Don't you worry. Ere, pour out."

"I aint got nothing. Mort took it."

"Two rings and a chain, a half-dollar, sixpence with a hole in it and a gold pin," Ginger says, counting the loot.

They swear they will never go out again, but Charley is found grinning.

"Wot you laughing at, Charl?"

"Wasn't laughing."

"Grinning, then."

"Toothache in me big toe."

He walks off into the darkness, still grinning, with his brass can wrapped in a piece of newspaper.

But when the next night he climbs up to the attic window he is received by Susan, who pulls back the curtain and tells him to go away.

"If you don't go away I'll tell Father."

Suddenly Charley turns sulky. "Ere, none of your business. Didn't come to see ya."

"Bessie'll tell you the same."

"Were is she?"

Susan brings Lizzie to the window. There is just enough light in the sky, full of bright cloud, to see her obstinate expression and angry eyes.

"Ere, Lizzie, brought ya something nice."

"You better take it away again. I filled up the hole in the cupboard and I got nowhere to put nothing more."

"Ere, Lizzie, it's a present, see."

"I don't want no presents from you."

"Wots the trouble, Lizzie?"

Lizzie is silent. Susan, just behind, says: "Tisn't no good you talking to her—she's made up her mind."

"You want me to go away, Lizzie?"

"Yess, I do, too."

"All right then, I will—see."

There is a pause. Susan says in sudden broad Doric: "Oh dearr, bant that booy gone yet? I'm slee-py."

"Go on," Lizzie says.

"I *am* going, see—going for good—you'll never see me no more, Lizzie."

"Good-bye, Charl."

There is another silence. Then Charley says: "Ere, Lizzie, wots wrong?"

"Good-bye, Charl."

"Oh, all right. Good-bye, Lizzie."

He is just descending the hurdle when Lizzie says quickly: "What about the little house?"

Charley stops and asks: "Wot about it?"

"Nothing. Good-bye, Charl." The window shuts with a bang and the curtain falls across the opening. Charley, going slowly home, throws the can into the quarry. Luckily it is not found for a week, and then by Mrs. Smith, who takes it home and says nothing about it.

60 The *Twyport Gazette*, reporting the robbery at Longwater Bridge, gave descriptions of three of the thieves as seen by one of the servants in the house. The descriptions of Mort and Harry were reasonably accurate.

Mort, as soon as the paper was out, came hurrying to Charley. Though it was in the middle of the morning, when Charley was in class, he asked for him at the back door of the Cedars. Mort came with a plan to loot Burls House in the hope of finding enough money to make it possible for him at least to go elsewhere, to Scotland or preferably Ireland, and lie low.

Charley, obviously amused by Mort's panic, answered that there was nothing in Burls. "But we might ave a farewell party there—jus for a send-off."

It was arranged at once that Ginger should have a car ready as soon after dark as possible, and that Burls should be rummaged afterwards for any valuables that the Wandles might have left behind.

"You won't get no cash and Ginger won't get no dimond necklaces, but it's just the place for a party. Less show the cops we knows ow to make a good finish."

At seven o'clock Charley is standing under the hedge in little Whiteboys piece behind Burls House with Harry and Mort. He wears two sacks folded and tied round his knees, and leather garden gloves borrowed from the Allchin shed. It is a dark and cold evening. The air seems heavy with darkness and a light watery snow is drifting through it as if unable to sink in its thick shadows.

Bert is hovering round Charley as usual when he can come near him; Lizzie, with a sack pulled hoodwise over her head, is standing behind him, so still and silent that the other boys have not discovered her presence. But Charley can feel her skirt touch his legs and sometimes a fold of her dress touches his back when she breathes.

He is startled by this silent visit of Lizzie. He knows that only some desperate resolution would cause her to break out from supervision and risk a beating. But he is too excited to wonder at her whims or ask himself what she wants.

A car passes along the road and Mort says: "If that ant Ginger, we're done."

"Go on, Mort, they aint going to cop you."

"All right for you to talk, Charley Brown, but you ant in the paper. You kep yourself out of that."

"It is Ginger," Bert cries, joyfully rushing towards them. "E's coming; e's got a car."

Ginger's thin, neat figure grows out of the dark and he says: "An old Vauxhall, but she'll do sixty."

"Were you put er, Ginj?"

"Through the gate in the Hall field."

"Thass no good for a getaway."

"Couldn't leave her in the road—people would know she didn't belong here."

"Thass right—and we aint in a urry—got all night—wot about ole Roy?"

266

"Just gone along."

"That gives us till closing time—we've two hours. Come on, chaps."

The party, including Bert and Liz, follow through the gate to the house garden and the kitchen yard. Charley, having climbed on the butt, affects to see Lizzie for the first time and says: "Ere, Liz, wot you doing ere? You better cut off now." Lizzie makes no answer, and Charley says: "Pinch er, somebody." But nobody pinches her. Liz, by some unseen emanation of character, has acquired a position of dignity. Ginger says to Charley: "She said she was going to stay."

Charley's nerves are like strung wires. He says impatiently: "But she can't stay and she can't come along with us or she'll be copped. Get us all copped likely—tell er, Ginj."

Ginger, with the very air of a man of good breeding obliged to take a liberty with a lady, bends stiffly towards Liz and mutters to her from at least a yard away. Liz, from beneath the hood, flashes her eyes at him and pushes out her thick lower lip in an expression threatening temper. But she does not move. "She can't ear—can't someone pinch er?" Charley says. No one moves to pinch her.

"You aint afraid of er, are ya?"

"She ears all right," Harry says, "but she aint going to listen. She thinks you cutting off somewhere."

Charley looks at Liz and feels both uneasiness and excitement. His nerves respond on two more notes as well as their former chord. He says in a peculiar tone which sounds both triumphant and disgusted: "Look at er, obstinate aint the word. All right, let er stay—I can't wait—me ands is getting froze." Charley swarms suddenly to the garage roof. He seems to walk up the wall on all fours. Four or five minutes later, Ginger, who has the keenest sight, mutters: "He's on the roof—we'd better go down." They file down the area steps into the basement yard and stand there in darkness. A handle rattles; Charley's voice says in a lively note: "Ongtrey, I opes I sees you well," then laughing: "Key was in the door this time—Roy's bin getting away with the coal."

As soon as the cellar door is closed he switches on the brilliant lights of the stairs and passage above. "Less ave some light on the scene—make yourselves at ome, gentlemen."

"Is it safe to turn on the lights?"

"Course it's safe," Charley answers, who has not considered the matter but wants the splendours of Burls to be admired. "Our blackout was done by Lord Blackout isself—ullo, Bert, wot you doing ere?"

"I never see in here afore, Charley."

"All right, Bert, but wipe your feet, see. Ullo, Liz, you come in, did you?"

Lizzie, reaching the top of the stairs at the tail of the procession, looks at Charley with a blank obstinacy. But Charley answers the look with a bland smile.

"Thass all right, Liz—you'll get off soons we ad supper, won't ya?"

"No, I ant—I bant going till I know where you're going."

Charley is already darting down the passage to arrive in front of Mort and Harry. He switches on the candle lustres which light the room from wall plates of mirror.

"This, gentlemen, is the royal dining-room—supper will be served at eight o'clock sharp with champyne and a band—Dick Gingers Hotspots."

Ginger, knowing every inch of Burls, goes straight through the far doors of the room towards the central hall and the drawing-room beyond. Charley rushes after him to turn on the lights. He wishes that he had a thousand guests to astonish by the beauty of the rooms. "The drawing-room, gentlemen, with pictures by world champions."

Harry, Mort and Bert are staring about them with open mouths. They huddle together in the doorway as if afraid to step on the carpets.

"Come in, genlemen, ladies——" Charley is delighted by

268

the effect of his display. "Scuse my butler being out, this evening, e's gorn to see a friend at the Green Man. The chairs is real gold and the table is Italian marble with gold legs."

"I seen better in the movies," Mort says. "Where's the safe?"

"In the pantry—second cupboard on the right under the slab."

Mort goes into the pantry and finds the safe, a simple butler's safe of sheet iron, swinging open with the key in the lock. He rushes upstairs to rummage the bedrooms on the first floor corridor and passes Ginger, with a face sharpened like a weasel's, going along from room to room. But he turns quickly aside from Ginger and takes care not to meet him in the hunt.

When he returns to the dining-room with nothing but four silver-seeming ornaments in his pockets, he finds Charley with a bottle in his hand, talking to Harry and Bert about the decorations. Other bottles and five glasses stand on the Italian table with cold bacon, cheese, a roll of margarine, pots of jam, pickles and marmalade. Lizzie has just laid six places with dessert plates of Crown Derby, black-handled kitchen knives and nickel forks. She is in the act of lighting the end of a greasy kitchen candle stuck in the middle of a magnificent seven-branch candlestick of Waterford glass. Another piece of the same candle is burning beside it.

Lizzie, having lighted the candle, puts her hands on her hips and frowns at the table, with a look probably caught from her mother or some aunt, before a party; a look that has descended in a straight line from forgotten generations of housewives.

She then looks again at Charley; her face changes in a flash from the sketch of a mature and slightly formidable mistress, to childish temper full of whim and defiance. She throws up her head and walks ostentatiously as far as possible from the table which she has laid with such anxious contrivance.

Charley, however, does not even see her table or herself. He is pointing, with the bottle, at a picture, the only one of which he has heard an expert description. "It's a cornfield, see,

Arry, and e's made it seem real corny, too, see—and see ow e done it—see them little bits of red——"

Bert is not attending to this lecture. He turns his spectacles up to the ceiling, then examines the furniture, the grand piano, the polished floor. The spectacles, catching the light, remove all intelligence from his eyes and replace it by two blank panes of glass. The sharp acute worn face of the child, full of a deep and narrow experience, surrounds two sheets of metal, as blind as the windows of an empty house.

"But wy as e done it all smudgy, Char?" Harry asks, frowning anxiously at the picture. "Wy aint e done it more careful?"

"Ere, Arry, I told ya—because e wanted to make it look real, see, like it was growing, see—like you could smell it."

"Corn don't smell."

"E says it do."

"Course it smells," Lizzie says, passing disdainfully behind Charley. "It could give ee a headache when tis ripe."

But neither hears her and she marches off again, red with her secret fury.

Mort has stood glaring angrily from under his projecting thatch of hair at this scene for some moments, waiting until someone shall notice his dangerous and awful mood. But when no one does so he lunges his shoulders forward and growls: "What's the game, boy?"

Charley turns with relief from his lecture which seems to carry no conviction to Harry and therefore begins to seem less striking to his own imagination. He cries: "Take a chair, Mister Morton—Liz, Mister Morton will ave a glass of wine."

Lizzie turns her back and disappears into the hall. Charley does not notice this rebellious action. He is already enjoying the game of acting as his own butler.

"Champyne or Guinnes, sir."

Morton refuses to play. He is playing out his own act.

"Look here, Charley Brown, I ant being funny. Where's the stuff—if there bant none, what you bring us here for?"

Ginger walks silently in from the hall. He is wearing a tall hat and carrying a silk umbrella. He looks at the umbrella, in the bright light, and feels the silk with obvious approval of its fine texture. Then he puts it down on a chair and says: "I can't find anything. I've been everywhere where they kept their stuff."

"Where did they keep it?"

"Cash in the library bureau, Mrs. Wandle kept her jewellery lying all over her room—there's nothing there now—and the silver was put in the safe every night."

"Come on, gentlemen, this is a party, aint it. Hi, Liz— bring those knives. Where's Liz—— Fill up, Mr. Morton."

"Here, Charley Brown—what you brung us here for—to get us copped?"

Charley himself cannot answer this. He cannot say:"So that I could see Burls House again and play the master of it," because he does not know this answer himself. Even to Charley, it would have seemed fantastic. His game of host seems to him a game, an amusing improvisation, and not the deliberate act of his real will, long fostered and cherished.

"He told you there was nothing you could take," Ginger says coldly. Ginger is still wearing the tall hat slightly over one eyebrow. It fits him and suits him well; as he seems to know.

Mort pours himself out a glass of stout and drinks it off. Then he sits down at the table and says: "May as well sit here till the cops come."

"Have another, Mr. Morton."

"Never got a break, I didn't. Never had a chance—fair sick of it, I am."

61 Liz, who has suddenly reappeared, with her nose in the air and in her hand a kitchen plate on which is salt, pepper and some mustard in an egg-cup, puts down the plate next the bacon and says: "There, don't say there ant no mustard." She is turning away when she notices that Morton's

elbow has pushed his plate beyond the edge of the table. She glares at the boy, takes the plate from him and says in a furious voice: "I think some of you bo-oys never see proper chiny afore."

"Wy, Liz, were you bin?" Charley cries. "Siddown and ave something."

Lizzie whisks away two dessert plates and says: "They'm too good for you—delf's good enough for pigs."

Bert is standing in the middle of the Aubusson carpet, with his shoulders at their lowest and his sleeves therefore seeming particularly long; his whole body more shrunk and formless even than usual. Suddenly he utters a shrill giggle. Liz whirls round and once more looks like the responsible house-ruler: "Now then, Edwud—don't ee git the laughs in here."

All look at Bert, and Charley goes to slap him on the back. "Wots the joke, Edwud?"

"Wots e laughing at?" Harry asks impatiently. "Ain't nothing to laugh at."

"Go on, Bert, get the cops in," Mort says in a mournful voice. "Charley Brown done for me anyhow. I never had no luck in this world."

"Ere, Bert, cut it out—wots the joke?"

Bert, with staring goggles, looks all round the glittering room, shakes his cap, flaps his right arm helplessly in the air and bursts into still louder giggles.

"He dreamt that he dwelt in marble," Ginger says.

"Sall right," Charley says, much gratified. "Sall real—you ain't barmy."

"Noa, he ant," Mort complains. "But us is—Bill was barmy, Bass was a barmy toad, and Charley Brown the barmiest a the bleeding lot."

Lizzie, who has withdrawn from the affair as soon as Charley entered it, now whisks away Charley's plate and glass and walks out of the room. Charley is too busy with his guests to notice the loss. "Sit down, Bert, and ave your supper. Gentlemen, drink up and eat up. The party as started. I just built this ouse, see, ony so's I could give this party to my friends. You all been my friends long time and we *good* friends, arn't we—we *good* friends." Charley is seeking the strongest emphasis—he wants to create the idea of an extraordinary depth of loyalty and affection. "We the best gang a friends in the world and we'll always be friends, see, in our gang—cos we can't elp it."

Mort suddenly gets up and says in a tearful voice: " Call this bubbly water booze—I'd be sha-med to leave it in a christin pot—where you hide the proper booze, Charley?" He goes out to the pantry. Lizzie suddenly takes her seat beside Charley and says to him: "When are you going to Lunnon?"

"Oo said we was going?"

"I know you be going—that's for what Ginger took the car —you wur going to slide away and leave me."

"But, Liz, you couldn't come—suppose you was copped?"

"Twas all your lie about Ammurca."

Charley has forgotten this plan, but now it pleases him again: "Wot, are you game to go to Ammurca?"

"Noa."

"But you said you could."

"Not with you—you're a liar—I was a fule to trust you."

Charley stares at her in mild surprise. "You're all right, Liz, aint ya?"

"They told me I was silly to trust you bo-oys—mum said you would do some hurtful thing to me—but you haven't, Charl. Noa, you coulddn do me any hurt."

Mort has come back with half a bottle of brandy, a bottle of gin and some dregs of vermouth. He fills all glasses except Ginger's, who always refuses to drink any alcohol, even beer or cider. Lizzie has no glass because Charley, not noticing the disappearance of his own, has taken both her glass and her plate for his own use.

"You coulddn do me hurt, you nasty little bo-oy," Lizzie says. But Charley is shouting across the table at Harry to drink his health. Then suddenly he notices that Liz, on his left hand, has no glass, and pushes his own towards her. "Go on, Lizzie, drink me luck. Thass lucky wen a moll drinks luck to er chap. I aven't dirtied it ony on one side——"

Lizzie pushes away the glass with a scornful gesture, but Charley is again attending to his guests. "Ere now, Arry——"

"I ates the stuff," Harry says. "It'll make me drunk and then I'll be sick. I ates being sick." He pushes forward his glass. "Ere's to ya, Mort—luck were it goes."

Mort, with a crimson nose and pale damp cheeks, mutters a long monologue of complaint on the usual subject, that nobody likes him and nobody treats him fairly.

"I never had a chance—everyone's down on Mort—even if they start friends."

He turns suddenly upon Lizzie at his right hand, and asks: "What you laughing at, Bessie Galor?"

Lizzie starts out of her bitter reflections and answers:

"I wasn't laughing at you, Morton."

"You wur too—you allays laughs at me. Serve you right that you wur made a deaf kind of fule. The fever was a fair christin punishment for ee."

In liquor Morton falls into a broader speech and an old-fashioned country eloquence. But for some reason, in spite of his ugliness, his nose, his everlasting complaint about the world, he remains dignified. Though Lizzie is suffering agonies that she had not believed possible, she can't help giving sympathy to Mort. But by instinct she avoids her favourite phrase. She does not say "Poor Mort " because she feels that it would enrage the boy to be pitied by her whom he despises. She says therefore: "You med laugh at me, Morton—but I coulddn laugh at you."

"Ah, but you do laugh—inside of you—you're laughing now. You be thinking I'm a fule. All the gurls allays laugh at me—that toad Milly sa-ays I have a noase like a cow's tit."

"She coulddn mean it, Mort. She spoke to spite ee."

"Ah, but tis too, zactly. I hate un, the fule of a noase—and me humpy back. Now I see you laughing behind my back,

Bessie Galor. You gurls is allays laughing at me behind my hump."

With voice as mournful as his own, Lizzie answers that his back is not a hump. "Tisn't a humpy, Morton, tis only a mite hoopy."

"Ah, but tis a hump too—and tis my Ma's fault. The gurls say to Tawleigh my Ma spoiled me for em. And you say that very thing too, for I heard ee."

"Noa, I never said you wur spoiled. Why, Morton, you be so big and strong as two men and you've growing to come."

"The gurls are right too, for I be spoiled. I be spoiled all through."

"You're not so baad, Mort. Tis only booys badness in you and you'll grow out of thaccy."

"You'm a liar, for I'm wicked too. All gurls be liars by nature, liars and fules. My Ma did spoil me all through—she was a woman too, the poor fule. And now, the gurls wont have nothing to do with me. Charley Brown there, a rubbishy runt from Lunnon, can get a gurl, but not me that was born and bred to Tawleigh."

"I'm sure you'll have a gurl if you look for one and treat un proper and don't frighten un with shouting and cussing."

"Ah, but I couldn't have un for nothing like Charley Brown has you, could I?"

Lizzie knows that this charge brought against her is a commonplace joke for big boys like Mort and Bill. She has often heard it called after girls from some road corner on a dark night. She recognises even, in a dim way, that they are urged to make the suggestion by their own appetites and that they get pleasure out of accusing a girl of the act which is in their own minds. But she can't prevent herself from turning deep red. Mort, thus seeing his random shot go home, cannot hide his triumphant delight. He grins and rolls on his heavy thighs: "Ah, you diddn think I knowed. Ah, I touched a spot that time. And what for did un have ee? For nothing, for a necklace—rubbishy glass and brass. My Ma spoiled me, but who spoiled ee, Bessie? I have a lump behind, but who med have a lump in front?"

"Someone's been telling ee a great lie."

"Tis not your face then. I never saw so much truth in a gurl's blood."

"I never did ee no harm, Morton—why are you so hurtful to me?"

"You're hurtful to me because you laugh at me noase, because you think I'm a fule—I hates all you gurls, cruel chattering fules that laughs in your fa-ace without a thought of what you med feel. Milly Roy, what's she know—she knows nothing, the ninnywit, nor you neether, Bessie. Shall I tell un all here—Charley Brown had Bessie for nothing—made a proper fule of her?"

"You'd tell a big wicked lie then."

"Then Charley is a liar, for he told me heself."

Lizzie is silenced by this unexpected blow. Her eyes look about the room with the desperation of one who would like to run away but dare not.

"Ah, you say I be spoiled, but so you be spoiled—and you laugh at me for a fule, for telling my faults, but so you be a fule and I'm laughing at ee. Shall I tell em now—shall I tell em loud?"

"It on't make no difference."

"Noa, for they all bin told—Charley tells everybody. Booys allays tell—tis a good laugh for un to get a gurl for nothing."

He stares at Lizzie in triumph.

"Charley made a proper fule of you, diddn e?"

Lizzie says nothing to this. Her deep ugly flush has faded to an even pink; her eyes are steady, she no longer looks lost and terrified. She is already accustomed to a new situation. Mort, looking at her, feels that disappointment common in the young, who are always suffering the chagrin of finding that their best effects upon the feelings of other children, either of pain or admiration, pass away in a few minutes. He says at last: "What do ee think of your Charley Brown now?"

Lizzie gives a long sigh which suddenly lifts up her breasts almost to womanly shape, and asks: "Tis a custom for boys to tell?"

"Of course it's the custom—when a gurl is such a fulish fule. Who could help making game of her?"

"Tis her own fault, as you saay," Lizzie says mournfully.

"Ah, but you diddn reckon Charley would tell."

"I diddn know twas custom."

"So now you're spoiled proper—he spoiled ee in the body and he's spoiled ee in the naame. Look at un there, laughing at the both of us, the dirty Lunnon runt. He thinks we're a lot o dumbhead fules. Cutting us over the head for nothing, and poking our fule gurls for a brass chain."

Lizzie seems to reflect for a moment and then murmurs: "Poor Charley."

All her bitter resentment has rushed away from her or her suffering, and she remembers nothing but her own bad feelings. She looks at Charley a yard on her right with an anxious and wary expression, like a wife gauging the temper of an insulted husband. Seeing that Charley's coat is dabbling in his plate, she pushes the plate forward and wipes the sleeve with her frock. Charley submits his arm and sleeve to this operation as if neither they nor Lizzie had anything to do with his private and sensible existence. The whole transaction might have taken place in some domestic interior between a couple so long and thoroughly married that they have ceased to make any exact distinction between their belongings or even the parts of the body.

Lizzie, having held Charley's wrist and carefully wiped his sleeve, is exactly where she was before.

Morton says in her ear: "Shall I tell un the very words that Charley said about ee."

Lizzie turns quickly to him and Morton moves his lips as if speaking a long sentence. "Did ee hear that?"

"Noa."

"And I was shouting at ee, too, you be surprising deaf, Bessie. Deaf as a stone."

"You med well laugh at me, Mort—I'm a laughable thing."

"Ah, so you are, too—an ugly toad and a fule by doctor's orders—he wrote it down in ink that your brains be rotted."

Tears flash into Lizzie's eyes and shake on her lower lids. Morton says with great delight: "Cry now—I've made ee cry," and he calls to Charley: "I've made your fule cry, Charley Brown. She bant laughing now."

Charley, however, more and more excited in his liquor, is shouting so loudly across the table at Ginger, Harry and Bert that he hears nothing. He is sweating with heat, beer and happiness. Universal benevolence beams from him, not only towards his gang, but towards the table, the plates, the chandeliers, the room, the pictures. He gazes even at the bottles with tender affection. "Fines stout I ever tasted. Gentlemen—special stout—see, Arry, it's wot they drink in the Royal Family in the House of Lords. Mr. Wandle never ad nothing but the best of everything."

62   Like many other hosts, Charley enjoys the party much more intensely than his guests. It is like one of his own stories come true. Beer and happiness excite him so that he cannot remember from one minute to another what he is saying. He makes a plunge at the centre of his meaning: "Genmen, I ope you're aving—appy party in Burls Ouse—fines party in fines ouse in the world. Ullo, Liz."

He has suddenly caught sight of Liz. "Ullo, Liz, you ere—ow you come ere?"

Lizzie smiles and colours with delight. She sees that Charley has no grievance against her, that he has forgotten her abominable behaviour. She says: "Yes, I comed at the beginning."

"You all right, Liz?"

"Yes, tis a proper party, Charl."

"Thass all right."

"They sa-ay you bo-oys going away to-night."

"Thass right. Hi, Arry, fill up—and fill up ole Bert."

"Can I come, too?"

"Yess, course you can. Thass all right—all in the gang, aint we, my gang. Hi, Ginger, you aint got nothing to drink. Ere, Liz, fill up ole Ginj." Then suddenly remembering Lizzie's recent request he says to her: "I want you to come—you got to come, see, I want you to come, Liz. Hi, Ginj, Liz is going to come along with us, see."

"What, in the car?"

"Unless she'd rather walk."

"She'll give us away. A girl will be spotted at once."

"Might as well drive straight round to the station to Tawleigh," Mort says.

Charley does not notice these objections. Lizzie, once more the hostess, has lifted Ginger's glass from the table in order to make sure when she fills it that any drip will fall not on the polished table but on the carpet. Ginger thanks her politely and, as soon as she turns away, exchanges his full glass for Harry's empty one. Charley does not notice the substitution because he is once more in the midst of his speech, beginning: "Gentlemen, this is going to be the fines party in the fines ouse in the fines country in the world, for the fines chaps."

An hour later, at half-past nine, he is still orating. Supper has come to an end, no one knows how or why, except Lizzie, who is preparing to wash up by boiling a kettle in the kitchen. Charley, having made his last speech at table, upon the extraordinary excellence of the Burls House beer, has now returned to the decorations, lights, furniture and pictures. He is wearing Ginger's top hat, which, since his head is smaller than Ginger's, has slipped down until it is supported, as by two rococo brackets, upon his projecting ears. He is standing in the drawing-room, slowly waving one hand and addressing an imaginary party of visitors. "Gentlemen, ladies, all the world

champions from the Royal Academy—see ere, cornfield—
Lommax, famous artiss—thousand pound—it's growing, see
—turn it upside down, gentlemen and lady—cost thousand
o pound." He stares at the picture with partly open lips and
frowning brows. His face is flame colour, sweat pours down
his cheeks, his expression is anxious and serious, and his speech
grows more and more urgent. "Mos famous picture in world
—genmen and lady—Mr. Lommax done it. It's growing, see
—it's rich—look at it upside down. Thass the way——" he
stoops sideways and downwards, trying to look at the picture
upside down. His hat falls off and, without changing his
position, he replaces it with both hands, and holds it on. His
voice, muffled by his coat which is falling across his mouth,
and by partial suffocation, comes from close to the floor. "Iss
the corn, see—iss so corny, see—iss growing, coo, aint it rich,
genmen and ladies."

Nobody is listening to him. Ginger has opened the piano
and is playing softly parts of one tune after another. Every
now and then he gets up, walks about the room, and coming to
Charley, says: "I say, Charley, we ought to be going. I'm
ready any time you are."

Mort is running about the whole lower floor, under the
blazing lights, sometimes swearing and sometimes complain-
ing, with dignified and melancholy feeling, of Milly Roy and
the Tawleigh girls. "And if the fules only knew," he says to
Ginger: "I'm the boy to give them jooy. I'm the hoss for the
hedge work. I'm the very booy they want. I bant expecting a
peach neether. Any female piece with a lump at one end and a
prang at the other'd be vitty to me."

Ginger walks past him and returns to the piano.

"Here I be meat for wenches so hoamly as a pig's foot—
that dursnt dream of a man below the collar for fear they'd
jump out of window or hang themselves—and they spit on
me, the dawted fules," and then raising his voice and throwing
into it almost a church note of denouncement. "And tis not
for pride they damn themselves, but only fulishness. Tis the

born fulishness of women that drives all that race a ninnywits like busted paper bags on Twyport muck heaps."

Ginger, getting up again, interrupts him: "If we don't go, we'll be copped."

"Ah, so we will," Morton says, then suddenly bends his knees and assumes his most idiotic expression, goggling his eyes, thrusting out his neck, stretching an enormous grin, "and that will be funny, too, won't it?"

"I'm ready if Charley is."

"And that's funny, too."

"I don't see the joke."

"Don't ee—why, booy, Charley's tight."

"He may be, but he's the boss." Ginger is unusually disturbed.

"Yah, and I'm tight and Harry's tight, we'm all tight cept you. But you're wa-aiting on us. Bant that funny?"

Ginger walks off. Mort slowly straightens his legs, gradually assumes his usual calm melancholy face, and says: "I would never speak to any of the fules agen—if twurnt my right."

Ginger is saying to Harry stretched on the sofa: "We ought to be going now, Harry—it's nearly ten o'clock."

Harry, with pale sweaty face and a terrified expression, is moaning among the silk cushions. He answers: "Ow, my ead —I been sick four times, Ginj. Wish I could die, I do."

"We'll be copped if we don't get a move on."

"All right, you go on, I aint going—I'll be sick again if I get up. Go on, Ginj—urry up, I don want nobody but Liz"

Ginger goes back again to Charley, who at once seizes him by the arm and points at the wall: "It's rich, see, cost a thousand pound—rich, corny." He stares at the pictures, and his perplexity gradually infects his whole face; raising his eyebrows, wrinkling his forehead, opening his mouth.

"We ought to get off, Charley—it's ten o'clock."

Charley mutters to himself and straightens his hat.

Bert has been wandering for some time through the upper corridors of the house in clothes stolen from various rooms, a

flounced dress in the Victorian style of 1939, and an extraordinary hat like a black witch's hat with a very high peak,
fixed to a schoolmaster's mortar-board. The mortar-board is
jammed upon Bert's round head almost to his ears. He is
wearing high-heeled white satin mules which he drags after
him across the floor with his toes. An enormous crimson
mouth has been drawn crookedly over his lips and two black
circles round his eyes. His nails and most of his fingers are also
coloured scarlet with the same lipstick. His little grey eyes
behind his spectacles and the two owl circles, are tearful with
laughter. Now he staggers into the drawing-room, wavering
to and fro, tripping on his gown, dropping the mules, and
taking the frock in his hands streaked with dirt and lipstick,
he tries to dance, kicking up his legs. No one looks at him
except Lizzie, who follows him from the door. She is shocked
and urges Bert in a wheedling voice: "Put them back, Bert,
you're making them all dirty—put them back."

She is troubled especially by the damage to the white satin,
which she feels to be expensive material of the best quality.
But Bert does not hear her. He laughs and says, "Bo-oomp-
sidaisy," then bows, kicks and loses a mule, goes down on his
knees to find it, and once more begins his dance.

Mort lurches by him, talking to himself, swinging his head
like a lost dog, spitting on the carpets; Lizzie goes back again
to the table and gathers another pile of dirty plates to be taken
to a safe place.

Ginger says to her: "We ought to be going, Lizzie."

"I know, but look at all this mess—I bant even got washed
up yet—the kettle only just boiled."

"But it's ten o'clock. Old Roy will be coming back from the
Green Man in half a minute."

Lizzie is perplexed. She looks anxiously from Ginger to the
table. Then she rushes to gather up the plates. "You take
some, too, Ginger—we could clear it."

"There isn't time, Lizzie."

"Yess, yess, if you take the plates—put the bottles behind

the sofa." She thrusts the plates into Ginger's hands and catches up the bacon dish in one hand and the bread-board in the other. "Come now, I'll show ee where to put em."

Ginger follows Lizzie down the room, protesting still that there is no time to waste on dirty plates.

Bert's dance meanwhile has been growing wilder. He whirls round with arms outstretched, carrying a mule in his hand. Brought up by the wall in front of an illuminated picture, he raises the mule and smashes the glass with the heel. He then throws the mule at the canvas and falls down in shouts of laughter.

The smash of the glass makes Mort swing into the room. He snatches up the mule, and throws it at another picture, a portrait: "Take that, you silly bitch."

The mule, striking on the toe, falls down without breaking the glass. Mort glares. "Awright, dem you, I'll show you." He rushes to the table and comes back with a bottle in each hand. In a moment, a bottle flies through the portrait, another through the Constable landscape, beside it.

Charley, in the middle of his speech, sees the picture glass in front of him fly into pieces; the canvas behind burst open. He stares with amazement. Then his brows smoothe, perplexity gradually leaves his face, he gives a cry of delight. He sees what can be done with pictures, expensive pictures, to produce a definite and glorious sensation.

He grabs at the neck end of Mort's bottle, rolling at his feet, and throws it through the next picture. Again there is a crash, succeeded at once by a burst canvas. Charley gives a yell of joy. "Come on, Genlm lady, newgame, smashpicture, thousands o pounds—gimme bottle, Liz."

Ginger, who has just returned at Lizzie's command, while she keeps watch at the back door, to fetch the empty bottles, stops, watches the room for a moment and then carries his armful of empty bottles to Charley. "Here you are, Charley."

Charley misses two pictures running, whereupon Ginger throws the next bottle himself, clean through the largest canvas in sight. He remarks: "That's the way to throw bottles—don't take em by the neck, but the thick part. Look here, Charley, like this."

Another bottle flies to the mark. Ginger then opens rapid fire. As usual he is by far the most efficient of the party. He uses his head, concentrates on his object, and after each shot, criticises his technique. "That one slipped a bit, you want to keep your hand dusty." He rubs his hand on the floor.

He does not seem to be enjoying the game, but simply to be performing a task. He says, looking round at the destruction: "May as well make a good job of it now."

Lizzie comes flying in. "Charley, Ginger—I blieve there's someone outside—calling out—come and listen." Then stopping in horror as a picture crashes, she cries: "Whatever you doing?"

"Aint nothing else to do with em," Charley shouts. He makes a rush at the table and tries to scramble upon it. "Gimme a leg, Liz." He is almost sobered by triumph. The intoxication of glory has driven out for a moment the milder intoxicants of stout and gin. "Gimme a leg, Liz."

Lizzie, protesting: "I'm sure there's somebody," nevertheless gives him a leg. Charley jumps upon the table and makes a leap at the great chandelier above. He catches it by the lower arms and swings with it.

"Look ere," he yells. "Look at me, genmen lady. Oos king of the castle now? You watch me—I'll smash the ole bloody ouse to flinders—that's wot I'll do wif it—king of castle," breathless he squirms, kicking at the table to make the huge pyramid of cut glass with its twenty electric candles swing. "Lookatme—king of castle—I'll smash olebloody everything— smash——"

The chandelier tears out of the ceiling and falls upon the display table with a crash like a ton of scrap metal dumped upon a stone yard. Every light in the lower storey of the house goes out.

For a moment there is silence; then a man's voice outside is heard shouting: "They're in the drawing-room now."

Inside, the darkness seems full of children and loud whispers: "That you, Ginj—were's Liz?"

Mort falls down the back stairs and finds Harry at the bottom. Lizzie and Ginger together drag Bert to the back door in mistake for Charley. Then Harry calls out: "Charley's gone off."

Charley half stunned by his fall and entangled in the chandelier, was the last to escape, and then only by luck. He was still creeping about on all fours in the big drawing-room when the caretaker, old Roy, came rushing in with a torch.

Charley was then able to see where the door was, and crept out of it, while Roy was searching with his torch for the chandelier. Charley was still bewildered, and not greatly anxious to escape. His feeling was that something which was bound to happen had now happened, and that he might as well yield to fate. But the same motive which made him apathetic caused him to go on, slowly and carelessly, upon the course in which he found himself. He crept through the yard, climbed the steps, and then, once more on all fours, crept through the garden.

The place was now full of searchers; all the evening company lately turned out of the Green Man and, still on the road to bed, had come to help Roy. Three or four torches were flashing in the yard and the garden, showing the snow falling slowly among the frost-blackened shrubs.

A torch shone on the path within a foot of Charley, as he crouched. He stopped for a moment, and the next torch was a yard behind him. Five minutes later he was struggling through a gap in the field hedge. He was swearing at the thorns, and wondering why the gap had become so much narrower, when Bert, running along the garden path, fell over his legs. Bert had left his long dress behind, and washed his face in snow; but it was still daubed like a clown's.

"Ullo, Bert, two lovely black eyes."

"Where you going, Charley?"

"Ome, John—aint no night to sleep out."

"Do you know where you are?"

"Not an idea."

"You be going to Twyport that way."

"You know, Bert."

"Shall I take ee home?"

"Thass very kind of ya, Edwud."

63 Bert, finding himself responsible for Charley, behaved with great sense and shrewdness. He did not lead him direct to the Cedars, but left him sitting behind the Whiteboys hedge until he had spied out the ground. He returned with the news that there was a police car outside the Cedars and that strange men's voices were to be heard from Mrs. Parr's.

"You can't goa there, Charley."

"All right, Bert." Charley was sleepy and seemed to take no interest in his own fate.

"Wish I knew where Ginger got to," Bert said. "You sta-ay there, Charley, while I look about."

"All right, Bert—you say."

Bert went off but returned in half a minute, full of anxiety.

"You mustn't move from there, Charley."

"Not likely, ole Bert—too comfable."

"I coulddn find ee if you went off in this weather."

"I'll stay, ole Bert. You can trust me."

Bert, with a last doubtful backward glance, as if fearful that Charley, as soon as his back was turned, would do something foolish, disappeared into the snow. In less than twenty minutes he was back again, breathless from running, to report that Ginger and the car had disappeared.

"But Bessie diddn go with un. Ginger took her to the car, but she woulddn go without ee, and I'm to bring ee along to Galors'."

"All right, ole Bert."

"You can lie in the apple loft till Ginger comes back for ee."

"An very nice, too."

"Shall us goa now, Charley?"

"Ave I really got to get up?"

Bert looked at him with perplexity. He resembled for a moment one of those highly efficient and responsible public servants who have no sense of humour.

"All right, ole Bert—give us a and."

Bert understood this. He smiled broadly, seized Charley's hand in both his and with a strong heave brought him to his feet. Charley took his arm and they made their way along the hedges to the Galors' garden patch.

The night now seemed much brighter; the snow was falling more slowly and stars could sometimes be seen between the thin vapour of dissolving clouds. A stronger light seemed to rise from the snow-covered ground. The scattered cottage roofs, thrust up, each from its own scooped hole, over the horizon of quarry field, could be seen at forty yards' distance. Charley himself felt conspicuous.

"Won't they see us, Bert?"

"They med see us, too," Bert agreed. "But most is aslape."

As they reached the Galors' garden patch Lizzie started forward from the dark flatness of the wall. She was wearing her sack over her head, but it was thick with snow, so that it reproduced in miniature the dormer above.

"Charl, is that you?"

"No, it's Bert—e's bringing me."

"What a time you've been, Bert," in a severe tone.

"I runned all the way, Bessie."

Lizzie is propping up the hurdle and urging Charley to climb. Charley puts one foot on the hurdle and says in a sleepy voice: "Cor, wot a smash!"

Lizzie gives him another heave and says impatiently: "Hurry up, Charl. They'll hear ee."

Bert pushes on the other side and tells Lizzie his adventures. "I coulddn see Ginger in the car."

"I told you they'd gone—I was there. Go on, Charl. I believe you're still drunk."

"Cor, did ya see it come down, Liz—with all the candles?"

Lizzie climbs through the window and pulls him to the sill. Susan is sitting up in bed with the candle balanced on the rail. She holds an open book on her knees and gazes at Charley with blank, exhausted eyes. "So you found him. Do hurry up."

"We won't be long now, Su." She helps Charley into the room.

"I should think not."

The hurdle top disappears. Bert has removed it. He, too, vanishes without another word, as if he had lived only to do this duty.

Lizzie is pulling off Charley's boots and breeches. The boy is now almost helpless with cold and sleepiness. He smiles foolishly, his arms and legs are as limp as boiled macaroni. Lizzie licks the edge of her frock and wipes his face. Susan is already at work. Her lips move and she gives a slow deep sigh. Then she says: "Keeping us all up to this time."

"But you wanted to do your history, Su."

"I could have done it perfectly if Mum hadn't put the candle out."

"Oh dear, he's too cold, Su; I coulddn put un in the cupboard now."

"William the second, ten eighty-seven; Henry third, eleven hundred."

"He mun come in with us, Su. But I'll keep un right over."

"Do hurry up, Bessie."

"You med give me a hand."

Susan, without taking her eyes from the book, puts out a hand, takes Charley by the shirt and gives an impatient tug. Lizzie heaves at the same moment and rolls him between the blankets. Susan winces and says: "He's frozen cold."

"He'll soon warm up, Su." Liz hastily jumps into bed and draws Charley away from Susan. "He won't bother you, Su."

Having collected Charley's scattered limbs to her outer side of the bed and taken firm hold of him, she looks anxiously at Su.

"Charles Second sixteen six-ty; James Sec-nd, six-teen eighty-five," Susan murmurs in a lilt, "and now he'll freeze you—Willyam the second, sixteen ateyate. But none of my business, of course, Anne, seventeen two."

At seven in the morning, when Galor thumps into the kitchen, shaking the whole building to its foundations, on his way back from Hall Farm, Lizzie springs awake to find Charley still tightly clasped in her arms. She shakes him and he murmurs: "Ere, ere, auntie, give me a chance," then he wakes up and says with surprise: "Ullo, ow did you get ere?"

"Quick, Charley, get in the cupboard. Mother med come up."

"The cupboard?"

"Yess, there's lots of room. It goes all along—see here."

Lizzie jumps up and opens between the wall beams a low wooden door which gives upon a long triangular space underneath the eaves.

Susan turns, asks sleepily: "What time is it, Bessie?"

"Father just come back—but he's early."

"Oh dear, I've got all my collect." She lights the candle, opens a prayer book and immediately sets to work.

"Get up, do," Lizzie urges Charley.

"Cupboard," Charley murmurs. "Nah, you can ave the cupboard."

Mrs. Galor's voice shouts from below: "Su-san."

"Yes, Ma."

"Don't you forget your colic for Sunday school."

"I'm doing it, Ma."

Charley is already creeping through the little door into the dark space beyond. Lizzie pushes the packing-case in front of

289

it. Mrs. Galor shouts from below: "Open that door. How can I talk to ee?"

Lizzie goes to open the attic door.

"Don't ee grizzle at me, Susan, I only doing it for your own good."

"Oh dear. Yes, Ma. O God, who knowest us to be—who knowest us to be—who knowest us to be—how long you going to keep him here, Lizzie?"

Mrs. Galor has thumped down her own steps into the kitchen.

"Till Ginger comes—or till the police stop looking for un."

"Ginger won't come back. He'd be afraid."

"Noa, he ont."

"The police will go on looking for years and years—and how are you going to feed him?"

"When mum's at the shop."

"Father'd kill you if he found out."

Liz says nothing and Susan reflects. Then she asks: "But if Ma comes to sweep out."

"I always sweeps out now."

"She often comes to see if you done it proper."

"She bant bin in for a week and her never looks in the cupboard. Bant nothing there but holes."

Susan sighs. "He's your boy, Bess. I'm only wondering. Set in the midst of so many and great dangers—set in the midst—set in the midst."

"He diddn keep ee awake, did he, Su?"

"His feet were rather cold, but I suppose you can't help that with boys."

"He'll have his stockings on to-night—I ony took em off because they wur so wet."

"That by reason of the frailty of our nature we cannot allays stand upright. Oh dear, collects are the worst, there's no sense in 'em."

"Poor Su."

"But he couldn't stay here for ever."

"Noa, of course not. I espect he'll be able to get off to-morrow."

"Are you going, too?"

"I suppose so, Su."

Susan turns her eyes towards her sister with particular attention. Then she frowns: "Where will you go?"

"Charley did say Ammurca." Lizzie says this in a doubtful and nervous tone. She is afraid that Susan will call this plan absurd.

But Susan accepts it calmly. She is startled only by the idea of Lizzie's disappearance. She says after a moment: "Must you go all that way?"

"It's the best place for jobs, Charley says."

Susan, now adjusted to the idea, answers: "Yes, I suppose so, but you'd better go soon."

"Soon as ever we can."

"It's a terrible long way, Bessie." Then after a pause she looks again at Lizzie and says: "But he's your boy, of course."

Lizzie makes no answer.

"Grant to us such strength and protection—Grant to us such strength—you don't mind, Bessie, going so far away?"

Bessie raises her eyebrows and frowns. She says at last: "I mun goa where tis good for Charley."

"Of course, he's your boy. I'll snatch you something for un if I can." Su's voice is resigned. "Grant us strength—oh God who knowest us to be set in the midst of what is it so many and great dangers——"

Susan pays no more attention to Charley. But after breakfast she suddenly reappears in the room with an old straw-stuffed pillow and a bundle of dry sacks which she pushes into the eaves-cupboard to him. Charley, shivering there, thanks her warmly, but she answers, rejecting unearned gratitude: "If you catch cold Bessie will worry herself to death, and then I'll never get anything done."

64 Mort and Ginger escaped in the Vauxhall which took them as far as Shaftesbury before the petrol ran out. From that point there was no trace of them. It was supposed at first that Harry and Charley were with them and so there was no careful search in the district round Burlswood.

It was a wonder in the Press, afterwards, that Charley was hidden nine days and nights in Burlswood without discovery; it did not so much surprise the hamlet which knew the old farm buildings, the self-reliance of the Galor girls and the daily absences of their parents.

But even then Charley was lucky. From the beginning he took risks. He refused, of course, after the first half-hour in the freezing eaves cupboard, to stay in it or even enter it again. As soon as the elder Galors were out of the cottage in the morning he took possession of it, above and below, explored their room and the kitchen, wandered in the old farm buildings and played a kind of fives against the wall of the old cyder house.

Lizzie, who watched him more closely than a private detective, dared not take her eyes off him or he would disappear. She would miss him in the kitchen, search the cottage and find him at last performing a back lift on one of the ancient beams in the ruined farm sheds.

"Charl, whatever you thinking of, coming out here?"

Charley, upside down, would answer: "Sall right, Liz—no one wasn't looking."

"However can you know? There's Albert just gone up the road."

"No one can see from the road."

"Albert could, he's eyes in his ears."

"Watch me, Liz—I'm just going over, see."

He gives a powerful heave and topples forward off the beam. Liz gives a cry, and Charley, picking himself up from the floor, says indignantly: "Me fingers slipped."

In the evening while she is cooking the family supper he disappears entirely. Liz, as soon as she can escape to the attic, slips out through the press-house and hunts the quarry, the field, the lanes and hedges as far as Wickens'. She returns at nine o'clock to be consoled by Susan.

"They can't have caught him yet, Bessie deurr."

"Don't you think so, Su?" eager for expert opinion.

"No, of course not, or we'd have heard; besides, he's clever, your Charley is."

"You do think he's clever?"

"Yes, he would have got a scholarship if he hadn't been so wild. They were saying so to-day at school." Susan obviously feels a new respect for Charley.

"If only he wurn't so wild."

"Yess, he's too wild."

"Booys have no sense."

"No, they haven't. But he's clever, too."

Charley returns at midnight in high feather. He has prowled all through the village, visited Burls House garden and the Cedars, and brought back mince pies from the vicarage larder, forced with his pocket-knife. Lizzie, hollow-eyed with anxiety and sleeplessness, says: "And a wonder you wasn't catched."

"Bessie was off her head waiting for you," Susan says severely. She may respect Charley's brains, but she despises him as a boy.

"You wasn't, Liz, was ya?" Charley uses a tone both curious and defiant. From the time of his arrival in the cyder house and his dependence on the girls he has behaved with an exaggerated liveliness and nonchalance. It is as though he resents their lack of enthusiasm for his deeds and their common-sensible discussions of ways and means. "You didn't come after me, Liz, did ya?"

"Noa, I diddn—if you're catched twill be your own foolishness."

"You think I'm a fool, Lizzie?"

"Noa, but you act foolish."

Charley laughs at her and looks at Susan for support. Susan glances through him with the piercing indifference only to be achieved by young girls using a woman's weapon with childish directness and cruelty. Charley laughs at her, too, but without pleasure to himself. However, he discovers a new source of self-satisfaction that morning in the *Twyport Gazette*, brought in by Galor, after circulation at Hall Farm. It contains Charley's portrait, from one of Lina's snapshots, a description, and a note beneath. "If allegations are true, Charles Brown must be the youngest cat burglar in England."

Charley, finding this paper in the kitchen when the Galors have gone to work, reads it to Lizzie a dozen times and takes it to Susan as soon as she comes from school. "Youngest cat burglar in England. You know wot a cat burglar is?"

"I should have thought you'd too much sense."

"Cat burglars is the fines kind of burglars—a sneak thief wouldn't dare speak to a real cat."

"If I was Bess I wouldn't have you for a boy. It will only lead to unhappiness."

"He bant going to steal in Ammurca," Lizzie says.

"Nah, course not; but look ere, wot they say ere—an extraordinary feat."

"It's a promise, bant it?" Lizzie firmly pursues her object.

"Course it is," in a very careless tone.

Susan, brushing her hair, says: "When are you going to America? You'd better be quick, I should think, before somebody catches you here."

"Yers, but we've got to ave some cash for the bus—I mean the first bus. We got to take the night bus, and so we got to ave some oof." Charley slides over the point that he cannot expect to snatch bags at night.

"I've got money in my money-box," Susan says. She flings down the brush and puts on her hat. "Six shillings. It's in Mum's drawer, but it's mine."

"Su, you couldn't give it to us?"

"I'll give it to *you*, Bessie."

"Then we can go this very day, Charl, and the sooner the better, if you ask me."

Susan is just leaving the room. She says over her shoulder: "I suppose you know the ships don't go every day to America?"

Lizzie is dismayed. Charley, to whom the American project is still rather fantasy than plan, says mildly: "That's a knock in the eye."

Susan calls back from the stairs: "If you want to know what's its name I'll find it out for you from Miss Thingummy."

In the upshot Susan organises the American plan. She finds out when the night buses leave Twyport for Southampton; she discovers from her mistress, by pretending an interest in the mercantile marine, that American liners still sail from Southampton and that one is due to leave on Friday next; she promises to recover her money-box from her mother's drawer on Friday evening, too late for a premature discovery.

"Mum will beat ee," Liz warned her.

"I know she will, but twill only be smacks. She dursn't really hit me with the brush because of my exams. Nor Father neither."

Susan's businesslike methods do more to convince Lizzie that the American journey is possible than all Charley's assurances. Lizzie is accustomed to depend on Susan's judgment in all affairs dealing with the great world. So that now she becomes both more hopeful and more anxious. She is anxious because she feels that Charley is not now fully resolved upon going away. He shows little interest in Susan's careful enquiries about buses and routes. He avoids the subject of America and talks a great deal about cat burgling. He tears out the *Gazette* notice and carries it in his pocket and is often caught reading it. He becomes bolder and more independent every moment, and spends most of the third afternoon lurking in the quarry and creeping about in ditches. At night, in a strong frost, he disappears again, and at midnight, returning half-frozen, he brings back as trophies a brass-covered blotter and brass inkstand, taken from a Tawleigh villa by an un-latched window. But he does not show them to the girls with his usual air of bravado and challenge. He seems almost ready to agree with the unspoken criticism in their calm, reflective air, which says clearly: "How childish, but I suppose it's not wise to say so."

He hides blotter and inkstand in the cupboard floor so quietly that the girls do not seem to notice their disappearance. But all know that they are aware of it.

This night, too, perhaps in return for a tactful silence upon this raid, perhaps because Liz, by allowing him freedom to range the country, has calmed some secret fear and answered some secret doubt, he is full of affection and gratitude. He comes back to her, not as an apparatus for providing warmth, but as to a place of privilege. He grasps at her and sighs: "This aint too bad."

"D'you like it here?"

"Nah," he breathes, "I ates it." After a pause he goes on: "And I ates you, too—like ell I do, because you aint no good for nothing, see, and because you never done nothing for me, see, and because you go on putting it over on me. You going to sleep, Liz?"

"What you mean, put it over on you?"

"What I sa-ay," Charley drawls sleepily. "You treats me ba-ad, Lizzie, you got a crool nature and bones all over ya— thass wy I ates ya."

Lizzie, finding Charley in so affectionate a mood, ventures to say: "And we'll go to Southampton on Thursday night to catch the ship for Ammurca." Charley answers still more sleepily: "Ates ya like pison."

"We'll have to take some clothes, too."

"An extrorany feat." Charley is now more than half asleep. Lizzie perceives that she will get nothing out of him. He is not going to talk sense. She lies silent, taking pleasure in his security. He goes to sleep and gradually her happiness sinks into the normal mixture of anxiety, responsibility, preoccupation. Already she can't live without the preoccupation of Charley, something to do, to think, to contrive every minute of the day.

65 Charley is sleepy still in the morning. There is deep snow on the ground and the attic is cold. He refuses to hide under the bed and remains among the bed-clothes. When Lizzie comes to sweep the room he tries to persuade her to get back into bed. All the morning he hangs about the kitchen. He does not once speak of cat burgling or recall his feats with the gang. He even remarks, with gloom, that Ginger is bound to be caught. He always said he would be.

Charley is mildly surprised, for the first time, at his own situation. He examines the cyder house and the cart shed attached to it with a kind of dejected curiosity. He marks down dangerous corners from which it might be possible for a tree-climber in the orchard to see him in the hollow.

It is as though the whole direction of his mind is suddenly heading into a new course, or rather, since the new direction is towards reason, as if a gradual curve, in the real nature of the growing boy, distracted by a temporary pressure or whim, has suddenly jumped back into its designed form.

He leaves his newspaper cutting on the kitchen table where Galor, at dinner-time, finds it, accuses Lizzie of treasuring it, and throws it in the fire.

But when Lizzie tells Charley of this loss he is uninterested. He gazes at her sidelong in a thoughtful manner and says: "It doesn't matter."

"You don't want the Ammurcans to know you wur a cat burglar in England."

"You really want to go to Ammurca, Liz?"

"Why, Charl, I thought we wur going."

"Course we are."

He begins to talk again about America, about its wealth, jobs and high wages. As he chatters he follows Lizzie about at her household tasks, helps her to wash up the dinner. Galor is now back at the Hawes; Mrs. Galor at the shop, Susan at school. They have the buildings to themselves.

Charley, turning to put a plate on the rack, comes face to

297

face with Lizzie, turning to put down a scoured saucepan. They bump together and Charley takes hold of Liz in an awkward manner, and says: "Aint you tired, Liz?"

"Noa, of course not."

"Don't you want to lay down for a bit?"

Liz looks at him with increasing surprise and says at last: "Me, whatever for?"

"I dunno—ave a bit of a rest. If you lay down, I'll lay down."

"I ant got the time." Lizzie goes on clearing the table and tidying the kitchen. Charley wanders after her with an embarrassed and perplexed air until she stops and asked: "What's wrong, Charl—you bant hungry again?"

"No, taint nothing—I was just going to lay down. We could lay down and talk a bit—about wot we'll do in Ammurca."

Lizzie says that she is too busy. But at night, when Charley creeps cautiously into her arms, she understands what he wants. As before she is at first startled, instinctively begins to thrust him away, then feeling him daunted, as suddenly hastens to assist his awkward movements. Charley, she finds, in growing older, seems to grow more easily daunted, more shy and clumsy. She has to be quick to understand his difficulties, and bold to solve them for him.

But now Charley does not wander from her. She has no difficulty in keeping him in sight. Whenever she turns round, he is there. Lizzie is not amused by this violent embarrassed passion which expresses itself in such awkward gestures and even asks for help. To her idea of things, Charley's desire and even his strange grotesque motions are a proof of his love. She thinks "Charley has fallen in love with me," and her heart swells with a happiness which is almost unbearable, which keeps her awake all night.

But she sees proof of this love and enjoys it every moment of the day. Charley is full of a new kindness and responsibility; a desire to please her which is sometimes so humble that it makes her shy. She takes a dust-pan from him and says: "That's not booy's work, Charl."

"But wy should you do it all?"

"Tis my work—tis woman's work."

"When you and me get our ouse, we'll ave a vacuum, like at the Cedars."

"Do they really clean proper?"

"Course they do—you can see the dirt inside."

"A floor ant clean unless you wash it."

"All right—we'll ave a washer, too—like at the Cedars, an a patent mop with a special bucket to wring it out."

"I'd rather get down on my hands and knees to my own floor."

"All right, we'll ave tiles then—and you wash em with a hose."

"Why, Charl, your feet'd be frozen on a tile floor."

Charley frowns and is silent for ten minutes. But he is never discouraged long in his plans for the house and garden. His imagination returns to them by mere force of its own energy which, having been directed into a certain course, pursues it of its own motion. He plans houses, gardens, kitchens all day, and even draws them on an old piece of drawing paper. "We'll ave the stove there, see—next the sink, sos you wont ave to walk arf a mile for a little water."

"That *is* a good idea," Lizzie says in a tone which condemns all the others.

Charley's imagination, since he is using it not for its own sake, but for a definite purpose, is now highly practical. He inquires how much stoves cost and wonders if tiles are cheaper than bricks. What does seem strange to Lizzie, even with the all-accepting happiness of her inexperience, is his new plan for a garden, to contain apparently neither fountains nor statues, but cabbages, lettuces, beans; and in one corner only, some rose trees. Charley actually paces out the Galors' patch one night as a model of what he has to work on and apologises even for that ambition.

"Course, we couldnt get as much at ome as you got ere, but in Ammurca they got bigger gardens—even the little ouses."

He spends half a morning on a plan of his garden. When Lizzie, to please him, speaks of a greenhouse and points out that Sam Eger, the blacksmith, has one, he shakes his head. "Aint no room—if we going to ave vegetables, too, and we need the vegetables. Ere, Liz, look at this, suppose we puts the roses over ere?"

His plan is like a thousand plans for little villas in the suburbs; and his talk like that of the millions of young husbands, a standard joke to the world, which does not, however, laugh at a poet who writes only little songs.

"If you gets a pound a day, Charl," Lizzie suggests, "you med have a little greenhouse."

He shakes his head. "Got to pay for the furniture first—don't want them tally-men round the door longer than we can elp—and good stuff aint cheap. Look ere, Liz, I bin thinking—ow you like one of those kitchen tables like in Burls Ouse with a top like a wite stove?"

"I should think they make the plates turble cold for dinner—wood is warmer."

"You are a cure, you are. Mrs. Noah wouldn't be nothing to you, but that's living all your life in the country. You aint got no enterprise."

Lizzie is not in the least put out by this criticism because she now feels secure of Charley. She speaks with easy and sometimes brutal frankness. "You can talk, but I know my work."

"You think everything's all talk."

Lizzie, seizing a pot, says: "Talk ont cook the dinner."

"All right, if you think it's only talk."

He disappears and for ten minutes is not to be seen. When she goes to look for him she finds him silent and gloomy, with the ridiculous mournful expression of a snubbed child.

For now Charley, as well as his old enthusiasm in invention, has a new set of moods. He no longer treats Lizzie's sudden little explosions of temper or tactless remarks as jokes. He is easily and deeply hurt. His sensitiveness, his strange embarrassments are a perpetual surprise to her. She cannot understand why suddenly the tough guy Charley, who forgot injuries and insults to or from himself, in a moment, should now be the touchier of the two. Especially when he is most affectionate; when, clumsy and tentative, he is making love, a smile at the wrong moment or a chaffing word will send him away to the most distant corner of the buildings; there to stand about for an hour, gloomy and miserable, in poses of wounded dignity.

This, more often than failure of her imagination, was the cause of those differences, which were sometimes nearly quarrels. For what to Charley was serious and important in their relation, a thing almost like a religious ceremony, by its very nature easily made absurd or brought to contempt, was to Lizzie amusing and often comical. She brought to it a delight not only in doing something with and for Charley, but a childish enjoyment of play. For her, every new development, even the most embarrassing to the boy, still ignorant of his powers and the strange whims of the flesh, was apt to be laughable. She would make little jokes, suddenly smile, or even chaff him, while he was serious and absorbed. Since, too, she was conscious of no wrong, since she knew that she was all his, body and soul, and felt so keenly their happiness together, as a new wonder of the world, she was often impatient with his moods, wasting precious minutes of those few hours when they were alone together in comparative safety. She would go to him, when he was nursing his disappointment, and, pretending necessity, sweep the floor about his feet.

"Mind out, Charl."

He would move a yard.

"What's wrong. Got a pain?"

Charley does not answer. An enormous force of nature, of insulted feeling, prevents him from uttering a word. He knows that Lizzie thinks him silly, like a sulky little boy, and he knows that he is not sulky, that his grievance is not on his own account. But he can't explain that without speaking. Even if he could speak, he can't explain why her levity, at a moment requiring the greatest possible tact and dignity, should wound him so deeply.

"Got a headache, Charl?"

"No," he moves away.

Five minutes later she comes to him again: "You bant looking well, Charl. Poor Charl." But the poor is sceptical.

"I'm all right, really."

"If you got a headache, I'll make you some tea and then you better rest."

"It aint so bad as that—you want to rest, Liz."

Lizzie, having cunningly brought up this idea, answers: "Wouldn't be good for you if you got a headache, would it?"

"I aint got so much headache now."

The headache in fact disappears within a minute and is replaced by desire. Lizzie has already discovered that the shortest cut to reconciliation is through Charley's desires. But this, to her mind, is perfectly natural and right. She makes no distinction between the physical and the sentimental. For Charley to desire her and for her to enjoy Charley's satisfaction, is the most perfect kind of explanation and apology.

66 Reconciliation was needed because of intimacy, and the effect of intimacy was the need and urge to talk, to confess and to explore themselves. Both tried, with consistent effort, to express something more than needs and passing sensations. They sought often to recall the steps of their own relationship in order to see themselves within it and to wonder at it as a new and strange event.

"Wot did you really think, Lizzie, wen I snatched that bag? Ere, you wasn't a bad girl, was you? Wy didn't you go off ome?"

"I thought you wur wicked."

"Then wy didn't you go off?"

"I wanted to stay too."

"To be along a me?"

Lizzie, cleaning a saucepan, reflects and says at last: "Noa, it wur the pictures. I allays bin mad on the pictures. When we're married, Charl, we mun goa to the pictures."

"You know wot, that officer said the pictures ad made me go pinching."

Lizzie, after another period of reflection, answered: "That med be, but I likes the pictures. They'm so good as books to me—better—the people is alive. They'm real people."

"Ever seen a theatre, Liz?"

"Yess, I seen Shakespeare to the vicarage—the choir did un —Peter Drake wore Miss Phylly's blue overall with stars on, and Albert had a donkey's head."

Charley set out to instruct Lizzie. "Thass real pretty, that is —Shakespeare is the fines poet in the ole world."

"Twas a nice party, but I'd rather go to the pictures, if it comes out proper."

Further discussion in the next hour showed gradually that Lizzie liked a picture in which the good people were rewarded with happiness and the bad people were severely punished. When Charley, who had heard such pictures criticised, pointed out that they were not true to life, she agreed at once, but said: "That's why I like em—tis a sweet change."

Lizzie's conversation, though more free and ready than ever before, was still confined to short statements at long intervals. But it expressed a very rapid development of ideas. Both children, by the excitement of their intimacy, their friendship, their solitude together, were changing and developing from hour to hour. Of most people, but especially of a child, it is possible to say: in this week or month, owing to such and such an event, his life took a new direction.

Charley and Lizzie, in a few days alone together, diverged

rapidly and far from their previous course. The mere possibility of frankness, of saying everything, so that the whole experience of each was thrown into their common stock, made hours as enriching as years.

67 On several nights, troubled by Susan's presence, Lizzie was persuaded to slip out through the cyder house and wander with Charley in the quarry or the orchard.

The snow was now a foot deep on the hill and drifted much deeper in the lanes. On a moonless night, it seemed to give the only illumination, a faint whiteness sufficient only to mark the position of the nearest trees and stones. Guided by this faint pallor alone, the children moved among the fields secure under a thick cloudy darkness. On a calm night, when the half-moon was passing among large thin clouds, very clearly defined, like a boat among the foam-circles of broken waves, though everything close stood out in sharp definition, and the children, with their blue-grey shadows, felt themselves conspicuous, they could see that objects even twenty yards away were indistinct. In spite of the moon's brightness, which dazzled the eyes, the sky behind it was as dark as slate, and this darkness, at a little distance, seemed to dissolve into the lower air, hiding the trees and the fields, with their white striped furrows, in a smoky mist.

They were more alarmed by the noise of their boots, pressing down the snow, which creaked beneath their soles like new harness, than the fear of being seen from any of the close-shut cottages.

But even that nervousness was quickly forgotten. It was difficult for them, in such a landscape, to remember that anyone else existed on the surface of the world. The peaks of the cottage roofs, distinguished against the sky only by their loads of snow, seemed like the tops of subterranean dwellings, inhabited by some race of earth-grubbers which no more belonged in this cold and austere earth, where nothing moved but stars and the arrow mark of a bird's foot was like a stain on its surface, than moles.

The children not only felt the beauty of such a night, the delight of their own exclusive possession of it, but they noticed it and dared to speak of it to each other. Though Lizzie had no more exact words than sweet, pratty, lovely and proper, she conveyed to Charley an appreciation strong and deep, enough to make him know that he and Lizzie had enjoyments of taste as well as sense in common. He was therefore very ready to confess to her that he thought the night real nice, the moon real bright, the snow real clean and white, and to say: "It was a good idea us coming out, wasn't it, Liz?"

"I like un, Charl. Proper I do."

"It was worth it, wasn't it?"

They stood arm-in-arm looking about them with an air of grave pleasure, like tourists enjoying some famous spectacle.

"I never seen Burlswood so pratty afore."

"It's a nice place, Liz. I like the country—I likes a nice place to live in—you can walk around and see nice things every day."

"Yess, I likes walking."

"We likes a lot a the same things, don't we, Liz?"

Lizzie does not answer. This lends great force to her agreement. Her calm expression says: "That doesn't need saying" —a faint smile—"but boys must have their say."

68 On Tuesday morning, Harry was found, half dead from cold and starvation, hiding in a barn at Crocombe. He had been trying to keep himself alive by robbing dustbins. He was sent into hospital.

Harry told no tales, but the police once more began to make inquiries about Burlswood. Farm buildings were searched, and Mrs. Brown, to her great amusement, was watched.

The police did not get any definite information, but they suddenly formed a conviction that Charley was somewhere in the neighbourhood. The truth was that a large part of the population of Burlswood, that is, most school children below the age of fourteen, knew that he was there. Many from cottages in the village, or from close by, knew even where he was. Lizzie and Susan were accosted every day by excited children wanting to know what Charley was going to do, how he was feeling and how Susan and Lizzie were feeling.

But Lizzie answered all inquiries by pretending not to hear them, or when she was frightened, by flying into a rage and shouting: "What are you talking about, what do you mean? I don know nothing about any Charley. His gone to Lunnon, I spose."

Susan, with more aplomb, would say simply: "Don't be so silly—how could he be here?"

The secret, though debated and discussed every day by dozens of mouths, was betrayed to no grown-up.

But though children are good at keeping even a tribal secret, their secrets, like most tribal secrets, in a few days or weeks, always leak out to the persistent and scientific inquirer. The reason is that a tribal secret is not preserved by any deliberate taboo. Its only preservative is distrust of the foreigner. When the natives or the children forget natural distrust of intruders, whether anthropologists or adults, they chatter among themselves and everything is disclosed.

Thus the police, though they had no real clue, acquired almost at once, as if from the air of the place, a strong suspicion that somebody knew something; and so also Gladys Eger, at the shop on Friday afternoon, heard a child of nine say to Lizzie Galor just outside the shop door: "I see Charley to-day —he was looking out of your window," and Lizzie reply: "No, you didn't—and don't you say nothing about it neither."

Gladys takes the story to her mother, who thinks nothing of it, but who, simply for something to say, tells Galor when he calls in at eight, on his way to the Green Man, for an ounce of red virginia.

Galor also thinks nothing of the story. The kids, he says,

have been kidding Bessie about that vacky for the last three months, ever since he warmed her the last time.

Then he goes to the Green Man and spends the rest of the evening there. At ten minutes past ten, when he goes to bed, he tells the story to his wife, who says at once: "Now that's a funny thing."

"What is?"

"Why, I just noticed—oh, it bant nothing."

"What's a funny thing, Allie?"

"Why, us used such a lot of bread last week—and I diddn see Susan eat so much more—I wish her would."

"Bread—what d'ye mean, Allie?"

"Only what the police said—to keep your larder window closed and watch un."

"Have ee kept un closed?"

"I do always this weather—but——"

"But what, Allie? Speak up, do."

"Somebody might hand something out of the window or the door either. Six four-pound loaves, and the marge has been running away too."

Galor stares at her for a moment. He is not very quick to grasp a situation. Suddenly he jumps up and says: "Her wouldn't dare——"

He rolls out of bed in his shirt and socks, climbs the loft stairs and opens the girls' door. The candle is burning. Susan's voice breaks off in the middle of the death of Gwinevere.

"Put out that light," Galor said. "Didden I tell ee forty times you'll spoil yourself with night work—noa, not now. Leave it now, I didden come to speak to ee. Bessie, I got something to say to ee."

Suddenly he stops, staring from Lizzie's terrified face to the heaps in the bedclothes. He steps up to the bed and suddenly turns back the clothes. He gives then such a shout of rage as brings Mrs. Galor running after him in her nightgown. She is in time to see a naked boy throw himself at Galor, who has lifted Lizzie out of bed by the scruff of her combinations.

307

Galor holds off the boy with one hand and says: "Here, Allie, you hold un. Thank God I haven't to do nothing with un."

Mrs. Galor catches Charley and drags him away. But she doesn't look at him. She is staring at Lizzie. "Shall I fetch the belt, Alf?" she says, in a wavering uncertain voice.

"I don know, Allie—I don know whatever to do with her. Seems there bant no way to teach her sense. Do ee want us to send ee away, Bessie, to one of they homes?"

Lizzie does not answer. She is either too frightened or too despairing.

The parents stare at her, half-suspended still on her father's powerful hand. Galor's large weather-beaten face expresses a mournful and hopeless perplexity; Mrs. Galor is at once angry and fearful. She is frowning, but her lips are compressed as if she fears to say too much. Now and then she gives Charley a jerk.

"Whatever shall I do with ee, Bessie—when you be so obstinate and fulish—seems like I'm beaten."

"Us's bound to do something, Alf," Mrs. Galor says, "and us don't want to send her away, do us?"

"What's the good a belting un?—her don't pay no heed."

There is a short pause. Charley's teeth are chattering and Mrs. Galor gives him another shake. Then she says: "Us don't want Bessie to go to one of they homes, but we'm bound to do something. It is a shame the way her goes on. And Susan's scholarship so near. We'm bound to do something."

"I suppose us must try agen. Bessie, I mus try to larn ee some sense and us know tidden no bit a good talking to ee."

"Shall I bring the belt, Alf?"

"Aye, but it'll be the last time—it's your last chance, Bessie, for I'm fair beaten by ee."

Mrs. Galor, handing the unresisting, dumbfounded Charley to her husband, goes downstairs. There she seems to have some difficulty in finding the belt. But at last she is heard ascending again, at an unhurried pace. The whole of this operation, which seems to Charley extraordinary and overwhelming, like everything that has happened to him in the last quarter of an hour, is carried out with a kind of reluctant deliberation, as if it is highly unpleasant but cannot possibly be avoided.

Galor, having handed Charley back and received the belt, carefully adjusts it so that the buckle is safely held in his palm, sits down, pins Lizzie's legs between his knees and beats her. He uses force and skill, but his expression remains perplexed and sad: so that the flying vindictive hand is in strange contrast with the serious, tragic face.

Mrs. Galor suddenly becomes agitated. Her face turns scarlet and she keeps turning away from the sight of the red weals on Lizzie's skin and then twisting back again. She is in a fever of distress. But this violent natural sympathy comes out in anger and bitterness against the child for causing it. Her anger grows with the punishment. She cries out furiously: "That's it, Alf, you take her hide off—the dirty hussy. She's done for herself, now."

At the same time, in her agitation, she jerks and shakes Charley so violently that his shouts of anger and fright come out in broken syllables. He is trying to explain that everything is his fault, but the words are incomprehensible. Susan, still in bed, has put her hands over both ears and looks at the scene with exasperated despair.

Galor stops suddenly, belt in air, and listens. He is perspiring and breathless, but he has not lost his temper. He says: "There's Hawes, Allie—in Wickens Lane—give un a call to phone up station to Longwater. Don't let the little bastard go. Call out from the window."

Mrs. Galor drags Charley to the window and shouts across the hill-side. A man's bass voice answers: "What's up there? Bit late to kill pigs."

"One of the children got a pain."

"Headache in the other end, eh?"

Mrs. Galor explains that the boy Charles has been caught in the building and asks the farmer to telephone for the police.

Hawes, greatly interested, roars advice. The boy is to be locked up. He offers the use of the cellar at Hall Farm.

"We'll look after un, Mr. Hawes—never fear."

"Ah, you've had your own troubles with un."

But Mrs. Galor does not like this reference to the Twyport affair. She is not going to discuss family scandals with the world. She shuts the window. Galor tells Lizzie to hold her noise and not get herself talked about, more than she is talked about already.

"Ah," Mrs. Galor says, "Her'll be lucky if her gets away with that—but I always said her'd come to the streets. Her and her boys."

"But she didn't do nothing," Charley tries. "It wasn't er ——" a terrific jerk knocks the wind out of him and nearly dislocates his neck. Mrs. Galor says: "You hold your tongue, the police are coming for you, or I'd set about you."

"Aye," Galor says. "Proper I would." He says to Lizzie, hanging limply across his knee: "You see what comes to ee, Bess, if ee won't listen to sense."

The child can only gasp and sob.

"It won't do no good," Galor sighs, releasing her legs and letting her fall to the ground. "Not a bit of good—her's always bin so obstinate as a pig."

Susan gets wearily out of bed like one exhausted by the tasks thrown upon her, unnecessarily. She kneels down beside Lizzie and draws her head into her lap.

"Don't take on so, Bessie," she sighs. "It's all over now."

"A lot you know about it, missie," Mrs. Galor ejaculates as she goes out. Galor hesitates a moment looking down at his daughters. His heavily wrinkled face, of the texture and almost the colour of the local red earth, expresses a perplexed tenderness and resignation. He rubs his hand, still holding the belt, across his bristled chin, and says: "Ar, who would have darters—seems you cannot do right with em." Then he, too, goes downstairs to wait for the police. Charley, since his clothes have not been found, is wrapped in a couple of sacks and locked up in the coal cupboard.

The police car arrives ten minutes later. A brisk young policeman receives Charley, makes him hunt for his clothes, finds them under the bed, washes him, dresses him, and whirls him off to Longwater. His treatment surprises and puzzles Charley very much. He is friendly and yet his manner is formidable. He is good-natured, but rather as a boa-constrictor is light of touch, as he bends his coils round the deer. Charley is suspicious of him but resigned to his authority. He obeys him with dumb patience. Though he seems unhelpful and stupid, puts his shirt on back before, and his right foot in the left boot, he is really suffering from shock. He does not know what shock is; though he gives still, now and then, a dry sob or gulp, he does not connect it with Lizzie's beating. He is not capable of thinking clearly. But depression and confusion together make him seem guilty and wicked. His swollen eyes seem to squint between narrow slanting lids; a fit of weeping will make any child look sly.

69   The station sergeant read over a long list of charges, dating from the first robbery at Tanborough, more than two months before. He asked Charley for a statement and warned him that he would be asked to sign it. Charley of course, denied everything, but in a manner which admitted everything. He was in such dejection that he was anxious only to do what was wanted of him and escape into some private place.

He was glad that so little was expected of him; that the sergeant recited the crimes as he might have read a time-table, and did not even look at the criminal while he awaited his answer. He was like a man in a parcels office, entering notes in one book, checking them in a second, and reaching out one hand for the date stamp or the telephone while still writing with the other. The very manner in which the sergeant read out his whole name, Charles Frederick Brown, instead of giving him, as perhaps was intended, a sense of responsibility, merely made him feel that he was being handled by people who did not really know him as himself or care about him. He was glad they did not want him to explain anything. He was too tired and miserable for such a gigantic task.

He felt relieved as well as helpless when the sergeant, with the same bored air of a parcels clerk, told him, as if reciting a by-law about the carriage of bicycles, that he could apply for bail to-morrow but that to-night he would be sent to the remand home at Twyport. "That's the usual course," the sergeant said to his book. "Anyone you'd like to see—I mean to-morrow?"

Charley gave Lina Allchin's name and afterwards his step-mother's. It occurred to him that the person he most wanted at that moment was Lizzie, and he actually opened his mouth to ask if he might send her a message. But the sergeant was writing a note in his book, scratching his neck under his uniform collar and reaching out through the air with his right foot for a swing-door. Before he had finished writing, or scratching, he pushed open the door with his toe and called: "Parker."

As Parker came in he reached for another book and made a note in it while he spoke. "He's under age, so you'll have to take him to the Twyport Home, the old one—the new one's full."

"Uniform all right?"

"No, change your coat, anyhow."

Charley looked apologetically at Mr. Parker, who was plainly annoyed at being made to change his clothes and drive twenty miles after eleven o'clock, because the prisoner happened to be under the age of seventeen and could not be kept in the cells. Mr. Parker did not notice the look; he had not yet glanced at Charley. But his annoyance did not seem to expect or require an apology. It was a bored annoyance set in the rigid lines of an official resignation which prevented both any great play of

Mr. Parker's features and any strong expression of his feelings. It was expressed only in an increased stiffness and blankness of feature like that of a parcels clerk who is asked to do just a little too much.

Mr. Parker, in complete silence, drove Charley to Twyport and handed him over to a good-natured buxom old woman in a red flannel wrapper, who showed him his bed in a room occupied already by three boys.

"We're a bit full," she explained, "but there, we always are last five years. You boys are so gamesome these days that we have to put you four in a room." The old woman made Charley clean his teeth before he got into bed. She treated him like a small boy, and Charley, though he liked Mrs. B., felt for the first time the inappropriateness of this treatment. He felt, without forming the thought, too old, too tired, too private within himself to have his ears examined by anyone. He did not mind what they did to him so long as they left him alone. Yet when at last he was alone, in bed, he felt such crushing misery that it surprised even himself. "Ere, ere," he remonstrated faintly. "Wots up, Charley? Aint the end of the world yet." But the wretchedness seemed to increase upon him, to press him down. He did not ask where it came from, but once he formed the idea: "Poor ole Liz, it's a shame."

He had expected, without particular thought on the matter, that he would again be let out on bail, and Lina Allchin had already applied for bail. It was refused on the grounds that Charley had broken his probation promises. He was told as soon as he got up that he must stay in custody until his trial.

Charley had not before seen the inside of a remand home. He had expected a kind of prison. He found something between an odd kind of school and a hostel or boarding-house. In the morning, after breakfast, he was set down with the eight other boys, of all ages from nine to sixteen, to do lessons. A little weary old man, a retired teacher, gave to each some task: first a sum, afterwards a chapter of history to learn, urged them now and then to work at it, and at last corrected the sum

313

or heard the chapter. All made a feint of working, but it was obvious that even the old man had no hope of achieving any instruction. The prisoners' faces, their very attitudes, seemed to say: "We have other things to think about, really important things," and the old man, by every word and glance, seemed to be agreeing with them and apologising for his lessons.

70   The house had little mark of a place of detention except the barred windows. But detention is a fact which needs no emphasis. It is present like a climate, so that public school boys who are surrounded by open fields and can escape at any moment nevertheless feel continuously the difference between school and home. They may not dislike the difference, and they know or believe that it is necessary and normal, part of a normal education; but they feel it in every moment and it modifies all their thoughts and friendships, the nature of their social experience.

Public schools have barred windows, but the bars say: "You mustn't break our rules because you are a normal schoolboy." The bars of the remand home, though no more obtrusive than many schools', since they were a standard defence bars built into all the kitchens in the row, said: "You are a prisoner, because you are abnormal, an enemy of society." This was the pervading consciousness which looked out of all eyes and seemed stamped upon all foreheads in wrinkles peculiar to the obsession. It made the place instantly peculiar, set it apart from the whole world of normal life, and made it certain that normal life could not be lived there, that normal friendships would be impossible, and that normal methods of teaching would be absurdly inadequate.

The sense of imprisonment did not at once make itself felt in Charley. He was at first more preoccupied by the domestic routine of the house and its surprising comfort. The beds were soft, the food was good. He had little to do. After lessons he helped to wash dishes and scrub the kitchen floor. In the afternoon, since there was snow on the ground and games were impossible, he was taken for a walk with the two elder boys.

In the evening the whole party sat in the little back parlour, called the recreation room, where there were cards, chess, draughts, a dart-board, books and even some illustrated papers. But Charley, though usually delighted with a book, found that he could not read more than a page. He began a game of draughts and suddenly turned to darts instead. He left the darts to go to the lavatory, simply in order to change his occupation and to leave the room. Wherever he found himself in the home he wished to be somewhere else, especially on the other side of the nearest door. At night he could not sleep and felt so urgent an impulse to get out of bed that in the small hours he gave way to it. He stole to the door, opened it and then did not know what to do. It was as though for three hours he had been kept awake only by the desire to open that door. There was a light showing in the passage. This light startled him, like an unexpected sentry. Then suddenly a bass voice spoke: "Hullo, there!"

The superintendent, an ex-constable, apparently slept with his own door open upon the passage.

He came out, a huge, bulky figure in gaudy striped pyjamas. "Hullo! who is it? Brown. What do you want?"

"Lavatory, sir."

"All right—end of the passage. Don't be too long, and put on your slippers. Don't want splinters in your feet, do you? Better put on your coat, too. It's freezing."

Charley puts on his coat and slippers and goes to the W.C. He sits on the seat and feels as it were suspended in existence, as if his personal life is dead. Suddenly he notices that there is a latch on the door. He turns the latch, locking himself in, and at once he feels released, as though he is out of prison. He falls back against the wall, puts his hands over his face and begins to cry, silently and desperately. An oppression is broken away from his heart, from his whole body. He thinks: "Wots appened to Liz?"

At once he sees Lizzie's broad serious face while she stirs a pot, and then she turns and looks at him with curiosity. Some incident of the hundreds engraved on his memory by happiness has reproduced itself upon his mind's eye. She smiles thoughtfully at him and says something about the time. It is late for dinner or early for the potatoes.

Charley cannot believe that he has ever lived such a life or enjoyed such freedom and happiness. He does not think now of his love-making. His mind never dwells upon those quick passing incidents whose quality is still strange to him and a little frightening. He sees Lizzie at work, and he hears her voice while they talk together enthusiastically about what they are to do, and how they will conduct their lives. He does not think of Lizzie as a wife but as Lizzie, the unique being with whom he has enjoyed happiness, and entered, as if by accident, into an existence together, where everything—work, play, the most trivial tasks and objects, such as pots, scrubbing-brushes, have suddenly become beautiful and dignified.

Charley does not know what dignity means, but he feels that with Liz he has become a mature being, that he has lived like a grown-up.

"It was a good time—bess time I ever ad," he says to himself; and what he means is that in that week he has made the discovery which transforms the world, that kindness is the dignity of living, which transforms the most grotesque gesture, the ugliest face into the expression of eternal beauty.

"Dear ole Liz—way she looked at me wen I fell off the beam."

"Hullo, there, haven't you finished yet? Don't hang about in this weather."

"Yessir. Jess coming, sir." Charley loudly crumples the paper to deceive authority and pulls the cord. Then he goes back to bed and tries to sleep. But once more something stiffens upon his body, not only upon his chest, oppressing his heart so that it beats more violently, but upon his very arms and legs so that they want to throw off the blankets. In the

316

morning, when again he sits at lessons, he has such trouble to endure sitting still for an hour in the same room that he can't think. He fails in the simplest sums. But the little old teacher, his face a mask of weariness, shows neither surprise nor irritation. He silently corrects the howlers, works over the sum and pushes the book back to Charley. He does not even say: "Try again."

71 Charley, on this morning, already had a close friend. This sudden devotion did not surprise anyone in the place. Within the dull stupid routine of the little house, whose clean paint looked senseless because it did not stand for anything but cleanliness, whose floors had been scrubbed till they spoke only of useless labour, there was always an abnormal excitement of personal relations. The boys, by their natures, their feelings and their situation, were like charged clouds, and produced between themselves, whether they liked it or not, the violent attraction and repulsion, the distortions of relations in space, the sudden tensions and discharges of an electric storm.

In such a place, where feelings must be abnormal, the normal dullness of routine, floor-washing, became itself abnormal, like farm fields on a volcano top.

Charley did not recognise a strangeness hidden from him by domestic simplicity, but he felt it all the more strongly.

When, as soon as the boys were alone together, they said to him: "You're Charley Brown, arn't you?" he refused at first to own the name. He did not know why he gave way to this queer impulse; for a whole afternoon he denied himself. Then suddenly, while he was washing up the tea-things with one of the older boys, he not only admitted his name, but told the full story of his crimes. In a moment he was offering friendship to the stranger.

He was called Toomer. He was sixteen, and he had already escaped three times from institutions. He boasted that no one could hold him. He expected to be sent next week to Borstal, but he would escape also, he said, from Borstal. At both his institutions he had made a practice of smashing crockery and starting fires. Once after smashing up a whole dormitory he had been locked in a padded cell. This fact gave him great pleasure to remember. "I puzzled em that time," he said.

Toomer's boasts were confirmed by another of the older boys in the home, Bailey, who had escaped with him.

Bailey was a thick-set, lazy youth, committed originally for small indecencies. He had been living since his escape by small blackmail. He proposed to return to this livelihood as soon as he could. "If you play fair you're all right," he said. "If you say finish, it's got to finish."

Bailey thought Toomer a joke and chaffed him all day. "E's Bolshy," he told Charley. "E aint got no sense—making trouble for his silly self. E's got everything all wrong."

But Toomer fascinated Charley.

He was a small lightly built boy, with an excessively thin face and long thin nose. His chin was small and sharp. He had very dark hair and dark brown eyes with long lashes. His whole appearance was effeminate, fragile, and his eyes were beautiful. He had a peculiar steadfastness and honesty in his glance which carried conviction. His look was masculine, full of assurance and experience. It seemed to say: "I know the world—I know what I'm talking about." But he had a peculiar trick, sometimes in the middle of such a speech, of stopping for a second and staring vaguely in front of him. For a moment his self-assurance would disappear, his eyes wander, his mouth fall open, so that he seemed to have received a shock of surprise. But these checks went off in a flash. In half a second he would recover himself and his confidence.

As an errand boy he had thrown up his job after some quarrel with the manager. Toomer had since picked up, in the institutions, a general grievance against society. He would say to Charley, with his steadfast candid glance: "It's a swindle, it's just a plant, to do the workers down. What we got to do is

318

to smash it all up. Then we can start fair. Tell you what I did at the last place, set fire to the carpenter's shop. Just before I left. They didn't trace it to me, of course. It puzzled em all round, and five hundred pounds of damage. That made em think a bit." Then his eyes turned aside and stared into the air with a sudden look of anxious doubt and perplexity.

72 Bailey, when he was not trying to flirt with Toomer, who received his advances with a cool indifference much more daunting than contempt, would tease him by suggesting that he was going mad.

"You better not set too many fires," he would say, "or they'll put ya in the loony bin."

"That's all you know," Toomer would answer, calmly and confidently. "You can't put a chap in an asylum unless he's raving, and then you've got to prove it. The doctors has got to be pretty careful what they do, I can tell you—there's a new law about it. Why, if a doctor tries to be funny, you can smash him up—you've only got to put the coppers on to him and they'll take away his licence. It's the law now, and you can't monkey round with the law." Then again his jaw would drop, his cheeks change colour and his eyes stare.

Toomer told Charley that it was easy to break out of any institution. "They put you on your honour but that's a trick. They know they can't hold you, so they try the honour plant; course, you just walk out whenever you like."

It was raining on the snow-covered ground outside, and all but two of the boys, in bed with colds, were sitting in the little back parlour.

All had books or illustrated papers, but no one was reading.

"I'll cut off," Charley said, "I aint going to stay in any of their bloody chokeys."

"Of course you arn't—you arn't a cissie," Toomer said, and the other children in the room turned their admiring or perplexed glances from Toomer to Charley.

319

The youngest, a boy of nine, found wandering in the streets and said to be out of control, gazed with round eyes full of a kind of miserable astonishment; two brothers called Hawke, of ten and twelve, on remand for robbing their mother in order to go to the pictures, listened with critical attention. None of the three could hide his interest, willing or unwilling, in talk charged with a real experience of life.

Sometimes the superintendent or his little round wife would look in, and once the former, in a significant tone, said to the younger boys: "Don't you believe all you hear from that lot," indicating Toomer and Charley by a movement of his head. "They haven't done so cleverly for themselves after all, have they?"

Charley noticed that he was included among the dangerous characters and this made him feel strange, as if he did not recognise himself. Years of experience seemed to divide him from the time when he had boasted of being the youngest cat burglar in England.

73 One night when Toomer was instructing Charley how to start a fire with a candle and a box full of shavings soaked in paraffin, Bailey said: "E don't go in for arson, Charley don't, e's a smasher-up."

Charley looked wise and waited to hear what this meant.

"Smashing up—no good—couple of quids' worth of old crocks and a kitchen table—they laugh at you."

"This chap smashed up a ole ouse full, thousands a pounds worth a damage the papers said. Didn't ya, Brown?"

Charley understood at once that the smashing up at Burls could be given a new important significance. Something in him, the old Charley, wanted to claim that importance for himself; another, more sincere, more experienced Charley, wondered how he did so senseless an act. He said at last with a nice balance between importance and sincerity: "It was the ell of an evening, that was." He turns to Harry, who has just been sent in from hospital. "Wot you say, Arry?"

Harry is too wretched to answer. He sits in a corner and stares at Charley as if at a wall.

Harry has already been told that he will be put on probation. He is being kept in the Remand Home only because it is held that a fortnight's detention there will do him good. He is in the same category with the Hawke boys. But his feelings seem more like those of the wanderer. He turns his eyes from one speaker to another with the same miserable stare.

"I didn't know you smashed it up on purpose," Toomer says, in his voice full of sincerity, the voice of one interested in truth. "I thought you were having a lark."

"We was tight."

Harry turns his eyes from Charley to Toomer. It is obvious that he can no longer make head or tail of the conversation, of his situation, of Charley, of Toomer or anything or anybody. He is too bewildered even to ask questions.

"Ere, wots the good a worrying," Bailey laughs from the sofa. "You aint ony got the one life and the tarts just sitting in a row asking for a nice clean young chap to eat out of their hands. I tell you another thing, too, chaps, go for the old uns like my Scotchy, that's kept off the booze. If they're boozy they're ell, they'll let you down as sure as Sattay comes before Sunday; can't trust em a yard—nothing but dirt and lies and owling matches. But if they've kept off the booze, it's a undred to one they'll do you proud."

"We got to bust it all up," Toomer says, following only his own ideas. "It's a plant by the cops and the boorjoys. They work it together."

"Oh, you're for the loony bin—I believe you're loony already. It starts like that, getting ideas."

Charley discussed their ideas all day. He had never before found philosophies so simple and coherent. Sometimes he preferred Toomer's and sometimes Bailey's. But they were only ideas to him, toys like darts and cards, to pass the time.

He was too restless, too preoccupied to feel the force of any idea. His life was still in his feelings, in his sense of oppression, his continuous longing for freedom and Lizzie.

74 Visitors at the Home were allowed at certain fixed hours, especially on Sunday mornings, when some of the boys' relatives came to take them to church or chapel.

Charley was visited on Sunday morning, first by his stepmother, then by Lina Allchin.

Mrs. Brown kissed him, shed tears, and said that it was a shame to lock him up and she wouldn't have him sent away. She promised to hire a lawyer to get him out of the Remand Home.

Charley was moved by his stepmother's warm sympathy, but it did not surprise him. He had seen her in the same mood and heard her use the same language about a slight acquaintance in the same street arrested for drink and disorder. He did not expect much from his stepmother and so he was grateful to her for her visit.

But he ran eagerly to see Lina Allchin. He knew, as soon as he heard her name, how anxiously he had been waiting for her. He did not know in the least what he expected from her, but he had boundless confidence in her friendship and her power to change his lot.

Interviews with visitors were in the little front parlour, supposed to be private to the superintendent. Here, among the plush furniture, in front of the souvenir mugs and comic dogs on the chimney-piece, Charley, with flushed cheeks, shook hands with his friend and tried to say how glad he was to see her.

But even before either spoke he felt frightened as of a new and unexpected calamity. He gazed nervously at Lina.

She began, however, to speak in her usual friendly manner, advising him to trust the magistrates and to confess everything.

"I simply couldn't believe it when I saw what you did at the

Wandles', that beautiful house, but now they say you were drunk."

"Yes, miss, that was it." Charley is eager to explain this act, so puzzling to himself. "I had too much at supper and then we began throwing things."

"I thought you loved the pictures."

"Yes, miss, I did." He frowns. "I don't know why I did such a stupid thing—cept I'd ad too much."

"I'm glad you're sorry."

Lina speaks now with a peculiar reserve and stiffness. Charley's nerves, sensitive to every mood in a friend, feel this change, and he looks up anxiously. "I'm sorry, miss—it was the drink—I bin a fool, I know—it was a wicked shame wot I done at Burls."

Suddenly Lina looks directly at him and says in a severe tone: "What I can't understand at all is what you did to poor Bessie Galor."

"Yes, miss," Charley turns very red.

"Do you realise the terrible trouble you have brought upon her?"

Charley says nothing. He feels at once confused. His forehead wrinkles in perplexity.

"Haven't you anything to say for yourself?" Lina is surprised by the boy's silence and allows her anger to grow. "Do you know what you've done? Do you know she's going to have a baby—and she's not fifteen till next month?"

"No, miss." He is startled, but he speaks still in a sulky tone. He is amazed by Lina's strange view of Lizzie. He has never thought of her as a poor country girl, unable to defend herself. To him she is Lizzie, a person full of odd and interesting characteristics, physical, moral and mental. He feels resentment against Lina but he says nothing. He does not know how to defend himself.

"I can't understand it," Lina says, but obviously she is sure that in this situation, at least, she can't be wrong. "I didn't think you were like that."

"Like what?" Charley thought. "What am I like?"

"It's so cruel and mean—and you don't seem to care a bit."

Charley is struggling against the woman's mysterious purpose, which he feels to be dangerous. He feels as if she is trying to push him into a dark place from which he will never escape. He has no words to describe a sense of guilt, a conviction of sin, but he feels by nervous imagination what they are.

"Arn't you ashamed of yourself, Charley—not even a little ashamed?"

A huge blackness rises upon Charley and he makes a desperate leap to escape from it. He exclaims: "But Liz didn't say nothing——"

"Bessie has tried to excuse you from the beginning, but that doesn't make it any better, does it? Charley, if you try to wriggle out of this, I don't think I'll be able to forgive you."

The young woman's voice trembles with disgust and anger, which works upon the boy with all the nervous force of its sincerity. He feels the pressure and fights more desperately against it.

"But I didn't—I didn't—it aint like that——" he wants to explain that neither he nor Lizzie are guilty of anything; that the same thing has happened to them both. But the idea is beyond him. The very feeling of it is already disappearing from his attempt to grasp it. He says desperately: "But me and Liz——"

"Think what you have done to her—she will have to be sent away from home—her own mother and father are ashamed of her—and you only think of excusing yourself. I wonder do you realise, Charley, how disappointed I am in you. I think I never want to speak to you again. A boy that treats a girl like that—a girl like poor Bessie, and then tries to justify himself."

At these words, poor Bessie, so skilfully chosen, the black wave rises again and this time Charley is overwhelmed. He bursts into tears. Lina Allchin says in a new voice, full of relief and happiness: "Thank God, Charley. You have got some decent feelings after all—I wasn't mistaken in you."

"Yes, miss, I'm sorry—I been bad—to everybody." Charley repents violently between sobs.

Lina, too, is tearful. She congratulates the boy on his repentance: "Now I do hope for you, Charley; and you know I will always be your friend."

She goes away happy and leaves him remorseful, still more confused than before. He complains to himself: "But she wouldn't listen—it wasn't like that."

His violent emotion, which was remorse, now becomes anger. "Wy did she go on at me? She didn't even listen. It wasn't like that."

He is enraged with Lina, not only on his own account, but because he feels that Liz, too, is involved. "It wasn't like that —she isn't poor Liz—and wot was wrong with it?"

But he feels also unsafe. For now he can't think of Lizzie and himself together, without hearing Lina's judgment and catching her contemptuous feeling. All his love-making with Lizzie, which an hour before had the beauty of its happiness, now suddenly takes ugly and squalid shapes.

He is angry, ashamed, bitter, and, above all, confused. He says to himself, arguing when argument itself is an expression of doubt: "It isn't like that—she don't understand. Lizzie and me——"

75 Next morning he was carried off to the Town Hall. He no longer expected an awe-inspiring trial. He knew by experience that he would be received informally and treated kindly. But he was now frightened of he knew not what. Since Lina had failed him he had lost confidence in all the world.

He at once expected the worst when, reaching the court, he found Lizzie in the waiting-room and heard that she was to be examined first. He had barely time to exchange glances with her, glances which, by trying to say too much, expressed nothing at all except anxiety and confusion, before she was taken into the magistrates' room.

Lizzie's examination was short, partly because the magistrates had already classified her, on information received, and partly because of her own plain answers. One or two questions made her flush her dark angry colour, and set her mouth in obstinacy, and then she was silent. But when the policeman, supposing or pretending that she had not heard, repeated the question in her ear, she answered with plain country words.

"When did this boy first have relations with you?"

"Night he fell in the water we first laid together."

"Did you realise what he was doing to you?"

Lizzie turns red and makes no answer. But being asked again, she frowns and says with a little surprise at the question: "Yes, m, I'm bound to know that."

She admits that she has been warned not to go with boys.

"But you didn't see the danger?"

"I did go with un still, m."

"Did he pester you to go with him?"

"No, m, I did follow un all the time."

"He gave you presents?"

Lizzie cautiously admits the presents and then that she knew them to be stolen. But she denies that Charley won her with presents.

Lizzie's anxiety to defend Charley is noticed, but makes little impression, because it is put down to whim. She has been classified already as childish and irresponsible.

The report on Lizzie, given by teachers and parents: that she was slow at school and can barely read; from the probation officer, that she is a problem child, out of control of her parents; and the doctor, that she is sexually too mature for her intelligence, have naturally more weight than personal knowledge acquired in five minutes' examination.

Even if any of the magistrates should realise, as probably all have done more than once, that the varieties of human character are infinite; and recollect, even in their own experience, illiterates whose judgment and wisdom made them sounder advisers, better friends, than many learned men, they have no right or justification to take notice of the fact, or time to attempt better acquaintance with a child, who is, in all probability, just what she is described.

They confer, therefore, as matter of form, read passages from the reports to each other, and agree that Lizzie must be sent to a Rescue Home. They make a note to enquire for vacancies and remand her on bail.

She is taken out once more through the ante-room, and sees Charley looking at her with an expression which is as senseless to her, as her own, to Charley, seems inscrutable.

Charley, brought in next, finds himself in the small comfortable room which he has known at his former trial. He sits even in the same chair. The magistrates are different, but again they seem kind and patient. One of them is a woman, who looks at him benignly through gold spectacles.

They ask him, as before, to tell his story in his own way. He gives them a full account as far as he can remember it, and then the policeman makes a statement. One of the gentlemen asks Charley questions on this statement and Charley agrees that it is true. He feels a little more confidence and strives to be cool. When the witnesses are called, he helps them to complete their evidence or corrects it as far as he can. He does not say, of course, that Lizzie or Bert was in the Burls House raid, because obviously no one suspects it, but he admits to everything they do know or suspect, and when the lady asks in surprise, why he has done so much damage, he says at once that he cannot tell.

"I don't know wy I was so stupid. It was a wicked thing."

"You had been drinking," the lady says.

Charley, knowing that ladies were sometimes severe on drinks, flushes and hesitates. Then he admits the fact. "I ad ad a drop, m." But the lady makes no further comment. The magistrates say so little on the destruction at Burls that Charley is nervous. What else have they discovered? What exactly has he done? He can't remember.

The chairman, however, asks no questions about the robberies. He begins a little speech about the dangers of drink and hopes that Charley realises them. Charley swears that he will never get drunk again. He is now greatly relieved. He thinks: "Lizzie put em right. She told em the right story." He is expressing his relief and admiration for Lizzie's sense and force of character, in the beginnings of a smile, when the lady magistrate says mildly: "And the girl, Bessie Galor, what have you to say about her?"

"I don't know, m. Didn't she tell you herself?"

"Do you realise, I wonder, what a terrible wrong you have done her?"

Charley feels again the impact of that will to shame him, to drive him down into a pit of remorse and despair. Startled, he turns red and looks at the woman; from her to the two kind gentlemen who have been talking to him in so friendly a manner. In all these faces, but more plainly in the woman's, he sees the same resolution. He exclaims: "But, Mum, Lizzie and me——" he falters and makes another attempt: "Me and Lizzie, we was——" He stops and tries to hold down a sudden impulse to weep, to allow himself to be shamed.

But angry and obstinate nerves within him stiffen against surrender; he feels he is not really guilty at all, that Lina and the nice magistrates still don't understand the situation. He can't explain it, but it isn't in the least like their idea of it. He frowns at them, looks sullen and defiant.

"To be honest, Brown," the eldest and the kindest of the gentlemen, with a little white moustache and round spectacles, speaks to Charley: "Your attitude to the whole affair strikes us all," he looks at the others who look acquiescent, "strikes us all as extraordinarily cool, to say the least of it, even callous, though I don't like to use the word. I am thinking not of the wanton destruction at Burls House, though that was bad enough, but of your treatment of this poor girl, Bessie Galor.

We are trying to help you, you understand—but it is difficult to do anything for you if you take up this attitude that nothing much has happened and that you've done nothing to be ashamed of."

"If you take that view," the lady said, "but I hope I'm wrong, there's no hope for you at all. None whatever."

In two minutes Charley is once more in tears. He can't speak. But now, underneath this violent hysterical emotion, there is fury like steel, a deep resolute anger. It is the protest of all his honesty against a lie, and a defilement.

76 Charley, brought back from court, still sobbing, could not recover himself for an hour. Then he could not eat his dinner. He was possessed by a violent excitement. He kept walking about the room, muttering to himself, going into the garden to look at the sky or the wall, or the little bare apple trees. Bailey bawled at him: "You gimme the willies opping about like that. You're as bad as Red."

Charley stared at him without understanding what he had said, sat down and picked up a picture paper, stared at that with the same uncomprehending blankness, and then threw it down and went out again to the garden.

Red was helping to wash up after dinner. As Charley passed the scullery window, he lifted up a plate to him, then opened his fingers and let it drop with a crash. Charley heard the old woman's surprised voice as she came hurrying, and then Toomer's explanations given in an angry voice which was full of guilt. "It slipped—it just slipped out of my hands. But you don't have to pay, do you, missus. It's government."

Charley takes no notice of the incident. He is standing in the middle of the little walled garden, staring at the sky. The snow is melting now in the long narrow garden, which is like a box with the top knocked out. There are patches of flattened grass, burnt by frost, between the snow wreaths, which have taken the colour of cold sago. The little apple trees at the far end are black and streaming with wet which makes round drops on every pruned elbow. The drops are the same colour as the snow and the sky, which is like an old dirty ceiling bulging downwards. On the path, the gravel has disappeared below a deep pinkish mud. The shrubs, with hanging blackened leaves, seem to be dead.

"Don't you worry, Charley," Red says at his shoulder. "It's always three years second time up."

"I aint worrying." Charley turns towards his friend a face so pinched and twisted that in the free world it would make people turn round and say: "What's wrong with that child?"

But Red has seen the expression before. He says: "Don't let em rile you. You got to fight em, see."

Red glances at the house to make sure that no one is looking and begins to water upon one of the little trees. "You can kill a tree this way if you do it often enough."

"Wots the good a that."

"You got to fight em, see."

"Killing apple trees—I'd kill em."

"You feeling bad, Charley—I know how it is."

"No, you don't neither."

"Don't you mind em, Charley—they don't matter. Lot of stuffed skins."

"I don't. I don't care wot they think either—think ya dirt——"

"Course they do."

"But I'll fight em—they don't know wot they've taken on— I'll bloody well smash the ole bleeding lot to ell."

Red, startled, gazes at Charley's face for a moment and says then, in an anxious voice: "Steady on, Charley."

"Steady on be——." Charley chokes in rage. "I'll puzzle em—I'll give em something to think about. I'll make em wish they'd never eard of me—I'll burn this blasted ole to start with."

"That's all right, Charley—of course we got to fight em— but you don't want to do anything in too much of a hurry. It needs planning. And you got to keep cool, you don't want to do anything silly."

330

"You yellow?"

Red is too fond of Charley and far too understanding of his state of mind to resent the charge. He takes the boy's arm and leads him slowly along the high wall, sweating its dirt in slow runnels of thick liquid. "You're all right, Charley, you got the guts. But you don't know the game yet—you don't want to get yourself into trouble."

"Cupboard under the stairs—that's the place to start it. It's full of firewood."

Red says in a hesitating voice: "And it can be tough, too, Charley. They got ways a getting at you. I don't mean punishment cells and bread and water and birching. I been tickled up twice. That's nothing. It's the way they get talking to you—get at your friends, too—get all round you. Sometimes you don know where you are."

"Oos the great burner up? Thought you was going to fight em."

"All right, Charley, I'll fight em." Another pause and then Red says: "Suppose I burn em up after you go. I'd do it, too."

"But I wants to do it. I'd like to do it."

"They certainly got you mad, Charley."

"Yess, I am mad, too. They'll find that out quick enough."

They are called into tea. Mrs. B. gives her sympathy to Charley. "But you're lucky—ten years ago it would a been nine strokes and the reformatory. Cheer up, lad, and praps I'll find a bit a something nice for your tea."

"Sall right, mum, I don care for em."

At night Toomer comes to him again and says suddenly: "You know what Bailey says."

"I don care wot the silly barstard says."

"About chaps going loony."

"You aint loony—you an me's the only sensible ones in the ouse."

"No, course I'm not," Red hesitates, and gives up his enterprise, whatever it was. But he says again with the same perplexed, regretful voice: "They certainly got you mad, Charley."

77 Charley's mind was now obsessed with the idea of a smash up. He imagined the Remand Home a ruin, with the rafters open to the sky, and invented elaborate schemes for unscrewing the nuts of the gas pipes and making an explosion. He hid under his mattress an old rusty tyre lever picked up in the back lane during the exercise walk. He studied the comings and goings of the staff and inmates, and decided that his best time was Sunday morning when the Superintendent took the whole party to church, and old Mrs. B. cooked the Sunday dinner.

Charley resolved to go sick that morning, stay away from church and lock Mrs. B. in her own kitchen. He would then be able to smash the house, from the top, at his leisure, and, if he chose, set it on fire.

This scheme was now so fixed and planned in his head that it did not seem even strange. To Charley, who had spent three days fitting it together in detail, it was a logical master-piece. He did not, however, tell anyone about it, not even Toomer. He had become secretive and suspicious. His very manner, though he did not know it, had changed, he had hardly spoken to anybody since the trial, and he rarely even looked at other people. He was absorbed in his bitterness and the exciting idea of the smash-up. He heard the crashes, the screams of Mrs. B., saw a crowd gathering in the street.

"There'll be the police an a fire-engine, two fire-engines with ladders, and firemen with hatchets and the magistrates, yess, and the mayor himself—ere, ere—they wouldn't ave the mayor, and I don't want im. But the magistrates would come. That ole girl with the nose-nippers an the general with the white moustache. They'd come—see em on the pavement wen I chucks the jerries through the winders and sets afire to the gas-pipes in the top room—course the firemen will chop the door down and then I'll just walk out and say: 'Ladies and genmen, jess a little bit of fun for a start. Nex time I'll do it proper.' And they'll say, wot did ya do such an awful thing for, ya bad boy, and I'll say because I've tumbled to yer little game, see—cos I see it's all a plant, see—ya thought you'd get me down, didn't ya, but I aint downed so easy."

On Sunday morning Charley refused breakfast, and when Mrs. B. asked him if he were ill, he said that he was not, but he didn't want anything. Mrs. B. at once gave him a dose of salts and made him lie down.

Meanwhile visitors called for the brothers Hawke, and a tall, bony old woman, Bailey's aunt, came, as she came every Sunday morning, to lecture him on his wicked life.

The coming and going below made Charley's nerves jump. Each time that the gate clanged he jumped off his bed and ran to see if it was the signal of the church party's going. Yet he knew that at least an hour must pass before church-time. He returned to his bed each time more impatient, and sliding his hand under the mattress, felt the tyre-lever with the nervous delight of an artist who handles the tool with which he will accomplish a masterpiece.

Suddenly a bell rang on the landing; a warning bell for any boy in the upper part of the house. Charley lay still. But no one answered the bell. It rang again, and he went to the stair head. Mrs. B.'s thin old voice came briskly to him: "Brown, Brown, a visitor for you. Mind your hands is clean."

Charley felt disgusted. He thought: "That'll be Miss Lina—to go at me." He stood for a minute. But Mrs. B. called again: "Brown, Brown, don't you hear?—it's visitors in the front room."

He descended slowly. As he came into the little front drawing-room, dark behind its lace curtains, he pulled the obstinate, disgusted face which had before so deeply offended the lady magistrate and Lina. But as he looked round he heard not Lina's voice but Phyllis's: "Why, it is Charrley—poor liddle chap—how are you, deurr?"

Charley flushed deeply. He was so much surprised that he could not speak. Phyllis was standing by the window with Arthur beside her and a little behind. Arthur's hand was

333

probably resting on her waist from behind because she made a little movement of her hips and said reproachfully: "Arthurr."

"How are you Charley, deeurr?"

"I'm all right, miss."

"Missus now," Arthur said.

"Noa, Arthur," Phyllis made a slight attempt, or feint, to shake off the hand; and then, turning her head, smiled at Arthur in that manner which is only seen in happy and unsophisticated brides and which seems to say: "I'm married, and I like it, and I'm proud of being a doting wife."

This smile appealed to Charley's sense of humour and pleased him too. He wanted to laugh at Phyllis and chaff her in the proper ritual manner; and yet he had never felt so fond of the girl. He stood looking at her until he realised that for the moment she had forgotten him. It was Arthur who first, with a slight nod of the head, warned Phyllis: "Now, Phyll, get it over—you said it'd only take ten minutes and it's taken a quarter-hour already."

"Why, Charley, I got something for you." Phyllis opened her bag and gazed inside, with an expression nearest to surprise of which she was capable. She said mildly: "Why, wherever is it?"

Charley turned very red and exclaimed: "Is it from——" he was going to say "Lizzie," but stopped himself.

"Yess—why, Arthurr, didden I give'n to ee?"

Phyllis to Arthur now sang the broadest vowels; as if only a traditional folk music, used by generations of Hawes brides to their men, could express her ritual sense of marriage.

Arthur, lofty and calm, seemingly deaf to all music, drew from his pocket a chocolate bar, which Phyllis handed to Charley.

"From your mother, Charley, and she sent her love."

"We'll miss our bus," Arthur said, "That's what!"

"Noa, Arthur. Poor liddle Charley—whatever did you go to break the pictures for?"

"I dunno," Charley said, not at all offended by this question. "It just appened."

"Well, now," Phyllis gazes at him with mild wonder, "and you so liddle—to do all that mischief. But it was a bit dull for you at Burlswood, I suppose, after London. It is dull, too, in winter."

"Please, miss——"

"Missus."

"Noa, Arthur, don't ee go on—yes, Charley?"

Charley is silent. He has lost his nerve. Phyllis looks at him and says: "Tell me, deeurr—I won't tell anybody."

Suddenly she says to Arthur: "You go on, Arthur—I won't be a minute."

"I'll not go without ee, we'll not get a seat as it is."

"Ah, go on, Arthurr—it's plenty of time!"

Arthur says firmly: "I'll give ee one more minute, by the watch." He looks at his watch and says, irritably: "I thought you wanted to be home dinner-time."

"We'll go this minute, Arthurr."

Phyllis beckons Charley. "Come and tell me, deeurr—you can whisper it, if you don't want anyone to hear."

Charley goes over and mutters into Phyllis's ear: "Ows Liz?"

"Liz?" Phyllis speaks aloud, forgetting her promise of tact. "Ah, you mean Bessie. She's not too bad. They're going to send her to one of those rescue homes, where she'll be looked after proper and taught the laundry."

"Where is she now?" Charley murmurs, turning crimson.

"Why, to home, last time I heard. But they keeps her close —ah, she's been a great trouble to poor Galor, Bessie."

Arthur for the first time looks directly and meaningly at Charley and says: "That was a bad job of yours, too, young chap."

"Noa, Arthur, how could ee know—he's too liddle; that Bessie was after un from the first day. I see her myself."

Arthur rises suddenly, and taking Phyllis by the arm shifts her from the sofa. "Come on, now, you said a minute, and this is twenty."

Phyllis allows herself to be dragged towards the door, smiling as if to say: "See how he treats me, the man. What a man."

Charley darts at her and catches her dress as if to hold her back. "Oh, miss—missus—will you take er a message?"

"Noa, she won't," Arthur says. "She won't do no such thing——"

"Oh, Arthurr!"

"What if the police heard of it? It would make nice trouble. Have sense, Phyll."

Charley makes a pull at Phyllis's skirt and stands on his toes. Half laughing at Arthur, she stoops down, and Charley says in her ear: "Tell er I'm coming, soons I can."

"She'll tell no one nothing," Arthur says. "She's got too much sense, or if she hasn't, I have."

Phyllis, laughing, is then dragged out of the room. She is so much amused and interested in Arthur's last assertion that she forgets even to say good-bye to Charley.

But Charley is left delighted; full of amusement and elation. Toomer, on the way to join the church party at the door, comes up to him in the passage and says in a low, anxious voice: "Good luck, Charley—you were right, too. All the time. You got to fight em." He squeezes Charley's free arm and, as he goes down the passage, turns to look at him again with an expression of anxiety and perplexity which contradicts his words. Charley, on his side, also has a wondering and confused look. He has forgotten all about his arrangements for a smash-up. Thus the two friends retreat slowly from each other with looks of mutual confusion.

Charley turns away and instantly forgets Toomer. He goes upstairs smiling, without knowing what he is smiling at or where his happiness comes from, even that he is happy. He feels only cheerful and very hungry. He lies down on the bed and thinks: "I'll op off—it's easy. Ony got to op out of Ned's winder."

78 Charley had no difficulty in slipping away from the Remand Home. Although, since his conviction, he was not allowed out except under supervision, he was never locked up. He had no difficulty, as soon as it was dark, in climbing the garden wall, by means of the dust-bin, and dropping into the next garden. He then stole a ride, on the back platform of a bus, for a mile down the Longwater road, and from there begged a lift to Tawleigh. He reached the Galors' cottage before eight, and in less than half an hour he and Lizzie were actually on their way to Southampton by the Exeter bus.

They paid their way so far with the contents of Susan's money-box. Lizzie, in fact, still had ninepence on her, at nine o'clock the next evening, when a young farmer found the couple asleep in an open cart-shed, with the rain drifting upon them. He, afraid that they would catch cold, waked them up and asked what they were doing there. They answered that they were going to Southampton, and had lost the money for their bus tickets. The farmer did not doubt this story, but thought that their relatives had better know of their plight. He therefore took them to the police-station. There they were at once perceived to be runaways. The station sergeant put them to dry before the charge-room fire, with a cup of hot tea, while he phoned neighbouring borough and county head-quarters.

Charley, through the thin door, could hear the sergeant's voice giving their description to Exeter, Taunton, Torquay and other places. "Blue eyes, brown hair, short nose, projecting ears, speaks with a London accent—says his name is Smith—girl about the same height, well grown and might be older than she's dressed, round cheeks, big mouth, brown mark on upper front incisor, yes, passing for brother and sister—girl says she's Betty Smith, but nothing like the boy and speaks broad. Seems a bit stupid and might be out of an institution."

Charley puts his hand on Lizzie's dress as if to feel it. He

337

realises that she has not heard these remarks, but his new sense of responsibility expresses itself in the gesture. He says: "Nearly dry, Liz?"

Liz is shivering. She says: "I'm all right, Charley," but she speaks sadly.

"Nice ot tea, aint it?"

Lizzie, recollecting her tea which stands beside her on the bench, picks up the mug and takes a cautious sip. Then she sits, holding the mug in her hands and gazing at the fire.

Charley feels that she needs encouragement, and says: "Soon's we're dry we'll go on, see. It aint far now—it aint fifty miles. One op in a lorry and there's always plenty going our way."

"You don't think they knew, Charley?"

Charley glances backwards at the wooden partition which cuts off the inner from the outer office, where the sergeant is at the telephone. He says in a rallying tone: "Ow could they know, Lizzie?"

"They do, though," Lizzie says.

"Go on, Liz—aven't you got no spunk? Ere, you aint going to chuck it up nah wen we jess getting there."

A constable comes in, takes his seat beside them on the form, pulls off his boots and holds out his feet, in grey woollen socks, to the flames. Then he glances at the children and says in a tone of friendly raillery: "Mister and Missus Charley Brown, I believe?"

Neither of the children speaks or shows a change of expression. Probably both had expected to be caught.

"Lucky thing we got to send along Twyport way, anyhow, so you'll be able to sleep in the old home."

Since they do not speak, the young man, good-natured and friendly, looks enquiringly at them and then reflects for a moment, eyebrows in air. He is obviously considering for the first time how they may feel. He turns up a foot, gives the sole a smart rub, and says: "Sixty mile since las night in this weather—good for you—you got the pluck, both of you."

The children make no answer and do not look at him. He glances at them with surprise, smiles, and is going to say something more, something funny, when he thinks better of it and once more looks at the fire. After two minutes, unexpectedly, he gives a loud, explosive sigh, which obviously startles himself, for he jumps up at once, becomes busy and active, feels his soles, reaches for his boots, knocks them upside down, on the fender, and says in a humorous voice: "Lot of good drying your socks when your boots is full of water." Then he pulls on the boots and thumps out of the room.

After a pause Charley says to Liz: "It aint so long."

"Three year."

"But I tell ya, if I behave myself, it might be only two."

"Two year."

"Wy, wots two year, and then we'll be grown up, see, and nobody can't do nothing to us. I'll ave a job and we'll get an ouse."

Lizzie reflects for a moment. Then she says: "They aint going to let us."

"Let us wot? Ere, they can't stop us—not after two year."

"No, they aint going to let us," Liz says in a mournful voice.

"Ere, Liz, wen we're growed up, see—then we can do wot we like, and we bloody well will, too? Ow they going to stop us?"

"They know how in those places—that's what they're for—to make boys different. The lady said so—she said they'd learn you different."

"They can't do it to me, Liz."

"Yes, they will too."

"Ere, Liz, wots wrong with you. It's ony two years—wots two years?"

Lizzie clasps her hands round her mug and shakes her head. "They makes you all over in they places—you comes out so nobody couldn't know you. Praps you won't even know me, Charley."

"Ere, and wot about you then? You goin to let that rescue ome make you any different?"

Lizzie is obviously surprised by this suggestion. After a moment she says, doubtfully: "Course they couldn't."

"If they do me, wy not you?"

Lizzie's fingers clutch the mug. She says: "I don want em to——"

"Then don you let em."

"I want to be like I am and I want ee to be like you are, Charl. But we can't do nothing, can we—when they get hold of us."

"And ow about getting married after and ow about the kid and the ouse and the bathroom and the garden an everything —wot you thinks going to appen to us?"

"I don know, Charley, and I don't care—if we're different."

"Ere, they aint going to do it to me, see. Let em try, thass all. I'll show em something."

"You won't do nothing silly, Charl."

"I will if they tries any of their games on me—I'll cut off."

"They'll catch you like they done to-day. They always catch you."

"Then I'll smash em up, see, that puzzles em."

"They'll make you different that way too—only worser— and you'll never get away from them."

Charley is stopped by this calm voice. His childish brag sinks out of him. For twenty-four hours he has been once more a man, forgetting himself and thinking only as maturely and sensibly as he can, for his woman and his home. He asks at last with a tone of surprise rather than indignation: "Wy can't they leave us alone, Liz?"

"We bin so bad."

"I mean now—wy don they leave us alone. We aint kids now. We wouldn't give no trouble to nobody. I could do a job, couldn't I, and you could cook or wash."

Liz gives a deep sigh. "We could, too, coudden we?"

"Wy can't they let us?"

340

"They won't."

"But wy, Liz?"

"Cos we're kids."

"But we aint kids now."

"Yess, we is too."

"Well, wot about it, if we are a bit young?"

"They got it in the laws—the lady told me."

"The laws about kids."

Liz says nothing to this. Charley says bitterly: "A bloody fine law that is."

"A lot of kids is silly," Liz suggests. "They can be a fair nuisance too. I suppose they got to have laws agen the bad uns."

Charley, after reflection, bursts out in sudden anger: "Nor you aint never been bad, neither."

"Lady says I bin worser nor you. They all says I didn't ought to've led you on."

"Led on nothing."

"Yess, I bin silly, too, like Su told me I wur, and the lady she said so too. Gurls did oughter have more sense than boys. They'm bound to be more forethinking."

"I'd rather ave you, Liz, than forty Sus and undreds of lady beaks."

"I done you a lot of harm, Charl—like Miss Lina said. A turble wrong, I done you. If twurnt for me taking you astray they medn't have put you away at all."

"Go on, Liz. Them beaks said it was me done you the arm. Thass the way they go on at us, see."

"They didden know about us—how could they if they wurn't us?"

"I did too."

"You never did me no harm, Charley—you made me so happy as I wish I could die."

"Ere, ere, Liz—don be si-lly."

"Course I ain't going to—doctor says I'm made so strong as a liddle mare. But I don't want us to be different—I can't bear that."

341

Charley opens his mouth to say once more that they will never make him different. But in the presence of Liz he is no longer a boy playing with words. He feels ashamed to strike attitudes, to turn from the truth. The two or three years, which stretch before him, become real to his imagination as to the courage and instinct of Liz. He feels even a tremor of excited anticipation. He sits still and says nothing. The sergeant next door is heard calling "Wilson, Wilson."

Gazing at the fire Liz says in a dreamy voice: "It's bin lovely, Charley, ant it?"

"Ere, it's going to be all right too—come on, Liz—cheer up."

"It's bin so lovely, I wish I could die."

The young constable opens the door and says in the brisk forcible tone of one who expects trouble and is not going to have it: "Now then, youngsters."

The children, expecting this interruption, get up obediently and put down their mugs on the floor. Their faces show no rebellious thoughts. Constable Wilson is relieved. He says in a tone almost of apology: "You can stay in the warm, missy, they say we got to take special care of you—you'll go along with Sergeant presently and his missus will put you up. It's you I want, Brown. Come along, you got a long way to go before you get your beauty sleep."

Charley, with stiff legs, clatters heavily towards the door; Lizzie looks at him, then turns away her face and sits down again on the form like a good little girl in a strange schoolroom. The constable, growing more kindly every moment as he sees that he is going to escape a scene, says: "This is goodbye, you know, youngsters, you won't be seeing each other again."

Charley turns like an automaton; Lizzie, the polite little girl ready to do the proper thing, gets up and comes forward. Suddenly her face twists and instantly both children break into loud gasping sobs. But they stand before each other stiffly, as if at a children's dance lesson.

"Come on," the constable says, already regretting his good nature. "Get it over—shake hands or something."

They shake hands, and then obviously thinking that perhaps this is not the full ceremony necessary to the occasion, they put forward their faces awkwardly and brush their dry lips together. It is the first time they have kissed.

"That's all right then," the constable says in a gratified tone. "Come on, Brown, wipe your nose, mind the step. Here he is, Cooper."

Charley, blind, deaf and senseless, not knowing what is happening to him, steps down into the glittering dark.

A small low black car with the hood up is below him at the kerb. The hood is shining in the rain like a new coal-scuttle. Charley gazes at this object with blank non-comprehension. He feels his arm gripped, and he is pushed head first under the hood into an opening so small, dark and narrow that he is sure it can never contain him. "They'll smother me," is the first thought that occurs to him for some minutes. But he submits, patiently and humbly, to be pushed. From the police station door a surprised constable's voice calls out: "Hi, Cooper, wait a minute."

"Oyay?"

"Funny thing, kid in here's passed out—fainted."

"Hungry."

"That's what Sergeant says. Think you could spare one of those sandwiches? We got tea."

"They got mustard in."

"That's all right—she can't be too particular, can she?"

Prefatory Essay by Joyce Cary

written especially for the Carfax Edition of

CHARLEY IS MY DARLING

CHARLEY is a small boy, an evacuee, sent to the West Country from a London slum. He is found to have a dirty head and has to be shaved. This gives him a bad start with the other evacuees, who, jostling for position among themselves, unite to jeer at him. But being a child with imagination and nerve, he recovers his position and self respect, and finally becomes a leader of gangs by various bold enterprises which at last land him in the courts.

I was once asked by an official of the Board which looks after young offenders, how I had come to know so much about them. It had not struck me before that I had any special knowledge, but when I reflected I thought that if I did have knowledge, it came chiefly from a good memory of my own childhood. And it has always seemed to me that every ordinary child is by nature a delinquent, that the only difference between us as children was the extent of our delinquency, whether we were found out in it and how we were punished for it.

I myself at the age of seven spent a whole afternoon in flight from the police. Playing with my gang (any group of children with a sense of community is a gang) about the village of Moville in County Donegal, I tore out several door-bells clean from their sockets. I can still remember that joyful shock when the wire came away at the elbow-crank, and I marched away with it over my shoulder, drawing yards of wire after me. And my terror when some larger boy (I have an idea it was one of the Montgomeries, perhaps the present Commander-in-Chief) warned me to run for it as the police were coming. Also I remember the wild relief with which, after lurking in various hide-outs about the Bath Green all the evening, I slipped down to the old wooden pier where I knew that all the family would be waiting for the steamer (the *Albatross*) to come in from Derry with the shoppers, and rushed into my mother's arms, or, rather, ran against her skirt and clasped her round the legs.

What is significant, I think, in the memory, is that I have no recollection at all of how or why I did this crime. I was only told of the being dared. My memories, vivid still after more than fifty years, in vision and actual sensation, are of the feel of the wire on my shoulder, the powerful effort which tore it loose, the triumphant joy of walking away with it. Then the shout of warning which is represented only by the silhouette of a head coming up behind a wall, and nothing else. I don't remember any words, though I do remember that I ran from the police. Then an equally vague memory of a doorway, or perhaps a shed in a back lane, leading to the mountains. And again the second sharp vision of my mother's face; her very expression of tender surprise and welcome; a group of relations and friends standing round on the pier, and my father smiling first at me and then at them with an air of great and rather proud delight. In fact, far from being arrested, I was greeted by my family as an adventurer, a dare devil, a true member of a sporting line; and on the next day (this again is merely legend and not my recollection) the police sergeant, beckoning to me from the door of the barracks, complimented me on my strength, and only warned me that if I again did the 'like of thon' I should be shut up in the Red Man (the lighthouse which still stands on iron legs, opposite Moville, in the midst of Lough Foyle) till the devil came to fetch me home. I say I don't remember anything of this threat, but I do remember, as well as those sensations (the bell wire, my mother's skirt), the brilliant visions, photographed for ever on my brain, of the warning head, of my mother's look, and then my feeling that I had done something at once dangerous and illegal.

I can also *see* myself pulling the wire and standing on the pier among my relations; but this, though also a vivid picture, must be an image, a very early one, perhaps formed that same evening, and produced by family remarks upon the event, remarks which made me see myself for the first time in relation with the whole circumstances into which I had plunged.

And perhaps it is these later but still brilliant images which combine with the pure vision, the direct experience, to give me the final complex memory, that what I had done was both grand and bad. There was not, I think, even then, confusion in my mind. I was quite clear that to tear out bells and defy the law was a bold, a terrific act, but also a wrong one, not to be repeated.

The significance of all this when I came to write Charley was the complex motives at work already in a child's mind; forces that are not different in kind from those that move a grown-up. The suddenness of temptation or, rather, inspiration, which (like many that come to an artist) is so quick that he doesn't even notice it, it leaves no moment for reflection. The imagination sees its opportunity, its prey, and instantly leaps upon it. You can watch this happen with any good talker, and you can see such inspired talkers carried suddenly away into brutalities. They drop bricks. That is to say, they are whirled into delinquency before they know it.

Such people, it is said, have given way to a sudden temptation. It has been too attractive for their self-control. For children, with their powerful imaginations and weak control, the wonder is not that they do some wrong, but that they don't do much more.

I was a lucky child, surrounded not only by affection but a lively family of cousins, aunts and uncles, full of energy and imagination, and also of very ready instruction in what was right and wrong. I had always new vistas of discovery and interest opening before me; I was encouraged to talk, to tell stories, to write and draw; I had freedom to range for miles over the little beaches of Donegal; and yet I knew very clearly (according to family ideas, which were old-fashioned perhaps but all the more definite) what was wicked, what was merely mischief, what was neither but, all the same, not done. I was neither bored nor confused. And boredom and confusion are surely the two prime sources of childish wickedness. I mean real wickedness which goes beyond mischief, the willed cruelty, the malicious damage. The child is a born creator. He has to be, for though in sympathy he is one with those he loves, in mind he is alone. He has to do his own learning and thinking. And Nature, for his very necessary good, sets him to enjoy it. Anyone can see how children enjoy discovery and reflection. But also how soon they are bored with what is known. It is as if Nature says to them, 'Go on, go on, there's plenty more that you must know'; and has made the joy of discovery evanescent; the imagination, like the appetite, perpetually greedy. So that being shut out from its need on one side it dashes after it on another.

Just as the grown-up world is for ever seeking new arts, new ideas, so children want change; and just as grown-ups who are bored take to drink or gambling or mere destructiveness, for the kick, so bored children get up a fight, or a dare, or steal, or smash. These too are novelties, adventures, and also explorations.

But the world that stands to be explored is also a moral structure which, simply because it is one of related ideas, is much harder for him to grasp. He perceives that it is there, he feels its importance to his comfort and security every moment of the day, but it is not present to his eyes and ears; he cannot see and touch it. He is not equipped with the experience and judgment necessary to put it together for himself. For this purpose nature has provided him (and many other small mammals which grow slowly in understanding) with parents. And if they refuse the duty of making the situation clear to him he will suffer. I am ready to bet that a good deal of what is called neurosis and frustration among young children is due to nothing but the failure of parents and teachers (often the most conscientious) to do so, that is, to give a clear picture without uncertainties. Without such a picture, children don't know where they are, and they do all kinds of evil (because it is just this sphere of good and evil that is puzzling them) to find out. A child will torture a cat or some other smaller child, in order to see what will happen, both to himself and the victim, and what he feels like in the new circumstances. The 'crime' is a moral experiment.

But beyond this experimental effort, a child, being still confused and frustrated, still unable to know, once and for all, what is right and wrong, will commit a real crime, a spiteful cruelty, out of rage and spite; he will choose some valued thing to dirty or to smash because he identifies it with a world which obstinately closes itself to his imagination. For of course the imagination is always looking for significance; both in the physical and moral world, that is its job, to put together coherent wholes, a situation with meaning, a place where the child does know, all the time, where he is.

The wrecking of the house in this story was taken from fact, when even younger boys did greater damage. And such raids are not at all uncommon. They are sometimes expressions of boredom; sometimes of hatred, a rage against beauty and dignity by those who have neither but feel the want; sometimes they arise from the ordinary dynamics of gangster politics (which now rule half the world), the leader's need to invent new and exciting enterprises for his band, but I think above all from the secret hunger of a starved imagination, not only for æsthetic but moral comprehension.

Knowledge, in short, the experience of the mind, is just as important to a child's happiness and 'goodness' as affection, adventure; above all, the knowledge of his own moral position. And the last is often most difficult for him to come by, not because he could not grasp a complex situation ('this is a grand deed but a bad one'), but because grown-ups do not trust the power of his imagination to form a picture in more than one dimension.

J. C.